A Girl Called Hope

A Girl Called Hope

Grace Thompson

CANELO

First published in United Kingdom in 2004 by Severn House Publishers Ltd

This edition published in the United Kingdom in 2018 by

Canelo Digital Publishing Limited
57 Shepherds Lane
Beaconsfield, Bucks HP9 2DU
United Kingdom

A CIP catalogue record for this book is available from the British Library.

Print ISBN 978 1 78863 146 4
Ebook ISBN 978 1 910859 28 5

Look for more great books at www.canelo.co

Printed and bound in Great Britain by Clays Ltd, Elcograf S.p.A.

One

Hope Murton pushed the pram closer to the front door of Badgers Brook, the house that stood just off the lane close to the wood. It had been a long walk, but she had wanted to bring Davy in his pram rather than take the bus, so she could get the feel of the area in which she and Ralph and their two-year-old son were going to live.

She had seen the house twice; once with Ralph and once with Ralph and his mother, Marjorie Williamson-Murton, a hyphenated name on which Marjorie insisted, but which Ralph and she had refused to perpetuate. This time, having arranged to meet the owner, Hope wanted to explore the place with only Davy for company. Without the others' opinions and queries and, in Marjorie's case, doubts, she knew she would begin to think of it as home.

She and Ralph had married very young. They had both been only twenty and since then they had lived with Ralph's parents in the modest house which had attracted the socially ambitious Marjorie by its name, Ty Mawr – the big house – standing, as it did, close to bungalows and a couple of Victorian terraces near the shopping centre of Cwm Derw.

The three years sharing a house with her mother-in-law hadn't been easy, especially after Ralph was called up. Their only private place had been the bedroom. Although even there they weren't safe from Marjorie bursting in to demand something or another. Living 'through and through' it was called locally, and Hope longed to leave.

Marjorie didn't approve of the quiet, shy young girl her son had married and she never tired of reminding Hope of how fortunate she had been to have been chosen by her son, who, she regularly insisted, could have chosen from the best the town could offer.

At first Hope had been miserable, unable to cope with the strong and aggressive Marjorie, but when Ralph discovered the extent of his mother's unpleasantness the misery vanished on the cloud of shared laughter. Ralph always turned a worrying situation into an excuse for laughter, although sometimes Hope wished he would deal with things rather than trivialize them. Now, when the end was in sight, she thought he might have been right. By smiling, turning away from the slightest disagreement, they had managed three years without a serious confrontation. It was easy to be benevolent towards Marjorie now, when everything was about to be perfect. With the prospect of a home of their own where she could live without constant criticism, Hope looked forward to nothing but freedom and happiness, and laughter based solely on joy.

A van came down the road and, as it slowed, Hope looked expectantly towards the driver. Parking the hardware delivery van on the wide grass verge Geoff Tanner stepped out, and hurried towards her.

'Sorry I'm late, Mrs Murton. I had a customer at the last moment.' He held up the key then opened the door. Taking hold of the pram, he said, 'Let me lift young Niblo inside, then I'll leave you for half an hour so you can do any measuring you need to do. I hope you like the improvements but if there are any questions you want to ask me, write them on this.' He handed her a notebook and pencil. 'See you in a while.'

There were a couple of information leaflets on the large scrub-top table in the kitchen. They referred to a new bathroom, with a geyser and a lavatory and even a wash-basin with a single cold tap.

Davy was sleeping, rosy cheeked and content. After making sure the door was shut and no one could walk in and frighten him, she ran excitedly to see the house's latest acquisition. In what had been described as a fifth bedroom, but was in fact hardly more than a box room, was a newly installed bath. The walls had been stripped of flowery wall paper and washed with white paint. A large bath on metal legs stood on the bare wooden boards. Perfect. She was longing to try her hand at decorating.

Everywhere was clean, and apart from wallpapering and painting, which she and Ralph would surely enjoy, there was nothing to do before they moved in. If only Ralph's mother would share their happiness instead of warning her that moving him away from the house he'd always called home was a huge mistake.

She could hear Davy moving and guessed he was about to wake up. She quickly measured the windows, relieved to find that the wires were there ready to hang curtains. Friends had been generous and given her some, so the money they had saved could be spent on more extravagant things, like furnishings for Davy's bedroom. Second hand of course, but good quality.

It was time to leave. The November darkness was creeping into the house, yet she didn't feel the expected chill. When she went to attend to Davy, he was warm and apparently content. She went to the door with him in her arms and looked out for the van returning. There was no sign of Geoff, so she tried to put Davy down on the floor so he could spend a little time exploring, but he hadn't quite shaken off sleep and he clung to her, head resting on her shoulder, his warmth and tightly clinging arms a delight.

The kitchen faced the lane, the direction from which people approached the house, and leading off a large hallway on the other side was a small breakfast room and a store cupboard. The front of the house was where the dining room and lounge faced the garden, which, as she walked around, carrying Davy, she saw had been well maintained since the departure of the previous tenants, Ivor and Marie Masters and their children. There was a greenhouse built from what looked like a collection of windows taken from various houses. Fruit trees and bushes filled an area and small plots had been roughly dug over for the frosts of winter to do their work.

Returning to the house, sleep was put aside and Davy trotted from room to room, Hope following. He climbed the stairs on his sturdy legs, chattering about everything he saw, Hope walking behind him and laughing at his enthusiasm. She scooped Davy up as she heard the door open and called down, 'We're coming, Mr Tanner, Davy is just deciding which room will be his.'

She opened the door and saw not Geoff Tanner, her soon-to-be landlord, but a man of about thirty, wearing a battered trilby and heavy country-style clothes. His eyes were bright blue and creased with a smile in his weathered face.

'Sorry I am to interrupt you, but I wondered if you'd like me to call each week with a vegetable order?' He held out a hand. 'Peter Bevan's the name. I usually call on Saturday mornings, but any day to suit, really.' He winked at Davy, who buried his head in Hope's shoulder. Not discouraged, Peter asked his name then he tapped the child's shoulder, saying 'When you're settled in, young Davy, you must come and meet Jason. He's my horse,' he explained to Hope.

Hope agreed to give an order to be delivered each Saturday morning, and Peter left, still trying to coax a smile out of Davy. He was almost at the gate before Davy called, 'Bye-bye, man,' to their amusement.

They were halfway up the stairs when there was another knock at the door, again Hope called, 'All right, Mr Tanner, we're coming.'

'Not Geoff Tanner,' a loved voice teased. 'You'll have to make do with me.'

'Ralph! Look, Davy, it's your daddy!' Ralph ran up the stairs to meet them and they hugged as though their parting had been days instead of hours.

They walked from room to room, looking out of the windows at the garden, and the trees edging the lane. The narrow roadway with green verges on either side was invisible, making the trees lining it appear to be a part of the extensive woodland on the opposite side.

'Badgers live in the wood.' Ralph told her. 'The stream giving the house its name is where they cross on their nightly foraging. The wood is so close to the house it's almost like living among its trees and sharing their home, isn't it?'

'We'll be so happy here,' she said.

Geoff appeared a few minutes later and smiled at their excited faces. 'No need to ask if you're still happy about renting Badgers Brook.' he said. 'You look as though it's woven its magic around you already.'

'Magic?' Hope queried.

'People say there's a special atmosphere in Badgers Brook that calms people, helps them to sort out their difficulties, that tenants come with problems or even despair, and leave having found peace.'

'We'll be the exceptions, we'll bring our peace and happiness with us,' Hope replied with assurance, hugging Ralph and Davy. 'It's going to be absolutely perfect.'

They discussed the few remaining queries, Geoff explaining the workings of the geyser and the water pump in the kitchen, and the gas lighting, and when their conversation widened Hope admitted that she wanted to change the colour of the kitchen walls from a dull beige to something more cheerful.

Geoff sold paint in his shop and he ran to the van and collected a colour chart. Hope looked at the colours on offer and pointed to a bright sunshine yellow.

'Perfect,' she said, showing it to her husband.

Ralph nodded agreement but added doubtfully, 'I think Mum will find it a bit bold, though,' which only confirmed her opinion that it was a good choice. As they walked home, pushing Davy in his pram, neither Hope nor Ralph could imagine a single cloud on their horizon.

Geoff watched them go. There was a local superstition that everyone who lived in that house moved in with a burden of unhappiness and left at peace with themselves. But there didn't seem to be anything threatening this family's happiness. He shrugged. Superstitions were for bored old women. It was a happy house in a beautiful setting, nothing more.

Although if the superstitions were true he might do worse than live there himself. He was happy enough, but when he saw young families like Ralph and Hope Murton and their son, a melancholy overcame him, a wistful dream of what might have been, if he hadn't stayed with his father and been a dutiful son after he was widowed at the beginning of the war.

After the years fighting in Hitler's war, he had been anxious to move away, find some new way of earning his living, perhaps go to college and pick up an interest he'd had in history, even become a teacher. But his father had almost run the hardware shop's business into the ground over the years he'd been away, and he had stayed, for a while that grew longer and longer until it seemed impossible to leave.

Now his father was dead and he was thirty-five and locked into a life he hadn't chosen without the energy or enthusiasm to try something different.

–

Hope and Ralph hurried home through the lanes and narrow streets of Cwm Derw, talking excitedly about their plans for when they were living in Badgers Brook.

As they passed the Ship and Compass, they saw Freddy, Ralph's father. 'I wonder what he's doing there?' Hope queried. 'It isn't open yet and he's going in through the side door.'

'Probably giving Betty Connors a hand with something. I believe he's done some decorating for her, and he and a few others help with shifting heavy barrels and the like.'

'Doesn't your mother mind?'

Ralph laughed. 'I don't think she knows, so don't say a word. The truth is, Dad's bored since he sold the business and retired. I think he's glad of something to do. He's done some work for Stella and Colin at the post office. He and Colin built a bathroom extending out from what was once a pantry. Very smart by all accounts. He'll help us, too, if we need anything done.'

'I wish your mother was more enthusiastic about our move,' Hope said as they approached Ty Mawr. 'I'd have thought she would be pleased to see you starting out, making a home of your own.'

'She lost my two brothers, remember. I'm all she's got left.'

'That's not really true, Ralph, love. Sadly, Richard is dead, but Phillip is alive. He isn't lost, he simply left Cwm Derw and doesn't bother to keep in touch.'

'You're right, darling, but Mum doesn't see it that way. Apart from a forty-eight-hour visit when Phillip was demobbed in 1945, she hasn't seen him. His letters are few and as brief as possible. She considers both Richard and Phillip her lost sons. So I'm all she's got.'

'Apart from your father. And little Davy and me,' she reminded him gently. 'We're her family too.'

'And she knows how lucky she is to have you.' He tightened his arm around her waist and touched her cheek with his lips. 'But I think we'll have to be extra kind to her after we leave home. Invite her often, ask her advice about things.'

'What things?' Hope tried to keep her voice light.

'Well, she's got such excellent taste and we could do worse than ask her advice about furnishings.'

'But I have my own ideas, Ralph. Choosing what we like, that's the fun of having a place of our own.' She determinedly kept her tone uncritical, disguising the disappointment flowing over her like an icy waterfall.

'In fact,' Ralph went on as though she hadn't spoken, 'I think we'll make sure to give her a key so she can call whenever she wants to.'

'To walk in when she likes, as she does now? Or to check up on me, make sure the place is as clean and as well run she thinks it should be?' It was no longer possible to hide her dismay.

'Don't be silly.' Ralph gave a derisive laugh. 'I know you're teasing me. Mum is very thrilled about everything. She won't want to interfere, but because she's so lonely I want her to feel very much a part of our lives, don't you?'

She wanted to shout, 'NO, I do not want to share what we have, Marjorie is demanding, possessive, greedy, she'll take over everything, including the way I bring up Davy.' But she knew the words must never be spoken. Ralph's loyalty to his mother was understandable, and good. She would hope for such affection and love from her own son. She just wished Ralph would accept that his mother had too strong a need to run their lives. Why couldn't Ralph see what his mother was doing? Was he saying the house would be Marjorie's second home? To decide what they needed and how things ought to be done? That wasn't what she wanted at all. She stopped, tucked a blanket unnecessarily around Davy as he sat in his pram, shouting at things he saw and pointing as another light came on in one of the houses they passed.

'What is it, Hope, darling? Is something wrong?'

'I don't know,' she said sadly. 'I suddenly feel very cold.'

Marjorie Williamson-Murton sat in the darkening kitchen, only the light from the hall revealing the table and the silent figure. Saving power was a constant governmental demand and no lights were lit unless absolutely necessary. She would turn the kitchen light on when the others arrived to eat. She glanced at the big clock in the hall and her fingers began tapping irritably on the old Welsh oak table.

Once she had reigned there over her three boys and her husband as they had eaten their meals or argued about homework, her husband getting as heated as the boys when there was a problem. A smile touched her lips and she looked across the hall towards the lounge door, beyond which her husband Freddy sat for hours, between visits to friends or to the Ship and Compass, day after day, doing crossword puzzles, jigsaw puzzles or playing endless games of patience, and in between just staring out of the window at some memory that he was unable to share with her.

Richard and Phillip had been called up but had survived until the last few months of the war without injury. Then, only weeks before Germany surrendered, a flying bomb had hit the building where they were staying and Richard had been killed. Soon after the funeral, Phillip came home and, instead of unpacking, he announced that he was going to live in North Wales and become an artist.

She kept telling herself this – chanting the train of events over and over, those few days that had ruined her dream of their returning to fill her home once again, to show how much she was needed – but sometimes it was impossible to believe. Even now, November 1947, more than two years later, it was still only a bad dream, a nightmare from which she would wake up to see them both walking towards the front door, demanding food and a bath, and clean clothes as they had a date with two fabulous girls.

Voices disturbed her and for a fleeting second she imagined it was her boys, then reality struck and she was abrupt as she opened the door to Ralph and Hope and the baby. Ralph was laughing, and he had no right to be happy, not when she couldn't feel anything but grief. 'You're late, I set the table for David half an hour ago,' she said briskly. 'He'll have to make do with a boiled egg, as the meal I prepared has dried up.'

'I promised him a few baked beans on toast, it's his favourite.' Hope said hesitantly.

'What a meal to offer a child of David's age! This isn't a "Joe's Café" you know. He'll have a boiled egg. Then once he's in bed we can start on supper. There's a little of that boiled bacon left for Ralph and his father – if he gets home from his nightly visit to the Ship and Compass before it's ruined. You and I can manage with the last of yesterday's corned beef.'

Hope turned to Ralph and mouthed, 'I hate corned beef.'

'I'll sneak you some of my bacon,' he whispered back. 'When she isn't looking, of course!' His blue eyes were laughing as he nodded conspiratorially towards his mother. Hope smiled. Only a few more weeks and, within the confines of rationing, she would be able to choose what she put on the table.

'Geoff Tanner thinks it will only be a week or so before we have the key and can move in,' she said later as she was peeling potatoes beside Marjorie, who was washing and chopping cabbage.

'What?' The knife clattered from Marjorie's hand and she called for Freddy and Ralph to 'Come here at once!'

'What is it, Mum? Have you cut yourself?' Ralph was concerned.

'Hope is talking as though you're leaving in a couple of weeks. Surely she's wrong? You can't be intending to move out before Christmas?'

'Well, yès,' Hope said, looking to Ralph for support. 'We want to spend Christmas in our new home. Surely you can understand that?'

'But not if it upsets you so much,' Ralph said soothingly. 'We can get the furniture in, but we needn't actually live there until after Christmas.'

'After New Year,' Marjorie contradicted loudly.

'But, Ralph,' Hope gasped. 'You promised. We decided that—'

'We thought it would be nice, yes, but Christmas is such a special family occasion and we'll have plenty of other Christmases, won't we?'

'Christmas isn't far away,' she pleaded. 'I want us to get settled.'

'And Christmas isn't a time for being selfish,' Marjorie snapped.

Hope stared at her and the most defiance she dared show was to say, 'You're right, it isn't the time to be selfish, is it?'

Hope watched as Marjorie picked up the fallen knife, washed it fussily and went on preparing the meal, which Hope knew she'd be unable to eat. Hunger had been driven from her at the prospect of having to stay here with her parents-in-law. After Christmas there would be New Year, then there would be other reasons for them to stay. Ralph's lack of support was no longer something for which she could make excuses. If only she were brave enough to insist.

Freddy disappeared for an hour or two but came back in as they were about to start eating. Marjorie thumped his plate in front of him and demanded to know where he'd been.

'Oh, talking to Colin and Stella. They want some help taking some furniture back from their country cottage,' he said with a smile. 'Bringing it home for the winter and painting the chairs and all that.'

'Country cottage. What a fool the woman is,' Marjorie retorted.

'It's a joke, Marjorie, a bit of fun.'

The country cottage belonging to Stella and Colin Jones was nothing more than their allotment shed. Someone had sarcastically called it that, and, instead of being offended, Stella and Colin had laughed and the name had stuck. Stella had made curtains for the windows, and had painted it a cheerful green with the windows and doors edged with yellow. Inside was painted white, regularly given a fresh coat to keep spiders and other unwanted visitors at bay. There was a piece of carpet on the floor for their dog, Scamp, a drinking bowl with his name on and a selection of toys for his entertainment.

Stella went there whenever her duties as the local postmistress allowed, and she kept it spotlessly clean. A series of boxes and tins held the makings of tea. An old biscuit barrel usually held a few cakes, and people often included the place in their walks in the hope of being invited in for a sit down and a gossip. Colin worked on the railway and his shift work enabled him to work on the garden while she entertained.

The name might make most people smile, but Marjorie didn't find it amusing.

–

When she and Ralph went to bed that night, Hope tried to persuade him to move into the house as soon as it was theirs. 'We can come here for Christmas, leave Davy's presents under the tree so your parents can enjoy watching him unwrap them, stay overnight if your mother would like us to, but we'd have our own home waiting for us. Isn't that what you want, Ralph?' she asked.

'Of course it's what I want, darling. More than anything. It's just that it isn't the right time.'

'For us, d'you mean, or your mother?'

'Both I suppose. Mum mostly. I'm longing for us to live in Badgers Brook; it's a perfect place for Davy and us. But I can't leave the house where I've lived all my life in an easy frame of mind knowing Mum is still grieving. And you can see how Dad is. No company for Mum there, is there? Him sitting in that room locked into his private unhappiness or walking the streets on his own? She'll be so lonely if we move now. This big house will echo around her reminding her of her losses, she and Dad rattling through its empty rooms like a couple of dried peas in a bucket. She'll hate it so much.'

'And you think after Christmas will be the right time?'

She felt him shrug. 'I don't know. After New Year, maybe. I just believe I will know when the time is right.'

'And what about Davy and me? Isn't now the right time for us?'

'Let's go to sleep now, shall we? I have a heavy day tomorrow, dealing with the accounts of that bad-tempered old man in the furniture shop.'

She chuckled, trying to lighten the mood. 'Don't be too impatient with him, he's given us a good discount on the furniture we've ordered.' She wanted to talk about the items they had chosen.

'Thanks to Mum's persuasion,' he reminded her.

Good old Mum, she thought sarcastically, and wondered why everything they discussed ended with a reference to Marjorie. Although, perhaps there was one subject that might break the pattern. 'How soon d'you think we should start thinking about a second baby?' she asked softly. But Ralph's slow breathing told her he was asleep. With a sigh she slipped out of bed, pulled on bed socks and wrapped herself in Ralph's thick dressing gown. She sat at the window for a long time, staring out into the November darkness.

–

In the bedroom at the front of the house, Marjorie also sat staring out at the almost invisible garden. She was engulfed in a rare moment of guilt. She was being unreasonable, and selfish – as Hope had boldly reminded her that evening. But how could she face an empty house? She'd heard that Freddy opened up in the convivial atmosphere of the public house, surrounded by friends, but when he was at home he was more like a ghost than an actual presence. She was as good as alone in a house meant to be home to a lively family. Life had been so unfair.

Three sons she'd borne and she had expected the house to be continually filled with them and their friends, then their families. Now there was only a seriously introspective Freddy, her least exciting son, Ralph, boring little Hope and a child they insisted on calling Davy. The child's name was David Frederick William Murton, the third Christian name, William, a concession to her demand they used the hyphenated name she had used since her marriage. Hope might be quiet and dull but she managed to persuade Ralph to do what she wanted, she thought with rising anger.

She turned away from the window and sat listening to the silence of the house. Once Ralph had taken his family away, the empty rooms would echo with hollow-sounding memories. She didn't believe in ghosts, yet sometimes she imagined she heard laughter, or footsteps running feather-light down the stairs as the boys set off for a late-night escapade, a midnight picnic, meeting their friends for a dare.

She smiled as she remembered how they had prepared, believing she hadn't noticed the surreptitious gathering of food throughout the day, hiding their cache ready for the house to fall quiet before slipping out, keeping to the dark shadows, to meet their friends in the old brick-built shed at the back of the house. There they would eat and giggle and play scary games before creeping back, while she sat and listened for their safe return.

She smiled as she remembered them tiptoeing up the stairs trying not to make a sound, holding back their laughter with great difficulty. Such a happy time when they had been young and she had shared their fun, every sunshine-filled day.

The house creaked and became a part of her imaginings.

Then the whimsical sounds became real, the footsteps slipping softly down the stairs were no longer her imagination. She went to the door and looked over the banisters. A torch led the way as Hope, in Ralph's long dark dressing gown, went across the hall into the kitchen. Silently she followed.

'I'm making a hot drink, would you like one?' Hope asked as she entered the room behind her.

'I couldn't sleep,' Marjorie said unnecessarily.

'Same reason as me I expect. The move. It's a difficult time for all of us. A huge change. I can understand how you'll miss Ralph and the baby. But I also know you want Ralph to move into a home of his own, to build a future for himself and his family, just like you and Father-in-law did here.'

'There's no need for you to go. There's plenty of room here.'

'We need a place of our own, to put down roots, build our own family home. I can't wait to live in Badgers Brook. Did you know there's an ancient sett not far from the house? It's how it got its name, according to Geoff Tanner from the hardware store.'

'I simply don't know how you'll manage,' she said harshly. 'Ralph is used to certain standards, he likes his meals on time and he won't tolerate David misbehaving while he's eating. You won't have me to help. Although I'll do what I can.'

I bet you will, Hope thought, but she said, 'I'll manage.' In an attempt to pacify the unhappy woman, she went on, 'Mainly thanks to you. I've learned so much living here with you and Father-in-law; you've helped me so much, and I'll always be able to call on you if I have a problem, won't I?'

'We all have to learn, I suppose, although it all came naturally to me. I'll have to learn to cope without my sons, won't I?'

'You still have Ralph and Davy, and me – if you'll accept that I'm a part of your family too.'

Marjorie gave a noncommittal grunt, stirring the hot water into the cocoa and condensed milk. They sat without a critical word being spoken for almost ten minutes, sipping their hot drinks, and Hope began think she and her mother-in-law might finally reach an understanding. Then Marjorie put the cup and saucer on the draining board and said sharply, 'I do wish you'd use his proper name and call the child David.'

Hope picked up the cups and saucers and began to rinse them under the tap. When she turned around, Marjorie had gone back to bed.

–

The following day, Hope went to the hardware shop to see Geoff. 'I don't want to pester you, but can you give us a date yet?' she asked.

'The previous tenants have paid rent for another couple of weeks but I'll have a word. And meanwhile I have no objection to you moving some furniture in, and starting on curtains, and things.' He looked at a calendar hanging behind the heavy wooden counter and said, 'What about the first of December, would that be all right?'

'Perfect, and thank you, Mr Tanner.'

'Geoff. Everyone calls me Geoff.'

Hope went to tell Stella at the post office then called at the office to tell Ralph, who, surprisingly, raised no further objections. She then hurried home to tell Marjorie, her heart in her mouth, prepared for trouble.

'Isn't it a wonderful surprise?' she finished, after telling Marjorie of Geoff's suggestion.

'Surprise? It's a shock that you can be so unfeeling. Richard dead, Phillip disappeared and now you're taking Ralph from me. Aren't you ashamed, Hope Morris?'

'Taking him? Mother-in-law, I haven't been Hope Morris for three years,' she said with a sigh. 'I'm Hope Murton, Ralph's wife, and we're not disappearing, just moving into a home of our own. Can't you be pleased for us?'

'You wouldn't even take his proper name. He's Ralph Williamson-Murton in case you've forgotten.'

'He prefers just Murton,' she said softly, 'and so do I.'

A couple of hours later, Ralph assured his mother that Hope had relented, and they would stay until after the New Year.

–

In the post office as everywhere, most of the conversations were about the wedding of Princess Elizabeth and the handsome Prince Philip.

'Best you and Colin come to the Ship and Compass this evening.' Betty Connors said. 'Everyone's invited. We've dressed the bar and there'll be a bit of a party in celebration of the royal wedding.'

Freddy was absent all day and when Marjorie asked where he'd been she was surprised to be told that, with Colin Jones, Geoff Tanner and others, he had been decorating the pub for the party. 'You're invited,' he said, watching her face for the expected response.

'Thank you, but I've no urge to involve myself with Betty Connors and her rowdy customers.'

'If you change you mind, I'll be leaving about half seven,' he said, knowing that a change of mind was unlikely.

There was a knock at the door and Marjorie opened it to a young schoolboy.

'Is Mr Murton in?'

'Mr Williamson-Murton,' she corrected.

'We needs him, see, down at the pub. The electricals is broke.'

'I'll give him your message, now hurry along home.'

'A peculiar child asks you to go to the pu— to the Ship and Compass to mend something, Freddy,' she called.

'It's all right, Marjorie, I heard.' He shrugged himself into his overcoat and went to the door.

'Please remind him your name is Williamson-Murton, Freddy.'

–

Phillip Williamson-Murton liked his hyphenated name. In his desire to become a sought-after artist he thought it gave added prestige when he signed his work. In spite of his name, his career to date hadn't shown much progress. After trying landscapes, seascapes and some portraits that had brought more ridicule than praise, he had tried abstract representation. This had also failed, as he lacked the under-standing and skill to give people what they wanted. His failure was the main reason he hadn't been back to see his parents.

The war had resulted in a restlessness and inability to concentrate. He gave up on every course he started, always thinking he knew better than the tutor. He wanted immediate success, recognition today not next year. He looked for short cuts, and impatience led to failure.

Blaming people for their lack of imagination impressed some of the women who supported him from time to time, but didn't solve the problem. He refused to face the face that he lacked both talent and tenacity.

He looked at the most recent letter from his mother but didn't open it. He had nothing to say to her and he didn't think she would have anything worthwhile to say to him. Gone were the days when she could bully him into studying, making him believe he would be famous if he would only work harder. He tore it across and threw the pieces into the fire.

He looked at the second letter that had arrived that day. It was from his friend Matthew Charles, another man who had failed to settle after demobilization. Matthew was a rep and they would meet up when he was in Phillip's area.

That night, Phillip's girlfriend Connie was at the cinema with a friend, and he and Matthew met at a local public house. As always their conversation turned to their present situation, comparing it to a kind of prison.

'Connie is good,' Phillip admitted, as drink began to make them maudlin. 'She's supportive and loving, but not someone with whom I dream of spending the rest of my life. She'll be broken hearted, but I have to move on.'

'I can't leave Sally,' Matthew said. 'She and the children depend on me.'

'Depend on you? That's rich.' Phillip laughed, too loudly. 'You're never home¡

'Sally's involved with her amateur dramatics and takes the girls with her. When I do go home they're often out at rehearsals and readings and castings and all that stuff.

I've tried going along, offering support, but it's so damned boring.'

'Thank goodness I'm not encumbered with children.'

'The girls aren't mine. As you know, Sally brought them from her first marriage – not that I don't love them. I do, very much. Beautiful they are. And they're the main reason why I can't ever leave. They've done nothing to deserve another upheaval. Losing their father was enough for them to cope with, don't you think?'

'I think you, Matthew Charles, are a brick.'

–

In Cwm Derw the weather turned cold and frost glittered on the hedges and sparkled like scattered jewels on the pavement. After a few days of being more or less confined to the house with little to occupy her, Hope was restless. Knowing the house that was to be theirs was empty, waiting for them, made her want to do something towards making it their home, but there was nothing to do except wait. The furniture was ordered and the curtains she had been given had all been neatly altered to fit.

Sewing was something she enjoyed and, although she had no specific training, she had a natural ability that even Marjorie had to admire. She gathered the remnants of the living-room curtains she'd been given and, while Davy played at her feet, found a piece large enough to make a cushion cover. By coiling smaller strips of material and using them to form a pattern at each corner, and adding embroidery, she made something beautiful and unique.

Ralph came home for lunch as his office was not far away, then, although the weather was not enticing she decided to take Davy for a walk. He'd be cosy enough in his pushchair to enjoy a little fresh air. Her steps took her to Badgers Brook. Almost without realizing it she found herself walking down the lane past the bus stop and looking for that first glimpse of the house.

The day was gloomy but it was still a surprise to see a light glowing in the kitchen, which faced the front path. She didn't know what to do, but curiosity was strong, as well as a growing sense of ownership, so she stopped at the gate and looked towards the house. A hand waved, then the door opened and Geoff Tanner called to her.

Easing the heavy pram through the gate and up the path she saw that he had been painting. He pointed towards the kitchen and to her delight she saw that the bright cheerful yellow paint she had ordered was now adding a lightness to the once dowdy room.

'It's as though the sun has come out!' she said, smiling her thanks. 'Thank you so much. Ralph will love it.'

'It was a good choice, I think. Even though it's a bit daring,' Geoff said. 'The house faces south across the garden and this is the darkest side, but your choice of sunny yellow certainly helps.'

'I like having the kitchen facing the lane. I can see people passing and greet visitors as soon as they reach the gate if I'm working near the sink,' she told him. Nothing about the house was wrong, everything was perfect.

'Now, I have to be off,' Geoff said wiping his hands on a rag. He offered her the key. 'You can make a start on any cleaning if you like, but unofficially, mind. Just between you and me, right?'

'Not long now.'

'A week or so, no longer. As I explained, the previous tenants have paid the rent for a few more weeks and I wrote offering a refund and to tell them their gardening tools are here but they told me to leave them for the new residents. It's best to be safe though, so we'll wait until the first. Okay?'

'As long as it's ours before Christmas. I'm still hoping to change Mother-in-law's mind.'

'Oh, don't worry, you'll be comfortable in your new home in time to celebrate Christmas.' He stopped to admire Davy and added, 'Don't forget to tell Father Christmas where you'll be, son. You don't want him to miss you, do you?'

It was at that moment that a determination to move in the moment they actually could overcame all other persuasions. This was her life, hers and Ralph's, and surely he wanted their own place as much as she did? His mother had had a lifetime of making her own decisions, forcing others to agree with her, and now it was time for Ralph to make his. He was twenty-three, he'd fought in a war, and it was ridiculous for him to allow his mother to tell him what he should do. She hurried home through the dark lanes and gaslit streets, filled with a determination that speeded her footsteps and narrowed her lips.

Tomorrow she would check on the furniture they had chosen. She wanted it to be delivered on the day the house was theirs. She would hang the curtains a few days before, with Geoff's permission, and the rugs she had bought for the floors would be quickly put in place. Between now and then she would wash the floors and clean the windows so everything was perfect. Then Ralph would be unable to refuse. Marjorie would have to understand.

Marjorie hated the colour of the kitchen. Hope didn't mind, she shared a smile with Ralph at her description of 'gaudy and ghastly'. Marjorie had insisted on going with her when she hung the curtains, and reacted in horror when she saw the kitchen with its bright walls and yellow and white check curtains.

A few days after Geoff had painted the walls, Marjorie arranged for a local decorator to re-paint them, in a subdued grey.

Angrily Hope demanded to know why. 'It's our house, Mother-in-law, the choices are ours, no one else's.'

'I agree, up to a point, but I simply couldn't allow you to do anything so ridiculous as paint the kitchen that awful yellow. Imagine what Ralph really thought. Believe me, he was horrified.'

'Ralph helped me choose it, or at least he agreed to it,' she said, fighting back sobs. 'He loved it as much as I did.'

'Trying to be kind, or he must have been too tired to know what he was saying. He works hard, you know, which is why you have to give him a home that's restful, calm, with peaceful decor to help him relax. Sometimes I think you don't understand my son at all.'

Hope felt the excitement of moving into her own home fading, drifting away as quickly as a dream upon waking. Ralph loved her but he loved his mother too. There was an ingrained obedience to her wishes that it seemed impossible for him to shed, Hope recognized with heartaching sadness and a growing certainty that Marjorie would never allow Ralph to truly belong to her and Davy. Marjorie was incapable of letting him go and Ralph was unable to offend her by insisting, supporting his wife when she needed him to so desperately. In this marriage, she, Hope, was alone.

Perhaps, if it hadn't been for the incident of the kitchen walls Hope might have softened towards her mother-in-law and given in about moving before Christmas, but that was the final straw. When Geoff called to tell Hope that the house was theirs from the following Wednesday, the first of December, she hugged the letter to her. Twenty-three days before Christmas Eve. It was easily possible. All she had to do was persuade Ralph. Christmas in their own home had once been just a dream; it was now more important: it was a means of establishing herself as Ralph's wife, sharing his life equally, and relegating his mother to her rightful place.

–

Everything was ready for the first delivery and Ralph, who had arranged for a day's holiday, stood at the door with Hope and tightened his grip around her shoulders. The furniture arrived: a dining suite in light oak and a leather three-piece suite for the lounge.

'Oh, excuse me, but there's a mistake. We chose uncut moquette in green,' Hope said, taking out the copy of their order.

Ralph hushed her. 'Darling. Mum changed it for a surprise. It was much more expensive, of course, but she paid the difference. She said leather is longer lasting and very smart.'

'Take it back. It isn't what I ordered.' she said firmly to the delivery men. They looked from one to the other and Ralph told them to leave it, that it was a surprise and his wife didn't mean it.

'Oh but I do. I hate leather. It's cold, uncomfortable and it's the same as you have at home. I want warm chairs, comfortable chairs not chairs that look nice.' Her voice was raised almost to a shout and Ralph looked most embarrassed. He apologized to the men, told Hope to calm down, and tried to lead her away while the men got on with the rest of the delivery.

'Ralph. Darling. We chose what we wanted for our house and this isn't it.' She angrily pushed an offending chair out into the hall and locked the door. 'Now, tell them to take it back or I'll burn it,' she said.

Alarmed by the fury of his normally placid wife, he unlocked the door and in hushed tones told them to return it to the shop and restore the previous instructions. In a tense silence the bedroom furniture and the rest of the deliveries were accepted and then, as the door closed behind the men, Geoff arrived with a delivery of household items from his hardware store. Ralph laughed. 'You realize we have a fully equipped kitchen and nowhere to sit except the dining chairs?'

'And whose fault is that?' she demanded.

'Mine, for falling in love with a girl called Hope.' He threw a couple of cushions on the floor and invited her to sit beside him. 'I know we'll be happy here, and when we get somewhere to sit we'll be happier still.' She threw a cushion at him and as he grabbed another and retaliated, laughing, kissing her between blows, Marjorie walked in with Davy. When she asked where the furniture was, they collapsed into laughter.

There are several kinds of laughter, Hope thought again, as they saw Marjorie on to a bus and began to walk back to Ty Mawr. Happiness and good company produced laughter that lifted the heart. This present laughter was a disguise for something deeply disturbing, hiding the fact that she and Ralph were continually patching over snags and breakdowns in their togetherness.

The false laughter trembled in her throat and she fought against it, knowing this time Ralph wouldn't join in. When they reached Ty Mawr and went in to listen to more of Marjorie's complaints about their refusal of the leather suite, it was certain to break out and offend her even further. And if she gave in to it then, she would laugh hysterically, embarrassingly, and alone.

Two

Hope's dream of spending at least a part of Christmas in their new home was fading away. Marjorie made it clear that the occasion was hers to arrange. Toys for Davy were wrapped and hidden, food appeared from mysterious sources that defied explanation in times of rationing. 'Favours owed,' was all the explanation her mother-in-law gave. The house was decked in holly, ivy and a huge amount of pre-war decoration, tarnished with age but giving the rooms a mysterious excitement that thrilled Davy.

Ralph seemed content with the arrangements and when she tried to persuade him they should at least sleep at Badgers Brook, he just laughed and said that Christmas had always been Mum's special time. 'She's strong on tradition,' he added cheerfully, 'and she does everything so perfectly.'

'But we need to start our own traditions,' she pleaded, to no avail.

The house that was theirs stood silent and empty apart from the eerie effect of the few formally placed pieces of furniture. With no sign of anyone living there it would be without warmth, unloved, and Hope badly wanted to bring it to life.

'It's like a stage set waiting for an audience, or a shop window trying to attract customers,' she said to Ralph one morning, in an attempt to make light of it.

'We'll soon make it untidy and lived in,' Ralph said. 'Mum will go there with a few pictures and cushions, she knows how to make a house a home.'

So do I, she wanted to shout. Instead she said. 'After Christmas then?'

'Probably.' His reply dragged at her heart. Marjorie was going to hang on to them for as long as she could. Getting her own way was something else Mum was good at, she thought with a sigh.

'Is there any news of Phillip coming home?' she asked, hoping that such excitement would allow them to sneak away and leave Marjorie to her celebrations, her welcoming of the prodigal son.

'That's unlikely, which is one reason we must stay,' he replied.

One Saturday, when she and Ralph had planned to go shopping, Freddy announced Marjorie's plan to have a party. 'It's something she's wanted to do for a long time,' Freddy told them. 'Originally it was to have been a welcome home party for Richard and Phillip, but the idea hasn't really gone away. I want your mother to have a reason to fill the house, even though it will only be for a few hours.'

'It will be a New Year party,' Marjorie explained to them later. 'We'll hold it a week or two into the New Year, though, when the celebrations are well and truly over and the weather closes in and people are in need of a bit of a lift. You and Ralph will host it, while Dad and I sit and enjoy ourselves. There'll be plenty of food and drink left over from Christmas. In fact, I've already put some things aside, tins and some sugar and, of course, friends will contribute. We can start the preparations straight after New Year, take our time, then it won't be a chore.'

'We'll help, of course, but remember we won't be living here,' Hope reminded her.

'Of course you will, dear. You can't go back to a cold house. In January? Far too risky. It'll take days of lighting fires before it's safe to take little David there.'

–

That night when they went to bed, which was the only time they were able to talk in private, she told Ralph that he must insist and tell his mother they were leaving as soon as Christmas was over.

'Not yet, darling,' he whispered. 'We'll have years on our own, just you and me and Davy. Let Mum have a few more days.' This response, this appeal for kindness, this thinly disguised blackmail, no longer made her feel any guilt.

'Tomorrow I'll take Davy and stay in the house, light the fires, make sure the beds are aired. I'll do that every day, and buy a few extras to make it our very own, and on Boxing Day we're going home.' She touched him, pushed against his shoulder demanding agreement, prepared to argue, but his breathing had slowed and his body was sluggish to her touch. Anger made her insist. Putting her lips close to his ear, she said, 'Whether you're asleep or just pretending, that is what I'm going to do. You can stay, or come with us. You choose.'

She lay still for a while, hoping he had heard and would reach out and comfort her, tell her he agreed, assure her that she and Davy were more important than his mother and they would move as soon as possible. After several minutes had passed, when she knew he was either asleep or had no intention of supporting her, she reached for her dressing gown and tiptoed down the stairs. In the dark kitchen she sat, unaware of the cold creeping into her bones. A creak on the stairs and she didn't move. It was probably Marjorie. The woman never sleeps, she's always aware of what I'm doing, even in the middle of the night, she thought sadly.

But it wasn't her mother-in-law. 'Darling, I'm sorry.' Ralph's arms wrapped her in their warmth and he held her close. 'Come to bed, you're freezing. I'm sorry about Mum's reluctance to let us go. But if we could give her a little more time to get used to the idea I'm sure she'll come round.'

'More time? This is our time, she's stealing our time, yours and mine and Davy's,' she said, the momentary relief and happiness of his coming to find her gone in a flash. He'd said just too many words and the brief joy had been destroyed. If only he'd stopped after 'I'm sorry'. Instead, once again, he had supported his mother.

Disappointed at the way his apology had been received, Ralph went back to bed, and Hope sat shivering in the cold kitchen until she was sure he was asleep before settling on the armchair in Davy's room.

-

By leaving Marjorie to prepare breakfast and busying herself with getting Davy dressed and fed, she managed to avoid speaking to Ralph the next morning. Explaining briefly that she was going to the shops, she put Davy in his pram and walked through the town and down the lane to

Badgers Brook. When she reached the house she found a rooted Christmas tree leaning against the front door. There was a label attached which read: *This tree is for your first Christmas in Badgers Brook. Put it in the garden in the New Year, and it will grow and remind you of how happy you are at this moment.*

Hope pushed it aside, dragged the pram inside and howled.

The coal entitlement she had ordered was in the shed with a load of logs. Someone, she suspected it was her kind-hearted landlord Geoff Tanner again, had chopped sticks and left a pile of newspapers. She had brought matches and although the paper was a bit damp she soon had fires burning brightly, reflecting on the walls in the almost empty lounge and adding a glow to the new polished dining table. Within a couple of hours the place had been given a life. If only Ralph were here to enjoy it with her.

A knock at the door surprised her. She opened it to a lady well wrapped up in a thick coat and fur-lined boots, a scarf tied around her head. She looked to be in her late fifties and had a smile on her small, thin face that warmed Hope like the sun. She looked at Hope expectantly, waiting to be invited inside.

'I'm Kitty Jennings and my husband, him down there by the gate, is Bob.' Hope looked to where she pointed and saw the man wave. She waved back as Kitty went on, 'Live on the lane, we do, and we wondered if you needed any help.' Her beady eyes looked past Hope and she saw Davy on the floor playing with a small wooden car. 'Oh, I see you're in. Welcome to the neighbourhood.'

'Won't you come in?' Hope stood back to allow her visitor to enter, then went to pick up Davy. 'We haven't moved in exactly. We're still staying with my parents-in-law until after Christmas. I just thought I'd light a few fires.'

'The rest of the furniture coming later is it?' Kitty said pointedly.

Hope laughed. 'It does look a bit sad, but the rest will be here soon. There was a mistake in the order.'

'Yes, I saw it come,' Kitty said without any embarrassment, 'then watched as they took it away again.'

Kitty boldly suggested a cup of tea might be nice and they talked for a while, and although the woman was obviously someone who liked to know all that was going on Hope warmed to her more and more, knowing she would be a good neighbour and friend.

'If you want me to look after the fires any time or open windows on a nice blowy day I'll be glad to help. The house needs both after being empty a while.' She opened the front door and dragged in the tree. 'Now, I've got some tinsel and a few spare dingle-dangles that your little boy would love. I'll just slip and get them. My Bob is sure to have a suitable container and some earth so we can set up the tree.'

'Sadly we won't be spending Christmas here,' Hope began.

'Go on with you! Christmas isn't a few hours, it's a season in itself. Weeks of fun, that's what Christmas is. In fact, why not have a second Christmas, once you and that husband of yours finally move in?'

Bob brought a pan of soup at twelve and they ate it with freshly baked bread. To Hope, her first meal in the new home was a feast, and Davy ate a bowlful and demanded more. He sat next to Bob and chattered in his sometimes indistinct way, with Hope translating his attempts.

Beside being blatantly curious to know all about Hope and Ralph and the family, Kitty and Bob told Hope a lot about themselves. Bob Jennings was a retired policeman and Kitty had once worked as a typist in a insurance office. 'Posh job, low pay,' she explained with a chuckle. Their children were grown up and had moved away.

The rest of the day was happy and busy as Kitty encouraged Hope to add decorations to the bare walls. The long oak table in the kitchen was covered in paste, paper and bits and pieces of the old decorations brought by her new friend. Even those that were broken were patched together by sticking and sewing, and it all helped to liven the rooms.

The results were not beautiful, Hope admitted, as she looked around the brightly decorated rooms, and she knew Marjorie would be horrified, but she hadn't felt so happy in months. She thanked Kitty and Bob as they left, and promised they would meet again soon.

At three o'clock she carefully damped down the fires, and, still warm from the hours close to the fire, she and a grubby Davy set off for Ty Mawr. She looked back when she reached the gate and thought that, even after such a short visit, the house was now her home, she belonged there.

They stopped to wave when they passed the home of Kitty and Bob, where a tree glittered in the window. She guessed that Kitty's would have been the first house in the town to have its windows decorated. Kitty Jennings was without doubt a lady who loved Christmas.

–

Several times in the days that followed, she packed a picnic lunch and took Davy to spend the day at the house. She was surprised that Marjorie didn't complain at her regular disappearances, and disappointed, too, that Ralph saw no reason to go with her at the weekend. The house was welcoming her, but in some mysterious way alienating her from Ralph. They wanted different things and, after three years of marriage, that was a frightening thought.

–

Christmas coloured the days as it approached, and hour by hour Hope felt less involved. Her thoughts, her future plans overrode the festival and she looked beyond the few days of Christmas to a time when she would be living in Badgers Brook. Although she tried in every way she could to imbue her husband with the same excitement, Ralph remained dishearteningly vague about when they would actually move in, seemingly quite content to remain with his parents for the foreseeable future.

When they went for a walk one Sunday afternoon, she deliberately led him towards their house. As they walked down the lane past Kitty and Bob Jennings's house she waved to them and explained airily to Ralph that she was already getting to know their new neighbours.

He didn't seem keen to go inside but she insisted, struggling with the pram when he seemed disinclined to help. Their visit had been pre-arranged by herself and Kitty, so the place was warm, the fires in both living rooms having been lit by Kitty.

'Good heavens, it's so warm,' Ralph exclaimed. She turned to look at him expecting to see pleasure on his face, but he wasn't at all pleased. 'Who lit fires for heaven's sake!

What a waste. Mum would have been glad of extra wood and coal instead of frittering it away like this.'

Hope looked at him sadly, her heart plummeting. 'Oh, Ralph. Only you could find a reason to complain when the house has been made so welcoming.'

'Sorry, darling, but you must agree, it is extravagant. It'll be a few weeks yet before we can move in.'

'The spring?' she asked coldly. 'The summer? Autumn?'

'Not that long, but I want to give Mum time to accept it.'

Hope didn't want to stay long. There wasn't any point. The happy visit she had planned was in ruins. Ralph collected the coat she had removed and waited impatiently at the door, his hands on the handle of the pram, pushing it to and fro, anxious to be gone. She put on her outdoor clothes slowly. Perhaps Ralph finally became aware of her dismay, because he turned away from the door and went up the stairs in a belated attempt to show interest.

He saw the bed all made up, and a fire glowing in the small iron fireplace and said, 'Darling, it looks so inviting. I haven't had a fire in my bedroom since I was a child, and only then when I was ill. Measles, that was the last time. The curtains drawn against the light and a flickering fire making pictures on the wall, changing the white counterpane to pink. I loved it.'

'Tell you mother we're moving in.' she pleaded. 'It's here, waiting for us, and I want so much for us to be a family in a home of our own.'

'The rest of the furniture hasn't been delivered yet,' he warned.

'Excuses, excuses,' she said teasingly, trying laughter as a means to persuade him as other persuasions had failed.

'We could christen the bed though,' he said.

'Davy might wake.'

'Excuses, excuses…'

As she smoothed the crumpled sheets an hour later, Davy woke, and at the same time there was a knock at the door. Embarrassed, certain the visitor would guess how they had filled the past hour, she opened the door to Marjorie.

'What on earth…? Who made this terrible mess?' she demanded, walking in and seeing the amateur decorations.

Ralph had followed Hope down and he put an arm around her shoulders and said, 'Don't you like them, Mum? We think they're perfect.'

A tiny wriggling glimmer of optimism filled Hope's heart, making it swell. 'Davy helped,' she said, leaning back and resting her head against Ralph.

Marjorie didn't stay long, but managed to show disapproval as she looked around the rooms, unnecessarily adjusting the curtains and silently straightening the bedding. She was quiet as the three of them walked home.

The following morning, as they ate breakfast, she said. 'I think it's time you moved into your home.'

Hope's heart began to race and she was afraid to say a word. She looked at Ralph, but instead of displaying the same excitement she felt, he only said, 'Only if you're sure, Mum. There's no great rush.'

There *is*, Hope wanted to shout but she dared not say a word. She stood up and began to collect the used plates, waiting for Marjorie's response.

'I thought you were in a hurry,' she said, and to Hope's disbelief Ralph shook his head.

'We're very happy here and Davy loves having his granny around to spoil him.'

'If you're sure. After New Year then, and the party.'

Hope beckoned to Ralph and led him upstairs to their room. 'Ralph, what is the matter with you? Don't you think I can look after you and Davy as well as your mother does? Or are you afraid to be responsible for your family? What is it that's stopping us moving out of here? Please tell me. I don't understand.' She stood in front of him holding his arms, forcing him to speak. 'The truth,' she demanded. He stared at her as though trying to make up his mind. Hope looked into his eyes and saw a stranger.

'All right, the truth, then,' he said at last. 'I didn't want to rent Badgers Brook. It was you who's been so persistent about leaving here. I'm comfortable and I enjoy living with Mum and Dad. I was born here and leaving the Ty Mawr will be a wrench, even with you and Davy. Besides, there's Mum. She's lost two of my brothers, one dead the other as good as. Phillip has cut himself off from us almost as permanently as poor Richard. If – I mean when – we leave she'll be faced with a rattling shell of a house that was once full of people and noise. She'll be here with time on her hands, waiting for a knock at the door, depending on our visits to fill it for odd moments, give her someone to look after. She's always been busy, always had people to care for, and the emptiness, the feeling of uselessness would kill her.'

'Living here, waiting to start our life together is killing me, Ralph.'

Outside, Marjorie was listening, and when she heard Ralph reply that in that case she was right, they should leave, she hurried down the stairs and prepared a brief pre-emptive speech.

'I've been selfish,' she told them with just a hint of dismay. 'Tomorrow we'll arrange with the removal men for the loan of some of my furniture so you can move into your own home.'

In her euphoria Hope turned and hugged Ralph, who looked a little stunned. Amazed, just like me, Hope thought happily. Instead his words shocked her.

'Only if you're sure, Mum. And if you aren't happy about it we can always come back for a while, can't we, darling?'

Determined there wouldn't be any further discussion, Hope arranged the following morning for the delivery of the armchairs that Marjorie was lending them. She also bought two book cases and an occasional table from a second-hand shop and a wooden toy box for Davy's room, which she intended to paint with a cheerful design.

She was so wrapped up in her plans that she was unaware of Ralph's lack of enthusiasm; she bustled him into dealing with things, her mind always on the next and the next, so it wasn't until they sat together, one each side of the fire in Marjorie's armchairs in the lounge on that first evening in their home, that she became aware of how subdued he was.

'Are you all right?' she asked a little anxiously.

'It's so quiet,' he said.

'I'll wake Davy if it's noise you want,' she said jokingly.

'We haven't got a wireless.'

'I've arranged for a rental set to be here tomorrow. Surely you and I can fill an evening without help?'

He smiled but it didn't reach his eyes. His taut expression frightened her. Had she made a terrible mistake persuading him to move away from his mother? It seemed the right thing to do, to start building their life together and making their own decisions, but perhaps the problem wasn't with Marjorie, perhaps he really hadn't wanted to leave?

It was a couple of hours before they could go to bed and she knew that unless she broke the evening up in some way the silence would become oppressive. He showed no inclination to share an armchair, had in fact moved away when she had tried to snuggle on his lap. The romantic homecoming dreamed of for so long had been a great disappointment. Was it because they had stayed too long with his parents? Had he lost the thrill of moving into his own home by waiting too long, becoming too comfortable?

Their marriage had changed very little in his life. He still went to the same office each day and returned to the same house. The bedroom they'd been given had always been his, and his meals had continued to be chosen, and often cooked, by his mother. She knew she had to do something to make this evening memorable, make him consider it the day on which their marriage really began. But everything she suggested resulted in a slow shake of his head.

As minutes passed and every attempt at conversation ended elicited a monosyllabic response, she asked, 'Are you hungry?' He hadn't eaten much of the meal she had so carefully planned and prepared.

'I am, rather.'

'Gwennie Flint's fish and chip shop is open until ten,' she coaxed. 'Shall I go and fetch some? It won't take long on the bus.'

'I'll go,' he said at once. She sensed the relief as he leaped up, grabbed his coat and headed for the door. The chip shop was near his parents' house and she wondered if he would use the excuse to call in. Surely not! He wouldn't, not so soon after moving out? But the thought refused to go away.

She sat making lists of things to do, things to buy, lists of people to whom she must send Christmas cards with their new address. The room grew colder as the fire dropped back, but it didn't seem worth adding more coal. Tomorrow, she told herself, tomorrow everything will be perfect. This is really our honeymoon. We'll wake up in our own home, Davy will run in and jump on our bed and we'll laugh and say how wonderful everything is, how perfect, and Ralph will be happy.

An hour passed and she began to listen for his key in the door. She found the silence strange and somehow unsettling. A glance at the clock told her it was half past ten and another half hour had passed. She presumed bitterly that he really had gone back home to catch up on what had happened during the few hours he'd been away. Irritated, she took the plates off the hearth where she had put them to warm and went upstairs to undress. She would ignore his insensitivity in leaving her and going back to Ty Mawr, and put on the gown she had bought for their first honeymoon. Their first night here could still be perfect, she had to give him time, that was all.

She was halfway up when she heard loud knocking at the door. Puzzled, she ran down and opened it. To her alarm two policemen stood there.

'Mrs Murton? Mrs Ralph Murton? I'm sorry, but your husband has been involved in an accident. Will you come to the hospital with us so you can see him and help the doctors by answering a few questions?'

'I can't, I have a baby. I mean, where is he? How badly is he hurt? Does his mother know? I'll have to bring Davy, I, oh dear, I can't believe it, he only went for chips, because we haven't got a wireless, and...' She went on gabbling as she ran upstairs and wrapped a sleeping Davy in blankets, then she picked up her handbag and followed them out.

In spite of her tirade of questions, they said very little about what had happened, just that he appeared to have been crossing the road near his parents' house and not seen a car approaching, being driven moderately fast. 'The driver was hurt but not seriously. There were a few witnesses, thank goodness. So we'll soon find out exactly what happened.' In fact, Hope didn't take in a word of what he said anyway. She didn't want to hear about the driver, it seemed irrelevant to be told who had hurt Ralph. Her only thought was how badly he was injured.

The first person she saw when she reached the hospital was her mother-in-law. She was walking up and down, and the anger on her face as she caught sight of Hope was a shock. Behind her, looking anxious and confused, was Ralph's father.

'This is your fault,' Marjorie shouted. 'If you hadn't made him move away from us he wouldn't have been hurt.'

'Not now, Marjorie,' Freddy said. 'Let's find out how bad he is before you start on everyone.'

Ignoring them both, hugging Davy as though he was a lifeline, Hope ran to talk to a nurse. Within a few moments she was talking to a doctor, while Marjorie complained loudly outside the door.

43

'How badly is he hurt?' Hope's voice was breathless, as though she had run every yard of the way. 'Can I see him?'

'It's too early to answer that yet, but he suffered serious back injuries. As soon as the doctors and nurses have made him comfortable you'll be taken to see him.'

In a daze she went out to where Marjorie and Freddy were standing. By this time Marjorie had calmed down and simply asked if Hope had learned anything new.

'As soon as they know the extent of his injuries they'll come and tell us,' Hope said. 'I can't see him yet, but soon, when he's comfortable.'

'What were you thinking of, sending him out for fish and chips? Can't you cook a meal yet?' Marjorie hissed. Freddy grabbed his wife's arm and led her away. Hope was trembling, and although she couldn't hear what was being said she guessed that Freddy was telling Marjorie not to apportion blame until they were given the facts.

Eventually the doctor took Hope, still carrying a sleepy Davy, into an office. Here she was told the frightening news.

'There's a serious spinal injury, I'm afraid, Mrs Murton, and for the moment we can't say how badly he'll be affected. It will take several days for the swelling and bruising to subside before we can properly assess the damage.'

'Will he come home tomorrow?' she asked, unable to contemplate what they were telling her. 'He'll be all right in a few days, won't he? Can I see him, please?'

'Too early to give a prognosis, Mrs Murton. But I must warn you the injury to his spine is giving cause for concern.'

She still looked at him blankly as though he hadn't spoken. 'But of course you can see him,' he said kindly.

'Although, he is sedated. Matron will take you to see him but then I think you should go home. There's nothing you can do here. He'll sleep through the night and you'd be better off doing the same, so you can deal with whatever happens tomorrow. Besides,' he added patting Davy's head, 'this handsome little boy of yours needs his bed too.'

Marjorie and Freddy were waiting outside as the doctor escorted her out still murmuring encouraging words. Freddy was clearly distressed but Marjorie was glaring angrily.

An immaculately uniformed nurse led her to the room where Ralph lay. He looked pale and so utterly still she thought for a terrifying moment that he had died. The nurse talked to her, about how much better things would be in the morning and how certain she was that Ralph was a fighter, and, as with the words of the kindly policemen, nothing she said penetrated Hope's dazed mind.

'Will he be home tomorrow?' she asked again, and again didn't comprehend the reply.

'I don't imagine he'll be home just yet.' The nurse tried to explain. 'It will be days before a decision is made on the best treatment. He had suffered serious damage to his spine, as the doctor explained, Mrs Murton.'

'There has to be a mistake. He's sleeping, that's all, he'll be fine once he's rested.'

'Try to understand. Mrs Murton. Your husband has been involved in a road accident and he'll be in hospital for quite a time.'

'But it's our honeymoon, we've only just moved in,' a stricken Hope cried.

'I'll take you to see your mother-in-law, shall I?'

'What's happening?' Marjorie demanded when she once more returned to the waiting area.

'I don't really know.' Hope shook her head, a frown creasing her brow. 'Tomorrow, they say we'll know more tomorrow,' she said in a low voice. 'He'll be home then, once he's rested. He looks very tired, and pale. You know how pale he is when he's tired, Mother-in-law.' She turned to Freddy. 'I wanted to go, to buy him some supper, a little treat for the first evening in our home. He insisted because he could call and see you two, that was why he didn't want me to go. Gwennie Flint's shop isn't far from Ty Mawr. He wanted to see you two. I should have gone. I'd have been more careful.'

The matron advised them all to go home and rest and come back in the morning, before walking away with a final reassuring nod towards Hope.

It was only then that Hope was aware of how tired she was after holding Davy for so long. She put a foot on a bench and rested him on her knee to ease her aching arms.

'I'll phone for a taxi, shall I?' she suggested.

'I'm not moving,' Marjorie said emphatically. 'You can go, if you aren't bothered about my son, but I'm staying until I know what happened to him.'

'The doctors and nurses don't want us around, Father-in-law,' Hope said with a trembling sigh. 'They'll get in touch if there's anything to report, but it's best we go home and come back in the morning.'

Freddy nodded agreement and went outside to a telephone box and ordered a taxi to take them home.

'We'll take you to Badgers Brook first,' he said.

'You mean you aren't coming back with us?' Marjorie gasped.

'No, Mother-in-law. Davy and I are going home,' Hope said firmly. Today they had made the break and had moved into Badgers Brook and it was there she needed to be, to wait for Ralph to come home.

Walking into the room with its sad, battered collection of Christmas decorations was the moment that shock really hit her. Putting Davy into her bed, she lay awake all night hugging him as though he were the one needing comfort. As the shock left her the words of the doctors and nurses flooded her tired brain and she began to feel afraid. Spinal injury! She thought of the wounded soldiers, sailors and airmen who lived their lives in wheelchairs or helped along with crutches.

She really was to blame. Ralph had admitted he hadn't wanted to leave his parents' house, and his reluctance to move in confirmed that. She had forced the move on him and the result was an accident that might have ruined his life. The doctor had been vague, yet his words – now clearly remembered – and the expressions on the faces of the kindly nurses all gave clear indications that the injuries were serious. For once she believed Marjorie's spiteful remarks; the accident was due to her determination to have her own way.

Marjorie went home but didn't even try to sleep. While Freddy dozed on the couch, she wrote a message to Phillip that she would send by telegram the following day, telling him to come home, that his brother had been seriously hurt.

–

When the telegram arrived at the North Wales address, Connie put it beside Phillip's plate on the breakfast table and he read it, considered it nothing more than a ruse to persuade him to go home for a dreaded family Christmas and lazily threw it into the rubbish as he had done with all of his mother's letters. Connie read it and tried to persuade him to at least phone the hospital and ask about Ralph.

'No need,' he insisted. 'Ralph has probably had a boil lanced or something. Very dramatic, when she wants her own way, is my mother.' Connie pleaded but to no avail.

—

The days following the accident were filled with hospital visits. Ralph underwent two operations and the results didn't offer much hope of recovery. The doctors told Hope that, for the foreseeable future, Ralph would be confined to a wheelchair.

'It's too early to know for certain whether there will be sufficient improvement for him to walk, possibly with aids, at some time in the future, but better you think of the short term and make arrangements for him to get the help he needs.'

'What will he need?' she asked, her voice trembling.

'A bed downstairs would be advisable, rather than having to arrange for someone to carry him up and down each day. I always think it's better for a crippled patient to be down, where he's part of the family during the day, rather than upstairs on his own.'

It was hearing the word crippled that upset her the most. With Davy in his pram, she walked miles through the roads and lanes trying to force herself to accept what the doctors were saying. Ralph was unable to walk and he would depend on a wheelchair for getting around, perhaps for ever. And the fault was hers.

Christmas came and went with Hope hardly being aware of it. She replied to greetings cheerfully called as she went about her tasks, waving to some of the new neighbours and accepting their kind thoughts, which she passed on to a completely uninterested Ralph.

Kitty and Bob called often, and it was they who gave Davy the fun of the season, playing games, admiring his toys and sometimes spending time with him while Hope visited Ralph.

Throughout the month of January, Hope visited the hospital every day, often sitting in the waiting area for most of the visiting hour, while Marjorie refused to leave Ralph's bedside. Sometimes a nurse, aware of what was happening, insisted on Marjorie leaving and allowed Hope to sit with her husband.

Marjorie rarely spoke to Hope and even Davy's cheerful and active presence, when Hope took him in an attempt to cheer Ralph, didn't take away the cold anger that distorted her face whenever she and Hope met. It was only Freddy who offered a little friendship, and even that was muted when his wife appeared.

Hope would try to amuse Ralph and make him smile at some of the things young Davy had done that day. She tried to sound positive and talked encouragingly about when he would be allowed home. The truth, the dreadful truth, was that he knew once he left hospital he would be confined to a wheelchair, possibly for life. His eyes stared at her from a pale face, and, although the words were never spoken, she knew he blamed her for insisting they left Ty Mawr.

–

When she wasn't at the hospital Hope spent a lot of time in the garden. Snow and frost made it impossible to do very much, but she cut away the dead remnants of the previous summer's display and cleaned the homemade, somewhat battered greenhouse ready for a new season. Freddy came once and helped her build a bonfire, but he didn't stay very long. She learned from others that he spent a lot of time at the Ship and Compass, although he never showed signs of excessive drinking.

Bob and Geoff called often, and they advised her on what she might grow. One day, when the three men were there together, glad of an escape from thoughts about Ralph's condition, they sat and wrote out an order for seeds and listed the plants she would need.

The garden hadn't been neglected, in fact the ground was in good condition and ready for planting. She had never had a garden before, and had no experience of anything larger than a window box, and the garden at Ty Mawr didn't have anything other than lawns and shrubberies and an area of soft fruit looked after by Freddy.

Forced to dig up lawns to grow vegetables during the war, Marjorie had employed gardeners to put it back to its original state the moment restrictions were eased. That Freddy had been disappointed, having enjoyed the delight of growing food, was something of which she was unaware. Ty Mawr had always been neat lawns and flowering trees and shrubs, and that was how it would stay.

One afternoon, Hope had returned from a visit to the town to place her small grocery order, when she saw that the gate was unlatched. They'd had a visitor. Her heart began to race. It was probably Marjorie, no one else was likely to call on a Monday. It was a busy day and the neighbours would be washing clothes and bedding, and clearing up after the weekend.

She took a deep breath for the condemnations to come. She pushed the door but it was still locked. Not Marjorie then. She wouldn't have hesitated to use the key Ralph had given her and wouldn't have needed to lock it again from the inside. She went to where she kept a spare key, saw it was missing and went inside.

It wasn't until she looked out of the lounge window into the garden that she saw that her visitor was her father-in-law. She went in to the kitchen and swiftly filled the kettle, set it on the gas stove and then went to greet him.

The ground was thick mud – in fact, she had been told by Bob Jennings that more harm than good would come of trying to work the ground at this time – so she was curious as she went out to see what he was doing.

'I thought I'd dig a trench for runner beans,' he explained. 'Nice and deep, then you can throw all your kitchen waste in and some old newspapers, too, to hold the moisture. Make the roots go down a treat it will.'

'Thank you,' she said hesitantly. 'But isn't it rather long?' The trench was only a couple of feet wide but the area he had marked out stretched for about twenty-five feet.

'They're so easy to grow.' he said. 'Wonderful to watch them. What you don't use you can sell. Everyone loves freshly picked beans.'

She doubted being able to sell them, but she told him it was a wonderful idea and thanked him profusely for his hard work.

'Bob Jennings helped,' he said cheerfully. 'He reminded me they need to be planted north to south so they get the sun one side in the morning, the other side in the afternoon. Now, what about a cup of tea, eh?'

Hope guessed that the activity was cathartic. The unaccustomed exercise was a time-filler and hopefully would encourage sleep.

She made tea and brought out a few of the oddly shaped biscuits she and Davy had made. In the chilly garden, dressed in thick outdoor clothes, Freddy explained how much he had enjoyed growing things during the war.

'I didn't want to lose the vegetable garden when restrictions were lifted, but you know how Marjorie likes everything to look orderly. Turned over soil, untidy planting, wheelbarrows, pots, strings and things just didn't appeal. She wanted smooth lawns and orderly shrubs. Even though the government still asks us to grow as much food as we can.'

As always the conversation led by one route or another to discussing the progress of Ralph. As they walked back inside, she said, 'I think I'd like to work on the garden. It's been well tended and it would be a pity to let it go. Will you help me?'

Freddy willingly agreed to spend a few afternoons with her, and she felt a surge of optimism. It was as though the promise of a garden blossoming and giving its bounty was a sign that other things would work out too. Ralph would recover, and even if he couldn't win any races he would be able to walk, even if it meant using sticks. Being an accountant, he would be able to return to work.

She went to see him that evening, having left Davy with Kitty and Bob, wanting to see him alone to tell him how hopeful she felt, to encourage him to think enthusiastically about his homecoming. The doctor asked her to go into his office and there she was told that after another small operation, mainly to ease the pain, he would be coming home, but the prospect of him ever walking again was too remote to consider.

Ralph's silence when she entered his room was frightening enough, but then, quietly and with apparent calm, he told her that he held her responsible for his situation. He spoke so gently that it was almost unbelievable that his accusations were so cruel.

'You sent me out knowing I was unhappy, knowing my mind was all over the place. We shouldn't have been there. Mum didn't want us to go. Dad liked having us there and I was happy living in Ty Mawr. Only you were insistent on us leaving.'

Stricken with shock Hope could only stare at him. The voice was Ralph's but the words were Marjorie's. He hit his useless legs and, still without raising his voice, said, 'These would still be working if it weren't for your determination that we needed a place of our own.'

Hope was stunned. Had he honestly forgotten his insistence on going out that night? Or, she suddenly remembered, that the initial idea of moving out and finding a place of their own had been his? Oh, she'd agreed, enthusiastically, but the original suggestion had been his. She had forgotten that, since he had become so reluctant under pressure from Marjorie. Now he believed the poison his mother was whispering into his ear.

Tears began to fall and Hope whispered, 'You know none of that is true, darling. Moving to Badgers Brook was what we both wanted. Perhaps we were wrong, and if that's the case we'll put it right. You get well again and, if you hate it so much, we can move back to Ty Mawr.

Anything you want we can do. Promise me you'll try to relax and concentrate on getting well. Davy and I need you with us so desperately.'

He didn't reply. From the closed expression on his thin pale face, she wasn't even sure he had heard.

A bell rang to warn visitors it was time to leave, and she bent over the bed to kiss him. He caught hold of her coat and pulled her close to him. She put her hands around his cheeks preparing for a proper, loving kiss, but he hissed, 'I overheard the doctors talking, so stop lying to me. They know I'll never walk again, thanks to you! Never, never, never!' He turned his head away from her and refused to say another word.

—

Ralph's homecoming was a sombre affair. Kitty and Bob stayed in the house with Davy while Hope went to the hospital and arranged for his transfer into her care. She was frightened, wondering if she could cope with all she would have to do for him, wondering, too, how difficult a patient he would be. At his insistence, he was taken straight up the stairs to the bedroom, where a fire burned cheerfully. Marjorie sat beside him while Hope prepared a meal. Kitty and Bob left, having been ignored by Marjorie, and promised to call later.

For three days he hardly spoke and then he asked to be carried downstairs to spend the day near the fire, where he could look out into the garden. Bob and Geoff would have helped, but before she could ask them Peter Bevan called with her order of vegetables and, hearing the situation, went up and carried Ralph down.

Hope had prepared the newly arrived couch to receive him and, with blankets and pillows and plenty of newspapers and books, he settled, again in almost complete silence, to fill his days. He insisted on having a bed set up in a corner of the room and declared his intention of staying there permanently.

Although the nurse called and tried to encourage him to do exercises and use the wheelchair that stood waiting for him, he refused. He made no effort to extend the severe limitations of his life. Until one day, when he was alone apart from his father, who had been working on the garden, he reached over and pulled the hated wheelchair close to the bed.

Ralph's arms were still strong and, with his father's help, he managed to get into the wheelchair. He manoeuvred himself from bed to chair and back again. He didn't go any further than the kitchen, but Freddy was delighted.

Hope tried to sound encouraging, loving, strong, but Ralph treated her like a servant, only speaking when he needed something done. Freddy was upset by this, knowing Marjorie was encouraging her son to continue to heap blame on his wife instead of coaxing him to rebuild a life for himself, and improve his existence by his own efforts.

Bob and Freddy built a ramp to enable Ralph to go outside, hoping that when winter gave way to spring he might be tempted to widen his world. Ralph told them to take it up as he had no intention of ever going outside to be laughed at or pitied.

Peter occasionally called when he had finished his delivery rounds, staying for a cup of tea and spending a little time with Davy while Hope did a few of her many tasks.

February was dull and bitterly cold but just occasionally produced a day of sun that confused people into believing spring had arrived. Marjorie came every day to sit with her son, firmly closing the door against Hope and little Davy. Their animated conversations left Hope feeling utterly alone, so rarely did they include her in their whispered words and laughter. The animation when his mother was there fell from him like a cloak when she left. He seemed unaware of Hope, and Davy had given up trying to interest him in his daily discoveries, or the pictures he produced.

The doctor called regularly, the hospital monitored his healing, and every time he was examined Ralph expected there to be an improvement. The day the doctor told him sympathetically that it was better to expect none, then if it came it would be a wonderful gift, was the day he gave up on the dream. The day was bright and sunny, the air crisp and fresh, a day for having fun, and the contrast was too much.

He ate very little lunch and refused a five o'clock tea-time snack, giving the plateful of small sandwiches and tempting cakes to Davy to put out for the birds. While Hope was bathing Davy and getting him ready for bed he made his move.

His arms were strong, and he managed with the ease of secret practices to get into his chair from the bed, where he still sat for much of the day, and go outside. The ramp made by his father and Bob, which he had sworn never to use, was wide with a rough finish and a gentle slope and easily managed. He spun the wheels and was soon making his way along the path and into the lane.

It was almost dark and the lane was never busy at this time. No one was likely to see him. There was a hill leading down from the other side of the woods, narrow, with a badly worn surface. The hedges had been neglected and were straggly, reaching out across the already limited access. Because there was a better road to make the same journey, this one was rarely used.

Pushing aside the over-long branches of bramble and the blackthorn, which would soon to burst into a beautiful display of white lace, he looked down the steep path and assessed its dangers. At the bottom, the road ran beside a long drop into a field beside the brook that ran through the woods. The fence had rotted and disappeared years before.

He reached the point from where the steepest descent began without seeing anyone and, with a strange haunted look on his pale, thin face, he lined up the chair. Covering his eyes with his hands and gritting his teeth, he released the brake.

–

Hope didn't miss him until the stories she had been reading sent Davy into a relaxed sleep. She stayed a while even then, watching him and wondering how this unhappiness was affecting him. Gathering darkness changed the room into a cosy place with night lights glowing from the top of the cupboard and near the window. Marjorie told her it was wrong to pamper the boy with a light, but she knew that the strange house and the utter darkness due to its position at the edge of the woods might worry him. Ty Mawr, on the main road, had never been so completely dark.

Darkness had fallen while she had been with Davy. Ralph was unable to turn on the gas light, but she was surprised that he hadn't lit his torch. Feeling guilty for neglecting him, she lit the centre gas light, pulling the chain and waiting for it to brighten fully, talking to Ralph as she did so. She wasn't surprised when she had no reply to her cheerful call and the promise of a cup of tea. When she looked at him to ask what he wanted for supper, she gasped. Ralph's bed was empty, the blankets folded neatly and placed on the pillows. Alarmed to see that the wheelchair was missing, she ran up and grabbed the sleeping Davy and went outside.

She called, ran around the house in case he had decided to look at what she had been doing in the garden, then ran down the path and called on Kitty and Bob. Others, including the police, were called, and the search went on with more and more anxiety as the night's chill brought added fears.

It was more than four hours before they found him, and that was only due to a poacher cutting down the narrow road to go into the wood unobserved. He had lifted him back into his chair, covered him with his coat and met a frantic Hope not far from the end of the lane.

The doctor was concerned. He spelled it out carefully, a warning to Hope that Ralph was seriously depressed and hadn't come to terms with his condition. That he had tried to kill himself was not said, but it was in the air between them.

The doctor reminded them, Hope, Freddy and Marjorie, that to attempt suicide was a crime, and if he had been convinced that was what had taken Ralph to that lonely place he should report it to the police, who had already questioned him. 'However,' he said, raising a hand to silence them. 'I've persuaded them to give him the benefit of the doubt as he insists he had been trying to master the wheelchair as a step towards returning to work.' He lowered his voice even further and went on. 'The onus is on you, as his family, to watch him, protect him. While you're with him, you must encourage him to be more hopeful of an improvement. Concentrate on what he can do, don't remind him of what he cannot. Don't remind him of his lack of mobility, but concentrate on his ability to cope.'

'But he will improve, won't he, Doctor?' Marjorie asked. 'There is hope of him walking again one day?'

'The chances of him walking again are, short of a miracle, almost nil.'

Ralph heard the whispered words and stifled a groan. When Hope and Marjorie took him his supper he threw it on to the floor.

Three

Over the following weeks Hope and Marjorie watched Ralph every moment possible. Rumours abounded as news of Ralph's attempted suicide spread. These were swiftly quashed by Marjorie, Freddy, and Hope and her friends but they didn't quite go away. Hope lived in a haze of exhaustion, day following day with nothing to distinguish them from each other.

Ralph had an uninvited visitor one morning, an ex-soldier who had lost a leg at Arnhem. Ernie Preece came with the intention of encouraging Ralph to be positive about his injuries. He began by telling him of a friend of his who had similar injuries to Ralph's own.

'I'm not interested,' Ralph replied rudely. 'How d'you think it can help me by knowing others have had the same thing to cope with? It isn't the same. I don't have the epithet "hero" to help me cope, do I? I wasn't injured doing something brave. I walked into the road and was hit by a car when my mind was under stress from the demands of a persistent wife!'

Ernie Preece didn't stay long and he walked past a white-faced Hope murmuring an apology, as though he'd been responsible for her husband's cruel remarks.

People came out of curiosity as well as to offer comfort and sympathy, many remarking that she was fortunate to have Ralph's parents to share her struggles as she cared for Ralph. Hope couldn't tell anyone that although she tried to help her mother-in-law to cope, Marjorie avoided doing anything to support her, and spoke only to make it evident she considered her daughter-in-law to blame for her son's situation.

Marjorie had written several letters to Phillip begging him to come home, explaining the injuries Ralph had suffered, but there had been no response. Phillip just discarded them unread. Eventually he asked his friend Matthew Charles to find out if his brother was recovered. 'Mother makes such a fuss, so I never take much notice of her wailing.'

'I'll be in Cwm Derw in a few days. I have to go home and see Sally and the girls, they're in some play or other,' Matthew sighed. 'I find it all so boring but I have to show my face at regular intervals. Thank goodness I work as a rep and can stay away for days at a time. Families, eh?'

–

Ralph's family had worked out a rota, managing to provide cover for all of the days and part of the nights. Marjorie sat with Ralph for much of the day but called Hope when help was needed.

It was Hope who fed him, changed his position, washed and cleaned him. It was hard, heavy work made worse by Ralph's determination not to assist her. Pushing when she asked him to pull, turning the opposite way from the one she wanted and all the time glaring at her with angry eyes.

He was rarely alone and he hated it. He tried to find odd moments, but it was almost impossible. When he did find himself minus his watchful protectors, he tried to increase his movements, exercising the parts of his body that still had muscle strength. He had never been a strong man but now he was determined to make his body do as much as it could. He didn't want anyone to learn about his efforts, knowing they would want to help and he would be smothered by their concern.

He invented goals for himself, stretching as far as this marker, then that. Straining to touch the floor without falling out of bed. He learned to drag his useless weight up in the bed by pulling on the metal frame behind his head.

The bookcase Hope had bought and which Freddy had fixed on the wall for her contained a book that Ralph wanted to read. *The Old Curiosity Shop* wasn't a particular favourite, it was simply out of reach and therefore a challenge.

His arms and shoulders were becoming quite strong and he stretched up and up until his fingers almost reached the spine of the book. A spine made of paper and thin imitation leather that was stronger than his own spine, he thought as he collapsed once more back on to the bed.

Reaching the book, pulling it from the shelf by his own effort, became an obsession, and at every opportunity, but only when he was unseen, he tried to fix his long slender fingers around it to pull it free. Every time, his fingers slipped and came away disappointed. Another couple of inches, that was all he needed, just a couple of inches.

He was tormented by the thought that if he asked it would be lifted with ease and handed to him. That was something he did not want. He couldn't admit to such helplessness. After days of struggling to free it from its place between *Hard Times* and *Oliver Twist*, he no longer wanted to read it. He just wanted to get it down, hold it in his hands, something achieved by defying his ruined body. He began to believe it would be an augury: to succeed was a promise that he would eventually recover.

At night, when the house was silent and there was little chance of being seen, he would force his body that little bit further, stopping when the pain was too much, then beginning again. A month after he had been brought home from hospital, Hope woke soon after midnight and went downstairs for a drink and to check on Ralph. She came into the semi-dark room silently and saw him struggling. She lifted the book from its place and handed it to him.

'Don't struggle, darling, you might fall. Just call if you need something, I'll always hear you and come.'

He felt a fury that was so strong, almost a hatred of her and everyone else upon whom he depended, he couldn't trust himself to speak. It was as though by retrieving the book for him she had lost him the chance of ever walking again.

He waited in simmering silence as she adjusted his bedding and kissed him before going back upstairs. Then he stretched over, tumbled out of his bed on to the floor and reached for the poker. Rousing the fire by stirring its ashes he threw the book at the back of it and, still on the floor, watched the prospect of his recovery burn, tears of despair running unchecked down his face.

He couldn't sleep. He also knew he couldn't face another day of this half-life. As the embers of the destroyed pages died he moved towards the chair. It took a long time to get into it. Usually he had reached it from the height of the bed or the couch; now the effort of pulling himself up from the floor exhausted him. After resting for an hour, getting himself out of the house and down the ramp was easy.

The night was moonless yet there was enough light in the sky for him to see where he was going once his eyes became accustomed to the starlight. A sob escaped his lips once as he stopped to rest and saw a badger cross his path. It stared at him with curiosity before slipping into the hedge on the other side. It would belong to the sett that had given the house its name. Hope would have been delighted had she been with him. For a moment he wanted to go back and tell her, share the thrill of such an unexpected encounter, but bitterness returned and after a while he moved on.

Apart from the crackling hum of his wheels on the gravelly surface the night was quiet, cold and clear. An owl passed overhead on silent wings; there wasn't the slightest breeze and even the trees were motionless. The world was sleeping and he was utterly alone.

He didn't go down the narrow lane beside the wood, the scene of his previous attempt to end his miserable life, but continued on towards the railway line. There he went up the steep incline where the road bridged the rail that went from Cardiff to Swansea and the west. It took him a long time to get out of his chair and on to the parapet. Before he had achieved it, a train passed below him, rhythmically repeating the silly words they had chanted as children, tuppence a mile, tuppence a mile, and he felt again a sense of failure. A threat of hysterical laughter threatened as he thought, foolishly, that he had missed the train. Through the cloud of smoke that filtered up into the sky he continued to struggle free from the hated chair.

Then he pulled himself painfully up and, balanced on the top of the low wall, he looked along the tracks and waited.

An hour later, as dawn was lightening the sky, a tramp saw the chair and, after glancing around and seeing no one to whom it might belong, he piled his collection of bags and string-tied bundles on to it. Like a child with a birthday treat, he sat on his worldly possessions and rode down the slope from the bridge then pushed it happily to the derelict house where he was living.

—

Hope was up very early and as usual she went straight in to see Ralph. He wasn't there, and looking into the corner she saw with a feeling of dread that his chair was gone.

She wrapped Davy in a blanket, ran to the telephone box and informed the police, then carrying a still sleeping Davy, she knocked on Kitty and Bob's door.

They dressed immediately, and with Bob carrying the child they went to await the arrival of the police. Bob left them to search the garden and those of their neighbours, opening sheds and going with some trepidation beyond the wood to where the brook widened and became deep before moving on to the field beyond.

As soon as the details had been noted, one of the policemen went to tell Marjorie.

'I'd hoped she needn't know until he'd been found,' Hope sobbed. 'He'll be found, I'm sure of it. He wouldn't try anything… stupid, not now when he knows how it would distress us.' Using a euphemism for suicide was a kind of protection. By not using the actual word it made it less likely to have happened.

Two days and two nights passed without a sign of Ralph. Hope and Marjorie sat in the living room at Badgers Brook without a word being exchanged. People came and went, leads were followed, but no one had seen him since Hope had reached up and handed him the book he wanted, the ashes of which they had found in the grate. Then his chair was discovered in the possession of the tramp and fresh searches were made.

On the fifth day he was found. Piecing together the bits and pieces of information, they gathered that he had fallen from the bridge where the tramp admitted finding the chair. He hadn't been hit by a train but had fallen into a truck. The delay of manoeuvring his body on the parapet and throwing himself off had meant the train was already passing below him when he fell.

Hypothermia had ended his life. Although it was March and winter had eased its frosty grip, the nights had been too much for him, injured, unable to move and wearing insufficient clothing. He had been found by a workman. Dirt and a light fall of snow had almost disguised him lying next to the small amount of coal left in a corner of the fifteenth wagon.

–

The days following the death of Ralph passed in a haze of bewilderment for Hope. His mother, red eyed with crying, rarely addressed a word to her and insisted on passing any necessary remarks via his father. When the news had reached them, Hope instinctively ran to Marjorie to hug and be hugged, seeking comfort in her grief, but she was pushed aside so fiercely she stumbled and almost fell. Days passed and still there was no chance for her to grieve as she concentrated on helping Marjorie and Freddy in any way she could. She had to be the strong one. Her own emotions were frozen deep inside her.

When Marjorie's outbursts were particularly hurtful Freddy looked embarrassed, but his own grief prevented him making a plea for sanity. Marjorie blamed Hope for Ralph's death and he guessed that she would have been less able to cope if that transference of guilt were removed. He only knew he daren't risk saying anything to support Hope in her grief, watching as the young woman tried to keep to a routine and protect Davy from the horrors of the tragic events.

Hope's first shock after hearing of Ralph's lonely death was learning his bank account would be frozen. She had nothing more than the money in her purse. Kitty told her that was normal.

Bob said nothing. She would learn the rest all too soon: that as a suicide all his assets would be forfeited. She would have nothing. Bob and Kitty took ten pounds out of their savings and handed it to her in one pound notes. 'With care it will see you through, pay it back when you can,' Kitty said kindly. 'No hurry, wait till everything's sorted, right?'

Hope dealt with every day and its problems with an outward calmness, which seemed to exacerbate her mother-in-law's anger towards her. But Hope knew that for Davy's sake she needed to keep everything as normal as possible. Davy asked where his father was but seemed to accept Hope's vague explanation that his had gone away for a while without too much concern. Unbelievably, almost guiltily, Hope was thankful for Ralph's recent lack of interest in his son, as it was making Davy's acceptance of his father's absence easier.

Both Marjorie and Freddy wrote to Phillip several times. Surely he'd come home now Ralph was dead? Without telling either of them, Hope also wrote to her brother-in-law explaining everything that had happened, and ending with a plea for him to come home and comfort his parents. She marked the envelope urgent and hoped that if he had moved someone would pass it on.

-

Connie saw the letters thrown into the fireplace and asked, 'Are you not just a bit curious?'

'I can imagine what they'll say. How much they miss me, and when will I be coming home, and have I sold much work lately, and how did the exhibition go.'

'But you say one was your father's writing, and another was from neither and marked urgent. There might be something seriously wrong.'

He kicked the letters closer to the flames and watched them curl, blacken and burn. 'They no longer interest me, Connie. Now, shall we go for a walk and find a pub for lunch? The day is perfect and I don't want it ruined by thinking about my tiresome parents.'

-

Marjorie went every morning to the gate to wait for the postman. Surely Phillip would come home now? She saw Matthew Charles one morning as he went into Mrs Hayward's grocery store. He and Phillip had been close friends when they were at school and he might have kept in touch.

'Matthew, d'you know where Phillip is living? He must have moved and forgotten to tell us. I've written many times but never have a reply. He must have moved.' she said. 'He would have come home once he knew about Ralph.'

Matthew hadn't heard about the suicide of Ralph, and was shocked. He promised to get in touch. He knew what happened to any letters Phillip received from home but he thought his own might rate a little more attention. 'I'll write to him and I'll also write to a friend who might know where he is. I'm sure he'll come, once he knows.' He hid his doubts well. Phillip had decided to cut himself off from his family and even the death of his brother might not persuade him to change his mind.

–

Kitty called at Badgers Brook every day and, on the first occasion after Ralph had been found, she volunteered to help prepare food for the funeral. When Hope went to Ty Mawr and mentioned this, Marjorie told her angrily – via Freddy – that the funeral was nothing to do with Badgers Brook, the house that had caused his death, and that the funeral would leave from Ty Mawr. Hope was too weary of spirit to argue.

Without saying a word against his wife, Freddy walked home with Hope and Davy that day and stayed a while, working on the garden. He gave her a list of the seeds he had ordered and wrote down when and where she should plant them. The garden was his comfort and he seemed to want it to be hers too.

Freddy insisted to his wife that Hope must be the one to arrange the funeral, even if the food afterwards was to be offered at Ty Mawr. With ill grace, the three of them went to discuss the arrangements and were told, sorrowfully and regretfully, that the church would not be involved. A place had been set aside for the internment of those who had taken their own life – again the euphemism helped – and they were told that it was in a corner of the cemetery away from the main avenues of graves.

Hope began to be aware of people looking at her strangely, and as soon as she realized they were uneasy at the way Ralph had died she determinedly smiled, ignored their uncomfortable demeanour, their superstitious fears, insisted on acting as though everything was normal until they reacted to her pleasantries without wanting to take flight.

Snow held off and there was a mellow feeling of a false spring. Freddy began coming every day, and in the garden the beds were neat and ready for planting far earlier than most years. While she waited for the results of the post-mortem, then the autopsy and finally for permission to arrange the funeral, Hope could do nothing and she began helping Freddy in the garden with a growing interest.

Vegetable and flower seeds were sown in the green-house Freddy and Bob had repaired for her and tomato plants were coaxed by a small oil heater. Already sturdy broad beans and summer cabbage were set out in the neat beds. Hope, with Davy's enthusiastic assistance, planted a herb garden, and the preparation for the summer months seemed to override the horrors of death with a plan for the future. Hope's grief and the guilt, constantly reinforced by

Marjorie, overcame her only at night when there was no one for whom she needed to be brave.

-

The funeral was a quiet affair, shameful and subdued. The undertaker was kind and did what he could, but without the comfort of the traditional service the memories were of a cold, indifferent and brief moment.

Marjorie invited a few people to call at the house but most stayed away. A suicide made it difficult for people to offer their sympathy. Aware of Marjorie's distress yet unable to find the words and not knowing how she would react to attempts to comfort her and Freddy, most settled for a card or a brief note.

Hope received a few cards; most held no message, but were just signed with a name. Callers brought flowers to Badgers Brook as a way of expressing the sympathy they felt. Kitty fielded most of them from entering the house; she and Hope didn't want Davy to be aware of the emotions of that terrible time.

When the last guest had left Ty Mawr on that tense and sad day, and only Hope and her parents-in-law remained, she couldn't decide how soon she should leave. Marjorie still hadn't spoken to her and it was Freddy who shared his feelings with her in murmured remembrances of Ralph as a child, and as a young man who would never grow old.

'Father-in-law, I think I must go now. Kitty and Bob have looked after Davy for long enough.'

'Of course. I'd walk with you, but...' he gestured to where Marjorie sat silently staring out of the window.

'Goodbye, Mother-in-law. I'll bring Davy to see you tomorrow. I have to go to see the solicitor first, so it will be late morning.' There was no response and she left the house feeling enervated, uneasy, having been deprived of the day of grieving that she had desperately needed. None of her friends had been present, Marjorie had made it clear they were not welcome, and she crept away from Ty Mawr and its eerie silence, the unmistakable smell of mourning flowers in her nostrils, as though she'd had no right to be there.

Kitty had invited the local vicar to visit. When Hope reached the house, he was waiting for her, being plied with tea, and playing a game of racing cars with Davy.

Kitty handed her a cup of steaming tea then took Davy out in the garden. Hope was finally able to burst into tears, and eventually explain to the sympathetic man all that had happened. He listened and tried to comfort her, take away the bitterness of Marjorie's grief, persuading her that the accusations were a mother's way of coping. 'She had three sons, and Ralph was the youngest. That often makes a child special. One of his brothers died at the end of the war, and another left home – an abandonment in her eyes. Ralph was her last remaining child, her baby, and we must see how impossible it will be for her to find comfort anywhere. Blaming someone else is her attempt to do so, and I'm afraid that means you have a double burden to carry.'

Although he was only saying what she had told herself time and again, his soothing voice and the authority of the spoken words, although only slightly different from her own, were a comfort. That night, for the first time since Ralph's accident, she slept for six hours, undisturbed by nightmares.

Until it was over, she hadn't thought any further than the funeral. Now, with an appointment at the solicitor's office, she gathered together the papers relating to the rental of the house, birth and death certificates and anything else she thought she might need. She took Davy's pushchair and went on the bus into the town of Cwm Derw and sat in the waiting room mulling over what she expected to be told.

His employers would have some insurance. He would have insured himself once they had married, possibly increased it when Davy had been born. Assets confiscated? She thought about the words and decided they were wrong. It was nonsense to think there would be no money. There was sure to be a lump sum, and a pension.

At least the house tenancy was safely theirs, hers and Davy's. Once probate was granted she wouldn't be rich but she would manage. She would have to earn some money, but she needn't hurry. When Davy began school would be time enough. Until then she would cope. She smiled, remembering Freddy's suggestion that she sold the runner beans he planned to grow in her garden. She wouldn't be wealthy but it wouldn't come to that.

The solicitor looked uneasy as she sat beside the heavy desk and looked at him expectantly.

'Is everything in order?' she asked brightly. 'How long before it's settled? At least my husband left a will and that speeds things up, doesn't it?'

'There is no will and I have no record of his ever making one,' he said solemnly. 'I suggested it on several occasions. There is no property and only a little money involved, but I advised your husband to make a will. He refused. Although it's irrelevant now, isn't it? Because of the manner of his death.'

'I don't understand.' She frowned. 'Even without a will there's a pension, isn't there? He'd have paid in to a pension scheme. And insurances. Those apply whether or not there's a will. Surely there won't be much delay?'

'I'm sorry, Mrs Murton, but none of those has been arranged. Your husband didn't think it important at his age to spend out on insurance, and there is no pension except that of the state.' He usually came straight out with any unpleasant facts but, looking at her young face obviously determined to disbelieve the rumours she'd heard, he was finding it hard to tell her the truth.

'But he was an accountant, he'd have known the importance of insurance. We talked about it and I understood it was all arranged.'

He rustled papers and said. 'I'm sorry, Mrs Murton, but there's nothing.'

'I don't understand. He was an accountant for goodness sake! Surely he couldn't have been so negligent?'

'I tried to warn him, Mrs Murton. Quite recently I explained what might happen, if...' He was referring to the suicide but Hope was thinking about Ralph's lack of care in not insuring himself.

'He was advised by his mother, I suppose?'

The solicitor heard but he declined to comment. He coughed nervously, silently agreeing with her. Ralph had more or less admitted it during one of his earlier attempts to persuade him to act responsibly toward his wife and child. Again he coughed nervously then said quickly, 'But its academic now, it would no longer be valid. Due to the manner of your husband's... from the way he – passed away – you cannot benefit in any way from his death.'

She stared at him as he muttered a brief explanation.

'It's considered fraud, you see. Cheating by obtaining an insurance on his own life then taking it himself, d'you see?'

All she saw was a bleak future.

–

Hope went to the bank as soon as she left the solicitor's office. She was stunned and very frightened. If she couldn't afford to stay in Badgers Brook, where would she go? There was little chance of Marjorie helping her. Wherever the circumstances finally took her, however she dealt with this disaster, she was undoubtedly on her own.

The bank manager was sympathetic but unable to help. He explained that it was imperative that she find employment to pay her way. 'Remember,' he said encouragingly, 'that a house is an asset, something you can use to raise income. You can perhaps take in paying guests, or summer visitors, although we're too far from the seaside to make that a strong possibility. Walkers perhaps. It's a popular place for walkers and cyclists. The owner's permission will be required, of course, and the council's approval obtained. Just a suggestion, Mrs Murton.'

She said she would pay two months' rental to Geoff with the money she had in her own post office account. At least that way the house was secure. 'That will give me time to decide what I'm going to do,' she said.

The bank manager was aghast. 'Two months? A payment before it's due? That's no way to get rich, my dear,' he said with a smile. 'Don't be too anxious or people will think the worst and you'll have people refusing you credit should you need it.'

She sat on the bus, pointing things out to Davy as they passed. And she looked at the people filling the pavements of the busy little town and wondered how many of them had met problems like hers and overcome them. So many families had lost their breadwinners and they had survived. At that moment she couldn't see any way out of the mess in which Ralph had left her. Their menfolk had died honourably. According to law Ralph had not.

Restless and unable to clarify her thoughts, when Davy went to sleep for an hour she began painting the wooden toy chest. It already had a coat of pale blue paint and now she gathered the assortment of colours and painted spitfires, fire engines, tractors and teddies, and a fearsome crocodile and a few books. When she looked up she was alarmed to realize that two hours had passed and she ran up to see if Davy had woken. He was on his back, his chubby face rosy with sleep, his plump arms above his head in a luxurious stretch as, smiling contentedly, he slowly awoke.

She didn't show him the toy chest. Better to wait until it was dry. Perhaps she would hide it until his birthday. Although October was too far away.

She went to see Marjorie and Freddy, hoping that once they knew the facts they would do something to help her. Davy was their only grandchild after all.

Marjorie refused to see her. Freddy explaining apologetically that she was resting as she had a headache. She told him about the situation, and although it no longer mattered – the manner of his death meant it would have been lost to her anyway – she asked if the lack of insurance had been Marjorie's idea.

'It was, and I tried to persuade him she was wrong. But he was very easily convinced by his mother. Always was I'm afraid.'

'Why?' Hope asked. 'He had a wife and a child, so why didn't he protect us?'

'Superstitious fear, I believe. That was his mother's reason – if you can use the word reason in such a context. He was only twenty-three and when Richard was killed, then Phillip left so suddenly and without explanation, she was afraid he was tempting fate by taking on life assurance.' He looked at her sadly. 'She persuaded him it was a waste of money. How could I persuade her she was wrong? Twenty-three he was and we thought he had years, decades, before he needed to worry about insurances against him dying.'

Before she left, he handed her a cheque for twenty pounds, a fortune when Ralph had only earned six pounds a week. 'Put it in the bank and use it only when and if things get really difficult. It will make you feel stronger knowing it's there.'

–

It was the following day when she showed the painted toy chest to Kitty that the plan began to form. Kitty said, 'It's wonderful. How clever you are. I know someone who'd buy that from you. And I might even know a couple more who would like one.'

Hope started to say, 'Buy it? What nonsense, I'll paint one for nothing, it only takes a couple of hours.' Then she stopped and realized that if she wanted to keep the house she could no longer allow herself generous impulses. 'No, forget I said that. Sadly, I can no longer be that kind hearted. I learned yesterday that I don't have any money. If I can sell them, then that's what I'll have to do. I'll do that and anything else to earn a few shillings. Whatever I have to resort to to earn money I'll do it. Davy and I will stay in this house.'

'Good for you, Hope, dear. Badgers Brook is a good place to be when you face trouble. You have a talent and imagination and people will gladly pay for what you do.'

'It will be hard,' Hope said. 'But I'll earn money in every way I can. We have to stay in this house, and, to do so, Davy and I will need every penny I can earn.'

'I'll spread the word,' the loyal Kitty said. 'Any good at sewing are you?'

'I'll sew and knit, and work in gardens, mind children, clean houses. In fact, there's nothing I'll refuse as long as I'm paid. I'll accept everything I'm asked to do. I'm here to stay, in spite of Marjorie's determination to the contrary.'

Her face showed spirit, but inside she was quaking. How could she earn enough to keep herself and Davy and pay the rent every month?

'The first thing to do is clear a part of the room where I can work,' Hope said. 'I've often made clothes for myself, sewn curtains and covers and altered dresses for friends, now I'll have to start advertising.' She relaxed her shoulders and drooped wearily. 'But it's hopeless, how can I earn enough to keep us and pay for this place?'

'Call me crazy if you like, but I believe the house wants you here. You'll find a way of staying.'

'Where do I start?'

'Stella Jones at the post office. Where else? She knows everything and everybody. Put a notice in her window and the news will spread as fast as greenfly on Bob's roses!'

Stella Jones had been in the post office for ever; at least that's what the locals said. She had started as a young girl helping her parents to run it and had taken over when she and Colin had married. Many could remember queuing with their mothers and now stood in the line of chattering women with children of their own. Her appearance had hardly changed. Her hair, pulled back into an under-roll and held firmly in place by a hair net, had remained a nondescript brown-grey. She wore no make-up and her only concession to fashion was incongruously bright red nail varnish. This, she admitted to friends, was to hide the state of her fingernails after the hours she spent on the allotment.

Besides dealing with the post office counter, Stella sold knitting wool, cottons and embroidery silks and a few items of clothing for young children. The varied stock and her willingness to order other things when requested made her shop a valuable service. Between them, the post office, Geoff's hardware store, a small shop selling ladies' fashions, a hairdresser and Mrs Hayward's grocery supplied most of the neighbourhood's needs. Trips into the larger towns of Cardiff and Newport weren't a necessity, more an occasional 'outing', a special treat.

Stella and her husband Colin had no children, and they filled their spare time with local affairs, taking part in the various fundraising events and, for most of the year, their allotment.

Every Wednesday, when the post office closed at one, Stella set off armed with brushes and bucket and soap and scouring powder to clean the shed. If he wasn't at work, Colin went with her and they would work on the plot

79

of land together. At the back of the shed, near the small section in which Colin was allowed to keep his tools, was a shelf on which stood a paraffin stove. A spring at the edge of the allotments provided fresh, clear water and Stella always managed to find the makings of tea plus a couple of cakes for anyone who called. Two chairs and a small bench were placed outside the door on the area Colin had paved, in the hope of a visitor or two.

It wasn't only gardeners who passed her shed door. People often walked around to admire the plots and see what was growing, sometimes exchanging plants or begging a helping of fresh produce. It was there that Stella saw Hope strolling, pushing Davy in his pushchair. She waved, found a sweet in her pocket for the little boy and offered Hope a cup of tea.

'Tea? What a lovely idea,' Hope said with a smile. 'I've just been wandering, trying to think out a problem. A cup of tea in this lovely place might just help.'

'If it's a gardening problem you're in the right spot. Between us all we're a living encyclopaedia.' Stella bustled in the back of her immaculate shed and Hope sat in the chair she had been offered and looked around her at the regular sized plots, which all showed signs of careful attention. Since the early years of the war, growing food had been a national occupation and although the war had ended there was no sign of the activity losing popularity.

'I forgot it was Wednesday half-day closing and went to the post office,' Hope said when they were sitting with their cups of tea.

'Damn-it-all, I can't get a few hours off without someone wanting something,' Stella said with a laugh. 'I don't know what the place would do without me and my little shop.'

'I wanted to put an advertisement in your window. I'm looking for work that I can do at home, or where I can take Davy,' Hope explained.

'Work? You a widow, daughter-in-law of the posh Marjorie Williamson-Murton of the Ty Mawr? Surely you don't need to work?'

'Sadly I do. There – there was some mistake in the insurances when Ralph and I married and, well, I need to earn money.'

'Him being a suicide you mean?'

Hope lowered her head. She didn't want to say any more. Marjorie would soon hear if she began spreading gossip, and her mother-in-law disliked her enough without adding giving her more excuse.

'Give the advertisement to me, lovely girl, and you can pay when you next come in. The sooner the better, eh?' She patted Hope's cheek with a grubby hand. 'Don't let it get you down, love. People soon forget. There'll be something else to talk about next week, sure to be.'

Hope left after watching with amusement as Stella washed the dishes and put them carefully away, wrapped in tea towels and stored in a large biscuit tin. She turned back as she left the allotments and saw that Stella was busily cleaning the shed windows.

'Pity help any spider who dares to enter Stella's country cottage,' she said with a chuckle.

The first response to her advertisement was from Stella herself. 'You any good at alterations, then?' she asked when Hope went in to pay. 'Our Mam's very short, not big enough to cut cabbage as they say round here, and she wants a couple of new dresses shortened. Olive Talbot doesn't do it any more.'

Hope went to see the old lady and saw at once that, being barely five feet tall and rather plump, simply shortening the skirt hadn't made her dress a good fit. It was too large and the waist was in the wrong place and the result was a shapeless garment that made the wearer look even more short and overweight than necessary. She took measurements and carried the dress home, promising to return with it on the following day.

She took the dress apart and remade it, taking out some of the unwanted length from the top, adding darts at the bust area, putting the waist where it should be and allowing the skirt to hang naturally. The result delighted Stella and she promised to recommend her to her customers.

With some regret, the toy box that was to have been Davy's was sold and two people brought plain boxes to be painted in a similar manner. Several requests arrived for dance dresses and for dresses for little girls ready for summer, and Hope thanked her lucky stars for the retirement of Olive Talbot – although her particular skills of altering clothes for those not easy to fit would have attracted more than a few customers once her talents were known. She turned shirt collars to give them an extra least of life, shortened and lengthened children's clothes as well as making new. In March 1948, clothes rationing was still making life difficult, and she was offered all the work she needed to fill her days.

A month after her devastating meeting with the solicitor, she sat down and worked out her accounts. She had been very busy but it wasn't enough. Without delving into Freddy's twenty pounds it would be difficult to pay the coming month's bills. And she still hadn't paid back Stella's loan. She had to look for something else. There were moments when she felt a real anger towards Ralph's mother. Marjorie seemed unaware of the implications of his death, or determinedly refused to face them. But the moments of rage quickly faded with the thought that always followed: if she hadn't insisted on Ralph leaving his mother's house he might still be alive.

She woke one morning to a strange noise. It sounded as though a tap had been left on, but there was no possibility of that. She would have heard it before this. An investigation quickly revealed that the bathroom was flooded and the running water she could hear was bubbling up through the floorboards and running down the stairs.

She ran to the phone box at the end of the lane, with Davy still in his pyjamas and a dressing gown covered by a coat, and called a plumber. The man promised to be there within half an hour. 'Have you turned off the water?' he asked and when Hope said she didn't know how, he said. 'I'll be there as fast as I can.'

On the way back to the house she stopped and called on Kitty and Bob. Bob came immediately and found the stop cock and the sudden cessation of noise was such a relief she whispered when she thanked him.

The plumber quickly discovered the source of the trouble and replaced a pipe and joint that had been carelessly fitted. The resulting mess was hers to deal with. The stair carpet of which she had been so proud ruined. She pulled it free of its brass rods and threw it outside. Whether it would be possible to reuse it was very much in doubt. Then there was the cost of the plumber.

Thoughts of Marjorie's satisfaction saved her from prolonged melancholy. It would have to be replaced, the insurance might help; as for the rest, well, somehow she would earn it.

In Stella's window she saw a job vacancy at the Ship and Compass. It was for a cleaner and she knew that, unpleasant or not, if she could take Davy with her she would do it. Just until the plumber was paid and the stairs had some sort of cover on them. The landlady, Betty Connors, was doubtful, but was persuaded to take her on for a temporary period until she found someone else. Knowing Freddy, and fearing the wrath of Marjorie, she hoped no one would see the young woman doing such menial work.

The previous cleaner had been far from enthusiastic and Hope found that the wooden floor in one bar and the slates in the other were in need of serious attention. This was not work she would look for again, but she knew that whatever she did she needed people to know that she did a good job, so she worked at the floors until every last stain was gone, finishing the wooden boards by scrubbing them with water to which she added bleach, and the result was very pleasing. Betty rewarded her with a bonus and the plumber got his money as soon as the bill was presented.

For two weeks she went every morning to clean the two bars, and although the smoky, beer-scented atmosphere was not an ideal place for Davy, she was determined to do it for six weeks so she would have a little money behind her. Money was security and that was something she desperately needed.

One morning as she was washing the last corner of the entrance steps a shadow loomed over her, and she looked up to see a man she didn't know. He stood threateningly close, his feet not far from her wet and red hands holding the scrubbing brush. She sat back on her heels to see him better. 'I'm sorry but we aren't open until twelve o'clock,' she said politely.

'What on earth are you doing? Trying to humiliate your parents-in-law even further? Driving your husband to suicide, and now this? This show of poor little hard-done-by widow?'

She jumped up, pushing a hand ineffectually through her untidy hair. She was hot and her flushed cheeks gave a glow to her eyes in which anger flared. 'Who are you?' she demanded. 'How dare you insult me!'

'I'm Ralph's friend Matthew Charles, and I've just heard of his cruel and lonely death.'

'Then you must also know that the reason I'm here isn't to shame his mother but to feed myself and his son. He left us without a penny.'

'That isn't what I heard.'

'It's the truth. Now please leave, I want to finish the work I'm paid for.'

'Is everything all right, Hope?' the landlady asked from inside the door.

'Yes, of course,' Hope replied, pushing the man roughly off the step and fastidiously scrubbing the spot on which he had stood.

'Another friend of dear Marjorie Murton, I presume?' Betty Connors said loudly. 'I remember Matthew Charles. He and Phillip were two of the most unpleasant—' She stopped and waved as Freddy appeared.

Freddy went into the bar but was waiting when Hope finished work. 'Please, Hope dear. Use the money I gave you and give up on this. Concentrate on the garden and your sewing. Marjorie would be most upset if she sees you working here, and little Davy with you.'

She refrained from shouting *good*, and instead said firmly, 'I have no one to help me, Father-in-law, and I need to keep the house. I'll do whatever I have to. I won't let it go.'

'I'm so sorry,' he said, and she hugged him and assured him that it was only for a few weeks, until things improved. 'I had a flood and the plumber had to be paid. I won't get into debt while there's a way I can earn money.'

'I thought you had sewing work.'

'I do, but a few weeks of this job and I'll have a few pounds put by. I still have the afternoons for Davy and the evenings for sewing. It won't be for ever. Although,' she said with a sad smile, 'sometimes is seem as though it will be. I look into a future that's unlikely to change for the better. How can it?'

'The only thing that's predictable about life is that it's unpredictable,' he said with an encouraging smile. 'Who knows what tomorrow will bring?'

'Do you know a man called Matthew Charles?' she asked him.

'Phillip had a friend of that name.'

'And you haven't seen him lately?'

'No, but he might have called to see Marjorie, she said something about a friend calling having heard the news. She asked him to contact Phillip and tell him to come home, but we've heard nothing.'

'There's no doubt that he's seen Mother-in-law! He's been to see me, too, criticized me rather unpleasantly. Tell him to stay away from me will you? Or I might just talk to the police about slander, and that would upset someone other than Matthew Charles,' she said pointedly.

'Give her time, Hope. She's very distressed.'

'And what about me? Am I not allowed to be upset? Losing my husband and possibly my home? Left practically penniless? Having to clean in a public house? A place I've never before even entered?'

'I'll have a word with Matthew, and try again to warn Marjorie about her behaviour.'

'Perhaps you could remind her that Davy is her grand-child? Perhaps you could ask her what will happen to him if we are made homeless? Will I be accused of allowing that to happen too? Just to embarrass her?'

'Ralph didn't just die, he killed himself, Hope dear. It will never be all right for her.'

'Nor me! I was abandoned in the most incomprehen-sible way. I've lost my husband, and instead of receiving sympathy I am accused of causing his death.'

He walked to the bus stop with her, pushing Davy in his pushchair, and got on the bus with them. He paid their fare and gave Davy a threepenny piece to buy sweets. 'There are no sweet coupons left until next month,' Hope reminded him sullenly.

'An ice-cream?'

Aware of his attempts to help and how uncomfortable he felt caught between herself and his wife, while he was himself grieving, she touched his arm and thanked him. 'I get very angry at times, but I'm grateful for your support,' she assured him.

Freddy didn't go straight home. He went to see Geoff Tanner at the hardware shop.

'Did you know that Hope had a flood?' he asked. 'A faulty bit of plumbing in the bathroom. She's had it fixed but she's scrubbing floors in the Ship and Compass to pay for it.' His anger showed. As the landlord he should have dealt with it and paid for the repair, not allowed Hope to arrange it.

'I'm sorry, Mr Murton, I didn't know. Why didn't she come to me? As the landlord it's my problem when something goes wrong.'

'Perhaps you can go and see her.'

'Of course. As soon as the shop closes.'

When Geoff found out what had happened he insisted on paying the plumber and for the cleaning of the carpet, which was still rolled up in a shed.

'Please,' he said once everything was agreed and Hope's savings had increased encouragingly, 'please let me know if there are any problems. I don't want your father-in-law telling me off, however politely he does it.'

Hope ran to tell Kitty what had happened and while she was there, asked, 'Do you know anyone who'd like Davy's pram? Davy walks well now, and I've the pushchair for when he's tired. I'll gladly give it to someone who wants it.'

'Sell it,' Kitty said. 'Don't give it away. For one thing it'll be more valued if someone has to pay and for another you have to think *money*. You can't give away a good pram and then go and scrub floors in the Ship and Compass. Where's your sense, girl?'

A young woman agreed to buy the pram but she needed it delivered. It was the greengrocer, Peter Bevan, who solved that problem. He lifted it on to the cart behind his patient horse, and with Hope and Davy sitting beside him delivered it to the other side of Cwm Derw. Davy pointed at all the vehicles on the road and the animals in the fields and Peter stopped as they approached their destination and allowed him to ride on the back of the horse. The little boy's blue eyes were round with delight and he patted the rough coat, safely supported by Peter's protective arms.

When Hope offered Peter some money to pay him, he pushed it aside, holding her hand for an unnecessarily long moment, and said, 'I should be paying you for the entertainment. I don't think young Niblo has stopped talking for more than a few seconds and I've enjoyed every minute. You don't have any more prams needing delivering, I suppose? Pity. Well, if you ever need me, just give me a call.' He offered a hand to Davy and said, 'Cheerio, young Dai. See you soon, eh?'

Dai? Hope repeated as they went inside. What would Marjorie think of that!

Marjorie came to see Hope the following day, and when she opened the door to her, holding Davy by the hand, Hope began to smile a welcome as she stood back to allow her to enter.

'You are embarrassing me and Ralph's father, and shaming Ralph's memory.'

'Because I'm working to stay clear of debts?'

'Scrubbing in a public house. Wandering around the lanes on a horse and cart with a strange man. What are you thinking of?'

'Staying clear of debts,' Hope repeated calmly. 'Will you come in? Davy has some drawings he'd like to show you.'

'Leave this house. It's too big. You must find something smaller and easier to run.'

'Far away so you don't have to see me struggle to keep us fed and clothed?'

'Just go, find something less humiliating to do with your life.'

'Oh no, I can't leave here. It's our home. Remember, Mother-in-law, if you had supported us, or if Ralph hadn't been so cowardly, acted so – so irresponsibly, I wouldn't be scrubbing floors, would I?'

It was the first time she had dared to accuse Ralph aloud, and she felt both frightened and brave. She immediately regretted it. She felt only sadness as Marjorie turned and hurried back down the path to the lane. What good would it do to upset Marjorie? The poor unhappy woman had suffered enough. Tomorrow she would go to her and apologize, let her rain more of her anger and hatred on her head. She would deserve it for what she had just said.

-

Winter ended and the air was filled with birdsong and the occasional sound of lawnmowers being pushed up and down on sunny days. Everywhere was the scent of blossom, and the earth, freshly turned, gave out its special smell, which Hope found exciting, filled with the promise of better things. It was the month of May and the glory of the fully leafed trees made every view a picture to be admired. Whatever happened, she knew she had made the right decision by staying in Badgers Brook.

As the days lengthened every moment was filled with sewing for the large number of weddings the coming months would bring. She was cheaper than most gown shops and her styles were individual, never seen more than once, as the designs were mostly her own. She still painted boxes and chairs and the occasional small table, and she learned to add colour to plain picture frames with sealing wax, a candle and a needle. Anything to earn a few shillings.

Peter called often and helped transport some of the furniture on which she was asked to use her skills. He sometimes stayed for supper, occasionally bringing a rabbit stew he had prepared, which Kitty and Bob would be invited to share. Peter, Freddy and Bob spent hours in the vegetable patch, laughing and talking while keeping the weeds at bay. She knew Freddy called in to the Ship and Compass on the way home and hoped Marjorie didn't complain at the way he chose to fill the still painful hours.

Only Betty Connors knew that Freddy also visited the bridge from where his son had fallen to his lonely death. She sometimes went there with him after the pub closed, leaving the pot man to clean the bar. They stood and she listened while Freddy reminisced about the boys' childhood.

The garden was still Hope's solace, and with Freddy's expert help the vegetables flourished. In July the enormous harvest of runner beans reached the picking stage. Bob made her a small cart out of pram wheels and a wooden box and, embarrassed at first, but with growing confidence, she began knocking on doors and selling them. Onions were harvested in August, and lettuce and a mountain of tomatoes had filled the greenhouse, which Freddy and Bob had now extended along the shed wall.

The money flowed in and she worked long into the evenings. After nearly three months, longer than she had anticipated, and partly because Marjorie didn't like it, she finally gave up cleaning at the Ship and Compass.

After her final morning there, an irate knock at her door made her expect to see Marjorie's angry face, but it was the face of a stranger. An angry stranger. A man in his sixties, well dressed in a smart overcoat and three-piece suit, well polished shoes and a smart hat. He looked prepared to meet trouble.

'Can I help you?' she asked politely, tightening her hold on Davy's hand as he tried to wriggle out of her grasp.

'My son helped you when you needed it and now you're stealing his business.'

'I'm sorry, but will you please explain what you mean?'

'My son, Peter Bevan. Heard of him, have you? He has a vegetable and fruit round and you're stealing his customers, selling before he arrives, door to door. I should report you, but Peter isn't vindictive, so I'm just warning you, stop selling your garden produce cheap. Got it?'

He didn't wait for a reply, just turned and hurried back down the path.

Hope sighed. How many more people would storm off down her path in anger? An hour later there was another knock at the door and this time she didn't automatically prepare a smile.

'Peter! I've just seen your father and I'm very sorry. I didn't think what I was doing would affect your business.'

'I've come to apologize. Dad means well but he shouldn't have called on you.'

'Will you come in?'

Davy heard him and ran from the kitchen, calling excitedly, 'Peter, did you bring the horse, can I have another ride? Will you come and see my painting? It's a picture of your horse Jason and the cart.'

Peter shrugged, grinned at her and said, 'First things first. Come on then, young Dai, where's this picture? It had better be good or Jason will be offended, mind.'

The painting, a blur of black and browns with the sun shining in a top corner, was duly admired, then placed on the kitchen table for Peter to take with him.

'There's always a sun shining in his pictures,' Hope told him. 'Unrecognizable shapes which he sees as his favourite things and the sun shining in the top corner. Or faces wearing wide smiles.'

'I suppose that means he's happy. He certainly seemed to me to be very contented with his life. A happy lad, aren't you, Dai?'

'Will you bring the horse when you come again? And will you play trains with me?'

'All right, trains it is, and tomorrow, when I go past, I'll call and if your mam isn't busy I'll give you a ride. Right?'

There was no answer; Davy was already bottom up, elbows going like pistons, searching in his toy box for his trains.

Peter was easily persuaded to stay for a meal, which Hope always ate with Davy, now there was no one else to worry about his rather flamboyant attitude to table manners. Peter didn't seem to mind the occasional mess and the meal was happier than most.

The day had been warm, and after Davy had been put to bed they sat in the garden for a while. Kitty and Bob arrived, and seeing Peter there Bob went home for a flagon of beer. Hope made some toast with Marmite and prepared a few sandwiches of salad with grated cheese she had been saving for the following day's supper. The impromptu party relaxed them and they talked late into the evening.

As the day ended, with the twittering of birds and the occasional call of a vixen, the alarming sound of a cat fight, the distant murmur of people strolling home along the lane, talking and laughing, no one wanted to move. For the first time in months, Hope felt at peace.

Four

Two days later, as Hope was putting the final stitches into a dress she had made for Stella's mother, there was a loud knock at the door. With needle and cotton in her hand, she opened it to two women. One was her mother-in-law, the other was unknown.

'We've called to see David,' Marjorie said peremptorily as she walked in.

After inviting the second visitor inside, Hope called, 'Davy? Come and see who's here. Come and say hello to Grandmother.'

Davy ran into the room, carrying a small piece of fabric he was wrapping around a teddy in an attempt to make a shawl. Hope laughed. 'Davy, I think you need something a big bigger. Here, try this.' She handed him a piece from the dress she had just finished.

'There!' Marjorie said, gesturing with a hand. 'She's making a sissy of him.'

Hope frowned, looked at the visitor and asked belatedly, 'Who are you?'

'I'm a district nurse, Mrs Murton. I have called to see how young David is getting on.'

'Why?' Hope asked with a frown. 'I've had no cause to worry. Just look at him, he's fine.'

'I've been hearing worrying reports about the way my grandson is being cared for. David isn't getting proper care.' Marjorie spoke with almost gentle concern in her voice. 'The dear little boy.'

'It's Davy. He's called Davy. What on earth are you talking about? Wrapping his teddy in a piece of material constitutes a lack of care?' She glared at Marjorie. 'What now, Mother-in-law? Haven't you harmed us enough?'

The district nurse, who introduced herself as Brenda Morris, said politely, 'Thank you for introducing me, Mrs Williamson-Murton, but now I think it would be helpful if you left us alone.'

It took a while, ploughing through Marjorie's protests and warnings of the deceitfulness of her daughter-in-law, but Marjorie was finally persuaded to leave. Her last words referred to an evening spent entertaining a man until all hours, and drink being consumed. Hope was too upset for her words to penetrate. She watched as Marjorie walked down the path, staying near the gate, looking back at the house as though prepared to re-enter at the first opportunity.

'A cup of tea would be nice,' Brenda Morris suggested politely.

'And then?'

'And then I would like to watch Davy play, if that's all right with you? I love observing children, don't you?'

'Davy gives me endless pleasure. My only regret is that he'll grow up without a father, but the town is full of children in that situation; the war robbed many families of their sons and daughters, brothers and fathers, and it will be a long time before the gaps are filled and the wounds healed.'

Davy brought out his cars and chattered as he played. He demonstrated with loud sound effects the way they rolled up and down a ramp Peter had made for him. Tiring of that game he then picked up his wax crayons and began scribbling with great enthusiasm, telling his mother what his drawing represented.

'What happened the other night when you had a man visiting until eleven o'clock, Mrs Murton? Where was Davy then?'

Hope frowned. 'A man visiting?' Her voice went cold. 'You must mean when Peter called. Peter Bevan, the greengrocer. He stayed to eat with us. He has done several favours for us and it was a small thank you on my part. When Davy was ready for bed and he was about to leave, Kitty and Bob Jennings came and we stayed in the garden talking. Bob went home for a flagon of beer at some stage. Kitty and I drank tea. Then they all left at the same time.'

She stared at her uninvited visitor with simmering anger, knowing the happy memories of the evening had been ruined by Marjorie, who had ruined so much.

'Is there something else?' she demanded, jumping out of her seat and rattling her cup against its saucer. 'I do have to get on. My mother-in-law might not have told you that besides coping with the shame of my husband committing suicide, we are practically penniless and I have to earn however I can, to keep us fed and with a place in which to live.'

'And you didn't think it unsuitable to take a two-year-old into a public house while you scrubbed floors?' Brenda was clearly embarrassed at having to make a further point.

Hope sat back down and buried her face in her hands. Then she straightened up and glared at her visitor again. 'I needed money urgently when we had a flood. A pipe in the bathroom failed and I lost the stair carpet as well as having the decoration ruined. Carpet and decoration could have waited but I couldn't tell a plumber that, because of my husband's lack of care and his decision to leave us in the most painful way possible, I couldn't pay him, could I? Yes, I took Davy with me, and whatever I have to do I always will. He isn't going to be pushed here and there with assorted "aunties", he'll be with me. If you think that's wrong then there's nothing more to say.' She jumped up and opened the door.

In a flurry of haste and anxiety, muttering apologies, putting down a cup and saucer, reaching for her coat and grabbing her bag, Brenda headed for the door. Without allowing time for her to put on her coat, Hope closed the door behind her. She ran to Davy and hugged him.

'She can do her worst, that grumpy old grandmother of yours, but she won't tell me what's best for us. Only you and I know that.'

It was a day when Hope felt anger towards Ralph. There had been several during which she'd blamed him for their situation, asking herself how he could have been so uncaring, how he could have listened to his mother and not to his own heart. How could he have died and left her to face all this?

She remembered other things, like the time she had made him a pullover with the most intricate Fair Isle pattern, and when his mother had muttered that it was rather gaudy he had refused to wear it. He had sided with his mother when she had disagreed with the flowers Hope

98

had chosen for their wedding. And there was his refusal to allow her to have a dog. And his unwillingness to allow her to work before Davy came along. The memories became more and more trivial as her mind searched for comfort through his failures.

Then she was swamped in grief, guilt, shame and an overwhelming sense of loss and loneliness, which ended in self-pitying tears.

-

Phillip was feeling put-upon. Connie was increasing her demands on him and he didn't like it. She constantly referred to other people's husbands, comparing him to them unkindly. He had never pretended to be like 'other people's husbands' and she shouldn't expect him to be suddenly transformed into a replica of them.

Her demands that they should buy a house were alarming. Responsibility was something he had always determined to avoid. Responsibility was a rope around your neck with someone holding the end and threatening to pull. Definitely not for him.

As she began again to glorify the vision of them running a small guest house, small being an attempt to make it sound enticing and easily achieved, he walked out. He headed for the local pub, where he was certain to find someone to talk to, a stranger perhaps, who would commiserate with him about the wiles of women. He also needed to escape her pleas for him to go and see his parents and comfort them after the death of his brother, about which Matthew had told them. He didn't want any of it.

Frustration led Connie to throw things out of the door: chairs, rugs, papers and books, details of the house she wanted to buy, and anything else she could lift. She then took it out on the floor, wielding a brush, swishing water across the flags and scrubbing as though her life depended on it, wishing she had an axe and she could smash everything that belonged to him.

She rarely lost her temper, although she was never afraid of speaking her mind, but today, when she had hoped they would start making plans for a future, no longer she supporting him, but working together towards success, her temper flared. She went to the door of the room he called his work room and to her surprise and delight found it unlocked. Normally she wasn't allowed in there.

The mess was worse, far worse than last time she'd managed to go in, and she stared around her in disbelief. Then she sobbed at the chaos and the utter waste. Pounds and pounds of her hard-earned money lay in the ruins of a lazy man's negligence.

Canvases daubed and abandoned, dozens and dozens of tubes of oil paint opened and left without their stoppers to harden and become useless. Expensive brushes unwashed and ruined. Top quality paper displaying half-finished amateur watercolours a child might do, which she presumed were intended to be "abstract" portraits. She sank down into a paint-daubed chair. No one in their right mind could believe there was any talent here. She must have been crazy to have ever thought it.

The old wardrobe where he kept his canvases was locked, but she didn't bother to force the door. It would only be more of the same half-finished, carelessly abandoned stuff only fit for the ash bin, and she'd had enough for one day.

The row, when he came home merrily drunk from a pleasant couple of hours with friends, was the worst they'd ever had. She went to bed and lay there, wanting him to join her and at the same time knowing it was best he didn't, for fear the argument would be resumed with even greater ferocity. She had to stay calm, it was the only way of getting through to him.

Phillip sat in the living room where the floor was clean – the furniture was still scattered outside – and wrote to his mother and father. He told them nothing of what was happening in his life and never mentioned Connie. His short note consisted of boasts about the exhibition he was planning and the commissions that were promised for the near future.

Before settling to sleep on the couch near the fire, he hid the clothes he had bought that day in his work room, and this time made sure the door was locked. Shirts, socks, shoes, slacks and a beautiful jumper. Connie didn't understand his need to buy good quality clothes and shoes. She'd be angry about the missing money, and the debts, when she eventually found out what had happened to their deposit on the dream house. But the thought of her fury would not keep him from his sleep.

As he sat there thinking about a next step, he was tempted to go home. He knew he'd have a hero's welcome. His mother would believe anything he chose to tell her and Dad rarely interfered. They would keep him for a time – a long time – if he told them how a gallery owner had cheated him and left him penniless, and too distressed to work.

It was only the thought of Hope being there that made him hesitate. Hope had always seen through his tall stories.

She had a way of looking at him that made her mistrust of him absolutely clear. And there was the awful child. No, he couldn't go home while they were there. How could he pretend an interest in the child? If only Hope and her brat could be persuaded to leave. He sat thinking for a while. Tomorrow he would write to Matthew. He might need his help in a while.

–

Matthew Charles had a job that took up only a few hours of each day. He was a rep for a famous supplier of tinned food-stuff. Strictly on allocation, he had a limited amount of the special items to sell each month and his only worry was to make sure that every shop had a share, so they would remain his customers when the rationing finally ended. Besides baked beans and spaghetti and assorted vegetables, the promise of a few of the luxuries were how he obtained his orders. Salmon and crab, and the rich spreads were what everyone wanted. With the points system for many items, people could choose how they were used. An occasional luxury helped them feel better and his products were always in demand.

It was so easy to sell what he had to offer that he had a lot of spare time on his hands. With little to do that could remotely be described as urgent, he amused himself watching people, particularly Phillip's family, so he could write amusing letters describing their antics.

He called occasionally at the Ty Mawr, making sure Freddy was out, and offered sympathy, egging Marjorie on to bitter comments about Hope, which he passed on to Phillip. The unpleasantness he and Phillip had practised as children hadn't really gone away.

–

Hope saw Matthew Charles again a few days after her encounter with Brenda Morris, the district nurse. She was coming out of the post office with a few reels of cotton when she almost bumped into him. She began to apologize, then, recognizing him, pushed him firmly out of her way. She was holding Davy's hand and as she walked off the little boy was running to keep up with her.

'Too fast, Mummy,' he said, stopping suddenly and dragging back.

'Sorry, Davy, I wasn't thinking.' She stopped and looked back to where the man was standing, watching her. What would he find to criticize when he reported to Marjorie about her visit to the post office? She wondered vaguely how he had learned about that late-night meeting of friends in her garden. She was convinced it was he who had told Marjorie, and he seemed so very interested in her and Davy. Why should he bother? Why would he be feeding Marjorie with complaints to discredit her as a mother? How would that help Marjorie, apart from giving her a vicious satisfaction? Surely even Marjorie wouldn't do anything that might affect Davy's happiness?

She turned again as she reached the corner and saw that the man was still there. Was he following her? Spying on her? The thought made her shiver as she turned into the lane and he was lost to her sight. Why would anyone be interested in her and her son? This is nonsense, she told herself, you're being foolish. But the thought of being watched by someone who wished her harm didn't altogether go away.

'D'you know a man called Matthew Charles?' she asked Peter when they met near the park later that day.

'Tall, skinny and with a lot of black hair? Talks with a plum in his mouth? He was a friend of Ralph's brother Phillip at one time, until he moved to Cardiff and Phillip went to live in North Wales. They've probably lost touch after all this time. I haven't seen or heard of him for years.'

'He approached me when I was washing the steps of the Ship and Compass and accused me of deliberately embarrassing Ralph's parents by accepting such menial work.'

'Always an odd bod. He and Phillip were...' his face curled with repugnance. He stopped and looked embarrassed, changed his mind about what he was about to say, then amended '...close friends. Very close for a while, but I suppose they outgrew each other.'

'You didn't like him.' It was a statement rather then a query.

Peter looked at her seriously as he tried to make up his mind whether or not to tell her the truth. When he spoke the words sounded angry as his memories grew. 'He and Phillip were partners in viciousness, always together. They bullied many of the younger kids and were inseparable, egging each other on to greater cruelties. The other kids, specially younger ones, were scared of them.

'Phillip used to boast a lot, and hated it if someone had something he did not. He threw my sister's bike into the stream once. New it was, and he couldn't bear her having something so wonderful.'

'And what about Ralph, was he Matthew's friend too?'

'Oh, don't think Ralph was a bully! He was a gentle soul. No, I think that for some reason Phillip and Matthew liked having him around. To show off to I suppose. Ralph was a nervous child and was probably thankful to have their protection. He was gullible, easily impressed, you know what some kids are like. Nervous ones that try to hide but can't. They stick out, so bullies spot them immediately. Some people are bullies and some are victims. Victims hero-worship bullies if they befriend them. Make excuses for their excesses.' He shrugged. 'Phillip has probably grown into a decent enough man, like most of us.' Softening his words with a smile, he added, 'When I remember what a lot of hooligans we were its a wonder we didn't all end up in borstal.'

'You remember Ralph well, then? I didn't realize you were at school with him.'

'I was a bit older, but I had a younger sister, and a couple of cousins, and, well, you know what it's like, the ages overlap more easily as the years pass.'

'Was Ralph sociable, friendly?'

'Of course he was, we didn't know how not to be. A small town, everyone knowing everyone. He was cleverer than most of us, mind. Instead of kicking around the roads looking for trouble, wasting time on daft and often dangerous games, he spent a lot of time at home, studying hard. Under his mother's thumb we used to say. Wouldn't help us with our homework, though. He didn't have the patience to explain stuff when we couldn't understand something that came to him with such ease. When he became an accountant and was taken on by one of the big firms he was absolutely out of our league. I don't think many of the rest of us could have achieved anything so grand.' He laughed deprecatingly. 'It's as much as I can do to tot up my incomings and outgoings at the end of each day.'

'I don't suppose many of us need more than that.'

'I won't. I'm not a great achiever, more's the pity. Although, perhaps if I tried…'

'Don't change, Peter. You're perfect just as you are,' she replied seriously.

The few simple words gave them a feeling of closeness that lasted as they walked on into the park where Peter pushed Davy on the swing and encouraged him to climb the big slide and whoosh down with screams of delight. Hope was left with a feeling of regret when they parted.

As she walked home she thought about their conversation and began to feel a worm of worry. The talk about Ralph had made her uneasy and she didn't know why. She hadn't known Ralph as a small boy. They had been about fifteen when they noticed each other amid the group of people that filled their lives. Ralph hadn't been a great talker, and they had spoken of little else but their love and the home they would share and the children they would have. Always their wonderful future, never the past.

Marjorie and Freddy had only spoken of his brilliance at academic subjects and his near genius when it came to mathematics. Now, after his death, Hope was alarmed at how little she knew of his inner self. Killing himself as he had, Ralph had become even more of a stranger. A chill drifted over her as though a cloud had hidden the sun. But the sun was beating down on her back as she walked towards the bus stop; it was a perfect late-summer day, but still she shivered.

–

Matthew approached her as she was setting out for her afternoon walk the following day. She moved to the side to pass him but he held the pushchair.

'You should leave Cwm Derw,' he said, smiling, his voice light as though simply passing a polite comment. 'It's killing Marjorie to see you every day, knowing you're responsible for Ralph's death.'

'Let me pass! And please watch what lies you spout when you're near my son.' Using the pushchair as a battering ram, she was gratified to hear him grunt with pain as the foot rest hit his shins. She almost ran the rest of the way to the bus stop.

She had intended going to their favourite place near the stream but she was afraid of being followed. She really would have to do something about Matthew Charles. But what? She had no intention of moving from Badgers Brook, whatever Marjorie said.

–

There was another problem with the plumbing a few days later. An unpleasant smell invaded the kitchen, and even after thorough cleaning and investigations by herself and Kitty and Bob they could find no cause. The source seemed to be outside and, trying not to become alarmed at the prospect of another expensive repair, and wondering if she could manage without resorting to another cleaning job to pay it, she asked the plumber to call. She couldn't expect Geoff to pay. The rent he was charging her was very low, and this could be an extensive job if outside drains were the cause.

On the day the plumber came he found the fault and, with a gang of workmen, opened the drains right down to the cesspit at the end of the garden. The smell was horrendous. An unexpected spell of warm weather made it worse, and after a few hours he suggested that she and Davy should stay elsewhere for a day or two until the area had been thoroughly disinfected and repaired.

With some trepidation, Hope called on Marjorie. As she approached Ty Mawr she began rehearsing what she would say. Her first sentence must say it all as Marjorie might not give her time for a second before slamming the door.

'Of course David can stay. He can have his father's old room.' Marjorie replied, obviously delighted, when she had briefly explained her dilemma.

'It will only be for a couple of days, three at the most; we can't stay in the house while the work is going on,' Hope explained.

'Davy can't be anywhere near all that; he must come here,' Marjorie said firmly, adding, 'You see again how wrong it was of you to insist on taking Ralph and Davy to that house, away from their proper home?'

'I'll go home and collect our things.' Hope ignored the criticism, which never seemed to end.

'David's things you mean,' Marjorie said.

'Our things, Davy's and mine,' she said with a smile. 'We won't need much, some clothes and a few of his toys. I'll bring a cushion cover that I'm embroidering. It's almost finished and I can work on it while I'm here.'

'I don't want you here. My son is dead because of you, and the family is shamed and disgraced. What makes you think I'd allow you to stay here? People might think I approve of you.'

The shock was severe but after so many insults Hope was able to conceal her emotions quickly. She put on the coat she had slipped off, put a protesting Davy back into his pushchair and left the house without a word.

Marjorie shouted, telling her she mustn't put the child at risk, that he had to stay, that Hope was an unfit mother, and then Hope heard the door slam as, struggling to hide her tears, she hurried down the front path.

Matthew Charles was just entering the gate, and she turned her head away as she ran past him without a word, but he was aware that she was crying. He knocked on the door, which was opened by an equally tearful Marjorie.

'I don't understand that young woman, refusing help when it's offered,' she wailed. 'And I've just had another letter from Phillip. He says he's too upset about Ralph to come home while she's around. On top of everything else she's done, she's keeping my one remaining son away from me.'

'And he's probably very busy,' Matthew comforted. 'He's increasingly in demand as his fame spreads.'

'If she would only move away, leave Davy and go!'

'When Phillip comes he and I will talk to her,' Matthew promised sympathetically.

–

Hurrying away from her mother-in-law's wrath, Hope went straight to see Kitty. By then her distress had transformed itself to anger, and she told Kitty of Marjorie's repetition of her belief that she, Hope, had killed her son.

'To be honest, Kitty, I feel sorry for the woman, but I can't take much more of her accusations.'

'I don't know what you can do except wait for the poisonous anguish to leave her. I don't think people like us want to get into suing for slander, defamation of character and all that.'

'Of course not. I could never do that to Ralph's mother, Davy's grandmother.' She gave a huge sigh, then said, 'Mind you, it might not be a bad idea to remind her that I could!'

'Stay here tonight.' Kitty waved away her protests and went on, 'The couch and a put-you-up bed. That do?'

Hope could only say, 'Thank you.'

Leaving Davy with Kitty, Hope went back to the house to collect what they would need for an overnight stay, but before she could begin there was a knock at the door.

A man stood there with a handkerchief over his nose and mouth.

'Sorry about the smell,' she apologized. 'The drains are giving trouble.'

The man looked at a clipboard containing some papers and asked, 'Can you tell me who lives here?'

'Just me and my son, Davy.'

'Who is how old, Mrs Murton?'

'Davy will be three in October.'

The man stepped back and looked towards the side of the house, where men were working in a foul-smelling trench.

'The child will have to be taken to a place of safety, I'm afraid. It's far too dangerous for him to be so near this disturbance.'

'Davy isn't here. We are staying with a neighbour until the work is finished.'

He checked his papers again. 'I understood—'

'You understood from my mother-in-law – who refused to help us – that I was putting my son at risk?'

It took a while longer but the man was finally convinced that the child was far away from the open cesspit.

'You can stay longer if you wish,' Hope said finally, 'but I have to get out of here. My son isn't the only one who'd be better away from this place.'

–

Marjorie was writing to Phillip. Although he didn't write to her often, recently he had done so several times, asking questions about Hope and her son, encouraging her criticism. She wrote a full description of Hope's apparent failings as a mother, her working in a public house and having men to stay, her free-and-easy attitude to training, social development and good manners. 'I know he's not quite three,' she explained, 'but these things don't suddenly start at the age of five, they have to be a part of his life from a very early age.' She had no one else to talk to as Freddy refused to hear a word of complaint about his daughter-in-law, who, he often repeated, had been courageous in her misfortunes. So when she wrote to Phillip she poured more and more of her unhappiness out to him.

In the past he had rarely replied to her letters, but on the subject of Davy he was surprisingly forthcoming. He suggested that, being a penniless widow, Hope might be persuaded to give him up and allow Marjorie to care for him. Then Hope could find a more suitable way of earning money. It was exactly what she had said to Matthew. It showed how well she and Phillip communicated.

He also told her that she wouldn't cope with the tragedy until Hope had moved far away from Cwm Derw. He repeated his sadness that he was unable to come home while there was a chance of coming face to face with Hope.

As Phillip had written the words suggesting his mother might take care of Davy, he had felt a momentary qualm. Hope would never allow it, would she? But what if his mother did manage to take him from Hope? What then? His own childhood had been so unhappy and here he was committing a not-quite-three-year-old to a similar regime. He always thought of the years spent at home as a regime rather than a childhood. Perhaps he would go home one day and see what kind of a child his brother Ralph had produced. Picturing a little boy similar to his younger brother, he put the letter aside. Perhaps he wouldn't send it. The memories of his regimented childhood and the inability of his mother to demonstrate her love for him had remained as a sad echo of what his early years might have been.

Still, he reassured himself, his mother bringing up the child wasn't the plan. He just wanted there to be enough pressure on Hope to make her leave and take the little boy with her. Then he'd be able to go home, allow himself to be kept by his doting mother and not have to worry about success, or the lack of it. He really wasn't cut out for working for a living and he'd had enough of Connie's nagging. Hope would have to go, though.

He contacted Matthew and told him he needed a 'boys' night out'. Matthew had promised to attend the play in which his wife and daughters were taking part, but persuaded himself that Phillip's need was the greater.

Since leaving home straight after being demobbed from the army in 1945, Phillip had lived with four romantically inclined women, who, in turn, had been attracted to the handsome, expensively dressed, well-spoken young man who dreamed of becoming an artist, and who had imagined themselves being admired for supporting him and becoming his indispensable and adored wife. Three had left him, unable to cope with his failures once they realized that the ambition to paint was no more than an excuse to avoid regular employment.

His mother had encouraged a small talent he had for drawing and painting and had convinced herself he should be an architect. That Phillip had neither the talent nor the ability to take on such intense study was ignored. Not only was he incapable of such dedication, he had no desire to achieve the end result. He had an idea that, given time to develop slowly, naturally, he might become an artist. Earning money by painting pictures as and when the mood tempted him seemed a perfect way to spend his life.

Leaving home had been easy. Soon after his return, facing more of his mother's plans for him, he had simply walked out wearing his demob suit and carrying a few clothes bought by his mother, in a suitcase provided by the government. His wallet contained all the money he had saved and some he had been given by his father to set himself up with the materials he would need.

He went to North Wales, where the rugged scenery appealed. Craggy mountains and lakes of breathtaking beauty, rich green fields, their shapes distorted by ancient walls and crossed by bubbling streams. He journeyed dreaming the idle dream of becoming a landscape artist, portraying picturesque farms filled with contented animals and fascinating characters. He wasn't prepared for the effort involved. He did try, encouraged by various women who stayed until they realized that his main characteristic was not talent but laziness. Janet believed in him for a while, as he tried pottery alongside his paintings, then she gave up on him and left. Kate encouraged him to train as a teacher until his constant absences ended that brief promise. Harriet lasted only a month before walking away with everything she could carry that she might be able to sell, her luggage containing none of his paintings.

Now there was Connie, a sometimes fiery character who, at thirty-three, was seven years older than him. She had made him face the fact that he had no chance of earning money by his art, and had persuaded him to apply for, and accept, a job as a school caretaker.

She worked alongside him, bullying him when necessary to get him out of bed when he didn't feel like going to work, and making the weekends so wonderful that he slowly accepted that the five days of working were worthwhile. She took control of the money, handing him a few shillings when he felt like walking to the local for a drink.

Routine was something he abhorred but gradually he had learned to accept it. Connie cared for him and for a while he hadn't thought he could cope alone again. Whatever happened to him he hadn't thought he would ever go home. But now things had changed. Connie had changed. She was no longer content to drift along as they had been, her ambition for more had ruined everything. Perhaps, if he went on a visit, making sure Connie would still be here if he came back, he might be able to persuade Hope to leave.

'I'll come,' Connie said at once when he mentioned his idea of visiting his parents. Phillip shook his head slowly, kissed her affectionately. 'I wouldn't inflict my mother on someone I love,' he said solemnly. 'In fact, I must have had an aberration when I suggested she might take care of Davy. I don't know the child but I don't think he could possibly deserve such a punishment.' He explained about his suggestion. 'Luckily, I changed my mind and didn't post the letter.'

'Oh dear, I think I did,' Connie said.

'I don't expect she'll take any notice of what I said anyway. If she does, I'll bitterly regret writing that letter,' he added sorrowfully.

'Let's go and see. I'll stay away from the house if that's what you wish, but I'll go with you. We have a half-term holiday coming soon.'

'All right, if we can afford it. I'll write to Matthew Charles and ask if we can stay with him, shall I?'

'I'll enquire about the trains.'

'No,' Phillip said, then, 'Why don't we make it a Christmas visit instead? We'll be back in time for the New Year celebrations here.'

Connie smiled. 'You are getting to be a social butterfly, Phillip, you really are.'

Phillip smiled contentedly. Maybe he and Connie were well suited after all. In fact, was it wise to risk going to see his parents? His mother had a well-honed knack for spoiling things. But then again, Connie had a way of sorting out troublemakers and the contest might be fun to watch.

He still intended to leave Connie, but not yet. She wasn't his future, he knew that now. She inhibited him, held him too tightly in chains of conventional, wage-earning orderliness. He needed freedom; something she was no longer willing to give him.

Hope was earning a growing reputation for making clothes for people less than easy to fit. One of her customers had a slight hump on her shoulder blade after an accident as a child, and Hope's jacket helped to conceal the deformity, making the lady feel more confident, more able to mix socially. Several of her regular clients were small, and the usual method of simply shortening dresses and skirts didn't work at all. Hope's skill at remaking a dress, or making one from new, was quickly recognized, and she had as much work as she could manage. She often sat up late into the night to finish a garment, anxious to please a client and to see her bank balance growing.

In September, she decided that if she were to accept all the work she was offered she needed to take on a trainee. Too much of her time was spent doing simple tasks, like tacking and felling, that a less capable person could do. Going to the employment exchange and sorting out all the paperwork, besides getting herself on to an official level, was alarming; but she knew that what she had begun as a way of surviving was becoming a legitimate business.

The girl she employed had shown her some of her work and the neatness of her stitches, as well as her gentle demeanour, quickly persuaded Hope that, although she had little experience, she would give her a try. The girl was Joyce, Geoff Tanner's niece. She was fourteen and had left school to work in a wool shop, but was not happy there. The prospect of working alongside Hope pleased her, and in the middle of September she arrived to begin work.

At first Joyce was restricted to tacking, binding the edges of seams, sewing on buttons and dealing with the tidying-up at the end of each day, but within a few days Hope realized she could leave more and more of the more important work to her. She made suggestions as Hope worked out her designs, a second sewing machine arrived and the business grew.

Every afternoon, leaving Joyce busy, Hope took Davy out for a walk. This time was always for Davy. At first he had enjoyed trips to the park with the slide and swings, but one day, when she didn't feel like going on the bus into the town, they had visited the brook where the badgers drank and crossed from one part of the wood to another. Hope had packed a picnic and after that, whenever the day was fine, it was there Davy wanted to go.

Besides paddling in the thin trickle of clear, cold water and shrieking with the painful delight of it, they made dens, and found branches that made perfect swings, and gathered fire-wood and wild flowers, and watched as the leaves began to change colour. While they were there Hope was able, for a while at least, to put aside her loneliness and her concerns about the welfare of her difficult mother-in-law.

As autumn changed the scene around Badgers Brook and a chill began to bite at fingers and toes, rumours reached her, usually via Kitty or Stella at the post office, that Marjorie had become almost a recluse. The shame of Ralph's death and the uneasiness with which people greeted her had spoiled any attempts to be friendly, even with people she had known for many years. She rarely went into the post office, and Stella had been abruptly refused admittance when she had called at the Ty Mawr with flowers in an attempt to help.

Freddy came out of the Ship and Compass one day as Hope and Davy were passing, having been fixing shelves for Betty Connors, and he told her that it had begun with

Marjorie waiting in for news of when Phillip was coming home. As weeks went past and no further plans were mentioned she had fallen into despair and become less and less inclined to leave the house. Hope called at Ty Mawr several times and left flowers and notes, but heard nothing in reply.

Stella was surprised to see the unhappy woman one day when she was about to close the shop door. She pulled down the blinds to discourage more latecomers and asked what she wanted.

'Oh, a few stamps, I have letters to write.' Marjorie seemed vague, unlike her usual loud-spoken pompous self.

Stella lifted the sheet of stamps and asked, 'How many?'

'I've had this letter from Phillip, you remember my son?'

'Of course I remember him, Marjorie! You daft or something? Seen him grown from a noisy little scrap in a pram to a man going off to war, haven't I?'

'Sorry, I'm a bit…'

'Look, Colin is out, up the allotment digging over ready for some Brussels sprouts plants he's been given. Come through and have a cup of tea.'

Without protest, Marjorie followed her into the over-full room behind the shop, where three cats curled up near a blazing fire and Scamp, the little terrier, raised a sleepy eye and wagged his tail before going back to sleep. Shirts hung from a clothes rack and a railway jacket hung on the back of a chair. Stella threw it carelessly aside and invited Marjorie to sit.

'Sulking, he is, because Colin went without him,' Stella said pointing a thumb at the dog. She dealt with the kettle that simmered on the black-leaded hob and made tea. Her movements were fast as she reached cups, saucers and plates from the dresser, cake from a cupboard and the tea cosy from under Scamp's head, muttering about how she'd kill him if he didn't stop stealing it. She put the tea cosy over the pot, hoping Marjorie hadn't noticed where it had come from. 'Now then, this letter from your Phillip?'

'He suggests that I – that is, Freddy and I – look after little David, and give Hope a chance to get a proper job. What d'you think?'

'Forget it, is what I think! I can't imagine Hope ever agreeing to such an idea. That child is her life!'

'She isn't a fit mother, you know.'

'What a lot of old *lol*! A happier little boy I've never seen. Copes wonderful your Hope does. You ought to be proud of her. And as for a proper job, what d'you think she's doing now? Making dresses for half the town she is, and she's taken on an assistant, trainee or whatever. Geoff Tanner's niece. Wonderful clever from all I hear. Worrying for nothing you are. Leave 'em be.'

Marjorie stood to leave. As always, when a response was not what she expected or hoped for she wanted to walk away.

Stella stood too, blocked her way and handed her a cup and saucer. 'Add your own sugar, not too much mind, I'm a bit short at the moment. Used some making blackberry jam, fool that I am, and it's only eight ounces a week we get. Terrible hard to manage on a pound with my Colin sneaking extra when I'm not looking.'

Marjorie was forced to sit back down. 'Sorry, I shouldn't have mentioned it. I don't need advice, I know what's best for my own.'

'Do you indeed.'

'I know David isn't getting the right training.'

'How old is he?'

'Almost three.'

'Two then. *Not* three. Always one to push it to win an argument you are, Marjorie Murton! Two years old is all he is and you're worried about Hope not training him? Being happy and knowing he's loved, that's all he needs when he's only two. God 'elp us, Marjorie, what sort of childhood did your boys have if you think a two-year-old needs "training"?' She regretted the words the moment they were spoken. Poor woman didn't want to be told she'd got it wrong, with one son killed during the war, one avoiding her by moving away and Ralph choosing to kill himself rather than go on living. 'Sorry, Marjorie. As usual I open my mouth too quick. I'm sure you'd look after your Davy well – a wonderful grandmother you'll be. But don't think your Hope will let him go, because she won't.'

'She isn't *my* Hope!'

'She's doing very well by all accounts. She's that clever with her needle, and she designs and makes clothes for all manner of people, rich, poor, tall, short, slender as a bean pole and those who can't get a tent to fit over their hips.' she added in an effort to raise a smile. 'Leave 'em be and let them know you're there if they need help. It's best.'

'Thank you for the tea.' Marjorie went to the door leading to the shop and Stella stopped her again.

'What else did that Phillip of yours say? You haven't told me all of it. Don't need to be a detective to know that.'

'He says he can't come home while Hope is still living here. He's too upset about Ralph.'

'And you believe him?'

'Of course. He's my son.' Marjorie glared at her, daring her to disagree.

Stella made a deprecating sound between a hmm and a groan, and said, 'Don't forget your stamps, Marjorie, and you haven't paid, remember.'

'Freddy will pick them up tomorrow.'

When Stella had locked the shop securely and began to wash the dishes she found a lot of undissolved sugar in Marjorie's cup. Knowing she was short of sugar, Marjorie had made sure to take more than she needed. What is it about the woman that makes her so full of spite, Stella wondered, as she scraped the waste into the rubbish bin. From all she remembered of Phillip, he'd inherited his mother's lack of compassion, and the thought of him being too distressed to face poor Hope was nothing more than a sad joke.

Marjorie walked home, a sickly feeling in her stomach not completely due to her over-sweet tea. A growing need to take her grandson away from Hope was crowding out other concerns and the thought excited and frightened her. With her three sons gone and no one to fill the large house, which she had imagined being crowded with grandchildren and their friends one day, she had to do something. Freddy wouldn't help, he was ridiculously fond of Hope, but perhaps if she could persuade Phillip to come home she would have an ally, someone who would sympathize with what she wanted to do. After all, she would be a better person to bring up little David than the woman who had caused the death of his father.

–

The object of her half-thought-out plan was in the garden of Badgers Brook. Davy and Joyce were playing skittles, but he was laughing too much to concentrate and Joyce was adding to the fun by missing the skittles every time she tried.

'Time to go in now, Davy,' Joyce said, and with a groan he agreeably collected the game and put it into its box. When she went through the door, leaving him to follow, she saw Geoff and Peter. They had been watching the game.

'Never play for Glamorgan, will he?' Joyce said. 'I've never known such a boy for giggling.'

She went to wash her hands and Geoff watched the way Peter was looking at Hope and Davy. 'I'd have loved a family, Peter,' he said softly.

'Why didn't you remarry when you lost your wife? Wealthy businessman, not bad looking, what happened?'

'I had my chances but I let them go. I stayed to revive the business Dad had let slide. I spent too much on that, then looking after Dad. It's true what they say about all work and no play making Jack a dull boy, you know. Then one day I realized I'd left it too late, I'd lost touch with people my own age. Most were married and I was left high and dry. Be warned, Peter. Don't make the same mistake as me. Don't let life pass you by.' He gestured with a tilt of his head towards Hope, who was setting out glasses for the fizzy drinks she had bought from the Corona delivery man.

'No chance there,' Peter whispered. 'I've got nothing to offer. I live in a room in Lena Parry's house and rent a stable and storeroom. When Dad sold our house and remarried I just took the first place I could find and I've never had the money to improve things.'

'Two people pulling together can work miracles, believe me.'

'Besides, there's never been anyone but Ralph for Hope.'

'But he isn't here, is he? Anyone can see how you feel about her. And I don't think she's going to live with sad memories for ever. She's already very fond of you. Sow the seeds and give it time,' Geoff said, nodding wisely. 'Just give it a little time. Not too long mind, time races past much too fast. Believe it and learn from my mistakes.'

Peter stepped forward and took the tray of glasses and bottles. 'Here, let me do that, Hope, it's too heavy for a slip of a thing like you.' Behind him he heard Geoff give a muffled laugh.

–

Phillip wrote two more letters. In one he advised Hope to get away while there was time. She read it and found it alarming but obscure. What was he saying, that she would be safer out of Cwm Derw? Safer from what, or whom? Marjorie was a bitter and difficult woman but she wouldn't harm her or Davy. She showed it to Peter, who said Phillip must want her gone for reasons of his own, but what the reasons were he couldn't think. 'Just don't do anything Marjorie could criticize you for. And remember,' he said, taking her hand in both of his, 'I'm here whenever you need a friend.'

Phillip's second letter was to his mother. He told her how desperately he wanted to come home, how much he longed to see her and his father, but repeated that he couldn't come home while Hope was still in the village, he would be far too upset. Sometimes he thought he was over-reacting but then he thought of a messy, dribbling child following him, expecting to be hugged and calling him Uncle Phillip, and his determination was strengthened anew.

Five

Freddy was on the bridge from where his son had fallen. It was raining and, with the day still dark and the chill in the air, the weather matched his melancholy thoughts. He stood there for a while, rain dripping from the brim of his trilby, the water dampening his feet and occasionally running like an icy river down his neck, and daydreamed of it all being a mistake, a dream from which he would awaken.

How could Ralph be dead? He was just a boy. A young man who had survived his short months in the army without even the slightest injury. It was easy to understand Marjorie's bitterness, but impossible to explain her resentment of Hope, who was being so brave, and her indifference to young Davy.

'I saw you go past and guessed you'd be here,' a voice said, and Betty Connors came up and belatedly sheltered him beneath her large umbrella. 'Come back with me and have a hot drink, or Marjorie won't be the only one complaining of a cold.'

He turned and smiled at her, kissed her lightly on the cheek. 'Thanks, Betty.' He glanced once more at the track below them then turned away, tucking her arm in his companionably. 'I don't know why I come here. It isn't any comfort. It's more like enveloping myself in renewed pain.'

'It's the place where he said goodbye to you all; perhaps you hope for an echo, to hear him call to you.'

'You sound fanciful this morning!'

He was more cheerful when they entered the Ship and Compass and he saw a fire blazing in the room behind the bar, and a tray set for tea. The toasting fork was at the ready and the bread was sliced. 'You were sure you'd find me,' he said with a smile.

'Oh, anyone would have done.' she said airily. 'If not you then I was bound to meet some other idle wanderer in need of sustenance.' She reached for the teapot and took it to the simmering kettle and handed him the toasting fork.

Although the brief visit was a comfort, Freddy was seriously worried about Marjorie. She rarely left the house. He had coaxed and pleaded but apart from her occasional visit to the post office, where she always arrived late and sometimes stayed for a cup of tea with Stella, she saw no one and was increasingly afraid of meeting anyone. Now, when a cold had developed into a cough and she complained of a pain deep in her chest, she refused to allow Freddy to call the doctor.

'Come on, Marjorie, this is getting silly,' he said when he reached home to find her lying on the couch. 'Ralph died in the most awful way, but life has to go on for the rest of us. He would expect you to hold up your head and not show such defeat. He was ill, the courts agreed that he was ill. He was in despair at the thought of living the rest of his life in a wheelchair. He would never have left us if he hadn't been ill. He loved us and wouldn't want us to destroy our lives, even though he chose to take his own.'

'People blame me, I know they do.'

'The doctor won't. Please let me call him.'

'No. I'll be fine in a day or so. It's nothing more than a cold. Just write to Phillip, persuade him to come home. That will be better than anything the doctor can do.'

He didn't tell her that he'd written more than a dozen times and had no response.

—

'But, Phillip,' Connie said in exasperation, 'you have to at least reply. Your father's writing, begging you to go home, telling you your mother's ill. Don't you care?'

'I can't do anything. They've lived in Cwm— in that town all their lives, they'll have all the help they need. I don't want to go sick visiting. Why should I?'

'Because she's your mother? Isn't that sufficient reason?'

He looked away from her angry eyes.

'Because deep down, you love her? Or is love something you can't feel?'

'I love you, Connie. I'd never want to leave you.'

'Then let's go and see your parents and tell them that. Tell them we're together for always and that we're buying a property and running a bed and breakfast, working together, and invite them to our wedding.' She was watching him as she spoke the words he clearly didn't want to hear. 'Phillip?' she coaxed.

'It sounds wonderful, Connie darling, but it's too soon. I thought we'd stay at the school for another year, then, if we're still sure, we'll think about it.'

'Let's give it six months, shall we? And in that six months we can both make sure it's what we want. I don't intend to carry you,' she said, kissing him to ease the sting from her words. 'I don't want to take it on and find myself doing all the work, especially if we have a child, do I? But if we're both sure that you and I can work together, then I know we'll make it a success.'

Phillip made an excuse to get out of the house. If he stayed he was afraid he'd be sick. What had he done, talking about loving for ever. He had to get away. But where? To his mother? Out of the frying pan into the fire that would be. But he had to get away from Connie and her crazy dream. A future of hard, boring work, being nice to people he was certain to despise. Guests who would treat them like servants. That life was definitely not for him!

–

Freddy went to see Hope and this time it wasn't to work in her garden.

'Marjorie's ill and I can't persuade her to see the doctor,' he said as soon as he walked through the door. 'Will you come and talk to her? I know she isn't the easiest of people,' he said quickly when she began to refuse. 'She's so depressed and I don't want this cough to take a hold. She doesn't seem to be in a frame of mind to fight it. She hardly goes out now, and a long illness would make her a complete recluse. No one would bother to call and ask how she is, because she has refused to see anyone who tried. Ever since Ralph…' his voice faded. It was the longest speech she had ever heard from him.

'Very well, I'll go, but I won't take Davy.'

'But she'd love to see him,' he protested.

'If she's as ill as you say, I can't risk him catching it, can I?'

'Shall I stay here with him?'

'That would be best.'

He gave her a key, knowing Marjorie was unlikely to open the door to her. Then she frowned and said, 'No, Father-in-law, I think it's best if you come with me. I might need help if she has to take medicine. Kitty will look after Davy for an hour.'

When she walked into the living room of Ty Mawr, she was shocked to see how ill Marjorie had become. She lay on the couch, untidily dressed, covered with an eiderdown. Her face looked wasted and lined. Her colour was high and it was clear she was running a temperature. Hope's anger toward the woman faded. Compassion overcame her dislike. She saw an unhappy, sick woman who needed help, and she knew she was the one to give it. She ran towards her and at once pulled pillows up to make Marjorie more comfortable, and, for once, Marjorie didn't object. After making her a drink and standing until she finished it, she slipped out of the house and telephoned the doctor.

She needed to find proper bedding and at first Marjorie reverted to her usual disagreeable self and stopped her, holding on to the eiderdown and glaring angrily at her.

'You can protest all you like, Mother-in-law, but I'm going to freshen you up and make you more comfortable. If you refuse to help it will take a little longer, but I will do it.'

Marjorie hardly said a word but her eyes, red rimmed and angry, followed her daughter-in-law constantly. She allowed Hope to wash her and brush her unwashed hair, remake the temporary bed with a blanket brought from the spare room, but although she must have felt a little better for her ministrations, she continued to watch her with silent dislike.

The doctor came within half an hour and Hope had a quick word before showing him to where his patient lay. 'I can't look after her here, I have work I must do, but if you could persuade her to come and stay with me I think it would be a very good idea. We need to get her out of this house which she's making into a prison.'

The doctor examined Marjorie and advised her to get to bed and stay there. 'You need constant attendance,' he said in a deeply serious tone.

'I can't stay in bed. How ridiculous to suggest it! Freddy won't be able to cope and there's no one else to help us,' she said, her eyes daring Hope to disagree. 'No one at all.'

'I can't stay here indefinitely, Doctor,' Hope said. 'But if she can be moved to Badgers Brook I can look after her there.'

'No,' Marjorie panted, perspiration running down her face. 'I won't enter that house.'

'Then I won't be responsible for what happens,' the doctor replied calmly, sharing a conspiratorial glance with the anxious Hope. 'If you stay with your daughter-in-law, and I arrange for a nurse to call, then you'll be home in a week or so, none the worst for this little setback.'

'I can't.'

'Then it's hospital, Mrs Murton.'

'Williamson-Murton,' the sick woman insisted weakly.

The doctor walked towards the door and beckoned Hope to follow. 'I don't think it's serious, yet, but you're right, it's an opportunity to get her out of the house. It's a chance to make her leave, escape from these four walls, as you so rightly say. A rest, a change of scene, meeting people, an acceptance that life goes on, might give her the necessary push to get back into a normal life, or as normal as possible after such a tragedy.' He patted Hope's shoulder kindly. 'You're so wise and you've coped remarkably well with your ordeal. Here you are, with all you've had to face, worrying about a woman who – a woman who can be very difficult,' he amended.

Pleading with Marjorie to go back with her to Badgers Brook and be taken care of wasn't going to work. Hope knew that even before she began to put her case. Instead she spoke as though the whole thing had been previously arranged. Ignoring her vicious complaints and determined refusal to leave her home, Hope arranged for a taxi. 'This way she'll be less likely to refuse or make a fuss than if you try to reason with her,' she explained to an anxious Freddy. Turning a firm face to Marjorie she said. 'It's either this taxi or Peter Bevan's horse and cart!'

Packing her cases was difficult as Marjorie threw out everything as soon as it was put in them. It wasn't until Freddy coaxed her to go back to her couch and rest that Hope finally succeeded in putting together the necessary items for Marjorie's and Freddy's stay.

Later that day, helped by Freddy, Peter and Bob, and with much complaining, Marjorie moved into Badgers Brook. That Hope suffered apprehension was clear from her nervous cleaning and constant rearranging of furniture. She owed it to Ralph to do what she could for his mother and was determined to do her best. Freddy was given the small back bedroom looking towards the lane and the woods beyond, which delighted him. Its smallness was a comfort after the large, rather gloomy rooms of Ty Mawr.

Hope and Kitty prepared a corner of the living room close to the fire, with borrowed screens to make it cosy, and it was there that Marjorie decided to reign.

With racing heart, sounding more confident than she felt, Hope firmly put down a few rules. 'I work on the garden every afternoon after taking Davy for his walk, and in the morning Joyce and I deal with the dressmaking.'

'I'll need some attention, or why did you insist on bringing me here?'

Ignoring the outburst, Hope went on, 'Father-in-law has promised to continue helping on the garden; I really don't know how I'd manage without him and Bob. It's earned a useful sum of money towards the running this place and I'm very grateful to them both.'

'And what about me?'

With a quaking heart and a voice that trembled, Hope said, 'You will be looked after, I promise you that, but you'll have to work your wants around the routine of the house. I have to work, the garden has to be maintained, and when a garment has been promised I will not let a client down. As long as you understand that we'll get along just fine, Mother-in-law.'

She wondered afterwards how she had managed to be so dominant and brave in the face of Marjorie's disapproval.

'Kitty, you should have heard me,' she said, hiding her mouth in cupped hands. 'I sounded more of a harridan than Mother-in-law on a bad day¡

'Good on you.' Kitty was gleeful. 'Do her good to face someone as chopsy as she is. Now, don't waver, mind. You're a businesswoman and the work keeps a roof over your head. Remember that and you'll be fine.'

There were a few difficult moments during the first few days, while Marjorie was obviously ill, when Hope began to weaken. She wanted so much to help Marjorie, longed for even the slightest glimmer of a smile. Sympathy for the unhappy woman almost made her forget her own priorities. But then Kitty's reminders came into her mind and she refused to deviate from her routine. She had so much to pack into her days she knew that if she succumbed to a few days of relaxation she would be overwhelmed.

The evenings were when she concentrated on entertaining Marjorie, once Davy was in bed and the house was quiet. For a few days Marjorie was too ill to argue, but as the days passed and she grew stronger her protests increased. She wanted attention. She would make a provocative statement, usually about the untidiness of the house, and when Hope tried to explain she would reach over and increase the volume on the wireless and blot her out. Playing her at her game became a joke between Hope and Freddy, and she refused to rise to the criticism. To Marjorie's intense irritation, she simply agreed.

The house was a busy one and Marjorie complained that it was exhausting her having riff-raff bursting in with their trivialities. Hope just smiled and, when she had the chance, explained that it was a business house as well as a home. Most who called greeted Marjorie politely but received no word in response. If Hope had imagined that a stay in the friendly Badgers Brook household would change her she was mistaken. The calm, quiet restfulness that overcame most visitors when they entered the old house didn't work on her irate and pompous mother-in-law for a single moment. After a few disappointments, the stream of callers ignored Marjorie completely, which gave her cause for even more complaints. Stella was the exception. She was not a woman to be ignored. She burst in after the shop closed and chattered away about the events of her day and insisted on Marjorie joining in the gossip.

A greater understanding arose as Hope watched her mother-in-law during those early days. The anger that so alienated her from others was aimed more at herself. It was Stella who had put it into perspective.

'Marjorie didn't have much of a life, with non-achieving parents who quarrelled all the time and gave her very little attention. I believe that was why she became twisted in her thinking about the way children should be reared,' she said one day as she was leaving the house. 'She set out these rigid rules and stuck with them, and now, besides losing Richard so cruelly at the end of the war, there's Phillip, running away like an ill-treated puppy, and Ralph killing himself rather than cope as a less than perfect person. She must feel bitter, wondering if all these years she's been wrong. Poor dab,' she added. 'Pity for her, but she doesn't encourage people to like her, does she?'

Hope hadn't suffered disapproval from the local people as Marjorie had. For reasons she couldn't understand, her mother-in-law was blamed for what had happened, the feeling being that Ralph's mental health on that fateful day was less to do with the dreadful injuries he had suffered and more to do with the way Marjorie had behaved towards her boys during their childhood.

No psychiatrist was needed to tell the majority that continuous harsh criticism, a lack of affection and too much urging to succeed did not make for a happy, well-balanced child. Marjorie had encouraged her three sons to produce better and better results at school, but Ralph, being the brightest and the more malleable, as well as the youngest and her last hope, had been under the greatest pressure.

Hope had been offered sympathy from the moment the news of Ralph's accident had broken and continued to receive constant offers of help, so it was with shock and disbelief that she was woken late one night by the sound of a window being smashed. She ran to Davy's cot to make sure he was safe, then, with a torch showing the way, ran down the stairs. Her first thought as she ran to deal with whatever had happened was that she wished Peter was there.

The living room was no longer in darkness. Marjorie had a battery lamp which she shone towards her as she called for Freddy to help her.

'It's all right Mother-in-law,' Hope called as heavy footsteps followed her down the stairs. 'I'll soon turn on the light and we'll see what happened.'

–

Peter had been walking through the wood on his way back from a visit to a local farmer, and had heard the unmistakable sound of smashing glass as he reached the lane. Anxiously, convinced Hope was in trouble, he hurried towards the dark looming shape of the house. A man was just hurrying through the gateway as he burst out of the trees edging the lane and all he had was a glimpse of a tall figure, heading away from him. He was limping slightly, but travelling swiftly using the grass verge to deaden the sound of his footsteps.

The sound could only have come from Badgers Brook and he ran up the path and knocked on the door. Inside, a light was flickering as the gas light in the kitchen was lit, its glow widening as the chain was slowly adjusted. Through the jagged hole, he called, 'Hope? Are you all right?' Inside he could hear Marjorie calling to Hope and

Hope's reply, promising to come as soon as she'd found out what had happened. The loud complaining voice of Marjorie demanded to know when someone was going to come and attend to her.

'Peter!' Hope said with a sob of relief. She was so relieved to see him. He had appeared as though by the magic of her thoughts. Through the broken pane she asked, 'Did you see who did this?'

'No, but you shouldn't have shown a light in case he was still here. You'd have made an easy target. It's all right,' he added quickly as her hand moved to pull on the other thin chain to turn off the gas. 'I saw a man hurrying away seconds after I heard the crash of glass. Tall, he was, and limping. I didn't recognize him. Shall I go to the phone and call the police?'

'It can't have been a grown man who did this. Surely it's more the act of small boys challenging each other for a dare?'

'Can I come in?'

'Sorry. I'll open the door.' She unbolted the door and let him in. He went straight to the hole in the glass.

'I'll get a piece of cardboard. That'll have to do until the morning. Then I'll measure up and get the glass.'

Freddy came in then, with Marjorie hanging on his arm. 'Marjorie had to come and see what had happened,' Freddy explained. 'She wouldn't sleep unless she saw for herself.'

If Hope expected sympathy she was mistaken. Marjorie stared at the broken pane for a moment, then, turning to Freddy, she said dismissively, 'What does she expect, riff-raff wandering through the house at will? Who knows what will happen next. Really, Freddy, I'd be safer at home.' As Freddy gave Hope an apologetic glance and led his wife back to her bed, Marjorie went on, 'It's peace I want, not neighbourhood hooligans threatening me. Take me home, Freddy. I want to go home.'

As her tremulous, complaining voice faded, Hope gave a sigh and looked at Peter. Lowering her voice to a whisper that brought him closer to her, she said, 'I had hoped that a few days here might soften her, but she's worse if anything. The only time she smiles is when she's with Davy, and even with him she's critical.'

'Critical of a not-quite-three-year-old?'

'She tells him his manners are poor, and he doesn't speak properly, and even that he doesn't try hard enough with his drawing.' She felt a tear falling as she went on. 'He's so proud of the pictures he gives her but every time she tells him to do better, that they're untidy. How can she be like that with a baby? So I try to be there when they're together, to interrupt or add a word to soften her words. It's so sad. She's lonely, even with a lovely husband like Freddy, but she doesn't seem able to stop herself from spoiling every relationship she has. I want to help her, Peter, I really do. She'd have me for a friend if she'd only come halfway.'

'The way she is with Davy must be the same as her so-called "training" with Richard, Phillip and Ralph.'

While they were whispering, Peter had taken a pile of fabric remnants from a cardboard box and, using the box, had tacked a cover over the broken windowpane.

'Sorry, Peter. I shouldn't be telling you all this.'

'Why not? You have to talk to someone and I'm always here.' He looked at her thoughtfully and repeated, 'I'm always here, remember that, Hope.'

'Thank you,' she whispered, looking away from his intense stare. It was only then that she became aware that she was wearing only a nightdress and gown, both flimsy items she had bought for her honeymoon. The thought unnerved her and she hurried away with less grace than he deserved.

'Peter saw someone running away, a man with a limp,' she told Freddy when she had added a winter coat to her attire.

'How very convenient,' Marjorie remarked. 'Disguising his own actions, no doubt.'

'Mother-in-law, how can you think Peter did this? Why would he?'

'Hope, you're so gullible. Bordering on the stupid at times. I wonder what my dear son ever saw in you.'

The words stabbed Hope in her heart; she longed to run away and cry out her misery, but she said nothing, aware of Freddy's anguish and shame, determined not to add to them.

Peter heard them, and saw how distressed Hope was after such venom. Her face was white, and as he left he hugged her close to him and kissed her cheek. He referred to it only briefly. 'Try not to take it to heart, it's misery talking.'

He walked home wishing he had made the effort to chase after the man he had seen hurrying away from the sound of the breaking glass. Although hadn't his instincts been right, making sure Hope was safe? She had to be more important than catching the man responsible. He stopped and looked back, although he couldn't see the house anymore in the darkness. She was filling more and more of his thoughts and with a stab of excitement he wondered whether she felt the same.

Then he laughed aloud. How could she feel anything for a man like himself? He had a small business selling vegetables door to door, not even a premises, unless you counted Jason's stable. Compared with Ralph and his family, he didn't stand a chance of her thinking of him other than as a helping hand. Yet he knew that no matter how cruelly fate had treated him, he would never have allowed himself to become so despairing that he'd have killed himself, leaving her in such a mess. If she had trusted her life to him he would never have let her down.

Over the next few days he watched people passing, looking out for strangers and particularly for a tall man who walked with a limp. Like most, he believed the attack had been directed at Marjorie, not Hope, even though he couldn't understand the reasoning behind it. It was too much of a coincidence for it to happen while Marjorie was staying. The only stranger he saw was Matthew Charles, who wasn't exactly a stranger, as Peter remembered him from school. He had been a close friend of Phillip and both had been very unpleasant. Peter had suffered slightly from their behaviour, which they excused under the heading of humour, encouraging others to enjoy the humiliation they inflicted on younger, weaker boys.

Peter watched now as Matthew strolled along the main road, pausing occasionally to look in shop windows before going into the barber's and sitting on the bench. He tried to compare him to the man he saw running away from Badgers Brook. It had been dark and now they were in bright sun, so it was difficult to visualize. Matthew was tall and thin but there was no sign of a limp. Besides, boys who behaved as badly as Matthew and Phillip usually grew out of it and became model citizens, protesting about the unpleasantness of today's youth like the rest. He clicked to the horse and moved on.

Matthew stared out through the doorway of the barber's shop and watched with distaste as a shopkeeper darted out to gather up the steaming pile left by Peter's horse and carry it around to his back garden. What was he doing here? Surely Phillip couldn't seriously be thinking of coming back? He was a free man; if he'd had enough of Connie he only had to walk away.

While he waited for his turn in the small, crowded barber shop, he drafted out in his mind the letter he would write to Phillip. Mother ill and still an absolute pain, father as weak as always, sister-in-law a drudge with a boring child. Nothing to come home for, surely? Even for a fatted calf which during this time of rationing might only be a tin of dried egg!

It was time for him to move on. His allocation of quality food had been ordered. He glanced through his appointments book. Nothing urgent for three more days. Perhaps he would go home and see his wife. He counted the number of people before him in the patient queue and took out a notebook. He began a letter to Sally telling her he would be home in two days' time.

He looked out through the shop door. Strange that this had once been home and now he was a stranger, no one recognizing his face. He and Phillip had moved on after coming out of the army, determined to make a better life somewhere else. He had succeeded, by getting an easy job and marrying Sally, a wealthy widow, and Phillip... well, perhaps being supported by a succession of women was his idea of success. At least he had escaped from his awful mother.

Phillip's 'awful mother' was sitting in the garden of Badgers Brook, wrapped in a blanket, sipping a glass of port. Beside her was Stella from the post office, and her husband, Colin, who had brought the port. At Colin's feet sat Scamp.

Marjorie didn't like port. She drank an occasional sherry and sometimes port, but she didn't like it. She drank it because it was the thing to do, like having parsley and thyme stuffing with chicken, when she preferred sage and onion. Keeping up a pretence was second nature to her. She sipped and murmured approval, hoping there would soon be a chance to throw it amid the chrysanthemums that bordered the path where they sat.

'Looking better you are,' Stella said, when Colin asked about her health and she was afraid they would have to suffer a minute by minute report. 'Have to think positive, that's what Colin always says, don't you, Colin, love?'

'Yes,' Colin said, a bit bemused.

'Colin always says it's no good going on being miserable, or people soon lose any sympathy they feel. That's right, eh, Colin?'

Stifling a grin, aware of Stella's intention, he could only nod.

'Now,' Stella said, slapping a hand on her knee. 'When are you going back home? Another week, is it?'

'I need to be fully recovered, because I need to take a hand in the care of my grandson.'

'To help Hope, you mean? Good on you. Hard worker she is an' all.'

'For the child's sake.'

'Davy's a wonderful little boy.'

'David,' Marjorie emphasized, 'is in need of training.'

'Aw, poor dab,' Colin said softly.

'Hope is wonderful with him. A happier boy you couldn't imagine,' Stella protested.

'He's neglected. There's been no attempt to teach him manners and social behaviour.'

Stella looked at Marjorie, reached out for Colin's hand and decided to take a chance on their friendship. 'Be careful what you do, mind, Marjorie. You need Hope and Davy, and a wrong word and you could lose them both. He's a fine boy and you should concentrate on enjoying him, and young Hope. A credit to you they are, the pair of 'em.'

'I'm feeling tired, will you help me to go back inside?'

'I'll call again, in a day or so, shall I?' Stella was anxious that her words had been ill chosen or ill timed.

'I do get weary,' Marjorie said. 'I've been very ill you know.'

Stella didn't know whether this was an apology for her sudden dismissal of them, or a request not to bother to call again.

Marjorie grasped the letter from Phillip, her hand hidden within her pocket. She had been on the point of showing it to Stella, and sharing with her the determination that she would take over the upbringing of her grandson. What a mistake that would have been. No one understood except Phillip. He was an artist and she had encouraged him, taught him to work hard and develop his talent. Only he understood the value of training. And poor Ralph, of course, taken from her by the selfishness of Hope.

–

It was Stella who found out the identity of the man Peter had seen running away the night the brick had smashed the window of Badgers Brook.

'Ernie Preece, you know, him as lost a leg at Arnhem. Bitter towards Marjorie he was when he was unable to work for months. She told him to pull himself together and act like a man when he was offered a job and he had to refuse it. He's been loud in his criticism of her, convinced that, with the right encouragement, Ralph would have dealt with his affliction as he has. He'd called on Ralph in the hope of helping, but she told him off for upsetting him and warned him to stay away.'

–

September, which seemed to be the end of the gardening year but was really the beginning, often kept Hope busy until darkness drove her inside, where Marjorie listened to the wireless and waited impatiently for her supper. There was no sign of her leaving, and Hope wondered whether she had made her too comfortable. She didn't think she could cope with her permanently, even with the visit softened by the kindnesses of the ever-patient Freddy.

So it was with relief that, on the day the bean sticks were taken down, Marjorie announced that she was going home.

'I'm glad you're feeling well enough to consider it, Mother-in-law,' she said, hoping her joy didn't show. 'We'll make sure the house is warm and clean and welcoming before you go back.' She wondered vaguely when she would find the time to do anything at Ty Mawr, when all her hours were so tightly filled here. Freddy told her not to try.

'Stella will put an advertisement in her window asking for someone to clean and make it all comfortable.' Hope knew she should protest, insist she could do what was necessary, but she didn't. Instead she thanked him, kissed his cheek and told him he was a wonderful father-in-law.

–

Phillip was worried. Half-term was approaching and Connie was talking about them getting engaged, with a view to marrying the following summer. He knew he was being a fool to even consider refusing. Married to Connie he would be able to drift through life, fed, loved and with every comfort provided. Although the temptation was there to stay with her, he felt a cloying, dragging sensation as he looked into a future that would be exactly the same as now. Whatever the years ahead held for him, he couldn't settle for that. Ambition had been a fleeting excitement when he had been younger, but even without that oh-so-brief urge to achieve better things, he had enough enthusiasm, just, to try once more to find a better way of spending the next fifty years. Fifty years! God in heaven, the thought of fifty years living with the same person was utterly terrifying.

He took out the letters he had received from Matthew with their cynical descriptions of his family and wondered whether he could stand them for long enough to find a fresh start. However difficult his mother had been, and however much he disliked her, she might be useful, and somehow, although he couldn't quantify just how, he knew she owed him that.

–

As with Phillip, but for different reasons, going home was something Matthew didn't relish. His steps dragged as he approached the rather grand detached house Sally's parents had bought for them. He slung his suitcase on the steps of the porch and rang the bell with its cheerful little ditty that made him cringe but which today resulted in ominous silence. Damn it, they weren't in. He searched irritably for his key.

Inside there was a tray set for him and a note propped against the teacup with a ticket for that evening's performance. Sally and the two girls were taking part in yet another theatrical event. This one was *Golden Days*, a celebration of autumn. Sally and the girls sang, Sally played the flute, appearing as the Piper of Hamlyn in one sketch, a sailor in another. Megan and Olwen were dressed for the chorus as chrysanthemums. Amateur dramatics was not his sort of thing. Not at all. Matthew had never seen them perform – it was certain to make him cringe. Without stopping for a cup of tea, he left. An hotel would be preferable. He'd come back full of regrets at having missed the show yet again on Sunday.

–

Phillip's journey home took a week. He thumbed lifts, and twice stayed in the home of someone who had believed his extravagant stories. He was rushing back to his sick wife and child; he'd been looking for work: he was an artist who had set up an exhibition of five years' work only to have all his paintings stolen. He was quite sorry when he reached his destination.

Marjorie moved back to the Ty Mawr at the beginning of October, three weeks before Davy's third birthday. She quickly recovered from the need to be looked after as she went from room to room complaining about the state of the place and the carelessness of the cleaner Hope had found for her. Freddy smiled and thought that the signs were good and she would be kept busy for long enough to settle back into her old routine. He just hoped that she would make the effort to get out and do her shopping and mingle with the local people, who were only too willing to support her given the chance.

He didn't see his son, Phillip, stop at the gate, stare for a while then walk away.

–

Hope concentrated on finishing a dress and lined jacket she was making for a new client. Mrs Amby worked in the kitchens of a café, cleaning and preparing the table linen for each day. She was overweight and very conscious of the fact. She hadn't worried about her size particularly, until her son met Rachel Grant. She now needed an outfit for her son's wedding; something to make her smart and give her confidence in front of her daughter-in-law's beautiful and rather daunting family.

Ignoring the bed still in the corner near the fire, and the oddments of litter scattered by her mother-in-law, Hope finished the outfit, promising herself that once it was done she would clean the room and return it to how she liked it.

'No more visitors, what a relief,' she said to Joyce, who was helping to fasten the last button.

Joyce sighed. 'Once this wedding suit is delivered and the curtains for Mrs Ham's are done we're up to date. Who'd have believed it, after having Mrs Murton to look after for all this time. You're a marvel, Hope,' she said with a smile.

'Nonsense. You know I didn't do it alone. Thank you, Joyce, you've been wonderful.' Hope stretched and gave a sigh of relief, before starting to clear away the evidence of Marjorie's prolonged stay.

Joyce had gone, taking the dress and jacket to Mrs Amby on her way home, and the room was back to normal. Hope was playing a game of Snap with Davy, who had been taught to play by Peter one afternoon and had insisted on a daily game ever since. The knock at the door was a surprise. It was after seven, almost time for Davy to go to bed, and she rarely had visitors in the evening. Thinking it must be Kitty she opened the door, her welcoming smile fading as she recognized Phillip, her brother-in-law.

'Hello, Hope. Surprised to see me? From the look on your face you're disappointed. Who were you expecting?' She continued to stare and he said, 'Are you going to keep me blathering here, woman, or can I come inside?'

She stepped back to allow him to enter. 'Sorry. I didn't know you were home. You couldn't have been here long, your parents only went home today.'

'Yes, I heard they were staying with you.' His attractive, boyish face, fair hair tumbling around his ears, and challenging blue eyes with laughter in their depths were so similar to Ralph's that she felt a warmth for him far stronger than she might have expected. His familiarity startled her, her reaction to him a surprise. He was someone she had never liked.

'Would you like something to eat? Davy and I have had our supper but I can easily find you a snack,' she offered. Then she saw that he had brought a suitcase with him. 'Oh, you haven't been home yet? I can't walk with you, I need to get Davy settled, but have a cup of tea before you go.'

'I was hoping to stay the night,' he said, pleading with his eyes and his pouting lips. 'I don't want to disturb the old folk this evening.'

Her impulse was to agree – he was after all Ralph's brother – but something stopped her. She shook her head. 'I'm sorry, but I can't. As I said, your parents were here until just hours ago and I'm not prepared.'

He nodded towards the couch. 'That and a couple of blankets will do.'

'Sorry, but I can't. Your mother would never forgive me for keeping you from her. There's a phone box not far from the gate, you could get a taxi or walk to the bus stop at the end of the lane. I'll bring Davy over tomorrow and you can tell us all that you've been doing.'

He refused the offer of food and left, and as she watched him walk down the path, coat swinging open, suitcase in his hand, she had a very uneasy feeling that his visit was going to cause trouble. He looked so like Ralph that she had been deceived for a while, but there was something about him that was disquieting. Not like Ralph at all.

–

Connie held the note in hands that trembled. She had read it countless times and still didn't know what she was going to do. Phillip had always been vague about his family and had somehow managed never to tell her their address. She had learned a few things, which she now tried to put together. It was in South Wales and not far from the sea. It was a small town, and his parents lived in a big house with a Welsh name. A big house, that wasn't much help. A big house on the coast somewhere in South Wales wasn't much to go on. The note gave no indication that was where he had been heading, yet she felt sure that was where he would be.

The alternative was another woman, but they were hardly ever apart so that was unlikely. Not that she trusted him completely, he would always have an eye for a pretty face and a tempting figure, but the opportunities weren't there. Living together, working together, when would he find the time? No, it was home he'd go, for a bit of spoiling by that mother of his, who sounded like a real bully.

The friend from his school days, Matthew Charles, had visited a few times, and she tried to think about their conversations, hoping to remember something to add a clue to the little she knew. He'd occasionally sent a letter or a card but these were usually taken before she could read them. In any case, cards rarely showed an address and the postmark wouldn't have helped much.

Why hadn't she taken note of the address on the letter she had posted for him? She had dropped it into the box with a letter to her own mother without a thought. His parents were so far away they had seemed irrelevant. Until now.

In a sudden burst of anger, she moved all the furniture in their two rooms, and emptied every drawer and cupboard. The piles of paper were mostly bills and receipts, but somewhere there might be a clue that would lead her to his family. He said in his note that he was leaving because he was holding her back. That was a joke. Phillip wasn't the kind to worry about someone else. When had he ever done anything else but hold people back? Selfish and lazy.

Thoughtless and useless. Every word she uttered made her fury increase.

Her anger was not aimed solely at Phillip. Why had she been such a fool? Like Janet, Kate and Harriet she had been blinded by the belief that she could help him achieve his dream. She was the one who would change him, make him a success. He had told her, with great passion, about the other women and how they had failed to understand his aspirations, the necessity of working, the feeling of incompleteness when he didn't have a brush in his hand and a blank canvas before him. How they had all walked away from him when his need was greatest, when success was just around the corner. Well she *hadn't* left him. She had stayed and supported him, coaxed him as his mother had done, and now she was going to find him and make him tell her to her face just why *he* had walked away from *her*.

Six

When Matthew walked into the house, the two girls looked up, smiled and said, 'Hello, Daddy,' but there was not the usual enthusiasm in their welcome. He took out two small parcels, gifts he had bought as an apology for once again missing their performances. They thanked him, opened the wrapping paper, admired the necklaces, hugged him in an automatic way and took them to show their mother. Sally hadn't even looked at him. He walked across the room and kissed the top of her head, then tried to turn her face towards him, but she moved away. This wasn't going to be easy, he thought.

He began asking Megan and Olwen about the concert and after a while their enthusiasm made them more relaxed, but Sally didn't contribute. Her coolness lasted through the traditional Sunday dinner and beyond. He took the girls for a walk to the park in the afternoon and they chattered happily enough until he asked, 'Has anything upset your mother?'

'You, of course,' Olwen said with a laugh, as though he were making a joke. 'You promised to come to the concert and she had arranged a party and you didn't come.'

'A party? A special occasion, was it?'

'Mummy said you'd be there and they altered the date of their annual get-together so you could be included.'

'I'm so sorry. I tried, I really did, but I couldn't get away.'

'"Rejection again," that's what Mummy said,' Megan told him seriously, and Olwen nodded agreement.

He was silent for the rest of their walk. When they arrived back home he went upstairs to find his case had been placed in the box room amid their suitcases and lumber and an uninviting single iron bedstead. He tried to apologize but Sally wouldn't talk to him.

In desperation he called to see her parents and invited his father-in-law for a drink. That he was angry was clear from his first words. 'You, Matthew, are an insensitive clown. They were so looking forward to seeing you at the concert. So many times you'd let them down but this time they really believed you'd be there.'

'I had intended to but—'

'Shut up and listen.' The man pulled a piece of paper from his pocket and showed it to Matthew. It was details of a house, his and Sally's house, advertised for sale. 'Sally doesn't have to stay with you. The house is still in my name and I can ask you to leave at any time, should Sally wish it.'

Matthew stared at him, a tic in his cheek revealing his anxiety. 'But she's my wife and I love her. And Megan and Olwen.'

'One more chance, Matthew, and that's all you're getting. Remember that they'll manage without you quite easily. After all, they've had plenty of practise, haven't they?'

Momentarily the idea of walking away was tempting. Sally organized the household so efficiently it seemed not to matter whether he was there or not. Any problem in the house was either dealt with by her father, or a tradesman was called and paid for by him. Her girls, her father, her house, he had never felt needed.

If he were honest, the need was in him, for a comfortable home to return to when he wanted a restful few days. But he admitted that his attitude towards it was little better than that he had towards some of the hotels and guest houses he used. He was welcomed as an occasional guest without question as long as he didn't cause trouble. Surely a homecoming should be more than that?

He began to tell Sally's father how he felt but quickly gave up the attempt. What was the point? He wouldn't understand.

-

At Ty Mawr the loud knocking at the door had Marjorie groaning, and it was with irritation that she stood to answer it. Then she recognized the voice from outside, asking if she was going to open the door sometime today, and she ran. She stared at Phillip in disbelief, then gave a kind of scream and hugged him, calling for Freddy to 'Come quick and see who's here.'

'Let the boy in,' Freddy said, laughing, trotting to the door and pulling Marjorie aside. 'Phillip, my boy, why didn't you let us know? We'd have met you at the station.'

'Hardly any need for that, Dad, I'm a big boy now.'

'Your mother would have so enjoyed it, watching for the train, complaining if it was late. You know what she's like, how she fusses.'

Phillip did know and he was already wondering how he would cope with even a few days of her tiresome ministrations. Absence was supposed to make the heart grow fonder, but as he looked at his smiling mother he knew that wasn't that case. Already, in these first seconds, memories flooded back of the constant urging to do better and better, the constant criticism, which was supposed to be character-building. It was like an itch that was impossible to scratch.

He looked around the house, his mind only half on his mother's excited chatter. Nothing had changed: the ancient leather chairs and sagging couch with patched cushions. The curtains, worn at the edges where the sun had rotted them with its kindly but treacherous touch. Why hadn't they bought new? They must be able to afford to make the place fresh and comfortable. The shops were filling up with goods for so long denied them, so why were they living with decaying curtains, dilapidated furniture and threadbare rugs over the parquet floor?

Perhaps, if he had stayed, he might not have been aware of the sad neglect. Happening slowly and being observed daily it might have gone unnoticed. Particularly as his mother had always gloried in the 'we are poor but respectable' variety of furnishing. The implication was that everything was of such a high standard it still looked beautiful as it fell into decay. To Phillip, walking into the house after such a long absence, it looked almost as bad as a hovel. Nothing shone, everything looked uncared for, as though the occupants had given up.

Connie had kept their home cheerful and sparkling clean.

'Well? What d'you think? Nothing's changed, has it?' Marjorie spoke proudly.

Good heavens, was she another Miss Faversham? Leaving everything at his departure waiting for his return? He swallowed the critical words that were souring his tongue and, instead, said, 'Is there anything to eat, I'm starving!'

He unpacked his small case in the bedroom that he had once shared with his brother Richard. Some of Richard's books were still on the book case: *The Three Musketeers* and *Twenty Years After*, a ragged copy of *Robinson Crusoe*, which had been one of Richard's favourites. Dreams of escape, he wondered idly? In a corner, half hidden by the clutter of a long-gone childhood, was Richard's tennis racquet. He smiled a sad smile. Richard had hated sports, as he and Ralph had, but their mother had made him practise, and tried to push him into the school team by promising the school financial help towards more sports equipment.

They sat down to a formal tea at four o'clock with the inevitable napkins and doilies, and with everything carefully set out.

'Tell us what you've been doing, dear. You must be a successful artist. Imagine! You earning your keep with your wonderful talent – what an exciting life you must lead. Have you brought any of your paintings for us to see?'

He lied politely, giving her what she wanted, a talented and successful son, but then he once again allowed himself to drift off and, as his mind closed to the predictable chatter, his thoughts turned to Connie. A smile crossed his lips as he thought of how much his mother would disapprove of her. Suddenly he missed her. Would he go back? The alternative was this place, and, even with her gradually strengthening demands, Connie, and the life of a school caretaker, was preferable. But surely he didn't have to choose between the two? Either, or. There had to be something more.

After tea had been cleared away, Marjorie plumped up the cushions on the armchair and they settled down for an evening of catching up. Marjorie did most of the talking; Freddy sat listening and smiling contentedly. Phillip wondered why he had come and how soon he could escape.

'I started by painting local scenes,' Phillip told an admiring Marjorie, 'but there are too many already doing that, so I did a few portraits – abstract, of course, nothing chocolate box about my work.'

In between the story of his 'successes', coaxed out of him by Marjorie, he asked about the death of his brother.

'Hope should never have persuaded Ralph to leave his home,' Marjorie said tearfully. 'He'd still be alive if I'd been looking after him.'

Freddy added nothing, but he managed to share a look with Phillip and between them understanding briefly glowed. Throughout the evening, until Marjorie left them to prepare supper, Freddy said the least. He was waiting for an opportunity to ask Phillip why he'd come home so unexpectedly.

He noticed the rather expensive new clothes his son was wearing and wondered how he had managed to buy them. He suspected that the boastful stories his son had told were for Marjorie's benefit and were completely untrue. He listened as Phillip recited in a modest, you're-forcing-me-to-tell-you-this kind of way, the commissions he had won and the satisfaction he was getting from doing what he wanted to do, earning his living by his talent, and didn't believe a word of it.

'Why did you come?' Freddy asked when the door closed behind his wife.

'To see you of course.'

'Why now, after all this time?'

'I had to get away from someone.'

'A woman? Or are you in worse trouble?'

'No, Dad. Just a woman. Connie is wonderful, but I get suffocated by her. She is getting ideas about us marrying and buying a property and running it as a business. I can't cope with stuff like that.'

'So you left her?'

'I'll go back, if she'll have me, but not yet.' He was lying, looking away from Freddy's quiet stare. He didn't think he would see Connie again. As with others before her, their relationship had run its course.

'Are you planning to stay? Your mother would be pleased if you stayed a while.'

'Perhaps.' He turned to look at his father. 'She doesn't change, does she?' he said, harshness in his voice. 'After a week she'd be trying to organize my life, telling me what to do, what to think, which is why I left in the first place. Is that why Ralph finally left?'

'No. To be honest I don't think he wanted to go. Ralph was too easily content. It was Hope who knew that unless he did he would never really grow up.'

'Dad!' His father's honesty was surprising.

'When you and Richard left and joined the forces I hoped that being free – especially after the years in the army with all the experiences that offered – you and Richard would become the men you were intended to be, and not what your mother was trying to mould you into being. But Ralph,' he shook his head sadly. 'Ralph was too satisfied with the status quo, taking the easy route by doing what was asked of him, being looked after by his mother and pretending at being married with poor Hope.'

'The war was a tragedy, no doubt about that, but it offered an escape for me and for Matthew Charles. He's never really settled since. He's married to Sally and has two stepdaughters but he can't find a gap in their lives that he can fill. He feels irrelevant. For me, I resented the strength of Mum's determination. The escape from home was a relief to us both – we likened it to men getting out of prison, but the truth is it's unsettled us and now we're both misfits and expect to remain so. We can't go back to how we were and we don't belong in the situation we find ourselves in now.'

There was silence for a long moment, then Phillip said, 'I called to see Hope earlier. Surprisingly, I suspect she's a match for mother, more strong willed than I'd remembered, and meeting her again she strikes me as an unexpected choice for Ralph to have made. Or did she choose him and he drifted along with it as the easiest option? I'd imagined him with his nervous little wife, behaving like two frightened mice, controlled by Mother, but Hope's no mouse, is she?'

'Hope has had to be strong, firstly to persuade Ralph to leave, then to cope with the aftermath of that terrible accident, then his death.'

'I'm sorry, Dad. About Ralph, I mean. And not coming home for the funeral.'

'I don't suppose you heard until it was too late. At least, that was what I told your mother.'

'Thanks.'

Dinner had been a strain and supper was more of the same. Using the pretence of tiredness after a long journey, Phillip excused himself and went to bed early.

He felt stifled sleeping in the room in which he had spent his childhood. It was over filled with memorabilia, things that brought back memories he didn't want, everything from which he had run away. The cricket bat and football shirts, which had represented a mild form of torture to him and his brothers, were still there. They had all hated games and whenever possible would hide in the shrubbery that surrounded the school grounds until it was safe to come out. The room was a mausoleum and he was expected to sleep there.

He missed Connie and woke several times to reach out and feel only disappointment.

At five a.m. he went down the cold stairs and sat looking out of the kitchen window at the brick shed, their only private place, where he and Matthew had dreamed their childish dreams and got revenge on the world by planning to torment others. Guilt for their unkindnesses had been brief, and self-pity had overridden it with ease.

–

Connie continued with her day-to-day routine and in her spare time searched for clues that would lead her to Phillip and his parents. A scrap of paper tucked into a pocket revealed a torn letter, but the only visible address was Ty Mawr. In an old diary, abandoned and forgotten in the lining of a suitcase now used to store books, she found a mention of the town of Cwm Derw. It struck a chord. She remembered Phillip explaining that it meant a valley of oaks, although she couldn't be sure it was where Phillip's family lived.

Writing down what she had learned, she checked on a road map, and when she found a town of that name she decided she had enough to start a search for him. The map showed her that Cwm Derw was a few miles from the coast in South Wales, west of Cardiff. It didn't appear to be a large town, and perhaps, with a name like Williamson-Murton, his family would be easily found. If it really was his name. She was beginning to wonder how much of the little he had told her had been the truth.

The hyphenated name was something he treated as a joke and he had mentioned it only once during a night out with friends. Normally such a brief reference would have been quickly forgotten, but his secrecy made every snippet of information stay in her mind, snatched up almost without a thought and squirrelled away with the rest.

An explanation that Phillip's brother had committed suicide was enough for her to be given a couple of weeks off work. Thankfully they didn't ask when the tragedy had occurred, so she hadn't needed to lie. She packed a suitcase and, with some trepidation, headed for the railway station.

She slept for part of the long journey and when she was awake she rehearsed what she would say, imagining Phillip's reaction in a dozen scenarios, some gentle and loving, others filled with anger or, worse, embarrassment at her unexpected appearance.

–

Peter was growing more and more attracted to Hope, although he knew that the time for doing something about it was far into the future. After the shock of Ralph's death it would be a long time before she could begin to imagine loving someone else.

There was no one he could talk to. His father had visited once or twice, without his new wife, and he made it quite clear that he didn't approve of Hope as a prospective daughter-in-law.

'Of course she's coping. She's driven a man to suicide, son,' he said when Peter began to tell his father how well she was managing. 'Self-centred people always cope. Putting themselves first, making others twist themselves into a spiral trying to do what they want, that's how they cope.'

'Hope isn't self-centred! She tried to do her best for Ralph, but the accident made his life unlivable. How can you blame her for that?'

'His mother knew him better than she did and she told him to stay where he was. She knew that the responsibility of managing a house on his own would be too much for him. But, oh no, Hope had to have her way, didn't she?'

'You're talking rubbish, Dad. Ralph was married and he had a son. Surely he could be expected to look after them, provide for them?'

George went on, repeating what he believed and re-stating what Marjorie had been saying, and Peter stopped listening. Although Hope hadn't heard the venom of his father's words he felt he had to make it up to her, ashamed for having listened, even under protest. After seeing his father off at the bus stop at the end of a visit that had been unhappy, he went to see Hope, taking a bar of chocolate for Davy.

Laughter met him as he reached the door of Badgers Brook, and he hesitated before knocking. To his surprise he heard, amid the laughter, the pompous voice of

Marjorie. What could have happened to make her laugh so uproariously? His knock was heard and a smiling Hope came to the door, Davy holding her hand, his face and shirt covered with chocolate. She invited him in and whispered that Ralph's brother had called with Marjorie and Freddy, and his friend Matthew Charles. Peter put the chocolate bar intended for Davy back in his pocket.

In the kitchen there was a party atmosphere that he could never have imagined. A couple of flagons were on the kitchen table, glasses and teacups spread around them. He was introduced and Marjorie said loudly that he was the man who went around with a horse and cart selling produce. She made 'produce' sound as unpleasant as rotten fish.

He felt like a stranger in the house where he had begun to feel comfortable. Even Davy preferred the attention of the newcomers, his Uncle Phillip and 'Uncle' Matthew. Freddy sat near him and tried to include him in the light-hearted conversation, mainly reminiscences about schooldays and their childhood. Peter said very little; what he remembered of their behaviour at that time it would not have pleased them to have repeated.

Their language and excessively loud, confident voices put him on edge. They made him feel gauche and clumsy, and to add to his growing discomfort, his vocabulary and his grammar were sometimes quietly corrected. Over the past weeks he hadn't needed an excuse to call but tonight he was an unwelcome stranger. He said briskly, 'Hope, if you can tell me what you have left in the garden that I might sell, I'll be off.'

She stood at once, amid artificial protests about his early departure, and followed him out through the door and a little way down the path. 'Sorry about this,' she said, gesturing back into the kitchen. 'I wish they'd leave, they make me very uneasy.'

'They're pleasant company; I've never seen Marjorie so animated.'

'Having Phillip home after all this time has made her forget the tragedy of Ralph, for a little while. She's even forgotten to be unpleasant towards me,' she added sadly. 'But I dare say things will be back to normal once Phillip goes back to wherever he lives.'

He risked a kiss on her cheek but she turned unexpectedly and their lips met. Her eyes looked dark and serious in the dim light flowing through the doorway. Unable to decide what to do, he stepped back and said lightly, 'Don't worry, even Marjorie will stop her taunting eventually. At least Phillip has proved she still knows how to smile.'

'Come for Sunday lunch. Just you and Davy and me. Hopefully Phillip will be gone by then and we can relax.'

He walked away in an uneasy frame of mind. She hadn't reacted to his kiss any more than she had when her father-in-law gave her a salutatory peck on the cheek. Did that mean he was so unimportant? Or had she moved her head deliberately? That thought stayed with him all the way home and until he slept.

–

Connie didn't find the town of Cwm Derw as easy to find as she'd imagined she would. Stopping in the busy town of Cardiff, she had thought a train would be available to take her there. The man in the ticket office hadn't heard of it, and there was no railway station listed. The bus stop proved as unhelpful. 'I'm a visitor here,' one man she asked there had replied. Another thought it might be near Brecon. A third suggested she ask in the post office, and it was there she had a first hopeful lead. There were buses but not many. She had missed the last one that day and would have to wait until the morning.

Finding a guest house wasn't difficult, and with relief she ate and went to bed. She vaguely wondered why travelling, sitting down for hours on end, was so tiring, as she succumbed to the comfort of the feather bed.

-

Peter arrived early for lunch that Sunday. Hope had managed to excuse herself and Davy from eating with Marjorie, Freddy and Phillip at Ty Mawr and had the diminutive roast in the oven, already sending out tempting smells. A cursory knock and he walked in, piles of vegetables overloading a trug in one hand. His smile widened as Hope walked in wearing a Fair Isle jumper depicting roses, which he had seen her knitting recently. Her figure was perfect, enhanced by the slim skirt and the new jumper, and he felt an attraction, desire, a growing love for her and a longing to hold her that made him hesitate to remark on it.

'I've brought a few vegetables,' he said unnecessarily, as he put the trug down on the floor near the sink. He turned away, afraid of what she might see in his eyes.

Davy came running in from the garden, where he had been overseeing the preparation of a garden swing being set up by Bob and Freddy. It would soon be his third birthday and already excitement was growing. His arrival relaxed Peter's mood and soon he was in the garden adding his assistance to the project. Freddy made an excuse and left, saying he had to spend as much time as possible with Phillip before he moved on. Peter and Bob completed the job and tied the swing up high so Davy wouldn't use it until the varnish was dry.

At one o'clock Hope came out, flushed from the heat of the kitchen, and called to them. Peter waved goodbye to Bob and, carrying Davy, strolled towards the house. He wished every day could be spent like this, being welcomed in to share the life of Hope and Davy.

–

Connie caught the bus that promised to take her to Cwm Derw at nine the following morning. The passengers had nicknamed it the Rambler, wandering as it did between the smaller villages, picking up people to go shopping or visiting, and collecting them for the return journey at one thirty. It was ten thirty before she stood at last in the town in which she hoped to find Phillip. The first shop she saw was a post office and, as she had learned, that was a good place to start.

Stella saw her come in and hurried through the few customers waiting, smiling at the stranger, determined to find out as much as she could about her.

'Would you be so kind as to direct me to—'

'Tourist, are you? What are you doing around here then?' she asked as soon as Connie opened her mouth to ask directions.

Connie pulled out a piece of paper and said, 'I'm looking for Ty Mawr. Is it near here?' She pronounced it Tie Moor and Stella frowned until Connie handed her a piece of paper with the name written down.

'Not far. What name did you say?' Stella asked suspiciously. She didn't want to send visitors to poor Marjorie if they were going to be troublesome.

'I'm looking for...' Connie hesitated, '...I have to see someone in Ty Mawr.' She was beginning to feel irritated. Why couldn't the woman answer a simple question? Her dark eyes glared unblinkingly at Stella.

'Well, you could try,' Stella said, dejected by failure. 'Probably out, mind.' She pointed out the home of Marjorie and Freddy and wondered how soon she would find out who the woman was and what she wanted.

Connie approached the house slowly, her heart racing as though she'd run a mile. She didn't knock. Better to watch for a while and see if Phillip appeared. He wouldn't be pleased to come home and find her sitting there talking to his parents. He'd be afraid of what she might tell them. Exploding a few of his myths would be so easy. And she was in the mood for it, too.

There was a café almost opposite the house, and if she sat in the window she would be able to watch for him. She ordered tea and a slice of cake and determined to make it last as long as possible. An hour later, when she was reduced to picking up imaginary crumbs with a moistened finger, she saw him.

It was easy to follow him. He didn't go far, just to a house near a hardware store with the name Geoff Tanner over the door. She went in to the shop and asked for a paintbrush she didn't want, taking her time deciding between the cheaper and more expensive range. She was handing over the money when the door of the house opened and Phillip came out with Matthew Charles.

'Good heavens! What's he doing home!' Geoff remarked. Connie waited in silence as Geoff followed the progress of the two men. With luck she'd learn something.

'Know them do you?' she asked, still offering the money.

'Oh, sorry, yes. Phillip Murton hasn't been home for years, not even when his brother died. So I wonder what he wants that would bring him here now.'

'Not someone you like, then?'

'Sorry,' he repeated. 'It was such a surprise, seeing him again.' He took the money, gave her the change and apologized again.

Connie went out and looked in the direction in which Phillip and Matthew had gone. There was a public house, the Ship and Compass, not far away. That was probably their destination. She went back to the café to drink more tea while she decided what to do.

Geoff came in later and ordered a meal. He saw her and smiled. It warmed her, made her feel less of a stranger.

'What are you doing in Cwm Derw, passing through, or staying a while?' he asked as he waited for his food to arrive.

Giving the impression she was a tourist, she asked him what she should see while she was in the area, and as it became more and more awkward to talk, with the tables filling up, it seemed natural for him to move to share hers.

'I left my suitcase at the station,' she told him. 'I wasn't sure whether or not I'd be staying.'

'And now?'

'I think I'll try to find a small guest house, perhaps stay a day or two.'

'I have a delivery to make lunchtime tomorrow. Nothing smart, only a van, but if you'd like a ride to one of the seaside places, I'll gladly take you,' he offered. When she hesitated, he said quickly, 'Sorry, of course you won't want to come. You don't know me, although I am quite respectable, ask anyone you know.'

She laughed. 'But I don't know anyone!' As he joined in, she called to the elderly waitress. 'Excuse me, but is this man respectable?'

'So, so, miss. Wouldn't trust him with a pretty girl, mind!'

'I'll be safe then,' Connie replied, still laughing.

Geoff knew she hadn't replied that way in the hope of a compliment. She seemed to be honest and straightforward and even so early in their acquaintanceship he just knew they could be good friends.

They arranged to meet at one o'clock the following day, and Connie went to find accommodation. She collected her suitcase and took out an extra scarf before starting her search.

'*Brecwast a Gweli*' confused her, until it was translated as Breakfast and Bed.

She asked if they spoke English, and told them she wanted a room for a night or two, and was invited into a warm, pleasantly furnished house shared by the family and the occasional visitor.

During the evening she found herself thinking about the following day with Geoff Tanner and wondering why she hadn't done what she had come for and confronted Phillip. There would be time in the morning, but the closer the moment came the less she felt able to face it. She had qualms about how Phillip would react when he saw her.

How would he introduce her if he was with his parents? As a friend? Someone he used to know? A landlady? With Phillip anything was possible, she told herself with a stab of misery. He said what suited him best at the time.

Perhaps it was wisest to just wait until they bumped into each other rather than visit his home. If they didn't meet by accident, she could wait a while. Why not have a few days' holiday first? Even in October it was good to be free of routine.

She was relieved at her decision, and, not for the first time, wondered why she had come. What she was hoping for, chasing after a man like Phillip? For a moment she was tempted to pack her few belongings back in the case and go home. Then, thinking of tomorrow, and Geoff, she wanted to stay, just a while longer. Phillip had to be dealt with. The chapter of her life with him must be closed and to do that she had to face him.

He probably would be with Matthew, and that fact alone made her want to delay it for as long as possible. Matthew and Phillip both had the same sense of humour, edged with a little cruelty. Making someone feel inadequate, wrong footed, was something at which they both excelled. If only she had someone to go with her, but she was on her own in this and she could either talk to him, find out why he'd left and what he intended to do, or scuttle back home and forget him. At that moment she would have preferred the latter, if it hadn't been for the arrangement to meet with Geoff Tanner.

–

Because Davy was an only child and would probably remain so, Hope often invited other children to come and play.

During the hours she set aside for Davy she continued to go out for walks when the weather allowed. But when it rained, or was too cold to enjoy being in the wood or the park, one of his friends would come with their mother and the house would be a playground for wild racing games, or there would be storytelling, and even concerts when the children would sing songs or recite rhymes.

There were many days when she desperately needed the hours spent in this way to finish a garment for an anxious client, but Hope never succumbed to the temptation of cancelling what she referred to as Davy's time. It was hardly surprising, then, that Davy was invited to several birthday parties. With his own not far away, he loved the thrill of going to tea with his friends, dressed smartly and carrying a gift for the birthday girl or boy, knowing his turn was coming.

Stella had asked Hope to make a jacket for her sister as a surprise, and when she found out her sister was going away for a few days she decided to ask Hope if it could be finished sooner than agreed.

'Sorry I am to fuss you, Hope, dear. But she's going to Weston to stay with a friend and I know she'd love the new coat to wear.'

'Stella, I don't think I can,' Hope apologized. 'Davy's going to a tea party and I have to take him, and be there at five to bring him home.'

'Can't you ask Marjorie?'

'No, I can't. I have to be there, he expects it.'

'Don't be so difficult,' Marjorie's voice from behind her called. 'I can help. He is my grandson after all.' The shop door, which she had just opened, closed behind her and Hope saw her walking away.

'Oh dear, perhaps I'd better talk to her,' Hope said, running from the shop and following her mother-in-law, calling for her to wait. However much she hated it, she had to agree, this once.

She saw Peter as she walked home and told him what had happened. 'I know I have to let him go sometimes, I can't expect him never to leave my side, but I hated having to agree. She's promised to collect him from Susan Davies's house at five.' She smiled sadly. 'The idea is for me to work, but I don't think I'll relax for a moment until he's home. I know she wouldn't put him at risk, but I'll be glad when he's back with me.'

'Don't worry, I'm sure he'll be fine.'

It was with trepidation that Hope left Davy the following day. 'Grandmother will be here to bring you home,' she promised, as he ran in to join his friends.

With an hour and a half in which to work, she forced herself to concentrate on finishing the jacket, and when five o'clock came she was standing at the window staring out into the darkness waiting for the beam of the torches to come dancing up the path to tell her Davy was safely home.

At five thirty she was beginning to panic. Joyce had gone home. She couldn't go to look for him as she needed to be here when he arrived. Perhaps Marjorie had taken him back to Ty Mawr. She's thoughtless enough to decide to do something like that on impulse, Hope thought.

Soon after, torches appeared and she sobbed with relief and ran down to greet him. But it was Marjorie and Phillip.

'Where's Davy?' she almost shrieked. 'Where is he?'

'How should I know? You never trust me to look after him, do you? Always tell me you can cope.'

'What d'you mean? You promised to meet him from Susan's party! Why isn't he with you?'

Marjorie turned to Phillip. In the light from the kitchen window, Hope saw her give a hard smile. 'I offered but she refused, as I told you, Phillip. Useless mother, she is. Imagine not knowing where her child is.'

In the utter silence the shock of her words had brought, the clip-clop of hooves and the jingle of harness penetrated her brain.

'Mummy, I held the reins,' Davy shouted as the horse clattered to a stop. With a large torch in his hand he ran up the path and jumped into his mother's arms. 'Uncle Peter was waiting for me. And I guided Jason. Peter says I'm clever.'

When Marjorie and Phillip left, blustering over Peter and Hope's accusations, Hope asked Peter again what had happened.

'I spoke to Stella and Colin at their allotment and they said Marjorie had told them you'd refused to accept her help. You'd told me different, so I thought I'd be there, just in case.'

She hugged him and murmured her thanks. He rested his check on her sweet-smelling hair and winked at Davy, and the boy contorted his face trying to return it. Peter didn't think he'd ever been happier.

–

Connie spent the morning looking around the town. She hadn't brought many clothes with her and she was tempted by a winter coat in the small fashion shop, but common sense prevailed. She didn't know how long she would stay and every penny had to be carefully considered before being spent. Philip had taken most of their savings and she needed to be able to pay for a room and food. A new winter coat was a luxury she had to deny herself.

When it was time to meet Geoff, she put on her smartest dress and shoes with a thick scarf and a matching hat, but had to add a waterproof and umbrella as it was raining. Not a day for the beach, she thought with regret.

'Come inside, for goodness sake,' he called when he saw her. 'I've only got to lock up and we'll be off, but you'll drown out there.' His smile was wide and she thought he seemed genuinely pleased to see her. She wondered if he had expected her to forget, or not bother to turn up.

The deliveries didn't take long, and with a little more time left of his lunch hour they went into a café for tea and cakes.

'I close the shop at one tomorrow and I do a round of deliveries of paraffin and other things,' Geoff told her. 'Not very exiting, but if you'd like to come I'd be very pleased to have your company.' Connie smiled and happily agreed. Delaying yet again her visit to Phillip was only part of her reason. She looked forward to what promised to be an enjoyable couple of hours.

She was waiting the next day when he came out of the shop and locked the door. He took both of her hands in his and his pleasure at seeing her was without doubt.

The regular orders for paraffin took more than two hours but then he drove to a beach west of Penarth called Lavernock, where to her surprise he took out a picnic hamper.

'I know this isn't the month for picnics, but if we find a sheltered spot I thought it would be a pleasant way to spend an hour.'

Connie was impressed to find that he had provided a small pie with a mysterious label promising assorted meats including rabbit, plus sandwiches, a few cakes and a flask of coffee.

'Nothing fancy, I'm afraid,' he apologized. 'I'm not much of a cook. Not much imagination, either.'

'But this is perfect, and you must have spent valuable food points on the pie. I'll really enjoy that.'

'Tell you the truth, I didn't. I have a few farmer friends who treat me to something special sometimes, and I swapped a packet of illegal farm butter for some tinned fruit which I swapped for the pie.'

Laughing at his secretive dealings, Connie began with a sandwich. 'Keeping the best till last,' she said.

Geoff admired the way she ate, unselfconsciously and with enthusiasm. He didn't have to coax her out of artificial politeness, and, when the food had gone and the coffee had warmed them, they went for a walk along the narrow pebbly beach. The small island just off the coast was not quite an island, and wouldn't be until the tide was fully in. Connie was intrigued.

'Only rabbits, rats and sea birds live there,' Geoff told her. 'Fishermen go out and sometimes brave picnickers stay for a few hours – or get cut off and wait till the next low tide.'

'I'd like to go there one day,' she said, shading her eyes against the weak autumn sun.

'I'd like to take you,' Geoff said quietly.

She looked at him and decided to tell him the reason she was there.

'I gather you know Phillip Murton and his friend Matthew Charles,' she said. When he nodded she added,

'Phillip is the reason I'm here. We'd been... together for a long time, but he walked out. I came to talk to him, find out why, but I haven't been able to confront him. I've either lost my nerve or, perhaps, I no longer care.'

Her hesitation over the word 'together' made him cautious about asking questions. He guessed they hadn't been married or she would have said so. For him to infer they had been living together without being married was an assumption that would embarrass them both if it was wrong, and even more so if it was right. So he said nothing, just waited for her to continue.

'He seemed to need me, and there's nothing more flattering than that. I took him in, then, well, you needn't know the details, except that when I suggested we get married he soon left.'

'You promised to support him while he made his name as an artist?' Geoff then surmised.

'Like several others before me, fool that I am. I thought it would be different for us. I believed he loved me, and when he agreed to the job as a school caretaker that proved it. Or so I thought.'

'A school caretaker?' That wouldn't please the high and mighty Marjorie, Geoff thought with a guilty feeling of joy. 'Did he actually work, or leave it to you?'

'To be fair, he tried, at first. But, gradually, more and more of the menial tasks were left to me. I thought that if we married, bought a place to run as a bed and breakfast, he'd behave more responsibly. Even now after such a short time apart I realize how stupid I've been.'

'Not stupid. You're a decent person, honest and loyal, and you expected everyone to be the same. You trusted him; isn't that what we all do when we give our life into another's keeping?'

'I was stupid. I knew what he was like, I pretended he'd changed, that I had changed him. Stupid and vain.'

They were getting cold as the short day ended: the shape of the island seemed larger, looming closer, and the sea, coming around and meeting in the middle of the causeway, seemed to chill them further. Connie pulled her scarf more tightly and Geoff followed her as she turned and walked back to the van.

'Sorry,' she said, as he opened the passenger door for her. 'There's me blathering on and spoiling your lovely afternoon treat.'

'Thank you for trusting me,' Geoff replied. 'And our afternoon wasn't spoiled. In fact, I hope we can repeat it before too long. That's if you're staying a while.'

She looked at him as he climbed in beside her. 'I don't know. I might go back home without even trying to see Phillip. Better, perhaps, to admit failure than get involved in arguments and recriminations that wouldn't solve a thing.'

Geoff started the engine and got them back on the road before he replied. With the engine purring efficiently he said, 'Please stay, at least for a while. I'd like to see you again, and perhaps next time we could eat in more comfortable surroundings? A warm café would be better than a picnic on a cold beach in October, eh?'

'I loved your surprise, Geoff. Thank you for it.' She touched his hand, lightly squeezed it. 'And as for going home, well, I think I'll wait a wee while, and see what happens when Phillip and I meet. I have to see him, close the door firmly, if you see what I mean.'

Geoff parked the van outside the shop, and as he began to walk her back to her lodgings a man opposite saw them as they passed into the light of a street lamp. He gave a low groan. Connie! What on earth was she doing following him here? He paled as he imagined what she would tell his parents. She was certain to be angry. The truth about how he had really survived in the years since he had left home would be hard to deny. Perhaps he should leave straight away before she found him. Or, better still, get his story in first.

As Connie took Geoff's arm and hurried through the dark streets, Phillip sat on a garden wall and began to invent his story. A word with Matthew to make sure of his corroboration and, really, this could be rather good fun.

Seven

Connie walked up to the door of Ty Mawr and knocked loudly. She stared at the door half hoping there would be no response. Her shoulders were back and she held her head high and wore an aggressive look which hid her nervousness.

She had imagined seeing Phillip's mother first, but it was Freddy who opened the door and asked what she wanted.

'I'm Connie,' she said. 'Phillip's Connie?' she added when a lack of understanding creased Freddy's brow.

'I'm sorry, I'm afraid we don't know many of Phillip's acquaintances.'

'I'm more than that.' Anger flared in her eyes. 'I'm – I'm his wife. We've been together for more than a year.' When Freddy still didn't say anything she went on more loudly, 'And I kept him for most of that time!'

'Please come in, Connie. Phillip isn't at home but I dare say he'll be back when he's hungry.' He showed her into the large, shabby room that overlooked the garden and invited her to sit. 'Forgive me, but I know nothing about this. Phillip isn't a good correspondent, and in the few letters he did write he told us nothing about his marriage.'

Connie slumped with disappointment. 'He just walked out. As he did with the others.'

'The others?' Freddy coaxed.

Her voice was low, as though she had forsaken any hope, and, to Freddy, it was more convincing than loud anger.

'Women who kept him,' she said, 'believing that he would become a successful artist, be grateful and love them for ever. They soon learned that he had neither talent nor determination. And the only love he knows about is self-love. Before me the record for his pretend marriages was four months. I had the determination others lacked and managed to persuade him to stay and take a job in a school.'

'Teaching?' Freddy seemed surprised.

'No. Although he did have a chance; being ex-army, he was offered opportunities. But no, not teaching. I managed to persuade him to take a job as a school caretaker, although I've always done most of the work. The truth is, Mr Murton, your son is an untalented, lazy dreamer and depends on fools like me who're prepared to share his pretence, even if it's only for a while.' She raised her head and stared at him, revealing the hurt and bitterness. 'I lasted the longest, so that must make me the biggest fool, eh?'

'These others, pretend marriages, you say?'

'That's all they got for all their efforts: pretence and promises.'

'And you, Connie?' he asked softly.

She stared at him, about to deny her status, then she lowered her gaze. 'I was a fool like the others, Mr Murton. We were to have been married. At least that's what I believed. But then, when I became a tiny bit too persistent, he just walked away.'

'Yet you came after him. Can you still want him back, after this?'

'I just need to know why.'

Freddy wanted her out of the house. He needed to talk to Marjorie before she and Connie met, and make his wife see that this was a time when she couldn't insult someone whom she would automatically dislike and disbelieve. He escorted her to the place where she was staying and walked back wondering how best to explain the visitor to Marjorie. He was convinced by Connie's story and he had to persuade Marjorie to at least listen before she went off into a predictable outburst of critical disbelief.

He didn't go straight back home after seeing her to her lodgings. He needed to talk to someone, and he went to the place where he usually found understanding and a sympathetic ear. The Ship and Compass was the one place where he always felt comfortable.

–

Days passed and Freddy didn't see Connie again. He began to think she had left, given up on Phillip and gone back to wherever they had lived, and he didn't think he could blame her.

He hadn't seen Phillip, either. His son was rarely in the house. He left early, before they were awoke, and returned long after they were asleep. The kitchen showed evidence of him preparing meals but that was the only sign of him having remained in the area.

In the days between his conversation with Connie and Davy's birthday, Freddy tried several times to tell Marjorie about their surprise visitor, but each time something prevented it, usually Marjorie's determination to avoid listening. He didn't want to come out with Connie's revelations without preparing Marjorie for the news, and every time he broached the subject of Phillip's idleness he was deterred by fears of her misunderstanding. Since he was never to be seen, he had said nothing to Phillip at all.

–

Preparations for Davy's third birthday party were slowly gathering momentum. Hope had decided that as the evening would be dark she would decorate the room to add extra brightness. When the children arrived they would be immediately caught up in the excitement of the event. Joyce helped and after they had completed their day's work they sewed banners and stitched together long lines of bunting made by cutting into triangles oddments of material left from garments they had made. They laughed as they remembered each piece of material, and sewed a piece of Marjorie's nightdress alongside serge from Gladys Morgan's husband's trousers. A bridal gown was in close proximity to lace from the christening gown made for the baby who had been born five months later. A section of Stella's summer dress was attached to one of Colin's gardening gloves. Pieces of Bessie Howells's summer blouse had pride of place in the centre, and each side of it was a strip of curtaining to which the words 'Happy Birthday Davy' had been appliquéd.

Days passed and people called with gifts of food, as was usual in the years of severe shortages, everyone combining their efforts to ensure the party was a success. It wouldn't be simply for the children. Any excuse for a celebration was met with enthusiasm. Even children's birthdays were something for the whole community and involved everyone within walking distance and many beyond. A list was made of who had offered what, and it showed promise of a good spread. Cakes, sandwiches, jellies and even a precious tin of salmon were on the list or in Hope's cupboard awaiting the day.

Hope looked around her at the house that lacked so many luxuries and knew that, whatever had happened to her, this place had helped. Its warmth and peaceful atmosphere had soothed her and helped heal the pain of Ralph's death as nowhere else could.

–

On the day of the party Marjorie was the first to arrive, and Hope began to look for tasks she might like to do, but Marjorie simply sat and watched. There was an undercurrent of disapproval as the children began to arrive. Marjorie warned them to behave, insisted they wash their hands and instructed them to whisper not shout.

Fortunately Kitty came soon after, and Joyce returned to help. Peter, Bob and Geoff called, too, plus a few of the mothers, and they helped Freddy organize a few games of hide and seek. Marjorie demanded headache tablets and a glass of water.

It was great fun, and it was only in quiet moments that Hope grieved for the absence of Ralph, who would have enjoyed it so much. In his place she had tried to involve Marjorie and Freddy with the preparations, but although Freddy had helped previously by making a couple of stools to accommodate the extra children, Marjorie had made it clear she didn't approve.

'It's only months since Ralph died,' she had said when Hope had asked if she would like to make some cakes. 'How can you celebrate anything, let alone his son's birthday? It's as though you were marking his absence with joy instead of sadness.'

'Davy isn't aware of how many weeks have passed since he saw his father.' Hope replied softly. 'It's his birthday and he's been longing for the day when he opens presents and invites all his friends to tea.'

'Encouraging greed,' Marjorie retorted.

'I want to make it special. He deserves that, doesn't he?' She tried to make her voice pleading, but could see from Marjorie's expression that, as usual, she had offended. She tried again to please. 'You are here, and that makes it special too. He loves you and Father-in-law; we're such a small family, and he needs and loves us all.' She turned to watch as Peter led them with a new game. 'Oranges and lemons said the bells of St Clements...' they all sang.

'Phillip won't come,' Marjorie said, covering her ears at the noise. 'He's too sensitive to understand how you can be so calm about it all.'

'Then Davy will be disappointed. But Phillip must make his own decisions.'

Again Marjorie took offence. 'Are you suggesting I don't allow him to decide for himself?'

Hope stifled a sigh. 'Of course not, Mother-in-law. Now, shall we have a cup of tea? I made some Welsh cakes this afternoon. Some for the party and some for us.' She walked away swiftly through the throng of excited children chanting 'Here comes the candle to light you to bed, here comes the chopper to chop off your head,' followed by screams as they made their escape. Hope laughed and clapped as the game ended, determined not to try to explain or apologize, as she had so often in the past when she had done nothing except try to cope with the difficulties life had thrown at her. Marjorie was exhausting when she was in this critical mood.

There were as many adults as children there as the afternoon wore on. The room had been decorated with the banners they had made, and on the walls she had displayed lots of Davy's cheerful drawings. On each one Hope or Kitty had written a title given to them by Davy, but which no one could see represented in the pictures. These were duly admired and Davy promised to make more "when he had time".

Hope laughed ruefully. 'I must say those words too often,' she admitted. 'He's used them several times recently.'

Marjorie didn't say it suggested lack of attention, but Hope read it in her eyes.

Peter had brought a gramophone and a pile of records and these were used to play several musical games. They tired of each activity quickly and, without the help of Peter, Joyce, Kitty and Bob, and the patient Freddy, who seemed to enjoy the occasion at least as much as the children, the lively three and four-year-olds would have run riot over the house.

When the last child had been collected and silence had settled over the house, and Davy was fast asleep hugging his favourite new toys, Peter went into the kitchen, where stacks of plates awaited washing. He returned to the living room with a tray of tea. Hope and Kitty were picking up the last of the muddle and Marjorie was wiping the table of its sticky remnants.

'Come on, you can finish off later. It's time for a breather,' he announced, and, gratefully, Hope sank into the soft armchair. Peter allowed Kitty to pour the tea, and sat on the arm of Hope's chair.

'I enjoyed that,' Geoff said, 'but I wouldn't like it every day, would you, Peter?'

'There's trifle on this settee!' Marjorie said in outrage. 'I told you you should have bought leather, Hope, then it would wash off.'

'I've got something in the shop that will clean it,' Geoff promised, winking at Hope.

Geoff left early, having promised to meet Connie – although he said nothing to Freddy, or to Marjorie, who still didn't know of Connie's existence. 'I'll bring the cleaner tomorrow,' he promised as he left the warm room and stepped out into the cold of the October night, sad to leave Hope but with a sense of relief to be parting from the tenseness created by Marjorie, in spite of Hope's efforts to overcome it.

As she lay in bed that night, trying to sleep, Hope thought that, although she had filled the hours with her automatic complaints, Marjorie had enjoyed the afternoon. Why did she pretend it was weakness to admit to being happy? Grief did odd things to people, she understood that, but Marjorie had always disapproved of anything under the heading of fun.

Her three sons had been brought up inhibited by strict rules of behaviour. Marjorie wouldn't accept that laughter was an essential ingredient for health as well as happiness. The war had taken them away from her and new priorities and values had distorted everything she had taught them.

A belated freedom to think and become aware of the less constricted lives most had led had made them consider with deep concern all they had been told, and had made a nonsense of their attitudes to learning and obedience.

Their ignorance and outdated views had at first made them the butt of many jokes.

Richard had told her a little of this, Ralph, a little more, although he seemed to settle easily back into life as it had been before the army had interrupted it. Both Richard and Phillip had changed considerably from the men they had been under Marjorie's regime.

–

Phillip had been waiting when Marjorie and Freddy reached home after Davy's party.

'I have something to tell you.' he said as he took Marjorie's coat. 'There's a woman called Connie who seems to have followed me and I'm afraid she might intend being a nuisance.'

'Friend of yours?' Freddy asked, not admitting they had met.

'Well, yes, I did befriend her for a while, but when she began to expect more than an occasional treat, like a meal or the pictures, a box of chocolates, you know the sort of thing, well then I had to back off. When I left to return home to you I thought I'd seen the end of her, but somehow she found out where you live and now she's here.'

'Connie, you say,' Freddy asked innocently. 'Pretty young woman with a delightful hint of a Birmingham accent?'

'You've met her?'

'We had an interesting conversation, yes.'

'Don't believe a word she utters. She's lying if she says we're more than casual acquaintances.'

'Not living together with the promise of marriage, then?'

Phillip sat down and hid his face in his hands. Useless hands, Freddy thought irrelevantly. Hands that wasted every day, allowed life to slip through without a thought, while he used other people to support him in his idleness. Marjorie sat beside Phillip and demanded that Freddy get him a drink.

'Let him get his own,' he said calmly. 'It's about time he did something for himself, even if it's only to pour a drink he hasn't paid for.' With a glance at the startled expression on both faces, he added, 'And for the record, I believe Connie.' He went to bed.

It was very late when Marjorie came to bed. He hadn't slept and didn't think he would.

'Are you awake?' Marjorie hissed. 'Phillip has told me everything. You've left a very upset boy down there. How could you be so cruel?'

'Easily when I know that our son is a cheat and a liar and will continue to be unless he's made to face up to things.' He got up, shivering in the cold night air, and went downstairs. He tried and failed to make himself comfortable on the leather couch, which was cold and unyielding, and stared into the darkness. After an hour he rose, relit the fire, made a cup of cocoa and settled to read. The next few days were not going to be easy. When he went back up the stairs, sleep was still a long time coming.

–

In Badgers Brook, Hope was also giving up on sleep. In a contrary way it was because of the hectic and long day. Rising early, running around getting food prepared and decorating the room as a surprise for Davy should have exhausted her. But instead of making her tired, she was left feeling effervescent, still filled with excitement. Sleep was a long way off.

Taking her mind away from Marjorie's unhappiness she smiled as she remembered incidents from the party: the chaos of tea time, the shouts of excitement as games were won and lost, Davy's rosy cheeks as he joined in with everything that went on, stopping occasionally to run and hug her. Giving up on sleep she rose, wondering whether a hot drink might help.

She wrapped herself in Ralph's dressing gown, which she had been unable to throw away, and with a blanket over her shoulders she was still shivering as she lit the gas cooker and put the kettle on the circle of flames. It was half past one and, for no particular reason, she opened the door as she waited for the kettle to boil. There was always the chance of hearing an owl, or perhaps a fox.

She often opened the door when she was alone, especially at night, and wondered what impulse made her do it. Was it an indication of her loneliness? A connection with other people, however tenuous? Invisible people, but out there, friends who cared.

A voice called to her and she began to close the door. No friends would be calling at this time of night. Memories of the broken window returned, scaring her.

'It's me, Peter. I won't come in, but I saw a light and wanted to make sure you and Davy are all right.'

Heart racing, she stood back for him to step inside.

'What on earth are you doing around here at this time of night?' she asked, going to deal with the kettle that was hissing and popping its lid, demanding attention.

'I've been watching the badgers. I took some food for them then hid while they ate it. They come out soon after nightfall, at different times as the evenings change with the seasons. I sometimes watch them leave, sometimes wait for their return. They can be a noisy lot, playing chase in the farmer's orchard as they make their way to the wood where they feed.'

'Oh Peter, Davy would love that.'

'One day, when he's older, I'll enjoy taking him.'

They were standing in the kitchen where she was preparing two hot drinks, and Peter saw her shiver. Instinctively he put an arm around her shoulder. 'Come on, I'll need to revive the fire if we're going to sit and drink this.'

While she wrapped the blanket more tightly around her, she watched as he efficiently dealt with the fire, which was soon emitting smoke and desultory flames and very little heat. 'It'll take a while before it's any use,' he said.

'Just to see it is an improvement.' She touched his arm affectionately.

Sitting either side of the gradually strengthening fire was so comfortable, so relaxing, that they stayed for a long time, reminiscing about the past, until Hope's wide yawn make him jump up and apologize.

'Hope, I'm so sorry, keeping you up all this time. After the party, as well. You must be worn out. It's almost five o'clock. what was I thinking about?'

'It was a perfect way to end Davy's birthday, Peter. Thank you.' She stretched rather inelegantly, and only then, having long abandoned the blanket, did she remember, once again, how unsuitably she was dressed. Peter was such an easy person to talk to, it hadn't entered her head. She pulled the collar up as high as it would go and Peter asked, 'Ralph's?'

When she nodded he smiled and said, 'It's good to hold on to something. Keep some of his things around you, and don't avoid talking about him. Otherwise it would be like pretending he'd never lived. You have years of happy memories and it would be a shame to forget them.'

Tiredness was taking its toll, which, together with the intimacy of the past hours, was making her feel weepy. It was so quiet, the only sound the occasional shifting of coals in the grate. They could have been the only two people in the world. She turned and clung to Peter and fought back tears. His arms were comforting, enfolding her in warmth and putting aside her loneliness. Slowly she raised her face to him and their lips met in a kiss. 'Thank you, Peter,' she said.

She slid out of his arms and he quickly moved away. 'Time to go, while there's at least an hour or two of the night left for sleep,' he said softly. As he opened the door a vixen barked close by, an eerie, wailing bark that sounded as lonely as he felt at leaving.

–

Connie was in her room at the guest house, counting her money, and, after working out how few days it would last, had decided to go back home. Apart from running out of money she knew she had been foolish to come, and now all she wanted was to get away. The job that had been Phillip's would be given to a man; it couldn't be hers, even though she had done most of the work. She'd have to find some other way of keeping herself. The rent of the room was small, and she could manage on very little.

The thought of going back to her family home on the outskirts of Birmingham crossed her mind, but she knew that it would be a retrograde step, that once she returned to the comfort and safety of her parents' home it was there she would remain, to grow old and end up alone.

She had left to take a job as nanny to two little boys in North Wales, and when they no longer needed her she had decided to stay in the area. She had been away too long, and to return home would have been stifling, even though the thought of being spoiled and cared for was a strong temptation.

She wished there was a way for her to stay in Cwm Derw, but that was impossible with Phillip's parents here and aware of the situation. She had seen Geoff a couple of times, but after meeting him tonight after Davy's party, she wouldn't see him again. Phillip had ruined that before it had begun.

–

Phillip was heading for Ty Mawr just before dawn, but didn't intend stopping. There was just time to slip home, leave his clothes to be laundered and collect clean ones, eat whatever he could find and leave again. As he passed Badgers Brook he was surprised to see a light glowing in the kitchen window. He slowed his steps as he saw the door open and a figure emerge.

It was almost morning, so who could it be? A doctor perhaps. He stood still. Perhaps he should go and see if Hope and Davy were all right. But that would make him late, and early morning wasn't the time to be faced by his mother. He darted across the lane and slid behind the trunk of a birch tree that glowed whitely in the darkness and watched as Peter hurried away.

So this is our innocent widow, is it? Hope hadn't waited long before finding someone to take Ralph's place! His indifference towards his brother shifted as he felt outrage, which was rapidly replaced by cynical pleasure. This was something to take his parents' minds off Connie, that much was certain. Bending forward, hands in pockets, his silhouette distorted by the heavy flying boots he wore and the thick overcoat, scarf and trilby, he was smiling as he headed for home.

—

Marjorie was awake. She had set the alarm clock for 5:30 and muffled it under her pillow. She roused herself but almost changed her mind about rising. The morning was dark and very cold. Her nose was tucked under the edge of the blanket to ease the discomfort of the icy night air. Sliding carefully from between the sheets she reached for her dressing gown, her feet feeling around for slippers.

This was crazy, she told herself. Phillip might already have been and gone; he might not come at all. He was clearly avoiding them, so if she showed a light he'd stay away. She hesitated on the landing in the utterly dark house, tempted by the warm bed she had just left and feeling the chill air around her feet, imagining the coldness of the living room with the heat of the previous day's fire dissipated.

She made up her mind, pulled the dressing gown more tightly around her body and went down the stairs. She had reached the last stair before she realized that there was a light in the kitchen. She opened the door and said calmly, 'Good morning, Phillip.'

'Mummy, I'm so glad to see you.'

'Are you, dear? Then why have you avoided us for so long?' She tried to keep recrimination from her voice.

He ignored her question and said instead, 'I've just seen something very upsetting.'

Marjorie waited for him to continue. He had filled the kettle and cut himself some thick slices of bread. Thank goodness bread was no longer rationed. Although whatever he took to spread on it would leave her short.

'It's Hope.' He raised a sad face, allowed a theatrical pause, and went on. 'She's found someone else.'

'What d'you mean "found someone else"! She can't have. Ralph hasn't been gone more than a few months.'

'I was walking back through the wood and I saw a light in the kitchen of Badgers Brook. I was worried, thinking there might be something wrong, Davy ill or something. I went towards the gate and saw Peter Bevan leaving. Him with the horse and cart. This was at five o'clock this morning.'

Marjorie covered her mouth with her hands, her eyes wide with shock, then ran to the stairs and called Freddy, demanding that he came down at once. Then, as always in moments of trouble, she made tea.

Freddy begged them to say nothing. 'Gossip is so easy to start but impossible to put a stop to,' he reminded them. 'If Hope is innocent she could be hurt by the rumours, probably for months. Please, Marjorie, let's keep it between us until we can talk to Hope.'

'I don't want to talk to her. After what she's done, and is doing, to this family I never want to see her again.' She was not being honest. As soon as four o'clock came and Joyce finished work she intended to confront Hope and tell her that her sordid secret was out.

It was sheer luck that Geoff saw Connie walking towards the railway station. Stella's husband, Colin, was on duty, and it was as he came out to take Connie's suitcase from her that Geoff looked out of the van window. He hurriedly parked the van and ran up the station approach. Stopping to buy a platform ticket, which he impatiently offered to Colin, he asked Connie why she was leaving without telling him.

'I'm truly sorry, Geoff. I didn't mean to be rude but I wanted to slip away without anyone noticing. It hasn't been a very successful visit, you see.' She looked up at him, saw the disappointment in his eyes. 'The best part was meeting you. I'll never forget our winter picnic. It was a magical day.'

'Then why say no to repeating it?' The heavy rumble of the approaching train drenched him with utter panic. 'Don't go. Or at least get the next train, please, Connie. Just another hour, surely you can spare me that?'

Leaving her case in Bob's care, they went to a café where they ate toast, drank tea, and talked. The conversation was stilted as it had never been on that picnic. Both were aware that there was so much to say and that many miles would separate them after the following few hours.

In the end, all they achieved was an exchange of addresses and the promise to keep in touch. As the train took her away from him, Geoff's spirits sank lower and lower. They hardly knew each other but over the short hours they had spent together Connie had become his hope of an exciting future when he had given up expecting one. He watched without blinking as the train moved away, its engine snorting and hissing with importance. When the tail of the train disappeared around the final bend in the track, he was bereft.

–

Freddy was standing on the bridge looking down at the railway line. He was concerned for Hope, knowing that, although she had promised to keep quiet about what Phillip had seen, Marjorie would be unable to resist spreading her suspicions. He couldn't understand her vindictiveness towards their daughter-in-law. The excuse of it being her way of grieving was no longer valid; she had a nasty streak and there seemed little hope of it fading.

He didn't feel able to go and see Hope and find out what had happened; there were no words that would discover the truth without offending, and he knew that Hope needed all her friends at this time, and they included himself. He would have to wait, and pray that this time Marjorie would behave with loyalty towards their sadly diminished family.

–

Before confronting Hope with accusations, unable to keep it to herself, Marjorie told Stella in the post office. Huddled in the corner where wool and cottons were sold, she repeated what Phillip had said. Stella's immediate reaction was that the story should not be spread. 'Don't tell another soul, Marjorie, there could be a simple explanation. Even you must see that it would be cruel to make Hope the subject for wicked gossip.'

'What d'you mean, even me? I don't like the girl. I never did, but I'm not spiteful. I simply can't ignore the truth! She wasn't the right one for Ralph and he'd still be alive if she hadn't persuaded him to marry her.'

Stella hushed her and pointed to the post office counter, where a few people waited to be served.

'Leave it be, for heaven's sake, Marjorie,' she hissed angrily. 'Let the girl speak before you spread wicked gossip on the word of your Phillip, of all people. There'll be an explanation, sure to be.'

'For example?' Marjorie hissed back. People waiting to be served moved slightly closer, hoping for a few words to give a clue as to what was happening. 'Come on, what can you suggest that would explain Peter Bevan leaving her house at five in the morning?'

Glaring at the curious women in the queue now murmuring among themselves, she said, 'A burst pipe? A door that got stuck? Davy unwell and needing the doctor? Anyway,' she said with a finality that made her forget secrecy and raise her voice, 'if your Hope is seeing another man it's none of your business. So my advice is stay out of it. Right?'

'She isn't my Hope!'

'Proves my point then, doesn't it?'

'But what if she'd been seeing Peter before Ralph died? What if that first accident wasn't an accident at all? What if she'd made him so unhappy with her shenanigans that the poor boy decided to—'

'Stop right there! I won't listen to such nonsense,' an angry Stella hissed. More loudly, encouraging the waiting customers with an attempt at a smile and a gesture of frustration, she pushed Marjorie, none too gently, into the back room.

'What rot you talk sometimes, Marjorie. Now it's almost time for my mid-morning tea, so stay and have one with me. There's some cakes, too, left over from your Davy's party. Kitty brought them for me to take to our country cottage. Help yourself. I'll be in when I've dealt with this lot, and you and I can have a serious chat.'

A queue had formed and one customer had a gleam in her eyes which had Stella seen it would have worried her. But unaware of anyone having overheard what was said, she cleared the queue and found the makings of tea quite unperturbed.

Outside the customers took a long time to disperse.

–

There were always a number of dances, parties and concerts held during the autumn and Hope expected a few more additions to the number of dresses she already had in her order book. Many women also treated themselves to a new dress to wear on Christmas Day when the family came, after the roast had been dealt with. Besides dresses there were the delicate items of underwear she and Joyce had added to their skills, and these were chosen for gifts. So they prepared themselves for a busy few weeks.

She had been asked to make a wedding dress for a bride planning a January wedding. Measurements had been taken, the style chosen and the material bought and carefully stored. The order book looked healthy and when Hope and Joyce went over the accounts it was gratifying to see how successful their small business had become.

Davy and two friends were playing with a train set that had rails going all over the floor, necessitating them crawling under chairs and behind the curtains as they pushed the train and its carriages along with loud chatter and enthusiastic sound effects. Peter had found it in a second-hand shop and presented it as a late birthday present. Davy had been delighted and played with it constantly.

Hope smiled at Joyce as they watched for a moment. 'I can't believe how fortunate I've been,' she said. 'Davy is so happy, and with your help I've made us reasonably secure financially. If everything continues exactly like this for the next twenty years I won't complain.'

'You have to work long hours to make it happen,' Joyce reminded her. 'People might look on and think you're lucky, but luck is mostly due to effort. If you'd sat and felt sorry for yourself you wouldn't have been successful, would you?'

'I suppose you're right. But luck does play a part. I found you and that was a very lucky day.'

The letter asking her to return the material for the bridal gown came a few days later, towards the end of October. There was no explanation.

'Perhaps the wedding is off?' Joyce conjectured. 'It happens.'

'Oh dear, I hope not; that's seriously sad, isn't it?' She shrugged. 'Perhaps I'll find out when I take back the material. It's quite heavy; I think I'll use Davy's pushchair, what d'you think?'

'My Gran would have said pushing an empty pram means you'll soon be pushing a full one,' Joyce grinned cheekily.

'Not much chance of that,' Hope said, sharing the joke. 'But perhaps I'll ask Gwennie Flint's mother to take it instead of me, eh? Eighty if she's a day, so she should be safe!'

She walked along the road to deliver the material back to its owner, and was surprised when someone she knew well turned away and hurried off as though not wanting to speak to her. Hope shrugged and presumed she hadn't been seen.

The afternoon was mild for late October, a weak sun shone and the day had that particular autumnal atmosphere. Dampness underfoot, a crispness in the clear air and the hint of smoke from garden fires. She knew she was happy, and could look into the future filled with optimism. Then suddenly the buoyant mood left her. Ralph shouldn't be missing this; he should be here to enjoy this wonderful afternoon.

'What's up?' Stella called, as, loaded with tins and cleaning materials, she made her way to the allotment. 'You can't be miserable on such a lovely day as this. Come to the cottage, and I'll make you a cup of tea. Cure for all ills, my cups of tea and the whiff of freshly dug soil.'

'No, I'd better deliver this in case I get it dirty.'

'What is it?'

'Material for a wedding dress, an order that has been cancelled. I hope it isn't the wedding that's been cancelled.'

'Me too. Sad that is. Who's it for then?'

'I'm returning it to Mrs Green. Have you heard about the wedding being cancelled?'

Stella shook her head. 'It's still on so far as I know.'

'Then why has she asked for the material back?'

A shrug from Stella, who quickly changed the subject. 'What's making you miserable then? Losing the order?'

'Oh, I don't know, the lovely day and Ralph not here to enjoy it. I miss him, and to tell the truth, Stella, I feel responsible on days like this. If I hadn't insisted, persuaded him we should leave his parents' house and find a place of our own, he'd still be here, wouldn't he? Marjorie is right, my behaviour was responsible, I did kill him.'

Stella hushed her. 'For heaven's sake, girl, don't talk like that! Rubbish it is, but there's plenty only too willing to listen to gossip. And joyfully repeat it! Look, go and get rid of the parcel and meet me at our country cottage. You need five minutes' peace and a good cup of tea.'

'Joyce is minding Davy, I have to get back.'

'Five minutes won't harm.'

Stella set out the little folding table and waited for Hope to come. She needed to know just what was going on. 'If that Marjorie's been spreading wicked rumours about the girl she'll get the sharp edge of my tongue,' she muttered to Scamp. Surely no one had heard her complaints that day in the post office?

Hope knocked on Mrs Green's door, and, smiling, was about to step inside. To her surprise the lady took the parcel, thanked her abruptly and closed the door. Hope was so shocked that, forgetting the invitation to Stella's country cottage, she hurried back to Badgers Brook wondering what had gone wrong.

–

When Phillip told his mother he was going back to Connie, she pleaded with him to stay.

'It's no use, I can't work here, the ambience isn't right. I need to get back to my studio,' he said.

Freddy listened and said nothing. Whenever he tried to make Phillip face up to his weaknesses, Marjorie defended him. When would the boy accept that he was chasing a dream that had died years before, and find some way to earn his living honourably?

'I hope Connie got back all right.' he said, secretly hoping she wouldn't be there waiting for him. 'She's a decent girl and she deserves a lot of kindness in return for hers to you.'

'Oh stop it, Freddy. You don't know how she's used him.'

Freddy walked from the room, muttering half to himself, 'Oh, Phillip, when are you going to grow up?'

He was startled when he called in to the Ship and Compass to see people huddled together whispering, only to fall silent when he approached. It didn't take long for him to discover that the latest rumours were about Hope. The story that she had caused Ralph's first suicide attempt, which she had insisted was an accident, by her 'goings on' with Peter Bevan was all around the town.

He stood up, demanded silence and refuted the accusations, but feared that the damage was done. Marjorie once more, he presumed angrily.

–

'I have something planned,' Marjorie said when she and Phillip were alone. 'A wonderful surprise for you, but it won't be ready for several weeks. Can you come back, or, better still, stay a while longer? It's something you need and which you'll love.'

'Any clues?' Phillip coaxed.

'None. You'll just have to wait.'

'I don't think I can stay. I'm running short of cash and I haven't brought any work to sell or—'

'Forget about money, your father and I will help out, you know that.'

Phillip smiled. He was in no hurry. Now Connie had gone he could stay home perhaps for a few months. His mother wanted it and she could always talk his father round. And his mother's attitude towards Hope meant he wouldn't be bothered by the presence of the tiresome Davy. He might see if he could take an evening course, he mused. Boring, but it might keep Dad happy.

Marjorie kept her secret as she could never keep the confidences of others. She had contacted a building firm and plans were made for the conversion of the brick shed into a comfortable room. That it was going to be a proper artist's studio wouldn't be revealed until the very last moment. She hugged herself. How thrilled Phillip would be. How his talent would mature.

Phillip was aware of nothing. He was so rarely at home. He met Matthew several times, and they commiserated with each other about their miserable lives.

'I try, Phillip, I really do. Sally doesn't need me, yet she's always complaining about my never being there. What am I supposed to do? I went home last Friday and they were on their way out to some rehearsal or other. I can't remember what they're involved in, can I? They never tell me, except when I forget to appear to clap and tell them all how clever and talented they are.'

'We all have to perform,' Phillip agreed vaguely. 'I now have to act like a five-year-old at Christmas and try to guess what boring surprise Mother is planning.'

'What d'you think it is?'

'I hope it's a car, that would be perfect. Something to take me as far as I can go from this place without actually falling into the sea!'

–

Over the following week several of Hope's customers cancelled orders. It wasn't until the fifth client had told Hope she no longer needed her services that she began seriously to worry.

'I had thought that, with the cost of Christmas, some of them were finding it hard to afford a new dress,' she said to Joyce as she deleted another name from the order book. 'Now I'm beginning to wonder if I've displeased someone in some way and the others are supporting her in a protest, without telling me why.'

Joyce said nothing, Hope saw her look away to stare out of the window, obviously ill at ease.

'Joyce? Do you know something that I don't?'

'It's nonsense, Hope. But there has been a stupid rumour. Forget it, you're good at what you do and people will soon come back and beg you to make clothes for them.'

'A rumour? Please, Joyce, tell me what's being said.'

'Let's say the sympathy people felt for you after Ralph died is now transferred to your mother-in-law.'

'But why? What on earth is being said?'

'That you and Peter – that you and Peter are lovers and were even before Ralph died. You're being blamed for his suicide.'

'Go on,' Hope said, trying to stop her hands from trembling. 'Tell me the rest.'

'They're saying you and Peter were the reason for Ralph falling in front of the car, that it wasn't an accident but a first attempt…' She couldn't go on. 'Oh Hope, it's so unfair and I feel sure your mother-in-law is at the bottom of it.'

'She usually is,' Hope said sadly. 'Can you imagine how it feels to be so disliked? It's horrible, it really is.'

By the first week of November there were few customers remaining in the order book, and Hope knew that unless something changed quickly and dramatically she would run out of money before the end of January. The business that had been an almost immediate success, and had seemed set to continue to thrive, was almost gone.

Eight

In an attempt to fill her time and put the alarming prospect of running out of money from her mind, Hope busied herself in the garden. Between times, when the weather made this impossible, she and Joyce made cushions in the hope that one day, when this recent lie had blown over, they might sell them.

–

The day when most people collected their pensions was Stella's busiest. The shop was filled from counter to door all morning. The customers chattered and for most of the time Stella was unaware of what was being said. She took books, stamped them, paid out and hardly looked further than the hands that offered and received.

Then a voice penetrated her brain.

'That first so-called accident, when poor Ralph was hit by the car,' Mrs Harris was saying. 'That was never no accident, more like his first attempt to end it all, driven to despair he was by the carryings-on of that wife of his.'

'Mrs Harris, I have to ask you to leave,' Stella said. Snapping down the counter flap behind her, she stood facing the woman in the small post office area, pointing a querulous finger towards the door. 'I won't have such gossip spoken in my shop.'

'Denying it won't make it untrue. I'm only saying the same as everyone else.'

Stella stood, pointing at the door. Mrs Green opened it and Mrs Harris stalked out unrepentant. Stella continued to point at the door until Mrs Green followed.

Hands on hips, Stella turned to face the rest of the wide-eyed people waiting to be served.

'The truth – supposing you're interested – is Hope hardly even knew Peter until after Ralph was dead,' Stella said to the other women waiting to be served. *That's* the truth, ladies. Boring, mind, but the truth!'

A few nodded, some smiled but most were unconvinced. No one argued; they needed their pensions, or stamps and postal orders and they didn't want to risk being told to leave, like Mrs Harris and Mrs Green.

'Peter Bevan never counted Marjorie among his customers, so how could they have known each other? Heavens above, can you imagine Marjorie buying her vegetables off a horse and cart? She'd die of starvation first!' A few laughed but most remained silent, hugging their own opinion close.

It was clear from the violent way she stamped the pension books that Stella was angry. People were so easily convinced of the bad in others, ignoring the facts for the sake of a good gossip. She decided to go and see Hope when she closed the shop for lunch. Take a piece of cake and beg a cup of tea. The poor girl had to be reminded that not everyone was as stupid as Mrs Harris. To talk to Hope, cheer her up, was a start, but surely there was something else she could do?

'Mam,' she said, when her mother called a few minutes later, 'you're having a new dress. Right?'

'Any special reason?' her mother asked. 'An outing or something¿

'Or something.' Stella snapped.

Hope and Joyce were making patchwork cushion covers with leftover material; Davy was playing with his train set.

'Can I come in?' Stella called, stepping into the kitchen. 'Any chance of a cuppa, then? Brought some cake I have, enough for four.'

Hope came out smiling a welcome. 'Stella. what a lovely surprise. We've made some sandwiches, won't you share them with us? Davy's favourite at the moment, Heinz sandwich spread.'

She led Stella into the living room and Davy looked up. smiled, then left his game and ran to greet her. 'Hello Auntie Stella, will you play with me? I need a signalman.'

Stella laughed. 'It's Uncle Colin you need for that – he's even got a railway uniform. Why don't you ask your mam to make one for you, eh?'

'That's a good idea,' Hope said, and Joyce at once began searching through the boxes of oddments to find some suitable material.

'He's missing his friends,' Hope confided, when she and Stella went to make the tea.

'Where have they gone? No one's moved away that I know of.'

'Stop pretending, Stella.' Hope gave a sad sigh. 'No one wants to know us since the rumours began. I'm a scarlet woman and tainted with evil. No one is safe around me, especially innocent children. Didn't you know?'

Evading an answer, Stella said, 'I came to ask if you'd make Mam another dress. Pleased she was with the last one. Fits like a dream.'

'You don't have to do this, but thank you.'

'Your clothes fit like no others. All those who're difficult to fit, who can't buy straight off the peg like most of us, thrilled they are at what you can do with your clever little fingers. Hope, Mam feels more confident that she has for a long time. There are many others who feel the same. Martha Powell for one, her with the damaged spine. Wore an old riding mac and trousers every day of her life she did, until you made her that dress and jacket. You designed it special, built up the shoulder, made it hang right. I bet she wouldn't go anywhere else for new clothes. You are good at what you do and people will soon forget the ugliness of today when they need something. Outrage and disapproval are all very well, but they won't get in the way of acquiring something of quality, believe me.'

'Thank you, Stella, I don't know what I'd do without you and Kitty and Joyce and—' She stopped as tears threatened.

'Where's that tea then? And didn't you say something about sandwiches? I have to get back for two o'clock. It's old Harold Francis's day to buy his postal order to do the pools and he'll knock the door down if I'm a bit late opening.'

A few followed Stella's lead and gave orders to Hope, including Martha, but it wasn't enough. With Christmas so close, and needing to buy at least a few surprises for Davy, she had to find other work. Her greatest fear was that, as with the dress making, no one would want to employ her.

'I don't want to lose you, Joyce,' she said a few days later, 'but I won't be able to pay your wages for much longer, unless the town has a dramatic change of heart. I have to get a job, and with Davy to look after it isn't going to be easy.'

'Don't worry about me, I'll find a job easily enough, and when everything settles I'd like to come back. Meanwhile, I'll help as and when I can. Perhaps I could look after Davy for an hour or two each day while you go out. And I've been wondering. This is a big house, could you take a lodger? If you explain to Geoff Tanner, tell him how unfairly you're being treated, I'm sure he'll allow it. He's a very reasonable landlord, isn't he?'

'Now that is a good idea. I think this house likes being filled with people. If I could find the right lodger, I might be able to leave Davy with her and do something like early deliveries of milk or even the post. They take women now, don't they?' Then she shook her head. 'No, that wouldn't do. I could never leave Davy with a stranger, no matter how desperate things become. And those who know me wouldn't want to live here now.'

An unexpected letter a few days later promised to solve at least a part of her problem. She took it to Geoff and asked if it were possible for her to rent out a room. 'It won't bring in much, but even a few shillings extra will help me at the moment,' she told him. 'Things have suddenly got worse, and I have to thank my mother-in-law's venom for it. How can she do this to her grandson? I don't blame her for hating me, but Davy's a baby and he's done her no harm.'

'Neither have you.' Geoff reminded her. 'Don't start believing the stories that are spreading or you'll ruin your life and Davy's. You were heard to say you killed Ralph. The words were obviously taken out of context but they were damaging.'

'I did say that. I even believed it for a while. He wasn't keen to leave his parents' home and I made him come away and start to build a home for us, Davy and me. Ralph was never brave, was he?'

'Marjorie was a very strong-willed mother, and of all the three boys Ralph was the most amiable.'

'The weakest.'

'All right, the one least able to defy her. He accepted everything his mother said and never questioned anything, until he married you. He tried to do what you wanted. He wanted to please you, Hope, never forget that.' He could see she was upset and rubbed his hands together as though putting the subject of Ralph aside. 'Now, who is this lodger you have in mind?'

She handed him the letter. 'It's Connie, the woman who said she was married to Phillip. She must have heard from Stella that I was looking for a lodger.'

'Connie?' he breathed. 'I don't believe it.'

'She wants to come back, but not to see Phillip. She needs a change, a fresh start, and thinks this town, this *friendly* town, she calls it, will be a good place to do so.' She looked at Geoff in surprise. He was smiling so widely he looked like a stranger; his eyes were dark and glowing with delight. 'Connie?' he whispered again. 'I think she'd be a perfect choice.'

With the agreement with Geoff settled and the promise of rent for the room, Hope was pleased, but knew it was nowhere near enough for survival. The sensible thing would be to move, find a room, somewhere cheaper, but that was something she wouldn't consider. Badgers Brook was her home and here she would stay. Every time she walked into the house she was surrounded by an atmosphere of wellbeing and warmth, the knowledge that the house was theirs. It wanted them there, and it offered a security that made her determined to stay. Each morning when she woke it was to a feeling of utter peace, the facts she had to face coming slowly, gently and without causing sudden shock and dismay. Everything was possible while she stayed in Badgers Brook. Whatever she had to do to earn the necessary money she would do.

There was a small dress shop on the corner opposite Geoff Tanner's hardware store, and, seeing a notice in the window for an alteration hand, Hope went there to apply.

The shop was a small one but it stocked moderately priced garments that appealed to the local women and was always busy. Customers called between finishing their shopping and catching their bus home, to browse and chat with others, so, like Betty at the Ship and Compass, Nerys Bowen was always up to date on local news.

She smiled apologetically when Hope asked about the vacancy. 'Sorry, Mrs Murton, but the position is now filled,' she said.

Geoff, watching from his corner shop guessed why Hope and called and went to see Nerys to ask what had happened.

'No, I didn't give her the job,' she said in reply to Geoff's enquiry. 'Sorry to my heart, I am, but I couldn't.' She admitted that she was worried the rumours about Hope might affect her business. 'It's terrible the way people gossip,' she added.

Geoff stared at her. 'It is, and you're no better than the rest, are you?'

Several days later, the advertisement was still there, which forced Hope into an unpleasant decision. No one wanted her skills as a dressmaker, but there was one woman who wouldn't say no to employing her.

Betty Connors welcomed Hope back as a cleaner. 'Sorry I am that it's necessary, dear, but I'd love to have you back. Truth is, it's never been done properly since you left.' Ruefully Hope accepted the compliment and the job.

—

Peter hadn't seen Hope since the accusations began. He wanted to call and apologize for his thoughtlessness in calling so late at night, and make unfounded promises that it would all blow over. He wanted to reassure her, tell her life would return to how it had been before the rumours began. Every time he approached the house he turned away. He could so easily make things worse. The attitude of the local people seemed set to continue. Once their mind was made up, most were reluctant to change it. He and Hope would have to wait until the stories died down from lack of nourishment, and that meant they would have to avoid seeing each other.

He had tried to write to her but each time the letter ended up in the bin. Better to wait and meet accidentally, then a few brief words would suffice.

He wanted to tell her how he missed her and Davy, and how he hoped that, once the unpleasantness had faded, he would return to regular visits to the warm, friendly house by the brook.

Blaming himself, he felt deprived of more than Hope and Davy's company: he missed the meetings with neighbours and new friends, and he missed the laughter. He felt his loneliness more than ever before. His mind was filled with memories of the past summer as being one pleasurable, continuous evening, long, lazy hours of uncomplicated enjoyment, and he wanted so much to be a part of it again.

–

Hope had heard that Phillip was staying with Matthew, and prayed he would be far away from Cwm Derw when Connie arrived. He was certainly no longer at Ty Mawr, according to Stella. Also according to post office gossip, he was working as an assistant in a shop that sold a few paintings and prints, calendars and cards, and glorified itself with the name: Grosvenor Galleries. Hope wrote to Connie telling her all she knew and invited her to move into Badgers Brook as a lodger, reminding her to bring her ration book and promising to look out for a suitable job for her.

She needed to go into Cardiff to replenish her stock of sewing accessories and buy a few gifts for Davy. Not as many as she'd hoped, but she was determined to make sure he had some parcels under the tree. While she was in Cardiff she would also have to dig deep into her meagre savings and buy some things for the room Connie would use. The house was not fully furnished and she wanted Connie to recognize that she had made some effort to make her comfortable. A small rug bought second hand, new sheets and a blanket were all she had so far.

Pushing a chattering Davy in his chair, she was lost in calculations, wondering whether she might afford a table lamp, when she saw Marjorie walking up the station approach in front of her. Oh, no. Surely she wouldn't have company all the way? She caught up with her as she bought her ticket and took a deep breath before saying, 'Hello, Mother-in-law. Davy, say hello to Grandmother.'

To her utter disbelief, Marjorie stared at her as though they had never met and walked to the furthest end of the platform. She ignored little Davy's greeting. Marjorie had ignored her before, but this was so blatant, Hope wanted to run home and hide. When would this end?

The train was rather crowded and when Hope alighted in Cardiff she didn't catch sight of Marjorie. Perhaps she'd be lucky and the day would pass without their meeting. She didn't know how to handle this, she really didn't.

She was edgy as she set about searching for her purchases. Only half of her mind was on the shopping, the rest was preparing for coming face to face with Marjorie, or someone else who disliked her, blamed her for Ralph's death. So it was with that dread she turned in answer to someone calling her name.

He wasn't her favourite person, but she was so relieved to recognize Matthew she greeted him with a smile. 'Matthew. Are you Christmas shopping too?'

He turned and took the arm of a pretty young woman beside him and said, 'Meet Hope, darling, the widow of poor Ralph. Hope, meet my lovely wife, Sally.'

After handshakes and the conventional remarks the two women didn't seem to know what else to say, until Matthew said. 'Come on, you two, let's go and find some tea and cakes.' He led them towards a café, and after seating them waved encouragingly at the waitress and placed an order. 'No point spending half the afternoon discussing what we each like, so I'll ask for assorted cakes. Is that all right?'

he asked belatedly. Hope looked at Sally and they shared a smile.

The rather unexpected introduction had meant Hope was unprepared and she groped through her memory to remember something about Matthew and his wife. Relieved she remembered their daughters.

'You have two daughters, I believe.' she said. Within minutes they were talking enthusiastically about sons and daughters, embarking briefly on the sadness of Marjorie's tragic losses. Hope quickly changed the subject, superstitiously afraid that the speaking of her would cause Marjorie to materialize and ruin what seemed to be a pleasant interlude.

Sally explained that she and her daughters sang and took part in amateur dramatics. Matthew interrupted and said there was nothing amateur about any of his girls, they were all extremely talented. Hope was aware that, when he made a little effort, Matthew could be utterly charming. Sally's glowing cheeks and her bright eyes supported her opinion.

'It started during the war,' Sally explained. 'I used to have quite a good voice as a child and I took part in concerts to entertain the forces, you know the sort of thing. But I began to enjoy it and later I joined the local drama group, and the girls joined in and, well, it goes on, we're all addicted.'

'Apart from me, sad to say,' Matthew said. 'Although perhaps I might have become a willing stagehand if my job hadn't made me so unreliable.' He looked at his pretty wife and said, 'I'm so proud of my three girls, and one day we'll all work together, won't we, darling?'

While they were finishing a second cup of tea, Matthew excused himself, explaining that he had some secret shopping to do.

'Something small and expensive for you, I hope?' Hope whispered.

'Oh, he does the right thing sometimes,' Sally said, watching as Matthew threaded his way through the tables. 'Just when I despair of us, he does something to make me change my mind.'

'You seem very happy together.'

'We are, or I think we are – when we're together. But he only comes home when he has to. He prefers to stay in hotels and spend the time among strangers than with us. D'you know he's never been to any of our performances?'

'He does cover a large area, doesn't he? It must be difficult to get home sometimes.'

'Sometimes, yes, but being near enough to get home and preferring to stay away is difficult to understand.'

Hope was unsure how to deal with the unexpected confidences. A hint of criticism would be remembered when Sally was feeling more benevolent towards Matthew, yet she didn't want to appear indifferent to Sally's unhappiness.

Sensing her embarrassment, Sally said. 'I'm sorry, I don't know why I said all that. Matthew is my problem, and only rarely do I seek comfort from discussing him with others. You have a very sensitive manner and it encourages confidences.'

Hope smiled ruefully. 'I don't think my mother-in-law would agree with you.'

'Look, shall we meet again, and perhaps talk of more cheerful things? Bring Davy, he's a darling and so well behaved.'

They spoke easily, and the conversation drifted to many things, including Christmas and the surprises they had planned for their children. As they stood to leave Hope said, 'I believe you have Phillip staying with you.'

'Yes.' Sally's face clouded. 'Not for much longer, I hope. He's making himself too comfortable and Matthew refuses to tell him to go.'

'I expect he'll go home for Christmas, his mother will want him there.'

'Like Matthew he seems unable to decide what he wants. I sometimes wonder whether it was the war that unsettled so many of the men, although after all this time you'd think they'd have forgotten the horrors and be thankful they're safe. wouldn't you?'

'It isn't my business, Sally, but remember it's your home. Why don't you tell Phillip to leave? You've nothing to lose, have you?'

Sally was silent for a moment and Hope began to worry that she'd spoken out of turn, then Sally looked at her and smiled. 'You're right, of course.' She went home with the words echoing in her mind. She would tell Phillip, the moment she got in.

Hope went through the busy market loaded with her packages, back to the railway station. All the time she looked around her, dreading seeing her mother-in-law, wondering what she was doing in Cardiff and hoping it would keep her there later than the train she and Davy intended to catch. She sighed with relief when she found a seat in the overcrowded carriage without seeing her.

Marjorie had called at a rather exclusive art gallery. She barged in, pushing aside a couple who were considering a seascape, and demanded to speak to an artist.

Bemused, the well-dressed young man said, 'I'm sorry, madam, but we sell quality art here, we don't employ artists to sell what they produce.' He spoke haughtily, but Marjorie's outdid him.

'My son is Phillip Williamson-Murton. You'll have heard of him?'

The young man shook his head. 'Sorry, but there are several new names appearing. Perhaps you could tell me a little more about him? But when I have finished attending to these ladies, if you please.' He spoke politely but firmly, turning aside from her, clearly displeased with her intrusion.

'I'm planning a surprise for him and I need to talk to an artist about my ideas. It has to be perfect, you see. His studio. North light, adjustable easel, sable brushes, you know the sort of thing.'

'Er, of course, madam. Please take a seat, and as soon as I'm free,' he said pointedly, 'I'll see if I can find someone to help you.' He raised a supercilious and disapproving eyebrow toward the purchasers, which fortunately Marjorie didn't see.

She was on the same train as Hope but made sure she wasn't observed. She didn't want anyone to see them together and think she had forgiven the girl who had stolen Ralph from her then driven him to suicide.

For Hope, starting back at the Ship and Compass was a sobering thought. Arriving home feeling filthy and wondering if the smell would ever leave her, day after day, was not a cheerful prospect, but money had to be earned. She thought wistfully of the life she and Ralph had imagined: two or maybe three children, a place they could comfortably afford, and perhaps one day, buying a house of their own; a typical middle-class family with enough money not to feel afraid.

After the first morning, while Davy sat near and Betty prepared lunch and restocked the bar, she wondered if she was right to stay in Cwm Derw. The world was huge and she didn't have to stay in one small part of it.

Connie gave Davy a chocolate bar. 'Lovely boy, he is, I bet Freddy's real proud of him,' she said, as Hope collected her apron and prepared to leave. 'Never had a chance to enjoy his own sons. Poor Freddy. Marjorie was always in complete control. Don't let her get her hands on Davy, will you?'

'No one looks after Davy except me or Joyce, and, on rare occasions, Kitty and Bob Jennings.' She sighed. 'Pity is, if I had someone to help I could find a better job than this. Oh, Mrs Connors, I didn't mean to sound ungrateful. I'm glad to be able to do this and be allowed to bring Davy with me.'

'If you were free I'd like you to work in the bar, but I don't think staying up till after ten o'clock would be right for young Davy, would it? Even though I'd love to have him here.'

There was something nostalgic about the way Betty said those words, and in the way she looked at a sleepy Davy as he settled into his pushchair clutching his chocolate bar and a favourite teddy in gloved hands. His cheeks were rosy and plump, captured by the knitted balaclava. Hope idly wondered what Betty's story was. She knew she'd been widowed when her husband was killed while working on an airfield and, so far as she knew, there were no children. Betty's brother, Ed, helped with the heavy work and a cousin was the pot man during opening hours.

Like me, once the door closes she's on her own, she mused sadly. The pub was busy all evening with customers coming to drink, chat, argue, play cards and darts and dominoes, and the contrast, once the place closed, must be worse for Betty Connors than it was for Hope.

Badgers Brook was her home, chosen by herself and Ralph, and she would have felt disloyal to have moved away, as though she was walking away from Ralph and their marriage. Now, looking at her dirt-stained clothes and rubbing her sore knees, she wondered if her decision had been a wise one. Had loyalty been the true grounds for her decision? Had her reasoning been emotional? Or was there an unwillingness to let go, step out alone, a fear of further change?

She closed her eyes and tried to imagine what Ralph would have suggested, but no answer came; all she could see in her mind's eye was him glancing at his mother for her to make the decision for him. She had never felt so alone.

As she headed for the bus stop she saw the bus approaching. On impulse she turned aside. It was time to tell Marjorie what she had been reduced to by her unkind and untrue gossip. She admitted to herself that she had taken the job offered by Betty Connors partly to embarrass her mother-in-law so she wouldn't have long to wait until she was seen by someone who would enjoy telling Marjorie about her daughter-in-law's latest shameful behaviour. She would go now, this minute, let her see what she had done to her and Davy, show herself in her shabby clothes and red, sore knees. The action was childish but that didn't stop her.

She knocked on the front door of Ty Mawr as she no longer had a key, and when there was no reply went around to the back. She was surprised to see several workmen there, near the doorway of the brick-built outhouse, in which several holes had been knocked, presumably for windows. The men were drinking tea and Marjorie was there offering biscuits.

'What's going on, Mother-in-law?' she asked, her anger subsiding and being replaced by curiosity. Marjorie saw them and came across. Ignoring Hope she held out her arms to Davy and said, 'Come and see what these men are doing, David, dear. We're planning a surprise for your Uncle Phillip.'

'What are you doing?' Hope asked again, and, when Marjorie still didn't reply, she went to one of the builders and asked him.

'An artist's studio, missus, that's what we're making.' He glanced at the other two men and added with a laugh, 'Never been asked to do one of them before, have we, boys?'

'Hurry up.' Marjorie bustled over to them with Davy in her arms. 'I have to get to the shops.' She put Davy down and snatched the cups and saucers from the men, waving her arms as though she were shooing geese. 'Let's get on, shall we? You promised this would be finished by the weekend.'

'I thought Phillip was going back to his job as school caretaker?' Hope queried. 'At least that's the rumour.' She emphasized the word rumour, but Marjorie showed no sign of guilt.

'Not a word to your Uncle Phillip if you see him,' she warned Davy, handing him back to his mother. 'Now I have to go.' Noticing for the first time how badly Hope was dressed she demanded, 'What are you thinking of, going around dressed like a skivvy?'

'That's what I am, Mother-in-law. Thanks to the untrue gossip that's been spread by some malicious tongues, I need money that the people around here won't let me earn, so I'm back cleaning for Mrs Connors.'

'You're taking David to that place?'

'Betty Connors loves to have him there.'

'You must bring him here, leave him with me and find a decent job.'

Hope didn't even bother to remind her that she'd had a growing business until it had been ruined by Marjorie and her friends. It was the unfairness that hurt. Ralph dead and his son without a decent standard of living. And Phillip, who had achieved nothing, was being treated to a studio.

She walked to the bus stop as Davy dozed, snuggled in a blanket and clutching his chocolate bar and his teddy, and felt a sudden sympathy for the woman who had tried too hard to make her sons succeed and had ended up losing all of them. If she were allowed, she would treat Davy in the same way, forcing him to follow the route she believed was the right one, and lose him too.

Phillip wouldn't thank her for offering him a studio. He'd be expected to show some output and, from what she could see, that was something he was unable to do.

-

Phillip was in a public house with Matthew Charles. Near them, a group of men were discussing a man from Scunthorpe called James Fielding, who had come home from the army to be told it was impossible to find him a house in which to live with his wife and children. Together with others they had taken up residence in an abandoned army camp, and more and more people had followed. Groups of families got together and removed animals who they considered better housed than they, cleaned the place, organized supplies of water, coped with primitive sanitation and called themselves squatters.

Candles had provided the only light at first, but gradually improvements had been made. Partitions were put in place, separating living from bedroom space, walls were painted, curtains and rugs appeared and the community took a pride in what they had achieved. When thousands enthusiastically followed their lead, local councils stepped in and, under strong and growing pressure, provided running water and electricity.

Phillip listened with amusement and was thankful that he had escaped from the tribulations of married life. Imagine being responsible for a family and having to go to such lengths to provide for them.

He'd been fond of Connie and he missed her. He felt a modest pride in the fact that he had actually accepted a job and had worked for Connie, unlike the others. It had begun to get him down eventually, though, and although a part of him wanted to go back to her, he knew it would be a mistake. Better forget her and start again in Cwm Derw where his mother would be on hand for a bit of financial help. Just as long as he handed her an occasional daub as a pretence of working, she'd look after him. Not a long-term prospect, putting up with her devotion; but being kept fed and warm would suffice for the winter months. Then he'd move on.

His mind returned to the men discussing the squatters, and one of them was saying, 'I wish I had the nerve to do something like that. Me and the missus still live with her mother. Three kids we've got, and still living in rooms in the home of my mother-in-law.'

'Go on, Arthur, find yourself a nice barn, kick the animals out and move in,' one of them teased.

'Lead me to it,' Arthur groaned.

–

It was Geoff who met Connie at the railway station. Getting off the train she glanced around expecting to see Hope, but there was no sign of her. She stood looking apprehensively around her at the scurrying passengers who all knew where they were going. Strangers, with their own lives, looking around for their own people and unaware of her standing alone.

Two young women pushed her aside, one after the other as they ran towards the exit. Another called to a friend and startled her with her loud impatient yell. 'Over here, come and get my case, for heaven's sake.'

Just when she began to think she was invisible a voice called and she looked up without much hope, to see Geoff waving and smiling widely.

'Hello, Geoff, what are you doing here? Have you seen Hope? She's supposed to be meeting me.'

'Sorry, but will I do instead?'

'Oh, is Hope all right? Am I still going to stay with her?'

'So far as I know everything's fine. I offered to come with the van in case you had a lot to carry.' He looked at the two small cases and asked, 'Is this all of your luggage?'

'I'm still glad to see you,' she said.

'Oh? Because it's me or for a lift in the van?'

'The van of course.'

The report of her travels and a brief update on all that had happened since she'd left filled the short journey to Badgers Brook, where Hope was waiting, with a table set for a meal and Davy impatient to show her his train set and offer a drawing he'd made for her.

Before she had removed her coat, Davy was on her lap, and she balanced a cup of tea in one hand while the other smoothed out Davy's drawing as she praised it.

'Anybody home?' Kitty called as she came through the kitchen, and Connie smiled and said, 'This is the best homecoming ever.'

Geoff didn't stay; he had to get back to the shop where he'd left the young boy in charge. 'I'll call tomorrow to see if there's anything you need.' he called as he closed the door behind him.

'Such a kind man.' Connie said. She looked at Hope and then Kitty. 'He told me what's been going on, with your parents-in-law making it difficult for you. I'll help all I can.'

'It's customers I lack,' Hope replied sadly. 'With half the village believing I was having an affair with Peter while

Ralph was alive, and the rest too scared of Marjorie's tongue to declare their disagreement, no one will offer me work.'

'Somehow we'll have to make her retract – publicly.'

'What we need is a bit of gossip about Marjorie herself, and I can't imagine her doing anything risqué, can you?' Hope forced a laugh, 'This teapot needs replenishing,' and she disappeared into the kitchen.

Connie's first priority was work. She went to look at the advertisements in Stella's shop window, and then to talk to Betty.

'I just told them I wanted a job and asked them to let me know if they hear of anything. The trouble is, I have no qualifications and little experience,' she told Hope. 'But don't worry, I have the money for four weeks' rent so I won't be a burden.'

'I wasn't worrying,' Hope told her. 'Welcome you are, by me and by Davy. And even more by Geoff, I suspect!'

–

Marjorie spent several evenings cleaning up after the builders and making lists of what they needed to be told the following morning. The new windows were in place and she had polished them to perfection. The door surround had been replaced with one from a yard selling items rescued from bombed buildings. It had once graced the entrance to offices of a shipping firm and was extensively carved and moulded. Although it was ridiculously unsuitable for what was only a garden shed, once it was painted a sombre shade of green she thought Phillip would be impressed with its grandeur.

Within the elegant surround, a stable door was fitted, the top and bottom opening separately seemed a useful addition. Phillip could get extra air on sunny days and she could stand there sometimes, leaning on the lower half of the door, and watch while he worked.

In a corner of the now painted room was a sink. Near it was a door leading to a toilet, 'For those times when he's so inspired he can't break away from his work,' she had explained to the architect.

A brand new easel was set up, which she had bought from the wife of a man who hadn't return from the war. She had also bought a few pots and jars filled with brushes and a dozen or so frames from the same source. Saddened by comparing stories of their losses, they swore to become friends, but Marjorie didn't think they had much in common. Richard would have been something important, like a barrister or Member of Parliament, Ralph had been an accountant and Phillip was a highly regarded artist. The woman's husband had been a bus driver. Artistically talented or not, driving public transport was not something she could contemplate discussing in any depth.

When the final coat of paint had been applied and the floor given its scrub, and everything was in place, Marjorie called Freddy to have a look at it. 'Perfect. It's perfect, isn't it?' she asked, expecting fulsome praise for her achievements.

He hesitated, glancing at her, wondering how much to say. 'I hope he likes it, you can never tell with Phillip.'

'Of course he'll like it. In fact, we'll go and find him now and bring him back to show him. I can't wait another day.'

They knew where Phillip was living, although Freddy didn't know how he could afford the rent. Having finally been thrown out by Sally and Matthew, he had a room in the guest house of Elsie Clements, in a row of houses behind the post office. It was Elsie who opened the door.

'Hello, Mrs Williamson-Murton. Phillip is in his room. You haven't come with the money, have you? He did promise a week in advance.'

Freddy glared at Marjorie but she pretended not to notice.

Phillip appeared to be sketching a group of trees, something he had to hand in case he was in when his mother called. 'Mummy, and Dad, what a surprise. Shall we go to the pub? I can't get on to the paper what I'm seeing in my mind, I need a break.'

'Your mother has something to show you. Get your coat.' Freddy said peremptorily. 'Come on, before it's dark.'

Phillip gestured to Marjorie and mouthed, 'What's up with him?'

'Hurry. Phillip dear. I can't wait to show you.'

Being led around the back of the house, for a fleeting moment Phillip envisioned a car. Surely his father hadn't agreed to him having a car? He'd been hinting for ages but had been given little hope. Then his excitement grew when Marjorie almost ran to the door of the shed and opened the new stable door. A motorbike. It had to be a motorbike! Not as good as a car, but welcome all the same.

Marjorie put a hand inside and flicked on the bare bulb in the centre of the white-painted ceiling. She stared at him, waiting for the cry of excitement to fall from his lips. Freddy was watching his son too, but his expression was cynical and he hadn't expected to see joy.

Phillip's spirits plummeted as he saw the fitted studio, and he wanted to run outside and scream his disappointment to the darkening sky.

'Mummy, you've thought of everything,' he whispered, 'How generous you are.' He walked around, picking up the tools of a craft he didn't want to practice, laughing as he opened the door to the flush lavatory. 'Everything,' he repeated.

'Of course, you'll have to live at home, leave that dismal room. You'll need a place where you can relax after working.'

They closed the door and Phillip pulled himself out of his blighted hope and said all the things Marjorie wanted to hear. She replied in delighted tones, utterly content with the way her surprise had been received. Freddy said nothing.

Later that evening, Phillip went to the pub and asked about the man called Arthur. He offered to sell him the key to the shed-cum-studio and recommended it as a suitable place for squatters. 'There's even a flush lavatory,' he told a delighted Arthur Gleaner. 'My mother thought of everything, apart from the small detail of my not wanting it.'

He was laughing as he walked home, imagining Marjorie's face when she arrived home after her usual Saturday shopping trip to find Arthur and family happily ensconced in her dream. If she'd achieved nothing else, she had made sure that Arthur's next plea to the housing officer would be considered with more interest.

He couldn't stay home. Perhaps he would go back to Connie, at least for a while. Once the squatters arrived he wouldn't be quite so popular with dear Mummy. Pity, he'd have liked to stay and see her reaction.

He counted his money. Having left the job in the gallery, considering it boring, there wasn't very much. He wouldn't be able to pay Elsie Clements for the few days he had stayed. He would make a run for it and shame would force his parents to settle what he owed.

He would have enough, just, to get him back to Connie and buy her a 'sorry' present. He was confident he could talk her round. She'd look after him and he might even manage to be a school caretaker again, at least for a while. As long as Connie didn't talk about marriage.

He saw Hope the following morning and mentioned going back to see Connie. He was alarmed to learn that she was in Cwm Derw, living in Badgers Brook. He went at once to talk to her, persuade her to give their love a second chance, but came away disappointed.

It really was time he left. But where would he go? He began to feel afraid. He couldn't go on depending on his youth, charm and good looks. He was getting older but certainly no wiser. He went to a café and sat, sipping weak, lukewarm tea, and allowed himself to wallow in self-pity.

Thinking of some of the men with whom he had served he wondered why he hadn't settled back into civvy life like them. He'd seen sudden death, but so had many others. He remembered an evening out to celebrate Jeff's nineteenth birthday. They'd all been in such high spirits, Jeff, Bobbie Vincent, Patrick Murphy and himself, inseparable, promising never to lose touch. They had made such plans for when the war ended. Then on that day, while they were celebrating Jeff being nineteen, a sniper had killed them. All three. Only he had survived. Jeff Thomas had lived for two days, his face distorted with pain, and Phillip had watched as he died.

Perhaps that was why he lived only for the short term, he mused. Commitment, children, that was the road taken by fools, people who didn't understand how all their tomorrows could be snatched from them in a split second, at the speed of a bullet. But his tomorrows continued to come and they had to be filled, so what road was open to him? Where could he go from here?

Nine

During the night Marjorie was disturbed by sounds outside. She roused herself a little, reluctant to move, knowing how cold the bedroom was outside the warmth of the blankets and fleecy sheets. There was a shuffling movement and what she imagined to be stifled laughter. Sleepily, unwilling to force herself to complete wakefulness, she wondered vaguely what was happening. They were on the main road and even at this time of night people passed and voices were occasionally heard.

She had a sudden wild thought that perhaps Phillip had come home and had brought a woman with him, but that was impossible. Phillip wouldn't do such a thing. The disturbances faded and she relaxed back until the sounds had merged with her dreams.

As dawn broke she woke again to a sound she couldn't identify. Freddy snored gently beside her and above the repetitious hum she thought she could hear singing. The wireless couldn't be on, surely? Besides, there wouldn't be music at this hour. She reached for her dressing gown and, shivering in the icy chill of the early morning, went to the window.

The noise had ceased and she made a step towards the bed, enticed by the thought of another hour of warmth, but it began again and this time she identified it as children singing. From the window she could see nothing; the frost had hardened into complicated designs, fern-like and utterly beautiful, decorating the glass and excluding vision. But at this moment she wasn't aware of its loveliness: the intricate patterns simply reminded her of how low the temperature had fallen and how warm a return to bed would be.

Braving the cold she opened the window and looked out.

The sound was stronger but seemed to be coming not from the street, but from the back of the house. Definitely children singing, interspersed with a low masculine voice telling them to 'hush, now'.

'*Oh Johnny, Oh, Johnny how you can love…*'

'Freddy, wake up! Some awful people are singing, waking the neighbours. I know it's impossible but they seem to be in our garden. Freddy!' Her voice became more agitated as he didn't move. She prodded him until he shed the remnants of sleep and sat up staring blearily to where Marjorie now stood beside the open window. He reached for the light but she stopped him. In the gloom of the early dawn she held his hand away from the switch and hissed, 'Don't let them know we're awake. They're probably burglars.' She began to dress using her dressing gown like a tent, unwilling to lose its warmth. 'Well, go on, then. Go and tell them to go away. I'll wait and run to call the police if they don't do as you say.'

'Come on where? If you think I'm going outside before a cup of tea and at least two more layers of clothes you're mistaken. And shut that window.' She shut off the sound of 'Roll aht the barrel' with a loud bang. Freddy continued to sing, 'We'll have a barrel of fun.'

'Freddy. Really!' She tiptoed into the back room and looked through the window, which, with no one sleeping there, was less affected by the delicate artwork of the frost. Lights danced around the doorway of the shed, which she now called the studio. There were several children waving torches and singing. 'It ain't gonna rain no more no more, it ain't gonna rain no more.'

'They're Londoners,' Marjorie gasped. 'not even local people.'

Freddy laughed as he struggled into a jumper and trousers, then his dressing gown. 'Of course they aren't, Marjorie, it's the way the song should be sung.'

'They sound very common,' she retorted.

He went outside and in the light coming from the shed saw that it was full of people. At first he couldn't guess how many as they were all dancing around. When they saw him coming, they squealed and darted back inside, slamming the bottom of the stable door with a bang. A head peered over the top, taller than the rest, and a man's voice said, 'We aren't moving, we've taken over this wasted space until the council gives us a proper home, like we were promised.'

'Are you squatters?' Freddy asked, bemused.

'Yes, we are! And there's nothing you can say will make us leave. Not until we've got the home we were promised. Fought in the war I did, and three years on I still haven't a decent home for my family.'

'Would you like a cup of tea?'

Switching on the kitchen light. Freddy filled the kettle, and while it was heating he stepped outside and called, 'Cocoa for the children all right?'

'Thanks.' came grudgingly.

'Thanks, mister,' came from the giggling choristers. There were more squeals and laughter and they disappeared from sight and closed the top half of the door. It opened again almost immediately and one of them called, 'Morning, mister. Mam and Dad say we mustn't talk to you, but have you got any biscuits?'

Marjorie stood, hands on hips, outraged that Freddy hadn't chased them away. Chuckling, and ignoring Marjorie's protests, he delivered a bag into which he'd put the biscuits from the coronation souvenir tin.

'That James Fielding has something to answer for,' Marjorie muttered, 'encouraging riff-raff to invade people's private property.'

While Marjorie threatened, cajoled and threatened again, the singing continued periodically, and voices were heard talking and laughing. Some homemade paper chains, presumably Christmas trimmings, appeared around the window, and, when the door was briefly opened, more could be seen draped across the room. Whenever either Freddy or Marjorie went out, the stable door was slammed shut amid screams. It seemed as though Arthur and Catherine Gleaner and their brood were enjoying their squatters rights in Marjorie's shed-cum-studio, and were planning to celebrate Christmas there.

While Marjorie stormed off to do battle with the council's housing department, Freddy talked to their uninvited guests through the partially opened top half of the door. He learned that they had been living with Catherine Gleaner's mother and were finding it hard to keep their lively children as quiet as her mother demanded, and sharing kitchen and living space for so much of each day was leading to tension and quarrels between Arthur and his mother-in-law.

'Where did you get a key?' Freddy asked.

Arthur shook his head. 'Not telling you that. I don't want to get him in trouble,' he said. It was enough for Freddy to guess.

Freddy wondered whether he dare defy Marjorie's wishes and give his word not to exclude them if they took the children out for a little while. Confined to what was in reality only a small shed was going to be hard on them.

'I won't interfere with your arrangements, Mr Gleaner, but if you need to go out I'll see if I can find the spare key for you. If you have them both no one will be able to get in without your permission.'

'Thanks, Mr Murton.' Arthur said, offering a hand through the part-open door. 'You are a gent. Perhaps this afternoon we could leave a couple of the older ones and do some shopping.'

'Of course. I'll take Marjorie out if she doesn't agree. What the eye doesn't see, eh?' He went back into the kitchen and washed the cups, wondering what Marjorie was doing and how their son might be involved. He had said nothing to Marjorie, but there was no one who had access to the keys but Phillip.

In a room in Elsie Clements's house behind the post office, Phillip – who had been unable to resist waiting to see the fun – woke, remembered and smiled.

–

News of the squatters spread and many laughed; others hurried home to make sure they weren't vulnerable to the same fate. It was Betty Connors who told Hope,

235

who hurried around to her parents-in-law to help. The normally quiet house was in chaos. Police were there, and council officials, mostly carrying clipboards and notebooks into which they were scribbling profusely.

Brenda Morris, the district nurse, was there to ensure that the children weren't in any danger. Many local people had come simply to see the fun, and, amid it all, the Gleaner family stayed behind the locked door of the studio and sang and laughed and shouted defiance to all.

There was no possibility of them going shopping as they had planned with all this attention, and, in a quiet moment, Freddy asked what they needed and promised to do what he could and deliver it later that day. He wasn't sure why, but he was enjoying this as much as Arthur's children obviously were.

Hope found Marjorie in the living room, Freddy beside her. She was sobbing. 'A laughing stock, that's what we've become. How did they get a key? How did they know when we were out and they'd have time to carry in all their furniture?'

Freddy was almost certain that the willing helper had been Phillip, who probably thought it a joke. He didn't tell Marjorie; she wouldn't have believed him anyway.

'They can't have brought much, there isn't room,' Hope commented.

'People like that don't worry about a decently arranged room. Everything is thrown in so they can hardly move, from what I managed to see before the door was slammed in my face. Beds, chairs, and a huge roll of lino, blankets, pillows and clothes, all higgledy-piggledy. It seems they plan to stay,' Marjorie wailed. 'We'll have to move; I won't be able to face people after this.'

Throughout the day the crowds increased, with people coming to look and offer advice, many bringing food, all ignoring the fact they were invading Marjorie's garden. Marjorie stayed inside, the wireless turned up to blank out the voices and laughter and merriment.

Hope did the only thing she could: she made tea. Within moments of the kettle boiling, two women came into the kitchen laden with cups, saucers and packets of tea, sugar and milk. Who cared about rationing at a time like this? Next week they'd be a bit short, but that was hardly a novel situation. Cakes were found and cut into small pieces so everyone had a share. The party went on all day with Arthur, Catherine and their children opening the top of the door to join in the party atmosphere and shutting it the moment Marjorie or anyone with the stamp of authority appeared.

Hope stayed with Marjorie and said very little. A brief word with Freddy had told her who he thought was responsible and she grieved for the unhappy woman who had brought so much misery upon herself.

'They tell me that we can't do anything immediately.' Freddy said after several discussions with the police and others. 'It seems they'll have to stay until accommodation can be sorted. They had a number of the points needed for re-housing, but not enough; staying here will increase their chances.'

'Seventy points for not having hot water,' someone explained. 'Thirty points for no proper bathroom.'

'I think I'll do the same as that lot,' another said stoutly. 'Time we were out of the two miserable rooms we live in.'

'I'll have you know *that lot* weren't in miserable rooms, and I'll thump anyone who says they were,' an angry voice declared. 'And that includes my apology for a son-in-law, Arthur Gleaner!'

Arthur, who had been listening to the debate on how many points he had earned, darted for cover when he saw his mother-in-law approaching. Catherine's mother was large, overweight and dressed in a man's overcoat and boots. With hair apparently uncombed, and red in the face with anger, she looked like a boiler about to burst.

'Cup of tea?' someone offered, taking one of Marjorie's better cups from the dresser.

Marjorie took a deep breath, about to complain, but Hope began to laugh. 'This is better than a farce.' she said, choking on her words, pointing outside. Marjorie looked out to where Arthur's mother-in-law was trying to hit him, leaning through the top of the door with an umbrella, while Arthur shouted for her to stop and tried in vain to close it.

Some of the crowd cheered, others growled in disapproval and wrestled to remove the weapon from the angry woman's hand. Arthur managed to get hold of the point of the umbrella, and it went to and fro, in and out, as first one then the other gained strength. The ferule came off in Arthur's hand and the victor leaned in. But a man from the crowd dashed forward and tickled the woman in a place where no one should have dared, and she turned around and began hitting him instead of the hapless Arthur.

Freddy was outside trying to restore order. A couple of women had gone home for fresh supplies and Catherine's mother had turned to telling everyone who would listen how good and kind she had been to Arthur, how she had loved him as a son. She followed this by calling him a very long list of names without pausing or taking a breath, which increased Hope's and Marjorie's laughter even more.

When the angry woman had been consoled and the excitement had eased, Marjorie was still laughing and, as they exchanged glances, Hope realized this had been the first moment of shared emotion between them. Even in grief after Ralph's sad death they had been alone. This laughter must surely break down barriers?

Building on what had been achieved, Hope said softly, 'How marvellous of you to help them, Mother-in-law.'

Marjorie seemed about to argue but relaxed and nodded agreement.

'Everyone will be so impressed with your kindness,' Hope added later after listening to another round of argument and watching strangers preparing further cups of tea, while the curious still filled the kitchen.

'Kindness?' Marjorie said honestly. 'I don't feel kind! The house is filled with strangers I didn't invite and who have taken over my kitchen and are offering me cups of my tea!'

'Hope is right: if people think you arranged this to help a family in trouble, they'll admire you.' Freddy touched his wife's arm, stroked it, as though to soothe her. 'How many others can boast of helping a family find the home they deserve? The man's an ex-soldier, fighting for us in conditions we can only try to imagine, then coming home to find there is nowhere to live. Most condemn them, call them troublemakers, but you offered them a home.'

'But I have complained, called them troublemakers.'

'That only makes your generosity more admirable.'

'Father-in-law's right. Keeping your support a secret shows you didn't do it for praise.'

Marjorie went into the kitchen where a muddle of cups and plates met her. She began to complain, but what Hope and Freddy said made sense, she could become a local hero if she held her temper for a while. 'More tea, anyone?' she asked with a rather forced smile.

–

Phillip fingered the money Arthur Gleaner had given him for the key to the shed–cum–studio and made a decision. Cwm Derw no longer had anything to offer. He'd made a mistake coming home. He might have settled into a uneasy peace with his parents, safe in the knowledge that the house would be his one day, if he could persuade Hope to leave and forget any claims her son might have, but after the joke of the squatters had been turned around and made into a victory, his mother and Hope seemed to be reconciled.

Being spoiled by his mother would have been just bearable, but having to share the house with visits from Hope and three-year-old Davy wasn't something he would enjoy. No, it was time to move on. He went to see Connie.

–

Connie had been dreading seeing Phillip. When she had returned it was in the belief that he would have left, and it had been a shock to find him still there. She had settled into the room in Badgers Brook and had been offered a job in the bar of the Ship and Compass by the kindly Betty Connors, which she had accepted. She felt completely at home in the house, considered Hope a good friend, and the town was filled with friendly people. Her life was beginning to settle.

Geoff Tanner was very kind and often called to see if she was free to go out in the van, usually providing a few cakes bought from the bakery and a flask of coffee. She looked forward more and more to seeing his slightly hesitant approach, guessing his insecurity but unable to reassure him without being too presumptuous. Besides, memories of the hurt she had suffered, when Phillip had made it clear she wouldn't be a part of his future, were slow to fade.

She was cleaning the kitchen in Badgers Brook when there was a knock at the door. She opened it expecting to see Kitty. and her welcoming smile faded when Phillip pushed his way in.

'Hello, Phillip,' she said calmly.

'Darling Connie. How are you¿

'The name is Connie, just Connie. and I'm fine.'

'I feel so ashamed of the way I treated you.' he said, his voice tight with emotion. He walked up and down, the epitome of a man under stress. 'The truth is, Connie, I was frightened of how much I love you. I've never intended to be part of a life-long partnership. Marriage and all that was for others. Feeling so strongly about you, loving you so much, I had to get away, try and settle my feelings.'

'And now you have?' For a moment she was tempted. It would be all right. They would go back to the job they'd had before and work together and— Pulling herself up she shook her dark head. 'I needed time to consider too.'

'Of course you did. I can understand that. Marriage is a big step.'

'Marriage?'

'If that's what you want then I want it too.'

'I do want marriage, Phillip.' She watched his face as it struggled with the attempt to show pleasure. 'But not to you. Not any more. Any chances you and I might have had are long gone. I don't think you're the marrying kind.'

'But I am,' he protested. 'Just give me the chance and I'll prove it.'

'Loving, sharing, and caring for each other? That isn't something you're able to do. Go away, Phillip, find another fool, there are plenty out there. But now, at long last, I can say I'm not one of them.'

–

Phillip was whistling cheerfully as he waited for the train the following day. His father and his mother, unaware of the double transaction, had each given him money to start him in a new life. He had hugged them both and promised to keep in touch, and with a package of food for the train and an extra few shillings – again from each parent – for a meal when he arrived at his destination, he was on his way.

He had booked the short distance to Cardiff and there he planned to call on Matthew and Sally. Their children were at least old enough to be less of an intrusion if he stayed a while.

For the first stage of the journey he was alone in the carriage, and he read the *Daily Chronicle* and thought about what he would do next. At Dinas Powys a young woman got on and he moved along the seat as though the empty carriage didn't offer enough choice, and smiled at her. A quick glance showed a lack of wedding ring. The way she sat opposite him and crossed her rather lovely legs, the wide-eyed smile, tempted him into conversation.

'Going far?' he asked. Not exactly a scintillating start but she answered in a voice that was low and utterly charming.

'Only to Cardiff. And you?'

'I'm not really sure. Cardiff to begin, then the world is mine to take what I will.'

'Lucky you.'

'Not really,' he said, putting on his downtrodden-but-brave expression. 'Drawing a final line under a romance that a young woman thought would last for ever is very sad. And now I'm forced into leaving my home town, when Christmas is almost upon us, utterly alone, with hardly any money.'

He looked at her and the gloomy expression vanished as his handsome face broke out into a wide smile before he threw back his head and laughed. 'I really got your sympathy then, didn't I? Truth is, I'm free and I can do what I want and go wherever the fancy takes me.'

'I bet you're an actor,' she said.

'How did you guess?'

'Oh, I can always tell. An observer of human nature, I am.'

Lying, flirting, changing seats to sit together as other passengers joined them, they were like close friends by the time the train reached Cardiff. Phillip had extended the lie that he was an actor with stories of his time in ENSA during a fearsome war through to his turning down a top part in London's West End when his mother was taken ill. The girl said little, just widened her eyes in admiration of his bravery and talent.

Arm in arm they walked from the station to find something to eat. The packet of sandwiches his mother had provided was thrown into a waste bin. He had money, so why not spend it? Tomorrow would be a cause for worry when it came, and that was soon enough to be concerned.

Over a generous meal and several drinks, she told him her name was Ariadne and she was a stage designer.

'Oh, I see. That's how you recognized me being an actor?'

She thought he was a charming waster, but she didn't say anything, just smiled and gave a saucy wink.

After the meal and a walk in Sophia Gardens and along the river Taff, she led him to a tall house with peeling paint and a door that didn't close properly, with cardboard where there should have been glass. He followed her up the stairs, smiling blearily, to a room for which she apologized, describing it as a temporary flat. 'I'm off to London in a couple of weeks. Perhaps, if you really are footloose, you might come with me. With our connections in the world of theatre we can help each other, can't we?'

'That sounds a perfect plan.'

He woke up the following morning with a severe headache and for a moment couldn't remember where he was or how he got there. Then he thought of Ariadne, and his face, creased from heavy sleep on the lumpy pillow, opened into a smile. His hand slid to the other half of the bed, and when he found it empty he sat up and called. The room, a very dirty and shabby room, was empty.

Filled with cold dread and holding his aching head he slid out of bed to find his wallet missing and only the few pounds he had cautiously stuffed in his shoes still intact. When he roused himself and went downstairs the landlord stopped him and demanded the two weeks overdue rent for the room.

Hungry and humiliated, he hitchhiked to Matthew Charles's house.

'I'm sorry, Matthew,' Sally insisted, 'but Phillip isn't staying here. With only a few weeks to go before Christmas we'd be stuck with him. I don't want that.'

Matthew didn't want Phillip there either. He hoped that over the festive season he and Sally might repair some of the damage he'd inflicted on their marriage. His friend being there would make it more difficult. 'You're right and, to be truthful, I don't want him here either,' he admitted.

'I'll tell him if you like,' Sally offered. 'Or you tell him and blame me. I don't mind, just as long as he goes.'

'We'll both tell him, together. It's what we both want, isn't it? I want Christmas to be just you and the girls and me.'

–

Phillip borrowed a few pounds and walked to the main road, where he stood holding out a cardboard sign with 'London' written on it. He knew very few people in London and couldn't imagine any of them welcoming him as a visitor at this time at of year, but he was broke and alone, and might as well try there as anywhere else.

–

Connie enjoyed working in the Ship and Compass. Betty was patient as she taught her the running of the bar, and Connie was a willing pupil, anxious to please, always doing more than she was asked. When Hope was there cleaning she would arrive early and help her, sometimes by minding Davy, sometimes with the cleaning.

'Wonderful team we three make,' Betty told them. 'Pity you can't work in the bar, mind. Wasted you are, pretty little thing like you, washing floors and hiding your trim figure under a sacking apron.' Before she left that day, Betty asked what they were planning for Christmas Day.

'There'll only be the three of us for dinner, so why don't you join us?' Hope said on impulse, liking the idea as soon as it was spoken.

Betty was delighted and, having been assured that Hope really meant it, promised to provide a chicken and vegetables, which she would order from Peter.

'Wonderful! Four is a much nicer number than three.' Hope said, wondering at the same time whether she might invite Peter and Geoff to join them too. 'Badgers Brook is large enough for several more, and the house always likes being filled with people,' she told Connie whimsically.

'If you trust me to look after Davy, we could perhaps share the bar work?' Connie suggested to Hope one day.

'I don't think I'd be any good at it,' Hope admitted. 'Not confident enough, really. I'm most happy sitting in my own room sewing for people who only see the end product.' She hoped that now she and Marjorie were better friends work might become available once again.

It was the end of November and customers were slowly returning, wanting a dress for a dance, a party or a special occasion. Marjorie had let it be known that she had been misinformed about Hope and Peter, and that the friendship had not been the cause of his death.

Although wary of criticism and a revival of the rumours, Peter began calling on Hope again, making sure it was always at a time when Connie was there. Initially he kept his growing feelings for her to himself. The uneasy peace between Hope and Marjorie could so easily break down. But after a more passionate kiss, stolen in the garden, while Connie was in the house with Davy, he declared his burgeoning love.

Hope pulled away from him in distress. 'What am I doing, encouraging you.' she gasped. 'I'm sorry, Peter, but I could never risk loving anyone again.'

'But why? Is it because I have so little to offer? I love you, and I adore Davy. I'll look after you both and do everything I can to make you both happy.'

'It isn't possible, and not because you aren't rich, Peter. Money isn't the reason.' But she refused to tell him what was. How could she explain her fears? That she had driven one man to suicide and was afraid she would do the same thing again. She was a determined woman, too strong minded, and a man needed a partner, not someone who forced him into doing things that made him unhappy to the point of desperation.

Tentatively Peter extracted a promise that when more time had passed and people began to forget what had happened, they would meet more openly, show the town how their love was growing. But he had the feeling that her idea of time passing would be a lot longer than his own.

-

The squatters were removed from Marjorie's studio after only a week spent providing entertainment for the town. The day they left was an excuse for more excitement, and people called with a few sweets and small gifts and the makings of tea to wish them luck in their new three-bedroom house. Many were still amused that it was the stiff, haughty Marjorie who had been involved in the plight of the squatters and were surprised to find her changed and on better terms with her much-maligned daughter-in-law.

Marjorie looked at the empty shed, now eerily silent, and wondered why she had bothered to make it into a studio. It had been far better used as a temporary home for Catherine and Arthur and their children. She began to wish another family would arrive and make the place into a home. She knew now that it would never have been the scene of inspired works of art. Although perhaps she could advertise it as a studio and give someone else's son a chance to succeed?

'What d'you think, Freddy?' she asked as they sat eating their toast and scrambled dried egg supper in the cold dining room.

'I think we should move. This house is too big for us and it makes sense to find something smaller.'

'But what if Phillip comes home?'

'He doesn't want three bedrooms, does he?'

Reluctantly Marjorie agreed. 'Not straight away, though, Freddy. I'll need the winter to sort out what we need to take and what we can throw away.'

'Then we'll make a start, shall we? I'll sort out the garden shed and the garage, and you can deal with the bedrooms.'

'We'll leave the studio as it is for a while, shall we?'

'Someone might be pleased to have a studio as part of the house,' he said, patting her arm affectionately.

On the principle of worst first, Marjorie began in the room that had been Richard and Phillip's. Since Richard's death at the end of the war she had refused to look at his room. All his childhood was represented there: old boxed games, various sports equipment, a recorder, a violin. She felt a momentary shame when she remembered how she had insisted on him taking part in everything the school offered.

Opening the door to a room she had previously entered only to clean was different on that day. The intention to begin to tear it apart made her feel like a murderer: she was going to kill all the memories the place held.

'Think of it as an exciting Christmas for Davy,' Freddy said, aware of her agony as well as his own. 'There are bound to be lots of things he would love, and many more that Hope can put aside for him for later on.'

Early in December, Marjorie began. Hayward's grocery shop provided boxes and she neatly labelled them Charity, David, Discard and Retain. She spent a long time preparing, unwilling to begin.

Freddy went up there one morning and found her sitting on the bed staring at a book of photographs. He took it gently from her. 'In the Retain pile I think, don't you?'

Emptying drawers was easy, and she put the clothes in the Charity box, ready to offer for distribution among the needy. Warm jumpers, an overcoat and shoes would go to the collection for vagrants, although she didn't really approve of these people who were unable to make the effort to sort out their lives. Then a voice inside reminded her that these men were other women's sons. Many, having suffered terribly during the war, still wandered the country confused and wounded, having lost touch with their families or learned of their deaths. She added two new jumpers and a good quality overcoat to the pile instead of putting them aside in the futile hope of Phillip returning and needing them.

Many of the toys she asked Freddy to take to Arthur and Catherine, *her* squatters, in their new home. She showed them to Hope, who happily agreed, delighted at the changes in her difficult mother-in-law.

It was Geoff and his van who delivered the surprising amount of unwanted items, and he added a few things from his own over-large, over-filled property. Connie helped him choose items he didn't need, and a growing affection between them was strengthened by sharing the simple task.

–

Christmas was going to be a problem for Peter Bevan. He had invited his father and his stepmother to spend it with him, with the willing agreement of his landlady, but the thought didn't fill him with the joy of the season. And with his landlady's family as well there wasn't really enough room. When he mentioned his dilemma to Geoff and Connie, Geoff at once suggested they all come to the room above the shop. He wished he could invite Connie there as his guest, three men and one woman wasn't ideal, and an extra person would ease the strain for Peter of dealing with his quick-tempered father.

'I know I can't ask you to join us. It would be such a cheek, inviting you for the purpose of helping me cope with Peter's dad,' he said as they walked home from the pictures one evening, cuddling together for warmth. 'But you'll have a happy time with Hope and Davy, and I gather that Marjorie has mellowed towards them too.'

Then Hope and Connie met Stella at her country cottage, and their discussion resulted in Geoff, Peter and his parents being invited to join the rest at Badgers Brook.

Everywhere these discussions were going on: who to invite and how to get out of an arrangement unwillingly made. Marjorie hoped that Phillip would appear and prepared, as much as rations allowed, for an extra place. She wanted to ask Hope and Connie and David, but, unsure of acceptance, unable to risk a rebuff, she did not. Instead, she waited, wondering whether she and Freddy would be asked to Badgers Brook, but so far, although she and Hope were more relaxed with each other, nothing had been said. Meanwhile she went on slowly and systematically emptying the bedroom.

–

Phillip was in London, working in a shop selling poorly made toys to objectionable children and hating it, staying in a basement flat that smelled of cats and stale cabbage. His days were spent forcing smiles for ghastly children and the life was far from what he had dreamed of, but there didn't seem anywhere else to go. North Wales, with the caretaker's job and Connie, was no longer a possibility. Although he did sometimes wonder whether she could be persuaded to change her mind.

He was a little embarrassed at his over-confident attitude in believing he could become rich by painting pictures for those he referred to as 'idiots who pretended to like art'. Who was the idiot now? It was a sour memory. He was sour.

His only enjoyment was flirting with some of the mothers who brought their brats in to look at what was available for their list to Santa. So when a tall, elegant woman came in near closing time, with a child that was evidently not hers – from the look of boredom on her face, the way she moved away from sticky fingers out of concern for her clothes and the refusal to hold an offered hand – his spirits rose. At least it would be a couple of minutes of amusement.

'Playing auntie for the day?' he asked, nodding towards the little boy, who was climbing into a wooden cart, pushing aside the notice asking mothers to stop their children from doing so!

'Heaven forbid! I have him for one hour only while his mother goes to buy some wonderful surprise for him. Ten minutes and I'm already at the end of my tether. Really, I don't know how my friend manages all day, every day.' Her voice was melodious and suggested wealth and education. Her clothes, hair and make-up were immaculate; even the way she walked and looked around her with a slightly disdainful expression told him she was way above his usual expectations, but he knew he had a certain charm and he used it.

'I can take you to a place I know where we can get a quiet drink if that would help,' he offered, as he wrapped a box of dominoes for another rather distraught customer.

'Don't be ridiculous. I don't know you!'

'I'm Phillip Murton, a failed artist, so now you know me, will you come?'

If he expected her to gasp with amazement and tell him how impressed she was to meet a real artist, he was seriously mistaken.

'A failed artist. How sad. Another with no talent, persuading himself everyone else was wrong, I suppose.'

Phillip laughed delightedly. 'Exactly. The worst was trying to persuade my mother I am completely lacking in the stuff.'

'Oh, mothers. Mine wanted me to become a teacher.'

'And did she succeed?'

'Heavens no. I own an exclusive shoe shop. You know the sort of thing, only three shoes in the window and no enthusiasm to show a customer more than two pairs. I do hate seeing people maul my stock.'

'A drink?' He was trying not to laugh; she really did promise fun.

She stared at him for a moment then nodded. 'Why not?'

Two hours later, replete and talking like old friends, she asked Phillip where he would be for Christmas.

'Parents, duty, I suppose,' he replied vaguely.

'Oh, duty, that old thing. Why not come to Norfolk with me?'

'Cold weather for Norfolk.'

'Not indoors it isn't.' She stared at him, an eyebrow lifted in amusement. 'Surely you weren't thinking of rowing boats and mud and rivers and things?'

'I'm thinking of a few days of utter enjoyment, with you,' he replied.

–

When Hope came to help sort out the bedroom that had belonged to Ralph's brother she found some diaries hidden in a sports bag, under some ancient football equipment: exercise books, filled with neat, small writing. Afraid of upsetting Marjorie, Hope waited until she could tell Freddy.

'Thanks, Hope, you're a thoughtful young woman. There might be things in here she'd hate to learn.' When Hope looked curious he smiled. 'Nothing criminal, but boys like to have their secrets and some might upset

Marjorie. Best I glance through them and then dispose of them, eh?'

Unfortunately, there were others, and these were found by Marjorie when she emptied a box of playing cards, old jigsaw puzzles missing half their pieces, and other useless games. It was as she tipped these straight into the box marked "Discard" that the books fell out. Three exercise books in Richard's easily recognized writing. She sat on the stripped metal bedstead with its rolled-up mattress and began to read.

–

Stella was in the allotment shed, watching as Colin picked a bowlful of Brussels sprouts. He was breathing out clouds of mist in the cold air, and as she watched she realized he was singing. She smiled and turned up the flame under the paraffin heater to persuade the kettle to boil a bit faster. A happy man, my Colin, she thought as he began grabbing the dead remnants of weeds and throwing them on to the compost heap.

There had been a layer of white frost that morning, almost like snow. Wonderful if there was snow in time for the children to wake and find the treasures left by Father Christmas, she mused. She had bought a new shirt for Colin and a pair of slippers to replace the ones he had worn almost into oblivion. Nothing exciting, but, then, we aren't exciting people. Just happy ones, she thought. 'Colin, love, tea's about to be poured.' He waved and threw the last withered sow thistle into the waste from which goodness would come again in the spring.

He sat in the chair next to hers, and, unwilling to close the door against the scene of orderliness that was their plot, they sat wrapped in blankets, and sipped in silence.

Hearing someone approach, Stella made a face. 'Now who is it? Three lots of visitors I've had this afternoon, in this weather, too. Lucky I brought extra milk.'

Marjorie knocked on the door and pulled it open, 'Stella, I have to talk to someone or I'll burst.'

'Whatever is it, Marj? You look awful.'

Marjorie was so distressed she didn't notice the objectionable abbreviation of her name. Stella gave an apologetic look at Colin, who stood and excused himself on the grounds of having to finish clearing before dark; and went outside.

Without preamble Marjorie handed Stella one of the exercise books, her thumb marking a place from where she should begin reading. It was a long piece, written by Richard and describing how he and someone called Barbara had celebrated their engagement with a party given by Barbara's family and many of their friends.

'Does this mean he was engaged to be married and couldn't tell me? It can't be true, can it, Stella?'

'Never! Fantasy, that's all this is, Marjorie. A story made up to amuse himself. What are you worrying about?'

'I'm worried because I believe it's true. I know how close he and Barbara Griffiths were, and how I forbade him to see her. Engaged, and without telling me or his father. That's what I drove them to, Stella.'

Stella stared; she didn't know what to say. She knew it was true. She and Colin had been among the friends invited to the celebration. Richard and Barbara had planned to tell his parents on his next leave, when they intended to book a register office wedding, but Richard had never returned. She had seen Barbara since and had tried to persuade her to go and talk to Richard's family but she had refused.

'Drink this tea, Marjorie, Colin didn't touch it. Sugar in it, too. Good for shock that is.'

Ten

It was a few days before Hope heard the news of the trag-
ically aborted wedding plans of Ralph's brother Richard.
Marjorie had shown the diary to Freddy and it was he who
explained to Hope about the surprising revelation.

They sat in the kitchen of Badgers Brook and drank tea
while Davy concentrated on drawing something he insisted
was Uncle Peter's horse, Jason, but which appeared to have
five legs, all in a row. One, he explained with patience, was
his tail. Hope didn't know what to say to Freddy so she said
nothing, just watched her son's chubby hands gripping the
crayons and scrubbing colour over the paper.

'So there it is,' Freddy said. 'Confirmation that Richard,
our first-born, couldn't even tell us something as important
as his marriage plans. We failed him, Hope, both Marjorie
and me.'

She tried to offer comforting words then, but Freddy
shook his head. 'If Marjorie hadn't found the diaries we'd
never have known.'

'And Barbara? She hasn't been to see you?'

'Not since the funeral. She came then with her parents
and some of his friends, but there was nothing to suggest
he was anything more than a member of the group. Not a
word.'

'Will you go and see her, now you know?'

'I don't even know where she is. The family moved away soon after the war ended. To live near a relation, an uncle who ran a clothing factory in East London I believe. We've lost touch. She might be married and she almost certainly wouldn't want me turning up after all this time and stirring things up.'

'Are there more diaries? Richard might have left a few more clues. They must have ended soon after his writing about the engagement party, but they would have stretched back a while: the proposal, choosing and buying the ring. He might have written something about her family, something that will help you to find her.'

Freddy stared at her as though she had given him a shock.

'What is it? Have you thought of something important?'

'I have to go. I have to read the diaries, search to make sure Marjorie doesn't read in the others something that might upset her even more.'

Hope nodded and handed him his coat as he stood to leave. He was agitated and Hope was alarmed; his skin was deathly pale and his face had sort of collapsed, the skin loosened, the jaw slack. He was suddenly older, as though the shock of receiving news from his dead son had added on several years. He hurried from the house and didn't look back, as he usually did, to wave to Davy from the gate.

Hope was curious but decided it was simply that he didn't want Marjorie to suffer more misery by reading the build-up to Richard's falling in love and his plans for their future.

Momentarily she compared the reaction to Richard's death and the continuing grief Marjorie displayed for both of her lost sons to the way she had treated her and Davy since Ralph's suicide. Hope hadn't been allowed the luxury of grieving, Marjorie had wanted it all. Being able to blame her for Ralph choosing to die had helped Marjorie to cope, and she had offered little sympathy to her widowed daughter-in-law during that terrible time, only hostility and rejection. Then Hope felt ashamed of her selfish thoughts and hoped they would find Barbara, and be comforted by sharing her sweet memories of Richard and adding them to their own.

–

Freddy hurried home and went at once to the room that had been Richard's and Phillip's. It was almost bare of anything that offered a hint of the lives that had been lived there. Just a couple of beds, with mattresses rolled and tied, and cupboards with doors hanging open to reveal bare shelves. The wardrobe door was ajar and he touched it open to see the empty space within. A waft of lavender polish teased his nose and be guessed that Marjorie had been cleaning everything preparatory to the move.

His heart was racing as he lifted the pile of books from the top of the chest of drawers and thumbed through them. No sign of the diaries. Perhaps Marjorie had already found them, and was at this moment reading things he'd prefer she never found out. He pulled the drawers from their slots and looked behind them; diaries were intended to be secret and Richard might have hidden some of them. But where?

Later he dared to ask his wife if she had found any more.

'No, and I don't expect to. I think he started writing what was little more than a journal after he and Barbara decided to marry. A romantic gesture, that's all.'

Freddy hoped she was right. 'If you do find more, please let me see them first,' he said. 'I don't want you upset any more than necessary.'

'I can cope. He was my son!'

'We'd be better coping with them together. Please, Marjorie, promise me you'll wait until I can look at them.'

'There won't be any more. I've emptied the room, thrown away his childhood!' She glared at a corner of the room, her face stiffened with resolve, defying tears to fall. 'I'd have found them if they were there.' She hadn't promised to wait for him to share any revelations. And there was still the spare room to be emptied.

—

Phillip and Fiona shared her small flat in Chelsea, London. He continued to work in the toy store and she went each day to her small exclusive shop in a corner of Mayfair. Once his meagre wages were spent, she gave him money so he could pay, and they went out to dine every evening, often before and sometimes after the theatre. The restaurants where they ate were always very expensive and he frequently saw people from the world of show business seated near them. They also met some of Fiona's friends and occasionally went out as a foursome with another couple. Phillip had the impression she was testing him, finding out if he could play the role she had given him, of wealthy man-about-town with moneyed background. He fell into the part with ease; his manner with waiters, doormen and other people put there to smooth their way was firm but gentlemanly and he knew she was impressed.

On one occasion six of them went to the theatre and for supper afterwards. At the end of the evening the three men settled the enormous bill and Phillip paid his share without demur. It was easy when it wasn't his money he was spending. He felt a long way from Ty Mawr, his parents and their neighbours, whom he hoped never to see again.

The nights when they slept in each other's arms were sheer joy and Phillip looked no further ahead, just lived for the moment. It was bound to end soon, he knew that and was half prepared for dismissal every time she came home from her business and greeted him with a kiss. It would be cold and abrupt, he was certain of that. He would be dismissed like a servant who no longer suited, and he daily tried to sense from the kiss whether it held a promise of more to come or signalled the end.

One day when she seemed a little preoccupied and he was more or less convinced she would tell him goodbye, she produced first-class train tickets and bookings for an hotel just outside Norwich. She also gave him money to buy new clothes, and explained what he would need for the several days they would spend there. She went with him to the exclusive menswear department and seemed pleased at his expensive choices.

Against all the odds, his immediate future was showing promise and, whatever happened in the New Year of 1949, this Christmas would be remembered as one of the high-lights of his scrappy life. Christmas Day was a Saturday and they were booked into the hotel from Thursday the twenty-third until the following Tuesday.

Phillip was a successful salesman, partly because he was handsome, immaculately turned out and well spoken, and also because flirting with young, wealthy mothers came as naturally to him as breathing. Pretending to adore the obnoxious infants who tore around the store causing irritation and creating noise was not quite as easy, but the thought of the commission, which represented an evening out with Fiona, made him hold his temper, even when he was hurt by toys being hurled at him and tricycles being driven over his feet. He would smile, wink at the distraught parent and whisper some flattering remark – 'Shows a lot of character, doesn't he?' Or, 'Extremely strong-minded, he'll go far' – wishing he could send the little monster into orbit with the toe of his well-polished shoe.

–

Sally hadn't heard from Matthew for over a week. Having a telephone in the house because of his business meant it was easy for him to keep in touch. But he rarely did. She had given up trying to contact him. She knew from experience that he was rarely where he said he would be, and having to ask his company office if they could find him was a shame and embarrassment with which she could no longer cope. Christmas was only a few weeks away and surely he'd turn up for that.

Tonight was the performance of *The Lost Children*, a seasonal story about a missing child being found by a donkey. Megan and Olwen were part of a group of dancers who appeared twice. The producers had borrowed a real donkey to come on stage at the end, and Twm would be led in by her daughters. The longing for their father to see them perform was heartbreaking, and Sally didn't think for a moment that Matthew would be there to take the seat booked in his name.

At six o'clock, leaving the girls with her parents, she went to the hall where the performance was to take place and began to help with the last-minute preparations. This would be the third and final performance. Everyone in the cast or involved in the many backstage activities had seen their families in the audience. Everyone except her. She was taking the leading role, of the shepherdess, their daughters had the exciting task of leading on the donkey at the end, and Matthew couldn't be bothered to come.

He had never supported either her or the children. Never appeared at sports day or school concerts, nor was he one of the proud fathers who went to the school to admire work on display. So she was used to being the odd one out; the woman whom new acquaintances presumed to be a widow. Why was this time any different? This time, when she played the lead and their daughters were a part of the finale, why was she coldly, calmly determined that she would make excuses for him for the very last time?

The local people supported their efforts so it wasn't a surprise to see that the hall was full, and Matthew's seat embarrassingly empty. At the last minute she allowed the seat to be filled by someone else. The story ended with a lost child being found and brought home, guided by Twm, the patient donkey. Sally's two girls walked one each side of the boy and the donkey, at the head of a procession. The roar and applause of the audience didn't faze the animal at all. He had taken part in many local events and seemed to enjoy the attention. The owner's only fear, that, typically, Twm might refuse to move, was averted by treats, and all went according to plan.

The celebratory party after the final performance was something Sally always dreaded, feeling the absence of a man at her side, being a single person among so many couples. There were several other people without a partner, but they were always alone because they had no one. Her husband had chosen not to appear.

She had always made the same excuses to her friends: he was tied up with work, too far away to break his journey, might miss appointments with valuable customers, excuses that no one believed. There would be a blankness on their faces; they would be lost for words, sympathy in their eyes, which she hated. This time she didn't mind at all.

The girls, who had been invited to stay and enjoy the party with her for the first time, were given lemonade and biscuits and flattery. She gloried in their success and walked proudly among her friends, smiling and not regretting Matthew's absence for a moment. For the next few years she would have her daughters to enjoy and, after that, when they had gone out into the world, she would find something else to fill her life, her need for Matthew nothing more than a sad memory.

–

Hope was surprised to receive a visit from Marjorie early one morning as she and Joyce sat sewing buttons on to the delicate material of evening dresses in the kitchen of Badgers Brook.

'You'll have to come and help me,' she announced as she walked in. 'Someone is interested in the house and I have to make sure everything is orderly. The boxes we've packed are going into store and Freddy can't manage on his own.'

Hope turned to Davy and beckoned to him. 'Come and say hello to Grandmother, Davy.' She said it pointedly, reminding Marjorie that he was there and expected a greeting, however brief.

'Hello, David. How are you?' She turned at once to Hope. 'Well, how soon can you come?'

'Tea, Mother-in-law?'

'There isn't time. That... horse-and-cart vegetable man, Peter, is helping. Geoff has his van, and your father-in-law is driving a neighbour's car. The viewing is at two o'clock and we don't want them to see the place looking like a shunting yard at the station.'

'Shunting?' Davy picked up on the word. 'Is Grandfather taking me to see the trains?'

'Don't interrupt, child. Now, I'll hurry back and expect you to follow.'

'No, I can't.' Hope's heart was in her mouth but she tightened her lips adamantly. 'These dresses are promised for this evening and Joyce can't manage to do them on her own. There are dozens of buttonholes to neaten as well as buttons to make. Joyce is actually making some, crocheting them out of matching cotton. I'll help another time, but I can't let people down, not now when the business is just recovering from – from the setback I suffered.'

'Very well. I'll find someone else. It won't be that difficult.' If there was a moment's guilt at the reminder of her behaviour, which had all but destroyed the business, it didn't show. Still bristling with irritation at her demands not being met, she left as rapidly as she had come.

Joyce gave a relieved sigh. 'That was hard to do, but thanks, Hope. I daren't think how we'd have pacified the Davies sisters if they didn't have their new dance dresses. And we'd never be forgiven by Mrs Amby if her outfit was delayed. Going to a christening, she is, on the early bus tomorrow, and she wants to be the smartest one there.'

'She will be,' Hope promised. She put the kettle on for tea, needing a few minutes to calm herself before getting back to the intricate stitching.

Once the day's work was completed, Joyce stayed to clear up and prepare for the following day, when there would be several more orders to fulfil, and Hope dressed herself and Davy warmly and set off on the bus to see if there was anything she could do for Marjorie and Freddy. The viewers would be long gone but she would feel slightly less guilty if she turned up, even though it was too late to help impress the prospective buyers.

It was raining, water dripping from the branches of the bare trees as they walked to the bus stop, the once beautiful grass losing its colour, sodden, collapsed and lying like a drab carpet on the verges. The wood on the opposite side of the lane looked uninviting, alien, making it difficult to remember warm sunny days and walks to where the badgers lived. The chuckling stream – which gave life to so many animals and birds – could now be heard, fast flowing and turbulent.

The bus was full, smelling of wet mackintoshes, with people going into town before the shops closed to search for treats and additions to the store cupboard, where a horde of luxuries was secretly waiting for the magic that was Christmas. Davy was surrounded by chattering voices asking if he had written to Father Christmas and whether he wanted a book or a toy as his present. He explained that he hadn't asked for anything but would wait for a surprise. Kitty was on the bus and she gave him a penny, which he clutched in his hand and discussed with others as to the best way to spend it.

When they arrived at Ty Mawr, Hope heard Marjorie and Freddy arguing before she reached the back door. Marjorie's rapid soprano complaints rose in counterpoint to Freddy's slow bass explanations. 'Both talking, neither listening,' she muttered to Davy, as she knocked on the open door and walked in.

'Mind your feet, I've washed this floor twice today already because of his carelessness!'

'Sorry, Mother-in-law, but it's either footprints or we go straight home. We can't stand out in this rain.' Since Ralph's death she had never given in to Marjorie's bullying and never would.

She turned to Freddy and asked, 'Did they like the house?'

'They want to move in immediately after Christmas. It's all such a rush. We only decided to sell a few weeks ago, and now we're having to find somewhere quickly or end up in an hotel.' He was looking at her as he spoke, a straight, unwavering questioning look, and she nodded.

'You can stay with us for a little while, Mother-in-law, just until you find a house you like.'

Marjorie nodded and muttered a cursory 'Thank you', spoiling even that by adding, 'We might be desperate for a short respite.'

'You'll have to put your furniture in store, of course. I can't take that as well; I need a work room and Connie has one bedroom.' She thought then that Connie might not like having to share a home with Phillip's parents and perhaps, as it was the festive season, accept his visits too. 'I'll have to check with Geoff first, mind, and Connie, of course, make sure she doesn't object. And you will tell Phillip that there isn't room for him to stay, won't you?'

If Marjorie thought of arguing she rapidly changed her mind. They needed a place to stay and it seemed unlikely that Phillip would be around. 'He might be home for Christmas,' she said with little hope.

'That's all right, you'll still be at Ty Mawr then.'

'We were hoping that we could share at least Christmas Day with you and Davy,' Freddy said. 'Everything packed away, it won't be very festive here.'

'Of course, but not Phillip. I'm sorry.'

Freddy shrugged. 'He's found a "friend" and will be in Norfolk, I understand.'

'You didn't tell me,' Marjorie complained.

'He wrote and asked me to tell you.'

'When did he write? Why didn't I see the letter?'

Leaving them to continue their argument in the comfortless house surrounded by boxes and with a fire that seemed incapable of warming the almost empty, abandoned room, Hope and Davy walked back to the bus stop and home. Kitty and Bob had called, leaving some logs and kindling. The fire burst into life at the first lift with the poker, and Hope looked around her and wallowed in the luxury of a home where she felt contented and secure.

The house was so much her own place, its silent but strongly felt welcome entering her very being and warming her with its feeling of peace. She was soothed by its atmosphere of security and couldn't imagine living anywhere else. In spite of the tragedy in her recent past, she was aware of being very happy.

It was daunting to realize that Marjorie would soon be adding her own special brand of supercilious disapproval to what should be a very joyous occasion, but there was nothing she could do about it. Christmas might weave its miracle around her, but somehow that possibility was in serious doubt.

When she next saw Marjorie it was as Peter was giving them a lift home on his cart. Davy was sitting beside him, holding the reins, Peter's protective hands over the child's small ones. Hope was on the cart, sitting on a box and surrounded with parcels of shopping. Slipping from one carrier bag was an assortment of vegetables, which she was trying to confine. Laughter filled the air as she groped with handfuls of carrots and potatoes and sprouts, all determined to escape. Hope heard her call and turned as a red-faced Marjorie approached the side of the cart with clear disapproval.

'Hope, will you stop a moment! I'm not chasing you all the way through the main road!'

'Why doesn't she ever speak without a growl in her voice,' Peter whispered as he and Davy called to the horse to 'Whoa, Jason.'

'There are a few things we need to bring over for the few days of Christmas. Will you bring Davy's pushchair so we can manage them?'

'I can collect them tomorrow if you like,' Peter offered as she drew closer.

She looked around as though he had made an improper suggestion. 'Thank you, but no, I don't want my valuables paraded through the street on a horse and cart.'

'Sorry, Mother-in-law, but I've given Davy's pushchair away.'

'Mummy, I want my pushchair,' Davy began to wail. 'I nee-e-d it.'

Peter suggested a taxi and, with a time arranged and Hope promising to book it, Marjorie left them.

'See what it's going to be like?' Hope whispered. 'For the first time in my life I'm dreading Christmas.'

'Don't do that. Just make sure there are plenty of people there,'

'Dilute her you mean?' She laughed and he joined in. 'That would be a useful trick!'

–

Sally was not looking forward to Christmas. She had made up her mind to tell Matthew their marriage was over. She had spent many sleepless nights contemplating this, but every time, until now, she had admitted that she loved him still and that the time they were together was happy. Now she faced up to the truth and told herself that the hours they were together were fewer than any other couple she knew. Everything she did, she did alone, while Matthew also sought other company for enjoyment and relaxation.

The house was her father's, some of the money needed to run it was also from him. Why had she been pretending for all this time that everything was fine?

She began the distressing task of sorting out his clothes and putting them in piles so he could choose what he wanted to take and what to discard, unaware that in Ty Mawr Marjorie was doing something similar for Phillip. She thought about Phillip and wondered whether, if he and Matthew had not remained friends, either one or the other might have settled more easily into civvy street. They seemed to encourage each other in ways that harmed them both. If only Phillip would stay away from them, even now there might be a way back. She went on sorting out the piles of clothes and daydreamed of a happy ending, wondering vaguely where Phillip had gone after they had asked him to leave.

–

In London, Phillip was dressing ready to take Fiona out for a meal. He heard the outside door of the flat open and close and, lacking a shirt, he went into the living room and held out his arms to greet her the moment she walked through from the hall. To his surprise she didn't run to him for that first kiss, but leaned against the back of the door and stared at him, her face pale, her eyes troubled.

'Darling, what is it? Have you had a bad day? Come, let me make it better.' As he stepped towards her she turned from him and went into the bedroom. Throwing her handbag, coat and hat on to the bed, she allowed her shoulders to droop and stood with her back to him in silence. This was it, he thought with the beginnings of alarm. This was when she told him they were finished. 'Darling, whatever is it? Have you had bad news?'

'The worst possible news. I am expecting a child.'

'But, you can't be. We've been so careful… and there hasn't been time, and… Don't worry, there has to have been a mistake.'

She turned slowly, raising her eyes to his. 'No mistake. And how much time d'you think it takes? You've been careless, Phillip. Utterly, inexcusably careless, and now we're landed with a child neither of us wants. You'll have to marry me. I'm not bearing all of this on my own.'

That night Phillip couldn't sleep. While Fiona breathed softly beside him, her face serene and untroubled, he began to work things out. Leaving the bed, he reached for a dressing gown bought for him by Fiona and, snuggled in its luxurious warmth, sat looking out of the windows. He'd been here a little over three weeks. Surely there wasn't time to conceive a child and know with any certainty, was there?

He remembered Matthew telling him that Sally's first child had been born just under nine months after her first wedding, and that had raised a few eyebrows, but 'honeymoon babies' were rare. Slowly, as dawn began to make silhouettes of some of London's buildings through the windows of the elegant flat, the truth began to dawn too.

He woke her with tea and toast, which they ate in bed, then, after a loving interlude in which Phillip was kind and concerned and reassuring, she left for work, his declaration of life-long commitment ringing in her ears. Phillip stared at the back of the door through which she had gone, walking backwards, blowing kisses to him in a very Fiona-like manner.

He had fondled her more knowingly the previous night, and realized that her slender body was already slightly swollen, something he hadn't been aware of until that day. His suspicions grew, although he intended to keep them from her. As the street door closed behind her he telephoned Matthew. A brief conversation and he was convinced that he had been duped. Fiona had found herself in a tricky situation and had chosen him to play the father for her unborn child.

He was amused and not a little flattered, as he realized he'd been put through a series of tests to decide his suitability. The highly expensive restaurants. The theatre visits and the intellectual discussions that followed. Meeting her rich friends and joining in with the fantasy that he was an artist who had suffered a setback because of his terrible wartime experiences.

'Don't be tempted,' Matthew warned as Phillip told him of his recent social life. 'She's wealthy but that doesn't mean you'll share it. You'll be discarded once you've made the child legal – or even before. She needs a father, and if you leave before the child is born you'll be a cad she'll have sympathy and support. Fiona isn't likely to be a gateway into a life of ease.'

Matthew convinced him. It was undoubtedly time to leave. Although, he mused, he might as well enjoy Christmas in Norfolk first.

'When you're in the area, will you tell my parents that I won't be home for the festivities.' he asked during a second phone conversation. 'Call it pressure of work, a touch of flu, whatever you fancy. Your wife isn't the only actor in the family, is she?' he said with a laugh.

–

The approach of Christmas was a confusion of Hope's plans and Marjorie's determination to do everything the way she considered proper. Nothing pleased her. The decorations were too gaudy, the tree so large it was vulgar. She straightened cushions, moved ornaments and generally made everyone nervous. When Christmas day dawned Hope and Connie were exhausted.

Davy awoke early and throughout the morning was happily unaware of the continuing disapproval, enjoying the gifts so lavishly presented by a constant stream of morning visitors. Kitty and Bob came and brought flowers, wine and a homemade garage for Davy's growing collection of cars. Betty Connors, who seemed surprised to see Freddy there, called with a painting book and a box of paints, but made the excuse of a headache and didn't stay for lunch as arranged.

Stella and Colin brought vegetables and a box of plasticine. Joyce came with her mother, having been invited to stay for lunch, as were Peter and his parents and Geoff. Gwennie Flint had told Hope she was alone for Christmas so she came, too. The borrowed chairs lined up around the table with hardly room to move an elbow once people were seated.

Peter, helping Hope to carry the food to the table, whispered, 'I see you took my advice and diluted your mother-in-law.'

'It seems to be working, too,' she replied, giving him a quick kiss on the cheek.

'If we can top up her port and lemon a few times she might even enjoy the day.'

'Don't you dare!'

'Oh, I dare,' he threatened, half seriously. 'I don't want her spoiling the day for you or for young Dai.'

There were a few small problems as Marjorie insisted on dinner being delayed so they could listen to the King's speech first then complained that the two chickens and the small piece of pork provided by the absent Betty were overcooked and the vegetables too salty.

Hope was aware of being scrutinized by Peter's father and stepmother. She saw them whispering to each other, and she suspected their comments were disapproving. Her instinct proved correct when Peter's father told her he wanted better for his son than a second-hand woman with another man's son.

Hurt but determined not to show it, Hope said calmly, 'Don't alarm yourself, Mr Bevan, I have no intention of remarrying.' The words were true. How could she think of doing so having driven a man to suicide? Ralph had chosen to die rather than stay with her, so how could she risk hurting Peter?

Nothing had been planned apart from a few silly games, which everyone enjoyed. Although Marjorie didn't join in, she did seem content to be entertained by the stupidity of others without resorting to criticism. Carols were sung and there were a few solos from those who, emboldened by drink, wanted an audience for a few minutes.

Freddy went for a walk at one stage and was away for a long time, although Marjorie didn't appear to notice. He told Peter he'd been to see if Betty was all right and reported that she was improved and was sorry she'd missed the fun.

It was after midnight before the last visitor left. Connie and Hope looked around them at the ruin of the kitchen and the glasses and plates that were dotted around the ground floor of the house. 'I didn't know we had so many plates and glasses,' Hope sighed, starting to gather them on to a tray.

'Betty lent us some glasses from the pub, plates as well. I'm working tomorrow so I'll take them when I go in at lunchtime.'

'Was it a good day, d'you think?'

'Wonderful. Even Marjorie was reduced to a sleepy silence. And how you managed that I don't know.'

'Port and lemon and too many people here to make herself heard. Poor Marjorie, she's had such awful luck. Three sons and only one surviving, and him too unkind to come home at Christmas.' She looked at Connie, about to apologize. 'Sorry, I forgot you knew Phillip.'

'You're right, he is unkind. It took me too long to realize it.' She frowned slightly, her dark eyes clouding. 'I wonder who he has supporting him now? There'll surely be some other stupid woman who believes she's the one to change him.'

'Be thankful it's no longer you, Connie.' She stood up and placed the tray of dirty glasses near the sink. 'Come on, I'm for bed. We can do the clearing up tomorrow. Thanks, Connie, for your friendship and your help today. I really appreciate having you here.'

'I should thank you for sharing your harmonious home and making me feel wanted. Today has been wonderful, I'll always remember it.'

'I think we'd better get to sleep before we get maudlin and start to sing sentimental songs and end up crying!'

Hope made sure the fire was extinguished and lit candles in two china candlesticks. She then turned off the gas light by pulling the little chain and listening for the pop. The candle flames bobbed, leading the way in ever changing patterns of light and shadow, the walls resounding with echoes of the singing and laughter of the past hours, as they went upstairs, tired and utterly content.

-

The weather became much colder once Christmas was over. The roads were covered with thin pools transformed into ice that glowed opaquely in the lights of passing cars. The trees glistened with the touch of frost that stayed all day without the strength of the sun to melt it. The grass on the kerb of the lane was brittle underfoot. Gardens were abandoned. The cold was painful to the skin and few people ventured out unless it was necessary. Heads down, wrapped up in extra clothes and heavy boots, shoppers did what they had to do and scurried home as fast as they could.

With clear reluctance, Marjorie and Freddy moved back to their cold, unwelcoming house and longed to be back in the comfort of Badgers Brook. The rooms were hollow without floor covering and with minimal furnishings, and when they slid between the sheets they were shockingly cold to the touch in spite of hot water bottles and extra blankets, bed socks and shawls.

With only a couple of weeks before the house had to be vacated, Freddy spent time looking for a property to suit their needs. It was Marjorie who finished cleaning the house, lifting the last squares of carpet and scrubbing the wooden floors, with the help of fifteen-year-old Hetty Gregory, a young girl who worked for one of Marjorie's friends. It was Hetty who found the notebooks.

Marjorie took them from her, surprised to learn they had been found under loose floorboards. Marjorie was tempted to read them, but Hetty would have to leave at twelve and they had to finish washing the floors today. With great reluctance she put them aside, promising herself a sad journey into the past as soon as she had prepared and eaten lunch.

Freddy had said he wouldn't be home until later in the day, and she was glad. She wanted to read Richard's words alone, imagine his voice as though he were reading them just to her.

When the girl had gone, clutching the few shillings she had earned, Marjorie abandoned the thought of lunch and, making a cup of tea, went to sit at the table and start on the diaries.

When Freddy came in about four o'clock, the room had grown dark and the fire had sunk to a grey ashy coldness. She was unaware of how cold she had become. Freddy was alarmed. After switching on the light he revived the fire with dry sticks and fresh coal, talking to her without actually looking at her.

'Are you all right, Marjorie? Not ill? Why are you sitting in the dark? And it's so cold in here.' There was no reply, and he stood, his face reddened from the closeness to the now blazing fire, and looked at her. 'What's that you're reading?' Alarmed, he strode to the table and picked up one of the exercise books. 'Richard's diaries? What is it? What have you learned to upset you?' As though to protected her, albeit belatedly, he snatched the small pile of books and held them away from her.

'I'm not upset, Freddy, just sad beyond measure. Why was life so cruel? Three sons, and two gone from us, in such a useless way. Richard only days before hostilities ceased, and Ralph, well, we'll never know the truth of that, will we? And Phillip, who's alive but can't be bothered to come and see us, knowing how we grieve. Was I such a terrible mother?'

'Of course you weren't. Don't ever think it. We all do what we think is best, and no one can do more than that. Come on, let's eat out, shall we? A special treat before we leave this place with all its memories for good.'

'No, let's go for a walk, bring back some of Gwennie Flint's fish and chips and eat them here, by the fire.'

'Why not let that be the end of it? Let's move out of here tomorrow. There's no point staying on surrounded by boxes and without any comfort. Let's start the new year in

Badgers Brook. Hope won't mind, she knows how difficult it is for you. She's a good, kind girl.'

'D'you really think we could? This place is no longer our home. It's cold and it doesn't seem to retain heat no matter how well the fire burns. I'm weary of hovering between being miserable now and feeling anxious about later, living a half-life.'

'Right then! Tonight it's fish and chips from Gwennie and tomorrow we'll arrange to leave.' He put the books in a box of oddments where he hoped she wouldn't find them, and they went out to buy their supper.

-

Phillip had a wonderful time staying at an expensive hotel throughout the Christmas weekend. Fiona had been loving and attentive, and bought him clothes and a few luxuries like a gold cigarette case and cufflinks and a pen, the accoutrements of a successful businessman. She constantly flattered him by showing him off as her *adored* husband, who was in retail, as she was herself. He was silently amused at the comparison between his selling toys for a wage plus commission and her owning a high-class shoe shop, but he enjoyed the subterfuge and acted the part to perfection.

When they got back to the flat she began looking in her diary for possible dates for their wedding.

'It must be a quiet affair, darling, so we can put the actual date back a few weeks to make sure we're considered respectable.' She laughed as he hugged her and shared the joke. After she had left very early to open her shop he carefully packed his better clothes and the gifts she had given him, and, with the suitcase filled to capacity and several other parcels on his arm, he stepped into a taxi and headed for Paddington.

On the way he posted his resignation to the toy shop, mentioning his brother's accident and suicide as an excuse, as though both had been recent. He was a little ashamed at using his brother's death, but not enough to rewrite the letter.

There was genuine sadness at leaving Fiona. She was fun, affectionate and generous, and rich enough to keep him in luxury he'd only ever dreamed of. But he knew Matthew was right: once the baby had been born and given his name, he would have been discarded. Someone like Fiona would never shackle herself to someone like him, with no money and no prospects. Handsome and charming, with the gift of the gab enabling him to bluff his way through most conversations, he fitted her needs for the moment, but sooner or later he'd give himself away to her friends and reveal the truth about his far-from-glamorous beginnings. He had arrived in her life at a convenient moment and, good looking, presentable and convincing enough to fool her friends, he had been taken for a mug.

As the train made its way towards South Wales he tried to remember whether he had left any clues to enable her to follow him, as Connie had so easily done, but decided that she wouldn't bother to try. He wasn't that important to her; there must be plenty of men in her life who'd oblige by marrying her, then leave with a generous parting present. Perhaps, he thought briefly, he'd have been wiser to have gone along with it a while longer, stayed and been paid for his trouble. He had been paid: with gifts of clothes and the expensive luxuries she had given him on Christmas morning, as they lay in the hotel bed, feeding each other the breakfast that had been left at their door. He glanced at his gold watch. Twenty more minutes and he'd be in Cwm Derw. He idly wondered whether there would be a porter available to carry his overloaded suitcase.

Unable to leave the dream too abruptly, he took a taxi to his parents' house and stood while the driver struggled up to the front door with his luggage. Leaving his suitcase on the front porch he knocked, and, having no response, walked around to the back. A glance through the window showed him that the house, Ty Mawr, his home, was completely empty.

He felt offended and filled with self-pity. His parents had moved without even telling him. What mother would do that? Now what could he do?

Marjorie was inside but she didn't open the door. It was her son, obviously wanting something. In need of a place to rest his idle head no doubt. Well he could go and find somewhere else. The house was no longer theirs. Hope might be kind but she wasn't stupid: she wouldn't ask Connie to leave Badgers Brook to accommodate a worthless waster like Phillip. She walked away from the window after watching him leave, struggling with too many pieces of luggage. Then she went back into the bedroom that had been his and Richards.

At that moment, as she sat on the floor in the bare bedroom, holding a final exercise book in her hands, she hated everyone, including her son. Within the pages of Richard's diaries she had just that moment learned that Freddy, whom she had trusted completely, had been involved in a long-time love affair with Betty Connors.

Eleven

Marjorie sat with the diaries in her hand until she became aware of how cold she was. Stiffly she rose from the bare floor of the bedroom and replaced the loose board. Underneath she had searched with a hand and a torch, just in case there were other hidden treasures, secret items that would bring back some memory of her son. She wanted to hold things he had held, pretend she was touching him, telling him she loved him.

Having found the last of the exercise books filled with his neat handwriting she wished she had not made that final search and had remained in ignorance. Freddy and Betty Connors. It was so obvious, now she knew. She wondered how many others knew and were silently sympathetic, or smug that it had happened to her, Marjorie Williamson-Murton, who put on such airs. Other people knowing was one of the worst things. Privately she could cope – shouting and raging and making sure Freddy never forgot – but knowing she was the subject of gossip was unbearable. Oh, how she hated Freddy for doing this to her.

She was shivering as she went down the stairs and at the door she stopped. Where was she going? Not back to Badgers Brook to pretend nothing had changed. But, with the house sold and no replacement found, there was nowhere else. An icy wind was blowing and her coat felt as thin as gossamer. The chill that was partly the weather and mostly the cold shock of betrayal seemed to find its way to every part of her. She stepped back inside but knew she couldn't stay, she no longer had the right to be there, the place was no longer hers. She belonged nowhere and with no one.

She was surprised at how much she wanted to go to Badgers Brook, to its safety and warmth: feel the security of its walls wrapped around her, and relax in its calm peaceful atmosphere. She needed to talk to someone, but her friends were few and not close enough to listen to this. There was no one, except Hope.

She caught the bus and got off at the end of the lane. Darkness was absolute after the illuminated bus and she paused a moment until her eyes could make use of the starlight. The trees moved slightly in a soft breeze that was adding to the chill of the evening. Foraging animals were heard from the wood on her left, startling her from time to time, but she was too lost in her thoughts to be afraid.

As Badgers Brook came into view with its kitchen light shining like a beacon, she felt a relief, a momentary glimmer of optimism; the house had that effect and she vaguely wondered why. Then she slowed her steps. If Freddy were there what would she do? Not confront him, that much was certain. Not yet, and certainly not with David there while Hope listened, tried to help, reassuring her, promising that everything would be all right. Nothing would ever change how she felt at that moment, filled as she was with hatred and humiliation. Cold and friendless.

She went up to the kitchen window and looked in. David was drawing, sitting at the big kitchen table surrounded by crayons and paints and pools of water. Hope came into the room and pointed at the clock and Marjorie guessed she was telling him he had five more minutes and then he must clear up.

The cold was biting into her feet and the back of her legs. She had to take a chance on Freddy not being there and go inside. She pushed open the door and went in.

'Mother-in-law, you look frozen, come and sit by the fire,' Hope said with concern. A blanket was spread across the end of the couch and she took it and wrapped it around Marjorie's shoulders, then led her to the chair close to the blaze.

'Is *he* here?'

'Do you mean Peter or Father-in-law? In fact, the answer's the same. They've gone to buy logs from the farm. They've taken the horse and cart and will probably stop at the Ship and Compass for a drink on the way home.'

'Don't mention that awful place.' Her voice came out as a low, growl. 'Hope, I have to talk to you, can we put David to bed?'

'No, I promised he could wait up and have a story read to him by Peter when he comes back. I can't disappoint him.' She could see that something serious was on Marjorie's mind, so she added, 'I'll let him get the cars and garage out, that will keep him happy for a while, then we can go into the kitchen and drink tea, and you can tell me what's worrying you.'

Marjorie waited impatiently as Davy was settled and the kettle was put on the gas ring to boil. She wanted Hope to be told before Freddy returned, so they could forbid him to stay. Hope wouldn't allow him through the door once she knew what he had done. When the tea was made, cups set out and the tea cosy in place, she handed the exercise books to Hope with the relevant page open.

'Are you sure this is true, Mother-in-law?' she asked when she had read several pages. 'Richard might have got his facts wrong. He must have been very young using books like these – maybe he misunderstood the situation.'

'Look at the dates.'

'Oh, I see. So you do think this is true?'

'It's very believable. Think of the time he spent in your garden and the gaps between when he left and when he arrived back at Ty Mawr. It would have been so easy for them to meet. A man saying he's going to the pub for a drink always seems innocuous, doesn't it? Oh, it's true. The question is, what am I to do?'

'Talk to him. That's the very first thing. You might find out it's nothing more than over-active imagination on the part of Richard. He was in love, remember, and he might have seen romance everywhere.'

'Not his own father. Children never believe their parents could be caught up in the emotions of love. They all think they invented it,' she added with a sad half-smile.

'Look, when Peter and Father-in-law come in I'll take Davy and Peter to visit Kitty and Bob. They won't mind. Connie is in her room, so you'll have the house to yourselves to talk it through.' She hesitated, turned away from Marjorie's angry eyes. 'Mother-in-law, I don't know a good way to say this, but I recommend that you say as little as possible, hold back on what you feel and allow him to talk. Let silences develop and make him break them. That way you won't allow recriminations and anger to block out the truth about what happened, and about how you both feel now.'

Marjorie thought Hope was very wise, but she couldn't say so. What she did say was, 'Easier said than done.'

'But you can do it. You're strong, use that strength now and get the facts clear, before you accuse and perhaps regret.'

'You don't think it's true, do you?' Accusation glistened in Marjorie's eyes.

'Like you, Mother-in-law, I simply don't know.'

-

Phillip arrived at Matthew's house to find the place empty. 'Damnation, where is everyone?' he muttered. Then, from behind him, he heard the gate-snick rattle and turned to see a group of peculiarly dressed people carrying what looked like all their worldly goods. There was a chorus of goodbyes, then a car drove off and he recognized the charming, musical voice of Sally. He called so he didn't frighten them by appearing from the shadows.

'Hello. I was beginning to think you'd left town.'

'Phillip? What are you doing here?'

'Hoping to see that husband of yours and maybe beg a bed for the night. Where on earth have you been?'

'We were performing this evening. A extra performance of *The Lost Child* in aid of the NSPCC. His wife and his daughters were taking part, a seat was reserved for him, so Matthew is certain to be miles away! Too far to come and see us. He'd make sure of that.'

'What do you mean? He'd have loved to be here but his job takes him all over half of Wales; you know how far he has to travel.'

'Yes, I do know,' she said, putting the key in the lock and ushering the two girls inside out of the cold. 'You'd better come in – for a moment,' she said pointedly. 'Matthew is in Penarth, hardly a long way away. Here, I'll give you the address of the hotel where he's staying. Probably nothing special, but better than home, obviously.'

While Sally was upstairs dealing with the girls and removing her stage clothes, Phillip phoned the hotel and left an urgent message for Matthew to come home and grovel.

Less than an hour later, after they had all eaten a snack of thinly spread jam on toast, Matthew burst in looking dishevelled and flustered, and said. 'Darling, I'm so sorry I missed your play again. I was intending to surprise you all and be in the audience, but I was stuck with a difficult customer who needed some serious pacifying. I came as fast as I could but too late. How did it go, Megan? Olwen? I bet you were wonderful. Did Twm the donkey behave?'

Sally let him finish then said, 'Time for bed, girls. You can comfort Daddy in his bitter disappointment tomorrow.' The words were sarcastic and Sally's face was a mask of controlled anger. Why did Phillip have to turn up, tonight of all nights, when she was ready for a showdown?

'Phillip, will you have another cup of something – before you leave?'

'Sally, love, we can't turn him out on a night like this. His parents have moved out of Ty Mawr without telling him, can you believe that? He can't sleep in a shed, like those squatters, can he?'

With bad grace she handed Phillip some blankets and a pillow and gestured towards the couch. 'What about the spare room?' Matthew whispered.

'The spare room is for you.' she hissed back. 'Don't dare to try and come into my bed. Tonight or any other night.'

'Sally?' He gave a half-smile and raised an eyebrow.

'Matthew?' she retorted, raising a reflecting eyebrow, but without the smile.

Before leaving them to settle she handed Matthew some post. The letter on top of the pile was from his employers.

She was heard going up the stairs, and then the bathroom door closed; there were more shuffled footsteps and murmur of voices before silence fell. Matthew asked Phillip to excuse him and slit open the envelope. 'Probably a pay rise,' he said casually.

Phillip saw at once that the contents were not good. 'Is everything all right?' he asked.

'No, it damned well isn't. I can't believe this. I've been sacked! They say they have to make cuts – demand is dropping off because of the competition.' He stared at the letter, read it twice more and muttered, 'Sally knew, didn't she? She knew what the letter contained!'

Phillip waited, expecting Matthew to want to talk about it, but nothing more was said and he made his excuses and began to make up his bed on the couch.

Both men retired to their beds but neither could sleep. At about two a.m. Phillip sat up, aware of someone creeping about, and heard Matthew hiss, 'Phillip, are you awake?'

They both went into the kitchen, closed the door and switched on the light. They met each other's eye and began to laugh. 'Like a couple of kids threatened with having their pocket money stopped, aren't we?' Matthew spluttered.

'Mine already has been!' Phillip replied, choking back loud laughter.

Turning on the tap slowly, so as not to make too much noise, Matthew put the kettle to boil and prepared a tray for tea, giggling at every unnecessary sound, hissing at each other to 'sssh' like drunks. Laughter continued as they tried to sip tea that was too hot; then suddenly the humour was gone.

'Matthew, my friend, I think it's time we grew up.'

Matthew stared, then nodded. 'I have to face facts, and those are that unless I stop acting like an overgrown schoolboy and give Sally the respect she deserves, show the girls that I truly love them, I'll lose everything.'

'That's what Connie called me, more or less. A child of twenty-eight who won't grow up.' He stared into his teacup. 'I regret leaving Connie, although I don't think it would have been a perfect marriage. Far from it if I'm honest. I regret Fiona much more. I was a fool to run away before I'd checked the facts. I wish I'd prolonged the dream a while longer. What if it is my baby? What if it isn't? I might still have had a good life. And before you ask, it wasn't just her money. There was something special about her. A confidence, an attitude to life that told people she wouldn't take any nonsense. She was special, really fantastic, and I acted like the fool I am and ran away.'

'After your mother, I wouldn't expect you to choose another strong woman, Phillip.'

'Oh, there isn't much resemblance between Fiona and Mum. Self-assurance makes the difference. Fiona knows exactly who she is and what she wants. She doesn't need to live through others like Mum tried to do.'

'Very philosophical for this time of night, Phillip! Why don't you go and see her?'

'I might try. There's nothing holding me here.' Getting up to replenish their cups he asked. 'What will you do?'

'I do love Sally. I'm really terrified of losing her and the girls. But I've slipped into the habit of using her more like a landlady and the house as an hotel. I want that to change, but how do I convince her I mean it?' Thinking aloud he went on, 'Before I plead my case to Sally, I need to get another job. Then I'll talk to her parents and see if I can persuade them to help me. I'm more likely to win Sally over with them on my side.'

–

Marjorie had been surprisingly calm when Freddy came in. She was sitting at the kitchen table, which was still smeared with Davy's paints.

'Oh, there you are, Marjorie. D'you know, I found a path about six inches below the ground as I dug at the top of the garden this afternoon. Quite exciting. Wonder where it once led. I started to expose it but it got too cold. Shall I make a cup of tea?'

'You won't be staying long enough to drink it, Freddy. I want you to leave now, this minute. Divorce proceedings will follow as soon as I've seen our solicitor.'

He laughed, then his eyes grew wide with surprise. 'Marjorie? What's this? Some game? A joke?'

She placed the exercise book on the table. 'No joke. Richard, Phillip and Ralph all knew about you and Betty Connors. I can't imagine why it took me so long. I always thought it was stupid to say that the wife was always the last to know. That any woman who was unaware must be stupid themselves. But it seems it's true.'

'What are you talking about¿ He tried to sound matter-of-fact, but his voice quivered a little. He took up the exercise book and read part of the page. He stared at her in surprise. 'This is nonsense. I don't know what Richard was thinking about, putting such a lot of rubbish in his diary. It's pure fantasy.'

'Then you won't mind if I ask Betty Connors about it?'

'I'd mind a great deal. She's a friend and I wouldn't want to embarrass her with such nonsense.'

'It's fortunate that we've just sold the house. It will make things a lot easier.'

'For goodness sake, Marjorie, listen to yourself! Tried and convicted before you even hear what I have to say.'

'All right, what do you have to say?'

'I call there often for a drink and to meet friends, have a chat, like dozens of other men. I sometimes helped her with jobs she couldn't manage herself. I wasn't the only one to offer help, but, being a landlady of a public house and living alone, she had to be very careful. She trusted me. It was no more than that.'

'I trusted you, too, but not any more. Now go, I don't want you here.'

'Go where? The house is sold. This is our home for the time being. I'm not leaving.'

'Perhaps, being a friend, Betty will find you a bed for the night?'

'I've never stayed in her bed.'

'What does that prove? Why do so many people presume that a bed is the only place in which to commit adultery? Go away, Freddy. I can't bear to look at you.'

Unnerved by her calmness, a restraint that was so completely out of character, he picked up the bagful of clothes she offered him and went out. His intention was to wait around until Hope was back and try again to convince Marjorie that their sons had been mistaken. He walked to the Ship and Compass but found it closed. There was no reply to his knocking. Cold and deeply afraid of the outcome of the revelations he had hoped to conceal, he went back to Ty Mawr and let himself in.

It was cold, no better than outside, and the still air seemed to seep into his bones. He lit a fire in the grate, which had been cleaned and polished ready for the new owners. No heat issued forth into the room and he sat there for a while, wrapped in greatcoat and misery, then went to see if Elsie Clements had a room to rent.

Head-on was never the way to deal with Marjorie. A couple of days, a word with Hope, a hint of what the gossips would make of it and things would change.

–

After an uncomfortable night on a couch too short to accommodate his long legs, Phillip invited Matthew to go with him and try to discover what had happened to the occupancy of Ty Mawr and the whereabouts of Phillip's parents.

'Ty Mawr is sold,' Stella informed them when they asked at the post office. 'And, just temp'ry, the post is to be send on to Badgers Brook until they buy another place. There you'll find them for sure. Although,' she added in a low voice, 'I've been told that your father stayed in Elsie Clements's guest house last night. Although that's probably temp'ry too, eh? Some trouble there is, but I don't know what. You staying local?'

'Not at present, Mrs Jones, but I'll be sure to tell you when I am,' he said, but the sarcasm was wasted on Stella. She thanked him and said to say 'Hello and happy New Year' to his mam for her.

'There's a terrible thing,' Stella whispered in a deep, confidential voice to her next customer. 'There's that idly waster Phillip come home to see his parents for New Year and they've moved without a word. And Freddy, he's staying in Elsie Clements's guest house. Kicked out by Marjorie. Everybody's locking doors on their own. There's bound to be a third. Always goes in threes, trouble does. Glad I am that I live over the premises or there's no knowing what would happen, eh, Mrs John? I'd better be sure to look after my Colin, mind. Mark my words, there's bound to be a third.'

–

Three days later, when Sally and Matthew finally managed to find privacy to discuss the sad state of their marriage, Matthew became the third to be told to leave his home. Sally was adamant and refused to reconsider, even for a few weeks while he sorted out somewhere to stay. He and Phillip, looking like whipped dogs, went to stay at Elsie Clements's guest house, where they met a dejected Freddy.

'Dad? What happened?' Phillip asked. 'What's the matter with everyone?'

'Love and happiness aren't always compatible bedfellows,' Freddy replied enigmatically. 'Have a drink and let time pass, that's what I intend to do.'

–

Matthew went to see Sally's parents and found them completely in accord with their daughter. 'But there's never been another woman, I swear it. I've never once strayed. I just don't spend enough time in the home, I admit that, and I will try, I really will. It's just the conversations I miss. Staying in an hotel, meeting strangers, listening to their views and experiences, discussing every subject under the sun, I find it fascinating. Compared with evenings like those, home can be abysmally dull.'

'Matthew!'

'I'm sorry, I know that isn't what you want to hear, but I wouldn't insult you with less than the truth.'

Sally's mother refused to look at him. In a grinding voice she said, 'And money? Are you fair about money? If so, why do we have to support them?'

'I admit it, I spend it on myself, staying at hotels when I should be home. I love them, I don't want to lose them. I will stop this selfishness and concentrate on my family, I promise you. I'll get a job and all the money will be for them.'

Her father shook his head sorrowfully and showed him to the door.

–

Phillip was fortunate enough to find his mother alone when he knocked on the door of Badgers Brook. Hope and Joyce had gone into town to buy supplies of cottons and zip fasteners and buttons, taking Davy with them. His mother was peeling potatoes and preparing to make a cottage pie.

She opened the door and without a word returned to her work.

'Mummy, what on earth has happened? Why has Ty Mawr been sold? Why isn't Dad here with you?'

'Your father is staying at the guest house until he finds something more suitable.'

'I know. I'm staying there too, until my money runs out, and I don't know where I'll be after that. Please, Mummy, tell me what's going on.'

She threw the vegetable knife into the bowl and ran upstairs, returning with the exercise book, which she thrust into his hands. Silently, he sat and began to read. Then he looked up at her and waited for her to speak.

'Is it true?' she demanded.

'Yes, it's true,' he told her. 'Dad used to visit Betty Connors and there was more than casual friendship and doing odd repairs for her.'

'Why didn't you tell me?' She almost shouted in her grief.

'Mum, how could I? It isn't a subject for a son to discuss with his mother, especially when it concerns his father. Dad never knew that we'd found out. Besides, Richard, Ralph and I thought it would blow over.'

'So you all knew?'

'I don't think anyone else did.'

'They do now,' she said sadly. 'I feel such a fool apart from everything else.'

'Perhaps it wasn't serious, just a need for friendship.'

'Friendship? What nonsense you talk, Phillip! He had me, and you three boys, his employees at work, why would he want friendship from the likes of Betty Connors, a common public house proprietor?'

He wanted to argue, to tell her not to be so harsh, that Betty Connors was a kind lady and far from common, but he didn't. He thought about the difficulties they'd all had in talking to his mother. The impossibility of trying to make her understand their point of view when they didn't agree with hers. Her unreasonableness was why he had left so soon after being demobbed at the end of the war, and it was also the reason Ralph had been afraid to leave and start building a life of his own. He thought all this but said nothing. It was still impossible to talk to her. She could still silence him with a sharp word or a glare from her constantly angry eyes.

Instead of discussing his father and Betty Connors, he told her about Fiona, and how he believed she had been trying to make him accept a child that wasn't his.

'It might have been yours. It doesn't take that long. And if you treat women like common prostitutes…'

He was silenced, shocked by her use of the word.

'I'd have liked to have the house filled with grandchildren,' she said. 'I imagined Ty Mawr being our family's home for generations to come.'

Irritation broke down his usual caution. 'Come on, Mum, you know you haven't got the patience for children. You treat them like little adults. Or animals that need training. Little Davy is yours but you hardly bother with him. All you do is crit—' He fell silent, looking at her face, knowing he had gone too far.

'All I do is criticize? Is that what you were about to say? It's called trying to help, Phillip. I want him to have a good start.'

'What if your help isn't needed, Mummy? And, worse, what if you're wrong? What then?'

She was excused answering by the sound of the door opening. Connie came in with Geoff, with carrier bags filled with an assortment of vegetables and fruit.

'Here are some leftovers; we might make a big pot of vegetable soup, what d'you think?' Then she saw him. 'Oh, Phillip. What are you doing here?'

'Hoping to see you, and to persuade you to forgive me and come back to North Wales.'

'Phillip, I like children, but, as I've said before, I can't cope with a twenty-eight-year-old child who won't grow up.'

'We'll talk later. When we're alone. Hope is sure to find me a bed.'

'You can't stay here. There isn't room.'

Geoff took Connie's arm and guided her back to the door. 'Sorry we can't stop, but we're going out, delivering paraffin.'

'How exciting,' Phillip said, giving her his special smile.

'It will be, with Geoff for company,' she said, walking out of the door through which they had so recently entered.

Phillip spread his hands. 'What did I say?'

'She won't want you here and neither will Hope, so you'd better go back to the guest house with your father.'

Phillip went to find Matthew and, dejected and despairing, they returned to the guest house. With Freddy they ate an unappetizing meal of cheese and potato pie in which there was a serious dearth of cheese with lots of pepper in an attempt to disguise the fact, and decided that something had to be done.

–

Geoff was quiet as they travelled around the houses delivering the fuel for heaters and stoves. Connie helped him, taking the money, writing the transactions into his book, offering change and a few polite comments. She wanted to talk to him, tell him that Phillip was no longer important, that she had seen him in clear and unvarnished truth for what he was, a lazy, self-centred man. She didn't know how to begin so she said nothing. Afraid of hearing something he dreaded, Geoff said nothing either.

There was an atmosphere, an edginess like there had never been before. When they touched by accident they would both move away as though the contact was objectionable. Their hands reaching for the same item, although wrapped in thick gloves, suffered a shock that was similar to electricity, jarring and no longer exciting.

As they left the last customer and the van headed for home, Connie said, 'Please, Geoff, can we go to our favourite beach?'

'It's almost dark, and we haven't even brought a flask. You'll be frozen.' He didn't slow down.

'I'll risk being frozen. Please, can we go, just for a little while, look at the sea and listen to the silence together?' She was aware of the silence that had kept them apart since they left Badgers Brook, but she imagined a different kind of silence, a shared peace, a chance to be aware of each other without intrusion. An opportunity to isolate themselves from the rest of humanity and allow honesty to enter.

He reversed into a farm gateway and she touched his hand as a thank you. It wasn't far and, as before, he drove in silence. When he stopped he turned, leaning away from her, his back against his door, and stated at her. 'Go on, then. Tell me,' he said softly.

'What d'you want to hear, Geoff?'

'It's not what I want, it's what I expect. You're going back with Phillip, aren't you? Tell me. Get it over with.'

'I'm not going anywhere. Except I'll have to leave Badgers Brook. I can't stay under the same roof as Phillip.'

Still he misunderstood. 'Can't trust yourself?'

'I couldn't stand by and watch him twist his mother around his finger and scrounge money from her. That's what he does, scrounge money, from one person after another, pretending love is in his heart, when he isn't capable of loving anyone except himself. Oh, I fell for it like all the rest, and it took me longer to face the truth than most. I don't know what Marjorie did to her sons, but I doubt if any one of them knew how to be happy.'

'You'll be leaving?' Darkness was closing in, settling around them like a veil, and she could barely see his face.

'Only Badgers Brook, and only if Phillip is staying there. If he's moving in, even temporarily, I'll find a room some-where, maybe with Betty Connors at the pub. She's very kind, and I don't mind asking her.'

'You will go home eventually, though?'

'Not in the immediate future. Perhaps one day I'll go on a short visit to see my folks. It's here in Cwm Derw I want to stay.' She leaned towards him a little, as though trying to read his expression. 'Unless you ask me to go, I don't think I'll ever want to leave.'

'You mean that?'

'I do. I've never been happier than since I came here, never more optimistic about the future.' Taking a chance on him not wanting to hear it, she added, 'Mainly because of meeting you. I'd hate us to say goodbye, Geoff. You make me so happy I'd hate for us to part.'

'Connie, could you be happy living at the shop?' He was so nervous he was breathless. 'It isn't grand but you can do whatever you need to make it more comfortable. I don't mean straight away,' he said as she was about to speak. 'I – I want you to marry me. Will you think about it?'

'I've thought about nothing else since we first met.'

'Neither have I,' he whispered as he gathered her into his arms.

Later, practicalities were discussed and Connie had to ask the question she badly wanted to avoid. 'Geoff, you do know that Phillip and I lived together, as husband and wife, don't you?'

'I try never to think about it.'

'You have to I'm afraid. I want you to think about it and make sure it won't come between us, tarnish our love with ugliness and resentment. I'm absolutely sure about loving you, but, given my past, it's you who needs to think about it carefully.'

'The past doesn't spook me and it never will. The present is all that matters, and the future is ours to make of it what we wish.'

'We'll have to wait a while.' she said as he held her tight. 'I own nothing but a few clothes. I need to save some money.'

'I have enough. The only reason for waiting is for you to be certain.'

'In that case, what about next week?' she said with a smile. 'Supposing Hope can make a dress in seven days.'

'Tomorrow I'll get a special licence. We'll go together, like we'll do everything from now on.'

'You have been thinking about this, haven't you?'

Repeating her words, he said. 'I've thought of nothing else since we first met.'

–

When Hope returned to Badgers Brook with Joyce and a chattering Davy, Phillip was there but she didn't allow him to speak. Without a glance at Marjorie she quietly told him to leave. With a kiss on the cheek for his mother and without a word to Hope, he did so.

Hope was afraid to look at Marjorie, aware of how painful it all was for her. She concentrated on unpacking their shopping. Before she and Joyce had put everything away, Connie returned with Geoff and it was at once clear that something good had happened.

'How soon can you make me a wedding dress?' Connie asked, her eyes shining, her normally pale face flushed and quite lovely, happiness enhancing her dark eyes. Beside her Geoff's face showed the same joy.

Hope's first thought was that she would have to leave Badgers Brook. It was Geoff's house and they'd surely want to live here. Her first reaction was spoken aloud almost before she thought it.

'You'll want me to leave Badgers Brook, then? How soon is all this going to happen?' Then, filled with remorse at her selfish thought, she ran to hug Connie, saying. 'Connie, my dear, I'm so happy for you. Congratulations, Geoff, you'll make the perfect couple. Oh, this is exciting, isn't it, Marjorie?' She turned to her mother-in-law in certain dread of the reaction being worse than her own, but Marjorie stood up and offered a hand.

'Connie, we haven't known each other long, but I'm sure you will be a good wife to Geoff. You, Geoff, are a very lucky man.'

Hope was speechless. She hugged Connie again, hugged Geoff and went to the kitchen cupboard to see whether there was anything drinkable with which to toast the couple. Marjorie being polite! And wishing them every happiness? It was a miracle!

'Before we drink a toast, I want to reassure you, Hope, that we won't be living here. Connie and I will live above the shop and your tenancy is safe for as long as you want it.'

'Thank you, Geoff. I can't ever imagine wanting to leave this wonderful house.'

'Oh, you will,' Geoff said mysteriously. 'The time will come when you're ready to move out. The house will tell you when. It always happens like that.'

Hope didn't question him, this moment was his and Connie's, and his assurance, strange as it sounded, was enough.

–

The following morning Phillip watched as the train puffed noisily and importantly into the station. Doors flew open and passengers emerged and he jumped in and found a corner seat. A change in Cardiff then he'd be on the way to Paddington. He could be talking to Fiona this evening. Why had he spoken to Matthew and allowed himself to be persuaded to leave, he berated himself.

As the journey progressed he considered his plans. Instead of going straight to Fiona's flat or meeting her at the shop he decided to get himself a room and a job, perhaps get himself reinstated in the toy shop. Then, although it was little enough, he would have some stability, and something to offer her. In his pockets were the beautiful gifts she had bought for him: the cigarette case and lighter, the gold watch, the cufflinks and tie pin. These would be returned to her whatever the outcome of their meeting. He would be sorry to lose them, but returning them and offering a sincere apology would be the first steps in the painful process of growing up.

Twelve

Marjorie didn't know what to do with herself. Living at Badgers Brook with Hope, Davy and Connie meant everything was organized and there was no place for her to fill. She was left alone for much of the morning but the meal was already planned and the vegetables done before she woke. Hope was well used to dealing with the routine of the house and everything ran smoothly.

Connie, too, had fitted into the way Hope worked and she had made certain jobs her own. In her enforced idleness Marjorie took to walking. Most mornings when the weather was reasonable she dressed in her smartest clothes and went out. Sometimes to the post office, where she shared a few comments with Stella and those waiting to be served; haughty, defiant, unbending, proud of her ability to face them all, knowing that as soon as she had left the conversations would be about her latest disaster.

Occasionally she went to the bridge across the railway line, drawn more and more frequently by melancholy over the fate of her young son, seeing in her mind's eye the wheelchair, and the occupant's struggle to free himself of its confinement, imagining him climbing over the high barrier and waiting with determination and utter despair for the train to approach. She allowed the events leading to the death of Ralph to pass through her mind like a film, time and again, wanting to become so accustomed to them that they no longer caused such excruciating pain.

This morning she hesitated at the approach when she saw someone standing where she usually spent a few minutes reliving her grief. The figure, hunched in heavy overcoat and a thick scarf, was gazing down over the shining, innocuous silver lines. She stopped and began to turn away. This wasn't a place where she would enjoy even a brief conversation. These moments were for herself alone. Her eyes were wet with unshed tears and she didn't recognize Freddy until he called out to her.

'Marjorie, wait.'

She increased her speed but he caught up with her easily and held her arm.

'Go away, Freddy.'

'Come with me, we'll have a cup of coffee and talk about Ralph. D'you know, we never have. Not really talked.' She continued walking and he still kept a hand on her arm. 'Walk away if you wish but I want you to listen to something I should have said a long time ago.'

She stopped then and glared at him. 'I see, you have more excuses, have you?

'I lost my son,' he shouted. Then he released her arm from his grip in an angry gesture as though throwing it from him in disgust. 'You and I have never shared in the grief. I loved him too, but you pushed me away, convinced that as a mere father I couldn't possibly feel the same sense of loss, the same agony at the stupidity of the ending of a life hardly begun. I lost him too, but you used your agony to blame poor Hope, who had lost her husband, her lover, her future. There is no compassion in you, Marjorie, not for anyone.'

He calmed down a little but didn't apologize as he might once have done. Instead he stared at her, demanding a response.

'Go away, Freddy.'

'You can send me away, you can push everyone away, but your misery stays with *you*. Remember that.' He walked off towards the main road and she stood for a long time staring at his receding back, allowing the tears to fall.

-

Geoff suggested they arrange caterers for the wedding breakfast when he and Connie married. He wasn't short of money and, although it was a rushed affair, he didn't want them to regret that they hadn't made more of their special day. A cake was planned, and, as usual during the years of shortages, many friends and neighbours contributed what they could spare towards making it. Cooking it was entrusted to Hope.

The dress was second hand, and it was a few hours' work for Hope and Joyce to alter it to fit and add a few decorations of their own, to make it unique. There wouldn't be a great variety of flowers available but the local florist promised to do something spectacular with whatever she could find. Amid all the excitement Marjorie's misery was swamped. Freddy's words had shocked her, and although initially she felt more anger towards him – how dare he criticize her after what he had done – she was beginning to accept that they were true. If Hope noticed a deeper misery in her mother-in-law's demeanour she said nothing. Marjorie had been given many chances but now she had to make the first move if she was ready to accept help.

In London, Phillip heard about the forthcoming wedding and for a moment felt regret that he hadn't been able to accept commitment and marry Connie. He discussed it with Matthew one day when Matthew came up to London in the hope of finding work.

'Other people settle for routine and family life, so what is it about us that we find it so hard?'

'We've blamed the war for so long I think we've begun to believe it,' Matthew said sadly. 'The truth is, we're fools, losers. My friend, you're right. It's time for us to grow up.'

'My biggest regret is Fiona. I just might have been wrong about her taking me for a fool.'

'Wrong to take you for a fool?' He gave a half grin.

Phillip gave a sad smile. 'No, she wasn't wrong about that, was she? I avoid decisions whenever I can and when I do make a choice I make the wrong one. But in some ways I've been a lucky fool. I talked my way back into the job in the toy shop. I've found a fairly decent place to live. And I'm going to try and see Fiona, take her out for a meal. I need to see her and try to make her understand.'

–

Matthew found work in a wholesalers, selling office equipment, and, after two weeks, filled with renewed optimism, he went home for the weekend to try and persuade Sally to move to London with him.

'No, Matthew. I'd need to have complete confidence in you to leave everything I know and start again. We have a good life here, Megan and Olwen are settled, Mum and Dad are close when we need help, they try not to intrude but they're there to provide support in every way. I consider myself a capable woman, but if there's a slight problem I can rely on them. They're always there and, sadly, you are not.'

'I will be from now on. I promise things will change.'

'You've lost my trust, Matthew. I don't feel able to put myself and the girls in your hands and move so far away from everything and everyone we know.'

'Then I'll leave the job and come home. I'm sure to find something closer to home. I want to be with you and Megan and Olwen.' He looked at her face, closed in with determination not to soften towards him, and regret and shame almost overwhelmed him. This pretty woman, whom he had changed from a kind, caring partner into this cold, determined stranger, who had given so freely of her love, had been treated worse than a servant by him, and the realization of how close he was to losing her made him weep inside.

She said nothing in reply and he went on. 'Will you help me find work? I don't really care what I do, as long as it brings in enough to keep us out of the red. I realize I've taken advantage of your parents' generosity and I don't want to depend on them any longer. I want to look after my three beautiful, talented girls. Please, Sally, give me a chance to prove it, and help me.'

She turned her head and stared at him. He smiled encouragingly but there was no answering smile, her eyes were cold, her lips thin and tight. 'There's a vacancy for a salesman in a men's outfitters.'

'I'll apply,' he said eagerly. 'Tell me where and I'll go straight away.' In his heart he felt a deep regret. Why couldn't he find another job as a rep, travelling from town to town, meeting new people and seeing new places?

Working locally and having no excuse for spending time away from the house was almost like a prison sentence. Pretend as he might, the loss of freedom, the confinement of hours spent at home would be difficult. But the alternatives were worse. He was no use on his own; he needed a base, a loving wife to come home to when he needed comfort.

'I'll do it,' he said, as much to convince himself as his wife.

–

Phillip opened the street door, walked up the stairs and knocked on the door of Fiona's flat. When a voice asked him to identify himself he found his own voice was little more than a croak. It took a second attempt before he could say calmly, 'Fiona, it's me, Phillip. Please can I have a word? I need to apologize and try to explain.'

The door was opened and Fiona stared at him before turning away, allowing him to step inside. She had moved to the doorway of the tiny kitchen to stand beside a tall, elegantly dressed man, who at once placed a proprietary arm on her shoulders.

'Sorry if I'm intruding, I won't keep you long. D'you think we could meet for a meal, or perhaps just a drink, so I can make my apology and perhaps explain?' He looked at the man who stood silently beside her and added. 'If your friend has no objection.'

'Tomorrow, twelve thirty? Lunch at Giuliani's?'

'Thank you,' he said, and, nodding at the man and giving Fiona a nervous smile, he backed out.

He was there early. The restaurant was small and he had booked to make sure of getting a table. Exactly on time she walked in. She wore an outrageously bold red and orange dress, with a tight-fitting top and a skirt that floated around her long, slender legs. There was a band of the same material in her hair and hanging down to her shoulder. Her dark green leather handbag was enormous and matched her ridiculously high-heeled shoes. She looked utterly stunning. How could he have let her go?

Eyes followed her, some with envy, most with admiration. Phillip stood to greet her and move her chair to allow her to sit, and felt pride such as he'd never known as she leaned over the table and kissed his cheek before sitting down.

'You are beautiful,' he said softly. 'Absolutely beautiful. I've never known anyone like you.'

'Of course you haven't. I am unique,' she said, matter-of-factly.

Waiters fluttered around them, anxious to please, and it brought back memories of the few weeks they had been together, when her obvious importance, exceptional beauty and dazzling outfits had brought them running to serve her. When they had ordered and drinks had been poured she looked at him and asked, 'Well, Phillip. What did you want to say to me?' Before he could gather together the opening words of his apology she went on. 'I suppose you thought the child wasn't yours and I was trying to trick you into marrying me.'

'No, of course not. Er, well yes. I might as well be honest with you or there's no point in taking up your time. The truth is, it was a shock, and I doubted it could be mine – after all, we'd known each other just a few weeks. I spoke to Matthew and be convinced me that you carrying my child so soon after we'd met was unlikely. So, like the fool I am, I ran away.'

She smiled then. 'You were right, it wasn't yours. But I thought you'd make a reasonable husband, for a while at least, and tried to convince you. I failed, obviously.'

'You've found someone else? The man in your flat?'

'That was Montague, my brother. No, I've decided I can cope alone. My parents have been remarkably civil about the whole thing; in fact, they're quite looking forward to being grandparents. So, no harm done, Phillip. It was fun, though, wasn't it?'

He reached into his pockets and handed her the presents she had given him. 'I want you to have these back. I took them under false pretences.'

'False pretences? We were both playing that game. No, keep them as souvenirs of a pleasant few weeks.'

They ate their meal, and while he paid the enormous bill, which would empty his wallet completely, she left, weaving her way through the tables, stopping several times to blow kisses, and giving a final sad wave from the doorway.

Phillip was like a ship without a rudder: he didn't know what to do or where to go, so he went back to the toy shop. Later he wrote to his parents to give them an address where he intended to stay for at least the immediate future. Perhaps, he thought foolishly, if he stayed in the same place he might see Fiona again, if only to make others envious by waving to her, blowing a kiss and sharing in the flamboyance of her personality for a moment or two.

–

Marjorie read Phillip's letter and showed it to Hope. 'It seems he's settled in London and won't be coming home.'

'Then you and Father-in-law can buy a small house without needing to plan for more than an occasional visit,' Hope replied. 'Two bedrooms will be plenty.'

'What he buys will have nothing to do with me. I'll choose a place to suit myself. Freddy can go and live with Betty Connors.'

Hope was still a little afraid of Marjorie, although she usually managed to hide the fact, but over this separation she knew she had to be strong. Freddy and Marjorie were both miserable and lonely. The fun of choosing a new home should have brought them closer, but since the revelations about Betty Connors they had never sat down and talked. She spoke of her concerns to Kitty. 'I wish I could lock them in somewhere, so they had no alternative but to talk!'

'Can you trust them to look after Davy?' Kitty asked. 'Telling them both they are responsible for him will mean they will have to stay.'

–

'Mother-in-law, I have to go out this afternoon, will you stay with Davy for an hour?' Hope asked, as they prepared their midday meal.

'Of course.'

'Father-in-law,' she asked Freddy when she took Davy for his walk, 'I have to go out for an hour later, will you come in and keep an eye on Davy? He loves to see you. Oh, and there's a letter from Phillip you will want to read.'

She let Freddy in while Marjorie was upstairs washing Davy after his rather sticky lunch and darted down the path to meet Kitty. 'Well, I haven't locked them both in but it's as close as I can get!' She raised her hands showing crossed fingers. 'I just hope they don't start fighting.'

'Don't worry,' Kitty said with a laugh. 'Bob's working in the garden and he'll listen out for the sound of World War Three breaking out.'

–

'What are you doing here?' Marjorie demanded, as she came down the stairs with Davy.

'Grandfather!' Davy ran to greet Freddy, who swept him up in his arms.

'I've come to play snakes and ladders with my grandson, haven't I, Davy?'

'*I'm* looking after Davy.'

'Hope asked *me*. Now, lovely boy, where's the box of games?' Without looking at his wife, Freddy asked, 'Where's Phillip's letter?'

Marjorie threw it on to the table beside him and he read it in silence. Then he reached into his pocket and pulled out a folded sheet of paper, which he, too, threw on to the table. Marjorie unfolded it to reveal details of a detached cottage not far from the bus stop at the end of the lane.

'Why are you showing this to me?'

'It's large enough for us. Phillip won't be coming back except perhaps for a visit. So I went in today and made an offer.'

'You have no right to make decisions for us.'

Freddy gave a long theatrical sigh. 'Davy, my boy, your grandmother can be such a difficult old lady. But even she can't carry on feeling sorry for herself indefinitely. Everyone's getting weary of listening to her. Even the kindest of people tire of a moaner in the end. She and I belong together and the alternative is loneliness for us both.' He spread the details of the house in front of Marjorie and smoothed it out carefully. 'Now the plan is this,' he said, still talking to Davy. 'Your grandmother's been unhappy for quite long enough and today it stops. We're moving into that house and you can have a swing and a see-saw in the garden for when you visit. And if Uncle Bob and Uncle Colin will help us, I thought we could make a tree house where you can invite your friends. There'll be a basket on a rope which you can lower when you want food and we can fill it with cakes and sandwiches and you can haul it up into your house. What d'you think?'

Marjorie said nothing, but with occasional sly glances Freddy could see the tension easing away from her.

When Hope returned, Marjorie opened the door and said softly, 'Father-in-law and I need to take a walk. I'll be back in time for tea.'

'I found some ghastly looking cooked meat in the butcher's shop. I daren't think what it's made from, but I'll make chips and set the table for the seven of us. Connie, Geoff and Peter will join us. All together like one big happy family. What about that, Davy?'

'I'm going to have a tree house,' Davy said.

The meal started off in a subdued way, but once Freddy started talking about the cottage he intended to buy, Marjorie began to open up and was soon arguing about what new furnishings she would need. Miraculously, the purchase of the cottage, although as yet unseen by Marjorie, seemed to be a fait accompli. Whatever had been said during their walk seemed to have sorted out their difficulties.

'I'm thinking of taking on a property too,' Peter surprised them by announcing. 'It isn't for definite, mind, I have to discuss it with others first, but there's a shop for rent at the corner of Gladstone Road and there's good accommodation above. Only a small garden but there's a shed for the cart and nice stable for Jason.' He looked at Hope as he said, 'You'll come and look at it, Hope? See what you think?'

Marjorie took a deep breath as though about to comment, and from the look on her face the remarks would have been unkind. But a glance from Freddy and his hand gripping her arm held her back, and instead she said, 'Yes, go and look, Hope. I'm sure Peter will value your opinion.'

'Why a shop, Peter?' Hope enquired. 'You don't need one, as you sell from the cart. You're out all day so you wouldn't be there to man it, unless you're planning to sell the cart, and Jason?'

This thought horrified Davy and he began to wail. 'You can't sell Jason, I n-e-e-ed him,' he complained.

'I'll never sell Jason, he'll live with me always,' Peter promised, 'but I'm thinking of giving up the round, selling it perhaps, it's quite profitable.'

They discussed his plan for a while, with Marjorie uncritical and even offering suggestions on what he might stock. Before he left he'd extracted a promise for both Hope and Davy to go with him to look at the property.

Bedtime came and there was an uneasiness in both Freddy's and Marjorie's movements. Neither seemed to know whether they were together or still separated by the hurt and quarrel.

Marjorie eventually said goodnight to Connie and Hope, and said quite firmly to Freddy, 'I'll see you in a day or so!' before going up to her room; Connie followed soon after. Freddy was about to leave for his rented room but Hope said, 'Won't you be staying, Father-in-law? I've got a few illegal eggs to boil for breakfast. Peter got them from one of the farms he visits to buy stock. There are plenty of blankets for the couch.'

Whether it was embarrassment or whether he was just unsure of how Marjorie would react, he stood up and kissed her on the cheek, thanked her for what she was trying to do and left to go back to the guest house.

Upstairs Marjorie heard the door close and wished she could be less difficult, and wondered sadly if she would ever learn.

—

At the last moment Freddy turned away from his destination, unable to face the clean, adequate but comfortless room. Ty Mawr was still empty, awaiting its new owners, and he had the key to the shed that Marjorie had converted into a studio for their so-called artist son. Why shouldn't he be a squatter? He was homeless just like Arthur and Catherine Gleaner had been, wasn't he?

—

The next morning Marjorie went out early and knocked on the side door of the Ship and Compass. 'I want to talk to you,' she announced with surprising calm. Betty was surprised to see her, and, taking a deep breath and preparing herself for a verbal attack, invited her inside. The first person Marjorie saw was Freddy.

He was wearing trousers but no socks and no shirt, and around his shoulders was a towel. His hair was mussed up from being dried and not yet combed. He stared at her, waiting for her to speak. At once she turned and began to hurry towards the door. He lunged forward and held her arm. 'Just for once in your life will you stop stalking off all fuss and feathers and damned well listen!'

'Freddy slept in the shed at the back of Ty Mawr last night,' Betty told her. 'He was unable to face another night in the room at Elsie's. He came here an hour ago and I offered him breakfast and a bath.' She looked from one to the other and added, 'I'll go and start frying the bacon, shall I? Mostly fat it is, mind, but you're welcome to join us, Marjorie.'

Instinctively Marjorie shook her head. 'I won't be staying.'

'Yes,' Freddy said firmly. 'Yes, you will. Thank you, Betty.'

The three of them sat down and ate, although it was doubtful whether any of them tasted a single mouthful. Marjorie was silent, and it was Freddy and Betty who talked, not about themselves, or the difficulties facing Freddy and Marjorie, but about the various customers that spent time in the bar. Although determined not to enjoy herself, trying to hold on to her anger and resentment, Marjorie had to smile as some of the more eccentric characters were discussed.

When she left, Freddy went with her. Taking her arm and pulling it through his own, he led her to the bridge from where Ralph had jumped to his death.

'We've lost so much, don't you think we ought to hang on to the little we've got left?' he asked as they stared down at the rails twinkling innocently in the winter sun.

'I want to look at the cottage.'

Content with her minimal response, he walked beside her down the approach to the road. For such a quarrelsome woman with opinions on everything, she said very little when words really counted.

–

The morning of Connie and Geoff's wedding started cloudy but there was the promise that once the early greyness lifted they would have a perfect day. The ceremony was arranged for eleven o'clock and at ten Connie was dressed in her beautiful gown of dark-blue taffeta, and Hope and Joyce were running around setting out the food for the reception to be held that evening.

Peter had borrowed chairs and a few trestle tables from the church hall and was putting them up for Marjorie to cover with white cloths and plates of food wrapped in greaseproof paper and moist tea towels. From before eight o'clock the door had stood wide open and callers had delivered gifts: wedding presents and offerings of food to swell the evening's celebration. Stella came, wearing a frilly hat with a drooping brim that had been to more weddings than the vicar; Colin wore a smart suit, which if a little tight was impressive on a man who usually wore either old or new uniform, depending on whether he was going to work at the railway station or on the allotment.

Freddy had taken Davy for a walk to enable the others to get on, and he went to show him the cottage which Marjorie had, somewhat edgily, agreed they should buy.

At half past ten they went back in time to see Connie walking down the stairs in her lovely gown and sparkling headdress. Hope, unable to get to a mirror, was trying to fix her hat on her curls. Joyce was wearing a pretty two-piece in a soft milky grey taffeta. Kitty, in a borrowed hat that constantly fell over her eyes, was trying to help and getting in everyone's way, and Marjorie was sitting on the couch dressed ready to leave and smiling at the happy confusion.

They shared a smile but when Freddy tried to join Marjorie in one of the cars queuing along the lane she pushed him away. When she left the house and walked down the path it had brought back a confusion of memories: her own wedding so long ago, and Ralph's marriage to Hope, as well as thoughts of Richard's secret engagement, and she grieved for the loss of everything she had once had.

The solemn atmosphere in the sombre, low-lit church was filled with ghosts, and the inescapable malignant shadow that was her own foolishness. Hope saw her sitting alone and went to stand beside her, with Davy and Peter. Davy offered her his tiny hand and she took it and forced a smile.

There was excitement as the organist began the Wedding March, and a gasp of approval as Connie entered, adding a brilliance to the building as so many others had before her. Peter felt for Hope's hand and gripped it tightly. 'I wish I had more to offer and it could have been you and me,' he whispered softly.

Hope was startled by his words. Did he still really believe that his lack of wealth was the reason she had refused him? She couldn't bear to have him think so badly of her. Staring into his eyes, she smiled. 'Just look at Connie and Geoff. Money isn't anything to do with the joyful expression on their faces.' She gripped his hand, affectionately moving her head towards his shoulder. 'Happiness isn't something you can buy.'

His grip tightened, and she moved just a fraction closer to him.

'Can I ride on your shoulders, Uncle Peter?' Davy's childish voice sounded extra loud in the solemnity of the moment. 'I can't see anything down here.' Peter smiled at Hope then lifted him into his arms and went to stand against the wall.

–

There were two unexpected visitors to Badgers Brook that evening, after the bride and groom had gone off to their secret honeymoon rendezvous. A knock on the door went unheard in all the clamour, and, pushing Sally before him, Matthew walked in. 'Hope,' he called when he saw her spreading out more plates of food. 'Forgive the intrusion, but I have a message for Connie from Phillip.'

'Too late, I'm afraid. Connie was married this morning and she and Geoff left more than three hours ago.'

Matthew handed her a neatly wrapped package. 'He wanted her to have this. It's a miniature gold bedroom clock.' He declined to tell Hope that Phillip had sold the gifts he had received from Fiona to pay for it.

They stayed a while, welcomed into the gathering of friends. Hope and Sally quickly revived the promise of friendship begun in the Cardiff café. Sally, who had come under protest, continued to be cold towards Matthew, determined to leave him. But she found herself relaxing, warmed by the house, the occasion and the company.

'This is such a friendly house,' she remarked to Hope after an hour had passed. 'It's as though I wore anger like a cloak but shed it the moment I stepped through the door.'

When they left, offering several people who had over-indulged a lift home, Matthew drove her to the beach where Geoff and Connie had often sat. Getting out of the car they looked across at the island, mysterious now in the darkness, its silhouette just visible due to a faint light over the horizon.

He reached out and gathered Sally into his arms and this time she didn't pull away. She allowed herself to snuggle into his shoulder and soon, with only a slight movement needed, they found each other's lips. Their kiss was a promise of a fresh beginning. Just as the dawn would prelude a new day, slowly sharpening the vision of the island, its contours and its colours, their life would reawaken to new experiences, new joys.

–

It seemed to Connie, on her return from honeymoon, that Hope had solved everyone's problems but her own. In her own happiness, she felt able to demand. 'Why are you refusing to marry Peter? I know he's asked you.'

Hope turned her head and looked out at the garden, where Bob and Colin were setting up the long row of bean sticks. 'Ralph died and I know I was at least partly responsible. How can I risk marrying Peter? I might be the kind of woman who demands too much, wants too much of her own way and pushes without reason until she gets it.'

'Did you know that Peter's been searching for the driver of the car that hit Ralph that night?'

'Why? He wasn't to blame. I was.'

'Ralph walked across the road without looking. There is absolutely no doubt about that. He didn't see the car until it was too late.'

Hope shook her head. 'He wished he was back in Ty Mawr and was deeply unhappy at the decision I'd forced on him. He was so depressed… The driver didn't have a chance of avoiding him.'

'That's right, he didn't. The man is quite clear about that night. And he said repeatedly that Ralph didn't step out deliberately.'

'How can he know?'

'Because he still sees Ralph's face caught in the head-lights of the car and— Sorry, Hope, but I have to make you see,' she said, jumping up to comfort Hope, who was convulsed with sobs. 'It was an accident. The driver saw that clearly in his face. The shock, the disbelief. He told Peter he still sees that face in his dreams. Ralph didn't step out on purpose. It was an accident.'

'He climbed on to the parapet of the bridge and let himself fall into a train. That wasn't an accident.'

'Ralph couldn't face life in a wheelchair. His mind was all over the place. You can remember how unreasonably angry and difficult he'd become, nothing like the man you had married. Some can cope – many people suffering such a devastating injury are brave and strong and do remarkable things with the rest of their lives – but sadly, Ralph wasn't one of them. You aren't to blame for any of it. No matter what Marjorie says. If you continue to think so then the accident ruined two lives. Three if you count little Davy. Is that what Ralph, the real Ralph, the loving, happy man you married, would want for you?'

'I was so wrong to make him come here.'

'You wanted a home for Ralph, Davy and other babies, where you could all be happy, away from an interfering and over-critical mother-in-law; how can that be wrong? You didn't drive him to suicide, his broken back did that. So for goodness sake stop torturing yourself and Peter.'

'He thinks I won't marry him because he hasn't much to offer.'

'Then it'll be easy to convince him he's wrong, won't it?' Connie became aware that she had been shouting and she hugged her friend and apologized. 'Hope, I'm so happy that I want everyone in the world to be happy too. Even Marjorie seems to have calmed down and accepted what happened between Freddy and Betty. She wouldn't want you to let this chance of real happiness pass you by.'

'It's this house. It makes people see the important things, relaxes them so they don't block their minds with trivia, exaggerate problems, become overwhelmed by anger.'

'Well then, listen to what it's telling you. Please, Hope, go and talk to Peter, tell him how you feel.'

–

Matthew went to see the manager of the men's outfitters and came away with a hint that he might be a successful applicant for the position of salesman. He had never felt more dejected in his life. How could he deal with boring customers day after day then go home to listen to small talk with Sally? He loved her but she wasn't enough for him. He wanted company, male company; he'd never been a womanizer. He needed stimulating conversation, arguments, some ribald jokes, laughter.

He didn't go straight home but walked to the small park in Cwm Derw, behind the row of shops that included the post office, and sat on a bench. Phillip was living in London so it was impossible for them to meet as regularly as before. Sally's father was building a lean-to shed and all his conversations were about his new lathe, wood, nails, screws and rawlplugs, and what he'd make once he had a decent place to work.

The house was empty when he eventually returned home. There was a note from Sally to say she had gone to the shops with her mother, and a letter addressed to him. With little optimism he opened it, then jumped out of his chair and began to pace the floor.

'Sally, love,' he called as he heard her key in the door. 'Read this.'

'Let me put the shopping down first,' she said, laughing.

'Give it to me, I'll take it through, just read this.' He thrust the page under her nose and she read it once, then again, more slowly.

'It's a job offer,' she said unnecessarily.

'From a firm selling different kinds of paper. Wrapping paper mostly, to shops. It isn't such a large area as before and I won't have to work on Saturdays. People in shops don't want to bother with reps on their busiest day, as I well know.'

'So we'll be back as we were before? Me here with the girls and you turning up when there's nowhere else to go?'

'No, Sally. I promise I'll be home most evenings. Instead of writing out orders in hotel rooms and pubs I'll make a corner of the dining room into an office and work there. I promise it'll be different. Please, let's try.'

Sally could see how animated the offer had made him and was well aware of the dread with which he was approaching work in a men's outfitters. She nodded. 'But it's a trial only. I really would be better off on my own than living with how things have been these past years.'

'Thank you,' he breathed, holding her, pulling her on to the couch with him, relief weakening his muscles.

–

It was strange without Connie sharing the house, and Badgers Brook felt surprisingly empty. Davy had started at a nursery class adjoining the school, which added to Hope's growing sense of isolation. Connie called often and sometimes helped Joyce and Hope with some of the simpler sewing tasks. Stella and Kitty popped in and usually left together, chattering about garden matters and commiserating about husbands who brought mud into the house. Peter hadn't called for several days.

A week after Connie returned, Hope asked her if she would stay with Davy while she went to deliver newly made curtains to Marjorie and Freddy at their new home. It wasn't theirs for another couple of weeks but permission had been given for measuring and cleaning. 'They're both there today pulling off wallpaper and washing walls, even though they aren't supposed to. Freddy doesn't want to dampen Marjorie's enthusiasm, so he's playing dumb,' she explained.

'While you're out, why don't you call and see if Peter's at the shop? He'll be busy preparing to move in, too.'

'I haven't got the time, there's Davy's tea and—'

'I'll take him home and he can eat with Geoff and me. We'll bring him back at seven tired out and ready for bed,' Connie promised briskly, not giving her a chance to argue.

–

The empty shop had once been a second-hand clothes shop, and the mustiness of the old stock had remained. Peter had hired cleaners and the walls and floors had been washed and the basement emptied of the clutter abandoned by the previous owners. He was busy tiling a wall when Hope walked in.

'Peter! I'm amazed at what you've done!'

'Hope, what a lovely surprise, I'll just finish this section and them we'll have a cup of tea. Where's Davy?'

'Don't stop, I'll find the kitchen.' She dropped the bags she'd been carrying on to the counter and went into the room at the back, calling, 'Davy's with Connie and Geoff, and I've come to help.'

They stopped for a few moments to drink tea and eat the cakes she had brought. Then, while Peter continued with the tiling Hope went through to where the walls were ready for painting. The brushes and paint tins had been donated by Geoff. 'Old stock,' he had insisted, but the colours were exactly what Peter had chosen after discussion with Hope and he suspected the gift was another example of Geoff's kindness.

They worked together for most of the afternoon and for several following. Peter's vegetable round filled the mornings and when he returned and stabled Jason he found Hope already there, working. He always asked her preferences when a colour or floor covering was discussed, but she was careful not to be too definite in her replies. 'It isn't my home and never will be,' she told Connie firmly. 'The choices have to be Peter's.'

–

It was about that time that things began to happen in Badgers Brook. Although the spring weather was warming the earth and everywhere new growth was appearing, inside the place felt cold. For the first time Hope felt a lack of welcome as she stepped through the doors. When Marjorie and Freddy moved into their cottage and left just herself and Davy it became even more apparent. 'Kitty,' she told her friend one March morning, 'I know you'll laugh at me but I feel that the house is telling me I should leave.'

'It's time to move on, your problems are behind you and your happiness is secure, if you have the sense to grasp it.'

'Oh, Kitty, don't get all mystical on me. My being fanciful is bad enough, but not you too. I depend on your rationality!' Hope said with a laugh, but although she jeered she knew she was right, the house wanted her to leave.

'It's nonsense, but if it were true, why now? I have nowhere to go. Davy and I are so happy here why should I want to leave?'

'Better things are out there.'

'Peter, you mean? You know I can't remarry.'

'You don't love him?'

'That isn't the reason for refusing. I'm afraid of hurting him, causing him unhappiness.'

'Shouldn't he be the one to decide on the risk?'

–

'Really, Stella, I could shake the pair of them,' Kitty said later when she called at the post office just as it was closing. 'Made for each other they are, and him afraid because he isn't rich and she afraid because, well, I'm not sure what she's worried about really. They want a good push.'

'I don't think her excuses are the real reason. I believe Hope's trouble is fear of offending Marjorie. Having a grieving mother-in-law hovering about when you remarry must be difficult to someone as kind and sensitive as Hope.'

'I wonder…' Kitty began. Then without explanation she added. 'It's about time Marjorie did something to make up for her behaviour, don't you think?'

Bemused, Stella could only nod.

–

'Stella has asked me to paint the outside of her shed,' Peter told Hope one Sunday morning. 'Want to bring Davy and sit in the sun and watch?'

'Don't you mean her country cottage?' Hope teased, explaining that Davy couldn't go as he was promised a visit to his grandparents' future home and a first sight of the beginnings of his tree house. 'But why ask you? You have so much to do on your new shop, and, besides, she and Colin love working on the place.'

'A surprise for Colin apparently.'

The weather was dull and there was a chill in the air. Peter called for Hope and they went down on borrowed bicycles to the allotments. They worked together and it didn't take very long. Afterwards they sat on Stella's garden chairs, inside the shed, sipping coffee from a flask Peter had brought. The sound of voices made them sit up. Could it be Stella and Colin to inspect their work? They soon recognized Marjorie's voice. Hope went to get up and greet her parents-in-law but Peter held her back.

The voices stopped at the back of the wooden hut and Marjorie was heard to say, 'I despair of Hope, Freddy. She's very stupid, isn't she?'

Again Hope struggled to rise and Peter held her close.

'She may be stupid, Marjorie, but it's only because she's so kind.'

'Kind? To deprive that boy of a decent father? Peter loves David as much as he loves Hope, anyone can see that. And Hope loves Peter. So why is she so afraid of offending me that she'll let it all go? Am I such an ogre, Freddy?'

Freddy's murmured assurances faded as the couple walked away. They didn't heard Marjorie ask, 'Did I do well, Freddy? Was I convincing, d'you think?'

Peter released Hope but didn't quite let her go. 'Marry me,' he said simply. 'It must be right if Marjorie agrees it would be a sensible thing to do.'

'Sensible?' she queried.

'Only in that I'll lose my mind completely if I don't get an answer soon.'

She said nothing as they began to clear up, but he didn't feel dejected. This wasn't the place for such a momentous answer, he knew that.

Back at Badgers Brook, where the evening sun shone through the back windows of the comfortable lounge and warmed them, she turned and smiled at him. He thought of all the words he'd planned, about having little to offer and how hard he'd work to provide for them, but in a moment of clarity he knew these were not the important things: they were taken for granted, part of caring, and the love he had for her and Davy.

'I love you, both of you, and I'll love you for ever,' he promised.

She moved into his arms, and, as a gust of wind touched the building, it seemed that Badgers Brook sighed in contentment.